Praise for *The Manning Girl*

"'Without that surge of mystery energy,' muses a neighbor in this wise and moving novel, 'no child would ever survive.' Nor would any novel. Fortunately, there are frequent surges of mystery energy propelling *The Manning Girl* and guiding the book's title character from swaddling clothes to wedding gown. Here is a compelling coming-of-age story, not just for the girl, but equally for the bewildered bachelor uncle who raises her. A beautiful book."

—Roderick Townley, author of *The Great Good Thing* trilogy

"Set in rural Kansas, Catherine Browder's *The Manning Girl* explores the redemptive power of parenting and community. Tyler Manning's life is transformed when a young mother leaves his own younger brother's baby at his doorstep. Tyler is of Free State Kansas stock, sturdy and deliberate, a meticulously organized industrial arts teacher who can make anything. Suddenly he must make a family. Uncle Tyler becomes Delia May's legal father, and a model caretaker. But beneath this tale of domestic striving is secrecy and strife, anger and resentment, the looming presence of back story. Browder contrasts a family's difficult past with a peaceful and hard-won present. *The Manning Girl,* heartwarming and wise, shows us that what we care about most can be made: hope, family, love, a bright future."

—Tom Fox Averill, author of the novel, *Found Documents from the Life of Nell Johnson Doerr*

"In a political climate that divides states—and people—into red and blue, Catherine Browder's stunning novel *The Manning Girl* is a gift. Browder delivers a vibrant and nuanced portrait of life, love, and family in rural America over generations. The story of

Tyler Manning's relationship with his adopted daughter, May, and his estranged brother, Mickey, is filled with pathos and compassion. Browder's novel triumphs as a retelling of George Eliot's *Silas Marner,* but its grand arc of love and strife also recalls John Steinbeck's *East of Eden* and authoritatively reclaims a place and time in American life that is all-too-often simplified and misunderstood. It is a joy to read."

—Whitney Terrell, author of *The Good Lieutenant*

"Stalwart Kansans people Browder's accomplished first novel, in particular the emotionally scarred, yet enduring Tyler Manning. His solitary peace on the old home place is turned upside-down with the arrival of an abandoned infant, a girl. Tyler seems an unlikely 'father' but rallies to the cause with the help of his neighbors and friends at the school where he teaches what used to be called shop. He's a fine carpenter. He's a good farmer. He's skilled at everything, even changing diapers and finding playmates for his precocious 'daughter.' May, whom Tyler adopts, turns out to be the one thing he needed to give life meaning. The counterpoint is Mickey Manning, Tyler's devious younger brother. Mickey threatens the sheltered, almost bucolic life Tyler has constructed for May, and, as if it didn't matter, for himself. Mickey is a snake who gives the novel a little of the flavor of a police procedural. He inspires in the reader a dread, a fear, threatening characters the reader has grown to love. In the end, Browder's novel is not so much an imitation of that sturdy high school classic, *Silas Marner,* as it is a thoughtful commentary. Ours are dreadful times, but good people exist, they outnumber bad people, and things could still happen this way."

—John Mort, author of *Oklahoma Odyssey* and *Down Along the Piney*

"Catherine Browder's *The Manning Girl* is a beautifully crafted book about the joy, pain, and growth that the advent of an abandoned baby creates in the life of an emotionally frozen man. In graceful, lucid prose, Browder examines important themes, familial estrangement, sibling rivalry, the immense challenge of raising a child alone, and the joys and perils of lifelong friendship. The heartwarming story of Tyler Manning's fumbling emotional growth as he fosters the childhood and adolescence of the baby dumped on his doorstep will entrance readers."

—Linda Rodriguez, author of *Every Hidden Fear*

"It is often said that great writers are in an ongoing literary conversation among themselves, and with *The Manning Girl*, Catherine Browder has created an American classic with the geographical richness of detail, sociological fullness, and psychological acuity of George Eliot's classic nineteenth-century British classic, *Silas Marner*. I rarely read contemporary novels that unfold with such a sure-footed compelling narrative voice that draws the reader into such a vividly realized community. A vividly realized family drama set in a vividly realized rural Kansas community, the novel reminds us of a kind of communal interconnectedness and genuine decency not on prominent display these days. Without any sentimentality, without ignoring contentious social issues such as racism, homophobia, drug cartels, or bullying, we are drawn into a community largely populated by good people. How rare and restorative it feels to inhabit this world! The novel is a quiet but strong tour de force."

—Marly Swick, author of *Evening News*

THE MANNING GIRL

Catherine Browder

Regal House Publishing

Published by
Regal House Publishing, LLC
Raleigh, NC 27605
All rights reserved

ISBN -13 (paperback): 9781646033942
ISBN -13 (epub): 9781646033959
Library of Congress Control Number: 2022920634

Cover images and design by © C. B. Royal
Author photo by David Remley

Regal House Publishing, LLC
https://regalhousepublishing.com

Printed in the United States of America

For the nieces:
Katrina, Jennifer, and Jayna

And their children
Kyle, Brenna, Lydia, Gabriella, Elyse, and Baby Crewe

And theirs
Malaya and Nyla

A child, more than any other gifts
That earth can offer to declining man,
Brings hope with it, and forward-looking thoughts.

—Wordsworth

"You'll take the child to the parish tomorrow?" asked
Godfrey, speaking as indifferently as he could.

"Who says so?" said Marner, sharply. "Will they make
me take her?"

"Why, you wouldn't like to keep her, should you—an
old bachelor like you?"

"Till anybody shows they've a right to take her away
from me," said Marner. "The mother's dead, and I reckon
it's got no father; it's a lone thing—and I'm a lone thing.
My money's gone, I don't know where—and this is come
from I don't know where. I know nothing—I'm partly
mazed."

—*Silas Marner*, George Eliot

PART ONE

1

Unexpected Arrival

May 1992

A few miles west of Lawrence, where Kansas Highway 40 veers sharply to the north, a county road intersects the highway and will take a traveler to the unincorporated town of Stull, famed mostly for its cemetery. Nowadays Stull sits on the northwest point of Clinton Lake, but back in the day, when Tyler Manning was still a boy living on his parents' farm, the lake was only a muddy, undeveloped reservoir. The Manning property was located off the Old Stull Road, on one of the smaller roads near the western edge of the county. And once the reservoir was expanded into a state park, traffic increased as people made their way to campsites and boat docks around the lake.

On the morning in question, Tyler paid little attention to the passing car headed to the lake, the sound as unremarkable as a birdcall or the bark of his neighbor's German shepherd. He was gazing at his wall calendar, coffee cup in hand, planning his week. He'd have preferred a larger calendar with space in each daily box for notes and reminders, but the one hanging over his wall phone was free, a gift from Hiram's Farm Insurance and Tractor Repair. He was in a buoyant mood. The first day of his summer vacation was his to shape entirely to his liking—no students, no staff meetings or study hall or bell. He'd already spent thirty minutes in the basement lifting weights, strengthening the already hard muscles of his substantial frame, and he felt flushed with well-being. He planned to spend the rest of the morning in the barn, half of which he'd converted to a workshop. He'd been up since five, a habit formed in childhood when his parents were alive and the place was a working farm.

The vehicle did not pass, however, but turned onto the long gravel drive that led to the house. Cup in hand, he wandered into the front room as the car approached, an unhealthy muffler growling through an otherwise peaceful morning. At the noise Tyler's golden retriever raised its head. Tyler observed the contrail of yellow dust until the car finally emerged. He didn't recognize it, a faded red Ford, a tank of a car, rusted and pinged with one huge dent in the front passenger door.

The driver spun the Ford onto the parking pad in front and slammed on the brakes. Rocks spewed, and Tyler took an involuntary step away from the window. Two small figures sat in the front seat. The passenger finally emerged, slamming the door, and then opened the right rear door to remove an elongated parcel. Tyler squinted. He didn't know this girl. He didn't believe she had ever been his student. She was tiny and blond, dressed in denim cutoffs and flip-flops and a man's red checked flannel shirt, her hair pulled back in a ponytail. It was an unseasonably cool Memorial Day weekend, too cool for shorts. As she slammed the door shut, she yelled something harsh to the driver that caused Tyler to straighten his back. The only word he caught was an explosive *fuck*. She carried the bundle in the crook of her left arm, the strap of a small bag in her right. The dog slowly rose to his feet, a rumble in its throat. Tyler glanced at the animal and muttered, "Trouble, ya think?"

The girl climbed the porch steps as if they were an offense, crossed the porch and banged on the screen door, rattling the frame. Tyler hurriedly opened the seldom-used front door. Before he had a chance to greet her or ask how he could help, her words accosted him.

"Mister, are you Mike Mann's brother?"

A seed of dread unsettled his stomach. "I'm Michael *Manning's* brother, if that's who you mean. Is he in trouble?" When was Mickey not in trouble?

"Shit if I know," the girl said. "But I am."

Tyler looked out to the red car and realized the engine was running. He couldn't make out the driver.

"Why don't you come in? The person out there too."

"No!" Her voice was high-pitched and reedy, like a cartoon mouse. "I just come to give you something. Mikey said if I ever had a problem to call you. I tried but no one answered."

He shrugged. "No answering machine."

"I noticed." She looked down at the zipper bag draped with a white blanket decorated in pink balloons.

"I got somethin' for you, a present from your brother. I can't afford it. He told me where you lived a long time ago. I didn't want nothin' to do with a person who threw his own brother out. But Mikey took off, so you get it." She elevated the bundle.

The dread bloomed, and his mouth felt suddenly dry. Tyler put the coffee cup on the hall table, opened the screen door and stepped onto the porch. "Who's in the car?"

"What's it to you? My cousin."

Tyler stooped and peered out at the car. The driver was also a girl, also blond, sporting oversized white sunglasses. The girl on the porch thrust out a bundle, startling him, as if she were handing him a wad of old clothes. As soon as he took the bundle, he knew what was inside. Quickly, he lifted the infant up, moving a layer of cloth aside to reveal a sleeping face.

"I drugged her," the girl said. "She cries all the time."

"You what?"

"Benadryl."

"Come in! Please."

"No way! I come here to give her to you and that's that. She's all yours."

"Is this your child?"

"Mike's too."

The yellow remnant of a bruise circled the girl's right eye and cheek. She couldn't be more than fifteen, and her hair needed washing. Tyler pointed to her face. "Did he do that to you?"

She shook her head and looked away from him, tilting her chin up. "He left way before that."

"Where is he?"

The girl let out a snort. She was high on something, he'd swear to it.

"Does the baby have a name?"

"Does it matter?"

"Yes! How old?"

"Young. New!"

"This is crazy! You gotta come in."

"I don't gotta do nothin'."

"How do I know this is his child?"

She gave a throaty laugh. "You'll have to take my word, won't ya?"

"But how can you—?"

"—I done what I come here to do, and that's that." The girl turned on her heel and thundered back across the porch, skinny arms swinging. The new floorboards seemed to tremble even though she couldn't weigh more than ninety pounds. *A slip of a girl,* Tyler thought incongruously, as if he were on the roof watching and not a part of the scene. It was something his mother might have said. *A slip of a girl.*

"Wait!" he yelled.

She didn't turn or even acknowledge him but stalked toward the car, her flip-flops crunching through the gravel. She yanked the heavy car door open and threw herself in. Tyler gripped the baby and walked quickly across the porch.

"Stop right now! You hear me?"

Before he could descend the steps, the driver threw the car in reverse and barreled backward beyond the edge of the parking pad and onto his well-manicured grass, whirled the old Ford around and sped toward the main road, followed by the same dust cloud that announced its arrival. The tires had left marks in his lawn. When he turned back to the house, he saw Rusty standing in the doorway.

"I got the plate number," he told the dog and then let out

a moan. He sank to the top step holding the child as though it were an heirloom vase. He'd been unable to move fast enough, stuck on the porch as if stunned by a blow. He remembered the only time his mother had slapped him, and for something he didn't do. He'd stood there, shocked, riveted to the spot, while his little brother sniggered from somewhere behind the shrubs. *Mickey.* Mikey?

He grew conscious of the weight in his arms: a child folded into remnants and rags. It wouldn't remain quiet for long. He rose from the steps and crossed the porch. By the door he saw the small zipper bag with the strap and grabbed it. In the kitchen he carefully put the baby on the table, dropped the bag on the floor, and peeled away the layers of cloth. A sleeping face emerged, its mouth a tiny heart, eyebrows like miniature feathers. When he pulled the blanket further away, he uncovered an incredible mop of dark curly hair, like his own. Like his father's. Mickey favored their mother with reddish-blond hair, fair skin and freckles. Like his mother in looks only. In temperament Mickey didn't favor any decent relative Tyler could think of.

The infant's face was too new to resemble anyone. He searched for clues of the young mother, but the encounter had been so sudden and unpleasant that he couldn't even remember the color of her eyes, only the green bruise and the streaky blond ponytail. The pale hair was natural though, for she was blond to her roots. He remembered that, oddly, but he couldn't remember a single feature.

The child stirred and struggled and scrunched her face. He loosened the cloth, and she balled her fists, tightened her eyes, and opened her mouth. A wail rent the silence. Two pampered house cats shot through the kitchen and out the pet door to the garden. He shushed and hoisted the infant onto one enormous arm and against his shoulder and strode to where the phone was attached to the wall below the feed grain calendar. Balancing the baby, he phoned Billie. When she answered, Tyler announced, "I need diapers. Quick!"

Billie Harrington lived in the only house visible from Tyler's front porch. After his call she put down her morning coffee, flinging on a jacket, and moved with deliberate speed to the pickup parked in the grassy side yard. She'd heard the wails before she'd hung up the phone. All she could imagine was a wounded cat except the sound wasn't right. Maybe a rabbit. They sounded very human. Ty rescued everything. *Everything!* Since they were children, you'd find jars of rescued pollywogs, moths, toads throughout the Manning farmhouse, plus the usual stray dogs and barn kittens. *Strong of arm, soft of heart, that's our Ty.*

She parked her truck in the space near the Manning back door and let herself in through his kitchen. He was standing near the wall phone, bouncing a bunch of rags.

"Ty?"

"Sit down," he said, his voice so faint she scarcely heard it.

Billie sat. He laid the jumble of cloth on the kitchen table in front of her and unfolded it, and she found herself peering into the face of a sleepy infant. For possibly the only time in her life, she was speechless.

"Mickey's," he said at last.

"You're going to have to explain that."

The story tumbled out: the dilapidated Ford, the girl and presumed mother relinquishing her child. When he finished, he shook his head. "What in hell am I supposed to do?"

The baby opened her eyes. Her face balled and she let loose another wrenching cry. Billie stood and reached for the child, her foot bumping against the zipper bag Tyler had brought into the house and forgotten.

"What's this?" Billie pulled it out and set it on a chair.

"Oh. The girl left the bag too."

Inside, she found three Pampers, a tin of formula, two prepared bottles of milk, and a very dirty pacifier.

"Thank god," she muttered. "I was worried we'd have to use tea towels. The kid's wet. That's why she's wailing. Hungry too."

She told him to run some warm water and moisten a clean

washcloth. She pulled the blanket away from the baby and removed the soiled diaper, throwing it in Tyler's trash under the sink. The infant had diaper rash, and she sent Tyler upstairs to the bathroom to find Vaseline and talcum powder.

"At least she's nice and plump," she said when he returned.

"Is that good?"

"To me it is. I wouldn't want a baby who wasn't thriving."

"The mother…she wasn't more than a child herself, Billie. And she was jacked up on something. Said she gave the kid Benadryl."

"We're gonna call Family Services right now. This isn't your problem."

Tyler gripped the back of a chair and leaned forward. "Slow down, please. I want to think this through. If this is my niece, if she really is Mickey's child, I can't just…" The words trailed off, his face knitted in worry. "How could I?"

"How could you what?"

"Turn her away. See what I'm saying?"

She glanced at his hands gripping the chair back, his knuckles turning white. "How are you planning to look after her?" she said.

"God, I don't know, but I guess we'll figure that out."

"*We?*"

The baby let out a wail. Billie grabbed a partially filled bottle, ran hot water over it and soaped the nipple, muttering to herself about filth, and rinsed it off. She picked up the baby and arranged her in the crook of one arm and offered her the bottle. After a fussy start, the infant began to suck freely.

"There you go," Billie murmured. She looked up at Ty who was watching with the most amazed smile on his face.

"It's like feeding a newborn calf or rabbit kit," he said in a dreamy voice.

"No, it's not. It's human."

"But it is the same. All creatures need milk and mothering."

"And you got the teats to feed her?"

He shut his eyes. "Jeez, Billie. You know what I mean."

"No, I don't."

"If she's my niece, she's not leaving this house until I get things sorted out."

"And what things, exactly, do you intend to sort out? Listen to what you just told me: A girl brings you a baby and says it's hers and your brother's, offering no proof, but you get to keep it now since she doesn't want it? Talk about crazy!"

The look he gave her was hard, defiant. *Shared stubbornness.* They'd once spent two hours in the cab of his truck, in the middle of winter, two teenagers arguing about something she'd long forgotten. Her husband Bud gave in to her. Sooner or later Bud always relented, but Tyler had never learned how to give ground, especially if he thought he was right. Billie was exactly the same. "Help me then," he said at last. "Please."

"You're gonna have to tell the authorities about this sooner or later."

"Why? It's a family matter."

"Ty, are you nuts? A bachelor. Living alone in a farmhouse. With an infant—a girl, no less—and no parenting skills."

"I got plenty of skills. I helped raise Mickey. Remember?"

"That was how many years ago? This is *a little girl.* What do you know about little girls? Someone is going to get suspicious, stick their nose where it doesn't belong, snoop around. And that somebody is likely to be from school. The very place you and I work and feel safe most of the time. It's not safe now. Nowhere is safe if you're trying to keep a family secret. When you go buy little girl clothes and someone congratulates you and asks if you're the proud papa, what're you gonna say? 'It's a family matter?' That won't do!"

"I thought you knew me better," he said.

"I'm not saying you can't do it. I *am* saying you're going to need help, and I don't want to be an accomplice to something that might be illegal."

"What's illegal here?"

"The girl says it's Mickey's child, but you don't even have a birth certificate."

"We'll find it. Can't we take a blood test or something? A DNA thingy?"

Billie barked a harsh laugh and then sighed while the baby kicked her legs, still nursing.

"So there." He crossed his arms, as if that settled it.

Soon the baby's eyelids sank, and the bottle slipped from her mouth. Billie lifted her to one shoulder and gently patted. In due course the baby let out a large belch. Tyler laughed out loud, and Billie stared at him. He just thought that burp was the most charming thing in the world.

"I'm going to the store," she said.

"Want me to go instead?"

"No! You wouldn't know what to buy."

"I might surprise you," he said in a hurt voice.

She smiled up at him. "I think you can do more good here. You can hold her till I get back or find a place she can sleep. I'll stop at home too. If memory serves, I still have a crib."

As soon as Billie put the child in his arms, he felt a surge of adrenaline. Maybe this was why children survived, that burst of energy that filled a parent on contact. Somewhere in the distance Billie's truck crunched through the gravel and accelerated down the road. Tyler carried the drowsy infant into the dining room and looked around. His mother's enormous buffet offered deep drawers filled with table linens. Tyler positioned the infant in the crook of one arm and slowly pulled open one heavy drawer. She'd fit. He removed a stack of damask napkins that hadn't been used in years, leaving the tablecloths, and gently slipped the child into the drawer.

Tyler watched the sleeping infant with wonder. She had such long eyelashes and a delicate nose. Then he saw it at last, the family resemblance: a remarkably well-formed chin that looked like Mickey's. Her head was well formed, too, ears delicate as split apricots. The baby's tiny fist lay against a cheek. Every feature fit together, nothing sticking out or irregular or poorly shaped. He felt something tug at him, something familiar, if he could only call it up. While he watched, her eyes fluttered open, and she gave him an unfocused look. The shape of her eyes was familiar too. Then the eyes closed, and the child went back to sleep.

Tyler walked quietly into the kitchen, placed his mug in the sink. A foggy image bothered him, burrowing into him. He stared out the window over the sink and ran the hot water. Sparrows and finches flitted to and from the feeder, but he scarcely saw them. Then his left hand strayed under the stream of hot water, and he yelled. The shock brought him back, bringing the lost thought up from its depths: Except for hair and eyes, this infant looked incredibly like Mickey as a baby.

Tyler abruptly grabbed a pen and wrote a sequence of license plate numbers on the phone pad.

Billie pulled her truck around and drove down Tyler's drive, feeling as if she'd just been beaten with sticks. What had she just agreed to? She glanced in her rearview mirror and took in the immaculate house, the tidy premises. If welfare people did show up at the Manning farm, they'd find a drive with no potholes and the grass mowed back neatly along each side. At the end of the drive nearest the road, he'd placed two tractor tires filled with spring flowers and an ornate letterbox he'd made himself. He kept beef cattle in the southwest pasture, poultry in a side yard, a well-tended kitchen garden his mother had started, not to mention the apple orchard. The house was always painted and repaired. The gingerbread around the porch gleamed a buttery cream. He'd painted the house yellow with a pale green trim and a subdued three-shaded green composition roof. Timberline, he called it. Even the barn was painted yellow. His retriever Rusty stayed by his side, and no yappy yard dogs scared off visitors. Some young social worker might pass this house and never imagine a woman didn't live here.

Billie blushed to her bleached roots. Ty's house put everyone near the Old Stull Road to shame. Of course, he had more time, not having to worry about a family. True, he'd stayed close to home the last three years, ever since Nancy left him and he'd sold the bungalow in town and returned to the family farm, throwing himself into needed improvements and long-neglected maintenance. Billie saw him at work every day, but since the Nancy incident he hadn't stopped by much or come to the house, except when she and Bud invited him over for a meal. It wasn't the woman so much but the manner of the jilting, Billie thought. Still, whether or not he was moping over his lost fiancée, Ty kept up his premises. Unlike her own house. Bud had been promising to repaint it for two years now.

She had a bad feeling about this child. What if the mother came back to reclaim her, which would be a blessing in her opinion? Ty would be powerless. Worse still, what if Mickey returned? She would have to look into the meaning of *guardianship*. If he was legal guardian, could anyone waltz back in and make a claim? And why was she thinking these things anyway? The situation was preposterous. Ty had no business taking on an infant. Any baby. He was a schoolteacher and a fine finish carpenter. All the kitchen cabinetry was his, as was the oak flooring throughout the downstairs and the new flooring on both front and back porches, plus that lovely little maple chest he'd placed by the front door. What would Ty do with an infant when August rolled around and classes started up?

A young clerk at the grocery smiled at her purchases and asked, "Newborn?"

Billie smiled, feeling as though her face was covered in drywall. *What a faker,* she mumbled to herself as she pushed her cart away from the checkout aisle. She placed her purchases behind the seat so Bud wouldn't ask questions she wasn't prepared to answer. On her way home, she glanced again at the peak of Ty's tidy roof. Maybe she'd feel differently if Bud ever took an interest in the premises or did more than paint the exterior every four years while she nagged at him for the three years in between. Bud knew how to fix a truck and anything mechanical, if he chose. Now that he was sober, the interest was rekindling, and she didn't want to push. At least he'd been a happy, sleepy drunk. First he got jolly. Then he went to bed: at eight, seven, six. Even though her elderly parents had lived with them, the only person she'd had to turn to was Ty. If only she could have loved *him*, been attracted to *him* when she was young. Besides, she'd had her eye on Bud Harrington. Fun-loving Bud.

She'd often wondered if Bud was ever aware of the competition. She'd chosen Bud Harrington for everything Ty was not: joking and romantic and venturesome. She had married Bud and had had several years of good, contented sex before it even dawned on her that he drank too much, until the alcohol took over while she raised two kids, cleaned, planted, sewed, taught school, and prayed. When Bud finally got off the juice, dragging his AA platitudes into every corner of their lives, she realized that instead of a drunken fun-loving ne'er-do-well, she now had a sober, supervisory quasi-ne'er-do-well on her hands. Throughout the years of this drama, the look in Tyler's deep eyes remained constant. More than once he'd rescued her in small ways: jump-starting her truck, tilling her garden, shoveling their drive with his snowplow while Bud snored on the sofa, sleeping off the booze. Maybe she was just plain dumb, but it was Bud she loved.

Billie bumped up the short unpaved drive. She needed to gingerly broach the subject of filling the ruts. In the drinking days, when he pissed her off, she'd yell at her husband, "Avery, get off your butt! I need help." He used to hate his proper name. But less than a week ago he reclaimed it and said he wanted her to forget *Bud*. It was a kid's name. *Call me Avery, okay? Bud's such a hick name, don't ya think?*

She parked the truck and slammed the door, storming into the kitchen, reciting the list in her head: crib, mattress, crib bedding, baby socks, layettes, rattles... Had she kept any of these things? Bud sat at the table sipping coffee, listening to his police scanner.

"Look," she said first off, glaring at him, hands on hips.

"First off, after twenty years I'm not going to start calling you Avery. Okay?"

He stared at her, puzzled. "Honey, what are you talking about?"

Billie shook her head and mumbled an apology.

"Did we keep the crib?"

He nodded. "Basement. Southeast corner."

"And the mattress?"

"Up in the attic."

She glanced at him, impressed. With or without booze, his memory remained specific. She opened the cellar door and switched on the light. Its dank, fetid smell wafted up as she stepped cautiously down the steps, gripping the handrail. She only came down in winter to get a jar from the canning room. Other than that, she didn't like the place. Her laundry appliances were upstairs in a little room off the kitchen. When she reached the bottom she surveyed the main room where boxes rose up along each wall—islands of marooned junk—broken chairs and stools and bedsteads. She strode to the middle of the room and pulled a light chain, hugging her arms to herself. Funny, at school she kept a meticulous desk, her home economics kitchen and sewing rooms orderly. Not a spool out of place. But at home she let herself go. The kitchen was clean and presentable, the house livable, but both attic and basement were disaster zones, dusty and unorganized, as if once the disorder set in she couldn't face the chaos.

Billie looked behind a tower of boxes wedged up against the south wall. Some vague memory hovered like a cloud, suggesting this was the spot for all the baby items saved for the garage sale she'd always meant to have. She tore open a box and saw clothes for school-age children. She pushed it aside to the box below and then the box below that, where she at last found clothing suitable for a baby less than one year. Then she saw the crib, collapsed and serving as a platform for the boxes.

Was she really such a pack rat? So much stuff, years of accumulation, a marriage registered in leftovers, packed and sealed and waiting for the kids to take away. How absurd to be saving the baby stuff for her daughter. Ginny was only twelve. This must be something mothers did: hoarded and passed on. The kids would probably sneer at whatever unfashionable items she'd saved. Billie retrieved the crib and carried it upstairs. Bud was still at the kitchen table, waiting for his breakfast. He watched her without comment until her second trip, when she dragged two bags of bedding to the back door, puffing under the weight. Bud chuckled.

"Is there something you haven't told me?"

"Nope. Just getting it out of our way." She was bursting to tell him but couldn't conjure up the words.

She returned to the basement for the box of baby garments and brought it upstairs.

"You planning to eat any time soon?" Bud inquired.

"I ate. There're some biscuits and gravy in the oven. If you want anything more, you'll have to make it yourself."

She had no intention of stopping now to fix the man whatever high fat, high cholesterol plate he pined for. She had stuff to do and he was in the way. Billie froze, her back to him. So that was how she felt. *In the way.* Her face grew hot. Shameful, to feel this way when there was nothing wrong with the man, considering how hard he was trying. *In the way.* She felt a stab of irritation toward Ty. Why was she bouncing back and forth between the needs of these two men? She took a deep breath, counted to five, leaned the crib against the door, and turned back to her husband. When had Bud not been a good listener?

"Glad you're sitting because you are *not* going to believe what I'm about to tell you."

"Try me."

She took the chair opposite her husband and rested her hands on the tabletop covered with a vinyl tablecloth. As she spoke, Bud's eyes rounded, his brows tenting, and a smile formed slowly. "I'm trying to picture Tyler as a father."

She nodded, suddenly weak from the telling. "Tell you what? If you go up and get that mattress and put it in my truck, I'll make us both bacon and eggs to go with the biscuits. How's that?"

Without a word he got up, heading for the attic stairs, while she took eggs and bacon from the fridge.

For the second time that morning Billie drove up the Manning drive and around to the rear, stopping so abruptly the tailpipe clattered. Tyler heard her and came out the back door as she climbed out of the truck. She gestured with her head in the direction of the truck bed, and Tyler pulled down the gate. He slid out the larger pieces and hoisted them both over his shoulder.

"Better clean it off. I didn't take the time."

In the kitchen, he set about moistening a rag with water and vinegar and wiped down all the rungs. Billie opened the box of baby items he'd put on a chair, searching for bed linens. Everything smelled musty. He'd need to launder the whole lot.

"Where's the baby?" she asked abruptly.

"In the buffet," he said.

He beckoned her into the dining room, and she followed. There she slept, snug in the middle drawer surrounded by table linens. Billie smiled. "Just like in the movies," she whispered. The dog strolled into the dining room and lay down protectively under the drawer. When they returned to the kitchen, she watched Tyler closely as he slowly, purposefully rubbed a damp cloth over every surface of the crib.

"Ty, do you have any notion what you're doing?"

He glanced up and shrugged. Why did he come across as such an ox, all mindless brute strength, when he was nothing of the sort? He simply kept himself a secret, concealed by his size and an undisturbed expression, as if he'd willed his face never to reveal a disturbing thought or joyful impulse. Like a giant sequoia. Even his students called him Moose behind his back. *Moose Manning.* The brown eyes and full mouth always seemed placid. No storm tightened the jaw line, like other men, until it occurred to her that what appeared placid might, in fact, be thoughtful. Or deeply, painfully reserved. But such reserve made her uncomfortable. She'd grown so used to Bud's expressive face, every amusement or anger or surprise playing directly across Bud's features. Every thought was telegraphed before Bud spoke. And Bud did speak, letting it "all hang out" as they used to say. Not like Ty.

"Tyler? Answer me. Now's not the time to hoard your thoughts."

He wouldn't look at her, turning his gaze toward the child. "Right now," he said, "I just want to set up the crib."

2

The Manning Boys

1964-1975

Delia Manning was the storyteller of the family, and Tyler grew up nourished by her tales of early Kansas settlers—her people—and the blood-drenched Civil War years, stories of Bloody Bill Anderson and perfidious politicians eager to drag the "peculiar institution" into the new territory of Kansas. There were the accounts of the Topeka convention and the honorable Dr. Robinson, then the history of poor Lawrence, sacked by despicable Missouri border ruffians in 1856 and set upon again by that madman Quantrill in 1863. She was a proud Free-Stater, tracing her family to settlers brought by the New England Emigrant Aid Company. Her stories were as thrilling and violent as any young boy could hope for, and it was through these, and his father's brief remarks, that Tyler gleaned his mother's abolitionist history.

Only later did he recall how often his father would slip out of the room when his mother was in a storytelling frame of mind. Still Tyler listened to her accounts—some mere nuggets of schoolroom history, others inherited from grandparents and embellished with pride.

"Did you know that Lord Byron's widow took pity on poor, besieged Kansans and sent sixty pounds sterling to relieve their suffering? That would be back in '56." She did not clarify the century, leaving the boy to wonder why Kansans were suffering and besieged only a decade ago. And who was Lord Byron anyway, and what was a pound sterling? He imaged a scale heaped with ingots.

"There's another side, you know," Hal Manning told his son. "Jayhawkers did their share of killing and burning. Ask your mother about Osceola, Missouri. Ask her about Order Number Eleven."

Delia's people were among the settlers who stayed on in spite of mounting conflicts between Missouri transplants and Free State arrivals, armed with rifles that arrived in boxes marked "Bibles." The territory of Kansas was a patchwork of conflict like its sister state: one town a proponent of abolition, the next town eager to allow its new residents to bring their slaves. Early on, Delia said, a family didn't always know if the folks on the neighboring farm were an enemy or an ally. She recounted the stories while he helped her wash dishes or feed poultry—an only child with diverse chores to suit both parents.

"What happened in eastern Kansas and all of Missouri was as bloody as anything in the Civil War. You'd think nothing happened here to look at the old daguerreotypes. That's because the photographers were all in Virginia. They could just ride out in their buggies and record the action of the day. All we have are drawings. But people don't believe in drawings."

When he was nine, she took him to the State Historical Society in Topeka to see a display of photos and diaries of post-Civil War settlers. He remembered only one picture of a grim-looking family seated in front of a grim-looking farmhouse, a child holding one chicken and the family mule standing to one side with a large dog nearby, as though the inclusion of livestock was a matter of importance, a display of worldly possessions that indicated good standing in a new community.

Tyler had asked if this was her family. She'd smiled and said *no.* When they returned home, she went to the trunk that stood at the foot of his parents' bed and carefully removed an heirloom quilt and then, beneath it, an album that included two photos of her ancestors. "There's my grandmother," she said and pointed to a small girl with long hair pulled away from her face and tied with a bow on top. Tyler looked hard for the family resemblance and found none.

"What about Daddy?" he asked.

"Oh, they came later. Your grandfather Manning moved here from someplace back east. Ohio, I believe. Came to take over his older brother's farm when he died. That brother had never married. Your grandpa Manning made that farm flourish."

Her tales always ended with someone or another *flourishing*, as though she couldn't abide a failure, as though not to flourish were a mortal sin and not a human happenstance, an attitude she carried with her throughout her life. Later, when his brother's failures became evident to Tyler and his father, his mother recast them as signs of unconventional success. Mickey marched to a "different drummer," that was all. Not even Hal could budge her from this notion, even after Mickey's adolescent brushes with the law.

When Tyler asked his father about "the old Kansas days" that meant so much to Delia, Hal would sigh and give him a tired look. "Your mother's legendizing. She needs the stories whether they're true or not."

This confused him. Why would his mother make things up?

"I wouldn't say she's making things up. She knows her history—some of it anyway. She's just imagining her family's part in it. Her people were just poor farmers like everyone else. Doubt very much they cared one way or another about the Black folks. Hell, she doesn't know any."

A joke between menfolk.

"Your mama just likes the old stories. But it was a bloody, awful time. Which is what happens when people get too full of righteous feelings."

Righteous feelings. The words meant nothing to him as a boy but would come back to him on the rare occasion when he felt unjustly treated, suffused with what he assumed were the *righteous feelings* his father spoke of, when the anger came so swift and strong, he knew he could have killed. He remembered his mother's history lessons of men like Jim Lane and John Brown who, under similar feelings, had done violent things, as if the acts were noble and thus worthy of reciting to a child of seven or eight or nine.

Delia wanted her second child born at home. She'd waited so long for this pregnancy and prayed so fervently. She suffered considerably during the pregnancy—morning sickness, edema, assorted scares and discomforts that worried the doctor. She did not wish to risk a wild ride into Topeka and told her doctor so, so he prescribed bed rest for the final term of her pregnancy.

When a neighbor sent over a bushel of newly picked green beans, she'd been so pleased she allowed herself the rare privilege of leaving bed to cook the evening meal. She was standing at the kitchen sink, cleaning a colander of beans, when her water broke. She went to the stairs and called Tyler down, instructing him to phone the doctor, fill a pot with water, put it on the stove, and to gather more towels. All of which he did without complaint.

As she lay moaning in the downstairs bedroom, there was nothing Tyler could do but wait, and Delia sent him out of the room. In the kitchen he looked at the pile of green beans in the sink and finished snapping them and wiped up the counter. He never considered his actions unusual; he thought of it as *helping*. But others—his childhood friend Billie's mother, for one— would look at the husky teenager and marvel at how those enormous hands could shape a tart as easily as plane a board. The greater marvel was this: no household chore appeared to diminish Ty's manliness or his quiet sense of self. He baled hay with the same ease as he swept a floor. He cleaned a gun as carefully as he prepared a cobbler under Delia's meticulous direction. Billie's mother once asked Tyler, still a teen, how he felt about the household tasks he was asked to perform.

Ty shrugged. "You hafta to eat, so you might as well enjoy making it. Dad always says all work's equal in God's eyes."

In the privacy of her own kitchen Ellen Markham told her daughter, "You snare that Manning boy, and you'll never be overworked a day in your life."

Billie still remembered her mother using that ridiculous word, *snare*, as if Ellen thought her daughter, and all women, were baited traps. To Billie, an only child, it made as much sense as "snaring" your brother. That's what Ty had always been, her playmate since babyhood, with the exception of one brief lusty period in high school, and another short chapter at the height of Bud's drinking when she'd lost all sense of herself and floundered.

Perhaps growing up in the Great Plains predisposed boys to choose service in the navy. That's what Tyler chose in the post-draft years after Vietnam. He did it by design: join, serve, see the world, and then go to college on the GI Bill. He thought it unlikely he could get the education he wanted without help. Since his parents were eager for him to take over the farm, they'd been disinclined to see him leave again, playing inno-cent, offering nothing. He knew what they were doing, but he'd made plans and intended to follow them, never once letting his feelings toward his parents harden. Tyler knew what else was on their mind: their younger son Michael was a poor prospect as a farmer. Even if he rented out the land, Mickey would not flourish, being neither hardworking nor thrifty, for Mickey's shortcomings surfaced regularly.

First off, as a newborn, Michael had colic. Delia was up with him day and night, sleepless and losing weight, walking him through the house for two solid months. She carried him down the drive and through the garden and out to the one-acre apple orchard. She seldom woke her husband, even though he told her to. She bounced Michael over her shoulder until it was time to cook a meal, at which point she gave the wailing infant to Tyler who took him and sat in the rocker and rocked. The infant took to his brother.

Sometimes Ty took the baby and sat in the old tire swing his father had put up with a stout rope, over a branch of the chinquapin oak that grew in the side garden. Ty swung back and forth, up and back, clutching Michael in his arms. And since

Delia didn't drive, finding it to her advantage not to learn, her husband drove her to the grocery store on Saturdays when Ty was at home and could watch the baby.

For two months Michael screamed. Then one day he stopped. The house cats, which had fled, spending their days under the porch or in the peony bushes or barn, crept back indoors while the family coonhound looked suddenly less put upon. The boys' father announced, "He'll be all right now." Delia wished it were true. What she actually felt was a roiling maternal guilt that she'd resented the infant's crying. In fact, there had been another reason for her guilt, a brief event so dark that Tyler would not learn, for forty years, what Delia had nearly done to her second son. Delia blocked the event from her memory, yet a lingering, amorphous guilt made her indulgent.

"You take that attitude, Delia," Hal said at the time, "and you'll ruin the boy."

Although Hal never once brought up "the incident," he did remind her that lots of kids suffered colic, and they turned out fine. Delia paid no attention to her husband's opinion. After all, he hadn't carried the boy for nine painful months and endured a troublesome birth or two sleepless months that had left her crazed. Mickey would need special attention, and that was that. Tyler had his own boy's life to live and did so without much concern over what his parents thought or said to each other in careless moments. He loved Mickey for who he was—"my little brother."

Meanwhile the Markhams down the road agreed with Hal: Delia favored the younger son and asked the older boy to do more than his share.

"She's turning that boy into the baby's nursemaid!" said Ellen Markham to her husband. Billie was old enough to soak up every word of gossip floating through the Markham house. Besides, Ty was her closest friend. The two mothers sewed, canned, and cooked together, letting their toddlers play. And until Bud turned sober, Ellen Markham would remind her daughter she should have married Ty Manning.

As for Ellen Markham's concern for Ty, she was right. Tyler became his little brother's nanny but didn't seem to mind. *All work is equal.* He learned how to change diapers, warm a bottle, purée peas and squash. He read Mickey books, played with him and his toys. There weren't any other boys nearby, Billie being his closest friend. Meanwhile, dismayed by what he was seeing develop under his own roof, Hal made sure Ty played Little League every summer.

"Does he want this or do you?" Delia asked her husband.

"He needs to spend time with other boys, not just his mama."

Delia knew this to be true and said nothing, even though she loved having Ty nearby. So Tyler played baseball every year from the age of ten until thirteen when he declared a keener interest in carpentry. Instead of playing ball, he spent time in Virgil Markham's home woodshop, "learning a useful trade."

He was also old enough to help his father. They mended fence, baled hay, doctored the cattle, the goat, and the pony Hal had bought for the boys. They repaired roofs and plumbing in the house and barn. Early on Hal had planted the orchard for his wife, and every fall, after the fruit was picked, the men pruned the trees. Mickey liked the orchard as a toddler, and Ty took him there so he could gather the windfall apples, turning it into a game.

When Mickey was about five and pestering his mother in the kitchen, Ty led him out to the orchard with the promise he could climb the ladder. Delia gave him a pointed look. "Don't do anything foolish." He reminded her he'd be close by. The fruit ladder was still in the orchard, left there from the day before when Delia had run out of storage space and asked them to quit hauling in fruit. The little boy ran ahead of his older brother among the trees. Only half had been picked, and the air was fragrant with the scent of fermenting apples. Mickey saw the ladder propped against a tree and called out his desire to climb it.

"Wait for me," Tyler cautioned.

Tyler followed the boy at a strolling gait. The boy made a

beeline for the tree, but Tyler assumed Mickey would wait until he'd arrived. In his mind he saw himself steadying the ladder while the little boy climbed up a couple of rungs, and then came back down. When the boy reached the tree, he turned to look over his shoulder, grinned back at his older brother, and gripped the sides of the ladder.

Like a snapshot, Tyler took in the scene. Only one half of the ladder rested against the tree; the other hung unsupported. Mickey began to ascend as fast as his five-year-old legs allowed. Tyler took a panicked breath and bolted for the tree. By the time he reached it, the child had made it to the third or fourth rung. Tyler reached for him, but the child laughed and climbed farther. At that moment, perhaps six feet off the ground, the boy's weight finally slid the unbalanced ladder away from the tree and out into space. Tyler yelled, reaching out. The ladder sailed into space, dropping earthward, taking the boy with it. Mickey hit the ground on his side, his rump breaking the fall. He wasn't down more than a few seconds before Tyler had scooped him up, yelling, "You should have waited!"

Under foot, the earth was soft with mulch and decaying apples. Tyler righted the boy on his feet and looked him over. Not a drop of blood and nothing broken. He'll be bruised, Ty thought. "You okay, buddy?" he asked the boy.

Mickey stared at him, still startled from his fall, mouth agape. Only after he saw the pained expression on his brother's face did Mickey pinch his eyes shut and begin to wail. Mickey's crying tapered off almost as soon as Ty started talking. Ty asked him what hurt, and the little boy said his hip but not too much. The fall was not as serious as it had appeared in that instant the ladder had flung the child off. But as soon as they reached the back porch, Mickey suddenly began to wail in a false, high-pitched, tearless lament that startled Tyler. When he'd picked Mickey up, he'd clearly been more surprised than hurt.

Delia flew out the back door and grabbed Mickey out of Tyler's hands. To her alarmed plea to know what had happened, Tyler accurately and calmly described the accident. Mickey finally turned down the noise and announced, "I fell out of the treetop," then turned up the crying. Tyler shook his head for his mother's sake.

"You fell off the ladder, Mick," he said in a low voice. "You were maybe six feet off the ground."

Then the irrational grilling began. "You know better, Ty. Why did you let him go up the ladder? How could you do that?"

Delia became as hysterical as the child. When he realized there was nothing he could say to make things right, he left the two of them to their crying fit and dragged his feet up to his room. His mother had never falsely accused him before. And why would Mickey fib? If it had been Tyler, he wouldn't have even told his mother because the incident seemed so ordinary. Later that evening, as he finished putting the balsa wing on a model Spitfire, his father tapped on his bedroom door. "What happened?" Hal asked. Tyler told him without excuses or embellishment. Hal nodded.

"It's okay, son," said Hal. "Your mother makes too much of your brother. You know that, don't you?"

Still puzzled, he looked at his father and said *yes.* Hal reminded his older son how afraid she'd been that she might lose Michael before he'd had a chance to be born, that mothers were protective creatures. Tyler nodded faintly and finally asked, "But why did Mickey tell a story like that? He made it sound worse than it was, made it sound like it was my fault."

If Hal knew why—and there was every reason to believe he might—he didn't share his suspicions with his older son. He patted Tyler gently on the shoulder and said, "We know it was an accident, and Mickey's fine. Your mother will get over it."

In the morning, Tyler heard Mickey go downstairs with the same bounce he always used. A few minutes later, Ty followed him to the breakfast table. He watched his little brother with a new wariness. He'd almost asked Mickey how he felt, almost said, "How's your butt," but thought better of it. Instead, when he pulled out his chair, he said, "Hey, champ." One of his special words for the scrawny boy.

Mickey acknowledged him back, friendly and normal, then poured milk on his cereal. Tyler grew conscious of his mother moving from sink to fridge to table. Nothing lingered of yesterday's accident except his memory of his mother's feverish response. The breakfast rituals were entirely the same, yet for Tyler the echo of that incident lingered.

"Bus is here," Delia said, looking out the kitchen window. She'd announced this event every day since Tyler started school. He got up from the table, grabbing his books and the windbreaker as he went out the back door—the only door the family used. He was stepping onto the bus when he realized that for the first time he had not kissed his mother goodbye.

Since they'd become teens, Ty's contact with Billie had been tapering off. She preferred girls now since boys had become the object of crushes. When he saw Billie, it was usually at the Markham house whenever he came to work with her father in his basement shop. He once heard a loud song sung by a trio of teenage girls. He gave Virgil a puzzled look, but the older man simply acted as though the girls didn't exist. Tyler worked silently beside his father's best friend until Ellen Markham called downstairs, "Tyler? I got a Coke for you when you're finished." When he went upstairs later to get the Coke, three girls, including Billie, were at the kitchen table eating popcorn. As soon as he appeared the girls squealed and fell into each other's arms, swatting each other, then lifted up like a flock of sparrows and swooped, laughing, out of the kitchen. What had happened to his childhood friend?

"What was that all about?" he asked Ellen.

"Teenage girls," she said with a conspiratorial smile. "You know how they are."

He didn't know. They were a complete mystery.

Hal Manning observed how serious his teenage son had become about woodworking and set aside space in his own basement shop. Not as dedicated or as skilled as Virgil, Hal still kept tools and a workbench for household repairs. Much of what he did was gluing things back together, not carpentry. It didn't matter how it was fixed, in his view, as long as Delia was satisfied.

Slowly, Tyler acquired his own tools: screwdrivers, hammers, planes, a poke shaver, scrapers, an industrial strength vice, wrenches, pliers, a Disston hand saw, and assorted other instruments—an item for his birthday, another at Christmas. His father put up a peg board behind the workbench where Tyler proudly hung the instruments of his craft. His dad shared the drill and sander, knowing Tyler would care for them.

At first he crafted small cars and trucks for his brother, the inevitable birdhouse for Delia, and then a bedside table for his parents' room and a treasure chest for Mickey. Tyler was sixteen, Mickey seven, when Ty's favorite screwdriver went missing. Delia thought maybe he'd used it when he fixed the dresser in her bedroom. He hadn't. The tool had never left the basement shop. He ransacked his memory but couldn't imagine where he'd left it.

"You just had a careless moment, son," his mother commiserated.

For the first time Tyler could remember, his father intruded. "Tyler isn't careless, Delia. It is the one thing he is *not*."

Delia looked at her husband in surprise and let it pass. Tyler had not considered theft—or borrowing—but Hal had and with a very good idea who the borrower was. After the boys had caught the school bus a week after the tool went missing, Hal went to his younger son's room and looked in every drawer and closet and cranny. He finally found the prized screwdriver inside the treasure chest Tyler had made for Mickey. He brought it downstairs and placed it on the kitchen table and spoke his wife's name.

Delia had been washing the breakfast dishes. Never one to rush, she shook the sudsy water from her hands, dried them on a towel, and then turned around. Hal pointed to the tool.

"And what is that?"

"Tyler's missing screwdriver."

"Good. That'll make him happy."

"Don't you want to know where I found it?"

"Is it important?" she asked, puzzled.

"In Michael's room. In his toy chest."

Which meant, Hal went on, the boy had taken it deliberately.

"It's possible he found it lying around and just picked it up to play with. You know how little boys are. And why were you poking around in Michael's things?"

At this Hal finally erupted. As a teen he'd discovered his disconcerting capacity for rage and had learned, as an adult, to control it. Thus, he appeared to his wife as a man who seldom lost his temper. The sudden burst of anger upset her deeply. Stunned into silence, she clenched her hands in her lap; her breathing turned shallow.

"You defend him this time, Delia, you'll do it again and again. And you'll have a thief on your hands."

She laughed but the sound was dry, defensive, and Hal heard this.

"You cannot cover for this child, woman. You cannot."

"I don't know what you mean?"

She did know, Hal believed. She must, for she'd been defending him against the world since he was born. Michael was no longer that colicky infant or the underweight toddler. And why on earth, Hal asked, would Mick feel he needed to steal something from a brother who loved him and would do anything for him?

"Maybe he doesn't see it as stealing."

"But it is, and we're going to tell him so."

Alarmed, Delia stared at him. "I think that's a job for a boy's father."

"Maybe, but you're going to be there to confirm we don't allow this in our house."

Tyler was not present at the kitchen conference. He'd not been invited although his father told him about it later when they were alone in the barn. It hadn't gone well. Michael turned his large green eyes on his father and claimed he'd found the

screwdriver although he couldn't remember where. Each time
Delia tried to speak, Hal glared at her and raised a finger until
the end when he asked his wife to confirm his position on taking the property of others. Finally given the chance to speak,
she refused, and in that refusal, Michael understood what Delia did not. Hal was dumbfounded. He concluded the family
conference by reminding Michael that neither his mother nor
father would abide taking other people's possessions without
permission.

Two weeks later a prized chisel disappeared off the pegboard above Hal's orderly workbench, never to be found. Hal
assumed the worst: the boy had taken it in retaliation and perhaps thrown it away. When Hal confronted Delia with this, she
refused to listen. "Ask your oldest son, why don't you?"

Tyler was coming in the back door when he overheard his
mother's remark. He turned on his heel before they could see
him and returned to the barn where he stood, incredulous
and burning with anger. Before Mickey was born, he'd felt
as close to Delia as to his father and admired each for their
own unique selves. Now that special bond had been ruined
by behavior he could not fathom. He took the ax and went
behind the barn to the wood pile where he split enough wood
for a week, his body moving in rhythmic swings and chops
until he broke into a sweat and he felt the anger dissipate. His
father found him there and stood watching his older son until
Ty lowered the ax, hurling it into the chopping stump, his
shoulders drooping.

"You heard your mother?" Hal asked. Tyler nodded. "I'm
sorry you did, but her words don't reflect on you. You may not
remember this but your mother was very ill after Michael was
born, and she feels guilty about that now. She'll say anything to
protect your brother."

Tyler nodded, but his father's information only made him
more dismayed. Nor could Tyler fathom the impact the theft
had had on his father. "Ask your oldest son." Delia's remark
made no sense to Hal at all. As he pondered why his wife would

abet such thieving, something vital inside Hal felt tampered with, as though trust in his helpmate was being extinguished. Trying to puzzle through this turn of affairs only confounded him, and he did not eat with the same relish as before and complained of heartburn.

As long as Mickey was not the focus, Delia remained a loyal wife, something Hal had long observed. So he tried not to mention the boy except in a positive light, but even this was a struggle. His teachers complained—he was a clown in the classroom; he cheated on his tests and when caught, implicated other students. No surprise there, Hal thought. From kindergarten into first grade, then second and third, Mickey scraped by, finding more pleasure in testing the patience of his teachers and coaches and bus drivers. He was once suspended from the bus for rowdy behavior. And in fifth grade he started bothering the girls.

After the chisel went missing, Tyler kept his distance, and a quiet heartsickness settled in. More than ever he spent time with his father or with Virgil Markham, giving the kitchen a wide berth. Mickey was lost to them, preferring Delia's company or the companionship of a string of fawning friends. ("Dolts, every mother's son of them," Hal told Virgil Markham.) These boyhood friendships would last until Michael alienated the newcomer in some manner, and then a new sidekick would take the discarded one's place until that one had been misused or a parent phoned Delia to complain, declaring that Michael Manning was not allowed, ever again, to play with her child. If these blatant clues disturbed Delia, she gave no indication but continued to defend her younger son as though he were the most misunderstood child in Douglas County.

Tyler spent the summer after his high school graduation helping his father around the farm or working in Virgil's shop. In July of 1975, Tyler would turn nineteen, and in late June he announced that he'd joined the navy and would be heading for the Great Lakes Naval Training Center in ten days. With his father's knowledge, he wrapped all his tools and took them to

Virgil's for safekeeping. He packed up the books he valued, his two Little League trophies, numerous model airplanes, and the animals he'd carved that took up one entire display case. These he also boxed and put in storage with the same prescience the spouse of an unrepentant gambler might hide the family silver. His father said nothing, but Delia was upset. This was his home too, so why did he seem to want to vacate it completely?

"My clothes are still here," he said with a smile. He didn't care about his clothes. Mickey could set those on fire, and Tyler wouldn't care. "Now you can have that sewing room you've wanted."

He meant it sincerely. He had no intention of returning to this house for more than a visit.

When Hal Manning drove his older son into Kansas City to catch the bus, he advised Ty to make his carpentry skills known. Conceivably, Ty could become a construction specialist, a builder, a finish carpenter. He might then not be stuck for long tours on the high seas. Ty had thought being on the water was the whole point, but he took note of his father's advice. Hal was mostly concerned that his son might be stuck in some mess hall kitchen.

"Whatever you do, son, don't tell them you can cook."

In the fullness of time, he was assigned to a mobile construction battalion, working alongside engineers, eventually doing the finish work he had first learned from Virgil Markham, growing more skilled during his naval service. His first overseas assignment took him to an airstrip in Puerto Rico for a few brief months, then to Guam to build housing for the sudden influx of Vietnamese, to Subic Bay for the bulk of his tour, returning to Port Hueneme, California, for the final six months of his three-year hitch. He'd enjoyed the lush and color-saturated island of Puerto Rico, his first foreign visit. He bought a handbook of Spanish phrases and practiced whenever he could. He liked the sounds of Spanish, its warm vowels and expressive sentences. Maybe he'd study Spanish when he finally attended college.

He met Manuel Robles, a petty officer, at Fort Hueneme, but not in the way he might have wished. Then again, if the fight hadn't occurred, he might never have gotten to know Manny at all. He'd joined a group of seamen for an off-base drink during a short leave. He couldn't remember if they'd only gone into Oxnard or had traveled up the coast to Ventura. What he did remember, on a cellular level, was the terrifying sensation of an angry man on his back. While he and his mates were enjoying their beers, he hadn't noticed the young men at a neighboring table, eyeing him. He'd learned that a certain type of man wanted to take him on for no other reason than his impressive height and shape. His father had taught him to ignore taunts and mind his own business. He'd never done much fighting as a kid because there'd never been any need. He knew everyone at school and they respected his size. But in the larger world, where respect was a tenuous and complicated thing, Ty Manning was unprepared for brutal provocations. He'd had no chance to learn about free-floating meanness, misdirected anger, or resentment. What he'd learned from his mother and brother seemed to apply only to the family.

The man and his two partners hurled themselves at Ty just as he was leaving the bar with his buddies: three men on his back, knocking him, face first, onto an asphalt parking lot. For Ty, the more shocking event was that the men were very young and Black. Tyler's mates fell into the melee as if they were born to fight. Tyler staggered to his feet with one accoster still clinging to his neck. Then his attacker, an arm wrapped around his neck, choking him, whispered, "Fuckin' peckerwood." He'd never heard the term but knew instinctively what it meant. When the man bit his ear, something in Tyler exploded. He whirled the man around, grabbed the restraining arm, and pulled it off his neck like you'd twist the horns of a troublesome steer to ground it for branding. With one additional twist, he broke the arm and flung the man on his back and shouted, "Stupid nigger!" Tyler reached down and pulled his attacker to his feet, ran him up against the rear of the building, bashing the kid's head repeatedly against the solid wall. Tyler then grabbed the young man by the throat and squeezed, pummeling his face with his free fist, over and over.

Suddenly, Manny was beside him, strong hands on Tyler's arms, pulling him back, talking him down from his rage. "It's okay, man, you did it. It's okay. Let him go…"

One of other Black men was screaming, "He's killing him! That cracker's killing him."

Manny turned and punched the screamer in the gut. "You brothers started it, asshole! This man didn't do nothin' to you. Nothin'! We got four of us who'll say so."

Tyler was trembling when Manny finally pulled him away, his legs a mass of jelly. The young man he'd pummeled slid down the wall, barely conscious, broken arm flopping at a sickening angle, nose flattened, a flap of skin hanging away from his face, eyes swelling, hair soaked with blood. Tyler stared at him in shock. If Manny hadn't stopped him, Tyler believed he might have killed the kid.

Stunned and deafened by adrenaline, Tyler didn't notice how Manny had taken charge, dealing with the bar owner, his fellow seamen, the young attackers and their partisans, moving the gawkers along, waiting for the authorities and an ambulance. Tyler's head finally cleared enough that he could make out Manny's voice establishing for anyone near the fight scene who was emphatically in the right. "You can't mess with a man and expect nothin' to happen… Can't do a man wrong and get away with it… Can't jump a seaman without consequences… Don't make no difference what you are—Black, white, brown, or chartreuse! Wrong's wrong!"

By the time the crowd dispersed, there was no doubt in anyone's mind that Tyler had done the only thing he could, in self-defense. "What were those dumbass kids thinking, anyway?" The only people of color Tyler had known were custodians in stores, cooks in restaurants or the school cafeteria. Not one schoolmate had been of color, a fact that would haunt him whenever he remembered that appalling fight. All he had done was stand on God's green earth, taking up his allotted space, and someone despised him for it. His battalion had taken him to the Caribbean and the Far East, but he'd had to return to the US to learn about hate.

Later one of his mates slapped him on the back and joked, "Hey, big guy. You're not in Kansas anymore."

Back on base, Manny made him a cup of tea, something healing that Mexican people drank, he told Ty. "You gotta learn to fight, man. Keep those fists up and head down. Lighten that big body of yours, dance on those long feet. This crazy pummeling business won't work."

And so Manny had taught him how to fight, how to keep focused and "cool." *Gotta detach, man.* What he learned from Manny, he would carry with him for the rest of his life. Without Manny, Tyler did not believe he would have learned how to control that secret cauldron of rage he did not know he owned. Never again, he told himself, would he allow himself to become so angry, so out of control. Like a rabid dog. He had frightened himself, he told Manny.

"Yeah, happens to all of us one time or another. Nothin' like the navy for learning life lessons." Then Manny gave a high-pitched *heeheehee* that took Tyler by surprise and made him laugh.

But Tyler suspected the rage had a different origin, that the seeds of his outburst had been sown in a Kansas farm kitchen. The *righteous feelings.*

"I used the word," he told Manny later, brooding about the man he'd pummeled. "Called the kid *a nigger.* Listen, I come from a long line of people who just don't say that. Even if you don't know any Black folks, you just don't say that."

He was thinking of his mother with her staunch Free State ancestors who traced their lineage to New England abolitionists, even if they'd been in Kansas since the mid-nineteenth century. His mother's larger sense of justice was something he could still admire because it wasn't personal. But when it came to her kith and kin? His heart beat uncontrollably just thinking of her and Mick. *Thou shalt not bear false witness.*

"Well," Manny answered, rocking back on his heels. The top of Manny's head came as far as Ty's chin. "He called you a cracker and a peckerwood, so I'd say you're even. Especially since you're not neither, and I've known some peckerwoods in my day. Maybe you gotta learn to be less nice."

For years after, he sometimes awoke with a cry, lurching up, his bedclothes moist. He'd dreamed again of the young man on his back choking him, dreamed of his own fist slamming repeatedly into the Black kid's head, the image of that destroyed face, dripping blood, as horrific to him as the weight of the angry man clinging to his neck.

He kept in touch with Manny after he left the navy. Christmas cards, joke cards. When Manny sent him a wedding announcement, Tyler sent a gift, wishing he could have gone back to California for Manny's wedding. Then Manny sent a picture of his first child: he and Maria had a daughter. Soon Tyler got so tied up in student teaching, he forgot to write. Over a year elapsed before he thought to send Manny a card, but the card was returned, address unknown. Years later he realized he could probably find Manny through navy channels but didn't try. In the last letter he received, Manny said he was thinking of leaving the navy. He wanted to set up an auto shop with his brother in Riverside.

His first adult friend and he had lost track of him. For the longest while, whenever he thought of Manny, he felt bereft. Now that more Mexican kids attended the high school where he taught, Manny Robles surfaced in his thoughts—little aphorisms, Mexican quips delivered in Spanish that Ty had tried to learn, Manny's fight instructions. "Keep your fists up and your head down… Gotta detach, man."

3

THE TROUBLE WITH DOCUMENTS

MAY-JUNE 1992

The evening the baby arrived, Tyler scarcely slept. Throughout the night he listened, getting up from time to time to make sure she was still breathing. Against the Harringtons' advice he put the crib in his bedroom. *Until I feel comfortable,* he told them. He'd never feel comfortable, Billie said, if he couldn't grab some shut-eye. In winter he usually closed the doors to the other two upstairs rooms to save on heat. One of those rooms, Bud pointed out, ought to be a nursery.

The following day became a blur of leaky diapers, acrid odors, talc and formula and bottles. By the third day he felt as if he were sleepwalking through his farm chores. When she woke him with a wail at one in the morning, he sluggishly threw off the sheet and stumbled toward the crib. On the fourth morning he fell asleep over his morning coffee. When the child went down for a nap, he lay down as well, becoming a nap taker for the first time in his life.

On the fifth day, Bud drove his truck to the back door and walked into the kitchen to find Tyler, eyes dark as a raccoon's, slumped over the sink while he slopped soap over a pan full of dirty dishes. Tyler glanced up.

"Man, have you looked at yourself lately?" said Bud.

Tyler glanced at his neighbor and grunted. "I've been busy."

"Billie said you looked like shit and I'm here to confirm it."

"Thanks...kind of you."

"We're taking the baby for the weekend."

Tyler looked at Bud with alarm.

"Relax…just so you can get some sleep. Understand? Friday and Saturday nights."

And sleep he did until he jerked awake at one or two or three in the morning, oddly anxious at the absence of a cry.

Diaper. Milk. Formula. For once he was grateful to be a creature of habit. Dull, predictable Ty. Someone had called him that once. Nancy, maybe… He'd pick the child up gently and place her against his shoulder, feeling the soggy edges of a diaper. Her voice rose into a wail while he removed the soiled Pamper and swiftly attached a new one, remembering with mild distaste the troublesome cloth diapers his mother had used with Mickey. He sang to her in a rumbling baritone and toted her to the kitchen. While the bottle heated he bounced the fussy infant, her urgent cries rising up into Himalayas of hunger. When he finally put the bottle in her mouth, the cries dropped like a radio abruptly turned off. She pulled on the bottle. Behind the sucking sounds were tiny grunts that made him smile. He carried her into the dark living room and sat in the old rocker.

How simple it was to make her happy. Her needs were sharp and clear. A moment of imbalance produced an immediate effect, but once her world was right side up—contentment. He pondered this unexpected thing, a growing infant in his parents' old home. The place surely had a distinctive smell, but what would it be? Not of pipe or cigarette smoke. No one had smoked, except Mick, and he hadn't been here in years. Perhaps that funny vacuum smell clinging to the drapes. Billie gave him some child-rearing books, but every time he set about to read a chapter, he fell asleep over the page. He rearranged the baby in his arms. She pulled deeply on the bottle, and her eyelids grew heavy. When she opened her eyes to look at him it was as if she were pushing up a great weight. Finally, the bottle dropped. Ty lifted her to his shoulder and patted her back. Funny, how all the steps came back to him from the days he'd helped his mother with Mickey.

He rocked her on his chest until she was fully asleep. He

ought to bring the rocker upstairs. In fact, he ought to get started on the nursery, open the room across the hall from his and make it suitable for a little girl. The weight of the child against his heart had the astounding effect of an amphetamine sharpening his brain, speeding him up.

Billie stopped by daily. On one such trip she asked if he'd bathed the little girl yet. He gaped at her. *Bathed?* How could he be so slow!

"You can wash her in the kitchen sink. Easy as pie. Washed all my babies in the kitchen sink until they got too big." She put a bottle of baby shampoo on the table before leaving. "Have fun. Babies love water."

Tyler got a bath towel, diaper, and change of clothes, then filled the sink with warm water. The little girl was awake and burbling in the portable bassinet Tyler had put in the living room, so he could watch both the morning news and the child. Rusty, the retriever, had lain down beside her. The first day Tyler had put her in the bassinet the dog peered curiously into it, leaned over and touched her face with his cold nose. The infant made a startled sound. Tyler calmly admonished the dog. Rusty lifted its muzzle, gazed at him mournfully before moving a foot away and planted himself on the rug, head on paws. He hoped the dog would be protective, but you never knew. He could just as easily be jealous. Tyler lifted the infant out of her bassinet and brought her to the kitchen and undressed her. He slowly placed her in the sink, one arm under the child for support. The baby kicked her legs and smiled.

"You're like a tadpole," he said aloud.

He laughed and swooshed a washcloth over the tiny body, then squeezed a drop of shampoo onto the mop of dark hair. An accidental splash over the baby's face produced an amazing uproar. The dog trotted into the kitchen and gazed at this creature capable of so much upsetting noise.

At the end of that first week, the Harringtons asked if he'd settled on a name, other than Tadpole.

"Yes," he said. "Delia May. *Delia* for my mother and *May* for the month she arrived."

Billie glanced at Bud before she spoke. "I'll be calling her *May* if you don't mind."

Billie didn't look at Ty after she said it. She didn't wish to offend, but surely he knew the reason. She could not bring herself to invoke the name of that unhinged woman, *Delia*, day in and day out. As she told Bud later, "That poor child comes with enough baggage if she's in fact Mickey's daughter. Can't her name, at least, be her own?"

As far as Billie was concerned, this baby was May Manning.

Billie couldn't put the issue aside. No child could go through life without documents. She'd kept the birth certificate and vaccination records of each of her children in Bud's basement safe. Ty remained adamant about not phoning around until they had more information. Where that information might come from she had no idea. They didn't even know the baby's age. Billie was sure May was less than a month old when she arrived. How could some young mother have taken care of her child for two or three weeks and then given her up? The cord was so strong in Billie, even now. Had the mother even gone to a hospital?

By the third week, Tyler's list of possible actions and resources grew longer. How do you find a birth certificate if you don't have any names? Besides, the girl knew the presumed father as Mike Mann. Which meant the girl could have used her own name—whatever that was.

"Now's the time to turn Bud loose," Billie told Tyler. "He's a finder, you know."

When she reached home, she found Bud seated at the kitchen table with a cup of coffee, his police scanner squawking. "Big pileup on 40 near the turn," he said absently before looking up with a questioning look as she walked through the back door. Billie pointed to the scanner.

"I'm turning this off a minute. Okay?"

He nodded, and she sat down.

"Do you suppose we could be this baby's uncle and aunt?"

"We can't rightly prove we're family. So why can't we be her godparents?" He said it hopefully.

"I think that's just for Catholics," she said.

"Not necessarily," he said and told her why.

"That involves church and baptism," Billie remarked.

"So? Ty's people were Methodists once upon a time. Members of that church east of Topeka, something-or-other United Methodist Church. He can rejoin, and we can stand by their side at the baptismal font. You see?"

She did.

"And when the social worker comes to check him out," Bud said, "we'll be there."

Relieved, Billie burst out laughing and slapped his arm lightly.

After supper she phoned Ty to ask him if he was sleeping any better. "I asked Bud," she said finally. There was brief silence, and she rushed to fill it. "He suggested we become the baby's godparents."

A grunt of agreement came from Tyler and then something else she didn't catch.

"Is that an *Amen*?" she asked.

"It is."

If she were lucky, this little girl would have the equivalent of three sets of parents, if Ty counted as a full set. They'd have to scratch the original pair who'd abandoned her. That would leave her with Tyler, who had the skill set to be as nurturing as a mother, and then her parents pro tem, Billie and Bud. Would that be enough? Was it ever enough if the original set cast you off? Watching her own children, she'd concluded that the advent of adulthood made people melancholy about what they'd never had. Floundering in a stewpot of hormones, adolescents discovered self-pity, abetted by a fresh rash of pimples and brooding moods, all the morbid muses rushing out of the box. Was a child ever allowed to move into personhood without passing through that torture chamber?

Her own daughter was passing through the chamber now. Aged twelve, Ginny was so insecure about her looks and her brain that she'd scarcely leave the house without an hour of preparation, all intended to make her look older, sexier, and smarter than she was. More than once Billie had to send her back to her room to modify her appearance. "That is not an acceptable outfit." Which always elicited a hurt response: "Mother, I hate you!"

Billie pulled herself back to thoughts of May Manning. Perhaps she should be giving May's young mother some credit. At least the girl knew what she couldn't handle. At least she hadn't tossed the infant into a trash bin. Still, she wondered if Ty had any idea how parenthood was an unbroken thread of worry? You'd think that woebegone young mother, when she appeared on his threshold, had come to deliver the Golden Egg.

Eleven days of parenting passed before Ty announced he needed legal help. He phoned as the Harringtons were finishing dinner. "Could you all come over tonight?" Billie grabbed the pound cake intended for their dessert, sliced two pieces for her children, located her handbag, and told her youngest child, Aaron, he could watch whatever he wanted on TV, but he had to mind his sister. The boy let out a whoop that his sister clipped with the reminder, "I'm in charge."

When the Harringtons walked into Tyler's kitchen, freshly brewed coffee perfumed the air. The three adults took chairs around the kitchen table (free of dinner crumbs or spots of any kind, Billie noted), mugs at the ready, while Billie divided the pound cake.

"Look at this linoleum," Tyler muttered in disgust. "Can't believe I haven't replaced it."

Billie glanced at the floor—older but not shabby, and clean. Tyler's standards were too high for the rest of us mortals, she thought. She pulled a pen and large yellow pad out of her tote and placed these in front of her. "I'm ready."

"Okay," Bud said and leaned into the table. "You want us to strategize, is that right?"

Without further prompting Bud tossed out ideas while Billie wrote them down. Ty pondered each one before giving what amounted to a thumbs-up or down. Bud ran through the usual choices: phoning hospitals, city offices, or emergency clinics. Billie was glad she was writing. It gave her hands something to do rather than flail around in frustration at Ty's slow responses. And as long as her fingers were busy, her mouth did not seem inclined to fling out a hazardous word.

Ty sounded reluctant to do anything, and then Bud dropped the bomb. "Man, you are so afraid they're gonna to take this baby away from you! You gotta get over that, or you're gonna sit there doin' nothin'!"

Billie held her breath, then reached over and gently patted his hand, grateful he'd had the courage to say it.

"You suppose that's it?" Ty said, as if Bud's comment was a revelation, which apparently it was. So here, on vivid display, were the assets of the masculine bookends of her life. Blunt Bud and Honest Ty who never turned a truth away, even if it reflected badly on him.

The baby gave a chirp of discomfort. Billie and Ty jumped to their feet.

"I'll get her," he said.

The first step was to follow through on the license plate number that Ty had had the wits to record. If that failed, they'd phone the hospitals, but so much hung on the mother's name.

Billie repeated her hunch that the baby was an emergency room delivery, that the mother might never have been to a doctor beforehand or used an alias.

Bud tilted back in the kitchen chair and gazed at Ty. "Where is your brother?"

Ty shrugged. "Haven't seen him in years. The girl didn't know either. He told her his name was 'Mike Mann.'"

He gazed down at the baby sleeping in his arms.

"You're lucky that kid's an easy sleeper," Bud said.

Tyler nodded. "Mickey had colic. Screamed for two long months. I thought Mom was going to lose it."

Billie harrumphed. "She did lose it."

The men looked up at her, startled.

"Sorry, Ty. That's just what Mother thought."

"Let's start with the plate number," Bud interrupted. "Her car?"

"No," Tyler reminded him. "Said the driver was her cousin."

"Doesn't matter," Bud said. "I know someone in the sheriff's department. We'll start there."

When Bud finally phoned, Tyler had all but given up. Bud kept his voice low as if fearful of eavesdroppers. Tyler had never understood why people were so attracted to intrigue.

"Strictly illegal, you know," said Bud, referring to the way he'd obtained the information. "The driver didn't list a phone number. Just an address on the northeast side of Topeka."

Bud knew the area, a neighborhood sliding toward the river: mostly bungalows, some two-stories, plus an assortment of shabbier shotguns. "We'll have to drive up there."

Billie advised Ty to take Bud, but he wasn't yet reconciled to such a necessity. It wasn't the company he minded, it was the chatter. Bud would talk all the way there and back, at a time Tyler would have preferred to think. Then Billie added, "He knows how to confront people."

"I don't want to confront them," he told her. "Just get the information."

On the chosen day, Bud insisted on driving, which gave him the chance to show off his new red Silverado with the extended cab. It was all Tyler could do to leave the child in Billie's care. Before climbing in beside Bud, he asked her, "Is she my niece or my daughter? I can't make up my mind."

"Do you need to decide right this very minute?"

He preferred daughter. It sounded more permanent.

Billie waited on the porch with the infant in her arms until the men had turned onto the county road. She had to wave Ty out the door while his eyes lingered on May. Indoors Billie picked up the child's windup swing and carried it with her free hand into Ty's large eat-in kitchen. She placed May in the little swing and wound it up. Back and forth the child went, content. She'd felt the need to keep busy even before the men had gathered their keys and their wits. Somewhere in this well-ordered room, Tyler would have all the ingredients needed to bake a pie or cake. The kitchen was brighter and more up-to-date since Ty had taken possession, refurbishing the old homestead, room by room. After Hal died, Delia had let everything slide.

Billie located mixing bowls, flour and oil, salt, baking soda, and sugar. Wesley had been five and her daughter Ginny not much older than May when she'd come to Ty for solace, creating the only secret she'd ever had to keep. He lived in town then. He'd offered to drive her home because her truck had been stuck in the shop for a week, and Bud had been too inebriated to arrange for its release, let alone fix it himself. She was grateful her parents lived with them and could watch the babes.

"Take me to your place," she'd said. She collapsed on his living room sofa in tears, all her dismay pouring out. What was she to do with two small babes and a sodden husband? She couldn't now recall the sequence, who kissed who first, as if it mattered. Still they had climbed the stairs to his bedroom and when it was over she'd whispered, "We can't do this ever again," knowing as soon as she said it that she would most definitely like to do it again and again. She came back the next afternoon and then another and another over the course of two weeks until it was his turn to say they must stop. She needed to make a choice, but whatever she chose he'd "have her back."

"What does that mean?" she'd asked, her voice trembling with anger and imminent loss.

"I'll support you, whatever you choose."

"How noble."

"No, it's not. It's just how I feel."

"You'd have me? Just like that?" she asked, a trifle amazed.

How could he be so certain? Had he, for an instant, considered the complications?

"If that's what you want."

She didn't know what she wanted, which of course was the problem. She looked around the master bedroom he'd rebuilt and decorated in a comforting dark green. She liked his airplane bungalow but didn't know if she could live with neighbors nearby.

She was coming to Ty for more than comfort. She was coming to enjoy the sex denied her at home. When she admitted this, she felt strangely relieved but also troubled. She was implicating Ty in a scheme of her own making, and it shamed her. One didn't do this to a lifelong friend, even if he was good in bed. She could walk out his door on those shared afternoons, to resume her own life. What did that leave Ty? It was either or. And so she confronted her husband: Either he sobered up or she was kicking him out. Exile. Curtains. Kaput. "You get what I'm saying here, Bud?"

He got it, indeed, and Billie stood by her wavering spouse and did not return to Tyler's bungalow, a fact he accepted with the same equanimity as he'd accepted her into it. A scab formed over this chapter of her life, then fell away, leaving only the smallest scar of a secret: they agreed Bud should never know. It was finished, an aberrant moment that had arisen out of her anguished helplessness. Tyler was again "the good neighbor," the childhood friend. She never asked how he felt; she couldn't bear to know. And now she had three children, her youngest, Aaron, the son of Bud's hard-earned sobriety.

The baby chirped and Billie glanced over. The swing had wound down and stopped. She'd do a pie, she decided. She'd seen the peaches in a bushel basket on Ty's back porch. Nothing consoled like a fruit pie.

Scorning the interstate, Bud took Kansas 40 into Topeka, continuing on Sixth Avenue when the state road ended. Tyler had no sense of this working-class neighborhood nestled into an east-

ern edge of the city, where the Kansas River bulged in a northerly direction before flowing southward toward Ward-Meade
Park. Bud turned right off Sixth and continued north, looking
for street signs. In the Oakland neighborhood, houses sat less
crowded together than he'd imagined, mostly one-story affairs
with front porches, the occasional two-story home mixed in.
Few of the houses had garages but some sported utility sheds
at the end of driveways. The homes were maintained for the
most part, some newly painted, while others stood unloved
with stained roofs and oddly affixed gutters. It was still early in
the summer and the lawns looked green and trimmed while the
occasional chain-link fence separated the properties.

Bud slowed the truck and parked in front of a mustard-colored house with a cluttered porch. Further away from the
house, a large round ceramic planter, bereft of flowers, stood
alone on the lawn. The most neglected property on the block,
Ty thought, and shot wary glances up and down the street.
They climbed down from the truck and walked tentatively up a
cracked concrete sidewalk. Dandelions sprouted in the broken
parts.

He'd assumed the "cousin" wasn't much older than May's
natural mother—only old enough to drive. Bud bounded up
the walk and climbed resolutely up the porch steps, waiting for
Ty. He wished Bud had stayed in the truck. It didn't feel right,
two strange men on a porch. Bud knocked.

Tyler heard voices but no one answered the door. Bud
knocked again, louder. A middle-aged woman in a faded maroon sweatshirt and polyester black pants opened the door part
way and looked them up and down. "Yes?"

"We're looking for Allison Smith," Bud blurted out. Tyler
poked Bud in the back.

"And who wants to know?"

Female voices murmured somewhere out of view.

"I'm Allison." A young woman appeared beside the older
one, a tough girl expression pasted across an otherwise unblemished creamy face. "What d'ya want?

"It'll take a moment, and we thank you for your time." Bud turned finally, deferring to Tyler.

Tyler cleared his voice and gave his name. "You or someone else drove a young girl with a baby out to my house near Stull. I'm trying to find her."

The younger woman's face clamped down, her jaw set in a rigid line. "That's news to me."

"Maybe so, but your car was at my house. Maybe you loaned it to a friend."

"Maybe."

"Look," Bud broke in. "We're only here to get some information. This man is taking care of your friend's child—"

"What child? I don't know nothing about a child."

Bud's eyes fluttered shut as he ignored her.

"He'd really like to speak with your cousin." Bud gave the word an unpleasant punch.

Both women had stiffened noticeably during Bud's speech. Then the older one announced, "We don't know what you're talking about. And I'd like you to get the hell off my porch. I'll call the law."

"You do that, lady," Bud menaced, "and we'll be happy to speak with them about child endangerment and child abandonment and a few other little things. You call the law and you're in a heap of shit."

Tyler caught a glimpse of a small figure moving quickly behind the woman, down a short hallway toward a door at the rear of the house.

"That's her!" Tyler said, pointing at the departing figure.

The door flew at them and both men jumped back as it slammed and locked. They hurried down the steps.

"They know," Bud said. "Guilty as crows—where you going, Ty?"

"Behind the house." He ran quickly around the side of the house, through some low tangled shrubs, before being stopped by a tall chain-link fence. Bud followed and pointed.

"This neighborhood has alleys. Look."

The girl could have taken off in either direction behind the houses or hidden in a shrub at the rear of the property.

"Get the truck," he shouted at Bud. "I'll meet you in the alley."

Ty sprinted across the yard and through the neighbors', looking for an unfenced break between houses. At the third house he found one, turned right, running along the edge of a tidy yard, past peony bushes and staked tomato plants until the property reached the alley. Here he stopped and waited. Bud pulled the truck into the alley and drove up in a flamboyant burst of speed. Tyler jumped in.

"Drive slowly."

"Too late, man."

"Just do it!" he snapped.

The truck grumbled in low gear. The alley was a single lane of patchy concrete, deteriorating badly along the edges. Tyler's eyes scanned the back of one property after another, left then right. A few premises had sloping tool sheds near the alley or old autos on cinder blocks.

"Dog patch," Bud muttered.

"Not quite. Better than I expected."

"Except the house we just left. That girl was definitely Daisy Mae."

They were nearing the end of the block when he saw a small figure running slowly along the edge of the alley in the next block. Tyler pointed. "There she is," Ty whispered. "Go straight."

"Crappy surface. Look at these potholes."

"It's an alley, Bud. Keep going!"

The truck lumbered over a rocky exit into the public street, then crossed the street and into the next alley where the surface had disintegrated even further into gravel. The figure ahead was running awkwardly now, and Tyler yelled for Bud to gun the motor. Bud shortened the distance until the girl stumbled and fell sideways. Tyler leaped from the truck and called out, "I got her!" When she saw who it was, she half-crawled along the broken pavement, struggling to climb to her feet. Tyler reached her before she could stand, grabbed her arm, and pulled her to her feet.

"Whoa. I'm not gonna hurt you. Relax."

"Let go of me!"

He thought she was about to turn hysterical and gave her a stern shake. The truck pulled up behind them and stopped.

"You can't leave a child on someone's doorstep and walk away. I need information."

She was crying now, her nose snotty as a toddler's, her upper lip slick. She looked even younger than she had at the farmhouse. He gave Bud a signal to stay in the truck while he tried to calm her. He kept his voice low, never once letting go of her, telling her what he wanted, assuring her again and again that the baby was in the right hands and everything was going to be okay. She looked him in the eye at last, her eyes watery. He pulled his clean handkerchief out of his rear pocket and handed it to her. When he asked, she gave him a name he felt sure was made up and gazed off into some shrubs. He'd seen the wallet in her back pocket, reached around swiftly and yanked it out with a quick apology. She swatted at his hand. "Goddamn you!"

Tyler tossed the wallet through the open window to Bud. "Tell me what you find."

The girl began wriggling to free herself, swatting at him, cursing. Holding tighter, he muttered, "Won't do you a bit of good."

Bud yelled down information as it revealed itself: a few bills, photos, an old school ID card but no driver's license. Finally, "The young lady's name is Sherlynne Smith."

"Okay, Sherlynne Smith. You belong with that bunch?" He pointed his hand in the direction of the house she'd just fled.

"I don't have to tell you nothin'."

"You might as well. We'll stand right here till doomsday unless you do." She thrust her chin in the air, her mouth pinched into an unattractive rictus. "I got all day," Ty said.

The girl gave a shuddering sob. "My aunt."

"And the younger woman?"

"My cousin."

He asked their names and she gave them. She was looking at him with wobbly defiance. He was afraid to ask about her parents since she might not have any.

"You live with your aunt, I take it."

"Hey, look at these," Bud called, reached out the window, waving pocket-sized photos. Pulling the girl along with him, Ty stepped over to the truck and took the photos. The pictures were grainy, taken at a mall photo booth where friends crowded in together for a photo shoot: Mickey and the girl were posed with their faces pressed together, smiling. Disgust swept over him. The girl snatched a small photo out of his hand.

"Give it to me, asshole!"

She was gazing at the photo of Mickey. An expression of longing had pulled her mouth open and caused her eyes to droop. My god, he thought. The girl misses Mick.

"So tell me about him," Tyler said.

She looked as though she might burst into tears.

"Forget it, man," Bud said through the window. "You got what you need. Let's go home."

The anger came in a flash. "For once, Bud, shut up!"

His hand still gripped the girl's arm. Slowly Ty let it go. She couldn't run anyway. He'd bet good money she'd sprained her ankle. "Okay, Sherlynne Smith. Just one more thing: where was she born?"

She looked downward, speaking to the pavement, "Stormont-Vail."

"And what name did you give the baby at the hospital— don't lie to me."

"Smith."

"Hopefully, I won't be seeing you again. Is that right?"

"Count on it!" she snapped while new tears leaked from her eyes and down her freckled cheeks. She took a step away from him, wincing as she stepped on her right foot. She still needed a mother, he thought, and didn't have one. Only the surly aunt on the porch.

"You can't walk with that ankle. We'll take you back to the house."

"You nuts? Think I'm gonna get in a truck with you two?"

He gaped at her. "You gave me your baby, for chrissakes!"

She dropped her gaze and shuffled the lame foot side to side. "Get in," he said softly. "You can sit in back. See? The truck has an extended cab."

It took a moment longer for her to decide. Ty opened the door. As he hoisted her up into the back seat, he asked, "What did you name her?"

The girl shrugged. "I didn't. We just called her baby?"

"Did Mickey know about the child?"

"Who's Mickey?"

"The man in the photo."

"That's Mike."

"Right. 'Mike Mann.' My brother. Did he know?"

"He split when I was only three months on. Didn't have the chance to tell him."

Tyler nodded. "Thank you."

The girl hung her head. Bud started the truck and inched down the unkempt alley to the street and turned right. When they reached the house, Tyler helped her down and she limped straight up the broken sidewalk to the porch without waiting. The front door opened before she'd reached the top step, and Tyler hurried after her. The older woman held the screen door open for the girl. Sherlynne disappeared indoors as the aunt stepped out, blocking the doorway, and waited for him. He came to a halt on the top step. The girl's return must have meant something to the woman. She didn't look surprised.

"If you all want me to take care of this child, we're going to have to do it right."

The woman cocked her head, and Tyler climbed to the porch and pointed toward a pair of faded white plastic chairs. "Will you sit out here with me? I'll only take a minute of your time."

"I'll stand," she said coldly and folded her arms, remaining in front of the closed door. The woman did not appear to have a single attractive feature: too small eyes, a bony nose, thin lips, and a wide face. It made him uncomfortable to look at her.

"Doesn't she want her child?"

"Christ! You saw her. Does she look like she can take care of a kid? She's a kid herself. She dropped out of ninth grade."

"Sometimes families help."

"I told her when she first told me—I've raised my kids, and I can't raise no more. Told her to put it up."

"Put it up?"

"For adoption. Whaddya think I meant?"

His hands flew up in a placating gesture. "Okay, so why didn't she?'

"She thought he'd come back."

"This Mike Mann person."

"Who else?" Her face rearranged itself into a scowl.

"Did he know?"

"Who knows? She didn't tell me."

"He's not Mike Mann. He's Michael Manning. I'm sure he never planned to come back."

"You oughta know."

He paused, curbing his temper. "How does she know this Mike Mann's the father?"

"My niece don't have other boyfriends. And she don't sleep around. Still a child herself."

"Look, I'm just trying to get information. You were pretty hostile when we first came to the door."

"And that other guy was pretty hostile himself." Her chin rose, pointing toward the truck. Her face softened briefly, and she tilted her head back in what he took to be agreement. "Thought you were bringing the kid back."

Tyler nodded. "I need documents. Can you help?"

"I can tell you some." She grudgingly squeezed out the where and when and the child's date of birth: May 14. He thanked her.

"There's something you all might like to know. My brother

never treated anyone well in his life. But he's real good at getting folks to like him."

The woman looked him in the eye for the first time. "He sure had Sherlynne fooled."

Tyler looked down at his boots. "One last thing," he said. "Sherlynne, and probably you, are going to have to sign some papers. She's going to have to give up all rights. Can you deal with that?"

The woman nodded once, grim-faced. "She should've done like I said to begin with."

Without another word she went indoors and quickly closed the door. He heard the lock turn. When he climbed into the truck, he felt more exhausted than ever.

"Did you threaten them with the abandonment thing?" Bud asked.

"Didn't have to. They thought we were bringing May back."

Bud shook his head.

"That little girl in there couldn't be a minute over fifteen," Tyler said. "She thought Mickey might come back. So she kept her newborn for over two weeks just in case. That's the saddest thing I've heard in a long time." Tyler leaned his head back on the rest and closed his eyes.

Bud waited until they'd reached the highway before talking, but Tyler was too tired to take in most of what Bud was saying.

"Mick sure knows how to pick 'em,'" Bud scoffed. "Underage PWT."

Tyler lurched forward, awake. "*PWT?* What're you talking about?"

"You gonna raise a kid that's half Mick and half poor white trash? Sherlynne Smith sure changed your life."

Tyler shut his eyes, craving sleep. His thoughts had moved away from the girl-mother and on to Mickey who'd also changed his life twice before. He stopped listening to Bud, his head swirling with the information the Smiths had revealed. Something resembling hope balanced the weight he felt whenever the subject of his brother surfaced.

4

TYLER, ALONE

1976-1985

When he'd completed his hitch in the navy, Tyler was twenty-two, lean and fit, his curly hair clipped short. After three years away, the arrangements inside his parents' home had not changed, and he didn't like what he saw. His mother sometimes addressed his father in a voice that sounded, to his veteran's ears, like a chief petty officer correcting a new seaman, making Tyler so uncomfortable he wanted urgently to leave. How lonely Hal seemed, so un-included. Tyler wanted to offer his father all the help he could as long as it did not require living under this roof, importuned by his mother. Within hours of his return, he sensed her pulling him toward her, threading her needs and wants through every act of maternal support until they disappeared into one seamless fabric.

"I'll go see if Dad needs some help," he said at his first breakfast at home.

"Don't rush, son. He'd ask for your help if he needed it."

The muscles in his stomach tightened until his breathing felt pinched. Meanwhile, Mickey chuckled to himself as he read the comics in the morning paper. Tyler gazed at the back of the *Topeka Capital-Journal* as though it were written in hieroglyphs. Hal was already in the barn, and Tyler pushed his chair back, smiling at his mother.

"You know me," he said carefully. "Gotta keep busy."

He kissed her on the cheek, grabbed his windbreaker off the hook beside the door, and fled. His eyes were burning by the time he reached the barn. He stopped and bent over, bracing his hands against his knees. Mickey had seemed indifferent to his return, going through the brotherly gestures and jokes and hand slaps they'd rehearsed so many times before. But, then, Mickey was still a teenager. He'd loved Mick once, when he was little. The pain in Tyler's stomach returned in one quick spasm. He groaned and bent over once more.

"Son? You all right?"

He stood up, feigning wellness. His father was leaning against the barn door. He got spasms sometimes, he told his father. Something he'd picked up overseas. A small fib. This pain was new.

"Better have a doctor look at it."

He nodded and walked past his father and into the dim barn.

He didn't linger. He told his father his plans and left again mid-year, this time to K-State. He rented rooms and worked and attended classes year-round, completing his education degree early, including his practice teaching. He returned to his parents' farm for brief holiday visits and for haying season. During these visits he took note of how little Mick did around the farm. Tyler was twenty-five when he confronted his younger brother on the second morning of the annual haying. Mickey was sixteen. If not exactly a strapping boy, he was sturdy enough to help. Tyler told him so.

"He's got plenty of help," Mick said. "Or didn't you notice?"

"Except for me, he's gotta pay those guys."

"You mean you don't get paid?"

"I wouldn't take it if he offered. We're his sons. It's the least we can do."

"Speak for yourself. I'm not that big a fool."

Tyler kept his face composed and his eyes level—something the military, and Manny, had taught him when smaller men, scrappy as terriers, tried to provoke a fight. Nobody likes a freeloader, Ty said finally. Mickey's eyes beaded and his nostrils flared. In case Ty hadn't noticed, the teen said, he had hay fever.

"Take a Benadryl."

The teaching position dropped in his lap. He'd sent applications throughout eastern Kansas, hoping to remain close enough to help his father when needed, but not too close. Then Billie Markham, now Billie Harrington, phoned him out of the blue: The high school where she taught, in a Topeka suburb, was looking for an industrial arts and math teacher. Was he interested? If so, she'd be happy to speak with the principal.

Billie.

He hadn't thought about her in months. Between his course work and his part-time jobs, scarcely a minute remained to reminisce over the first woman he'd ever cared for. It was hard to remember now if what he felt was merely the affection built up over a lifetime of contact. When had he first noticed her as more than a familiar fixture at holiday potlucks or get-togethers with the Markhams? Most of these events were lost in the fog of childhood.

When, as a gawky teen, he began helping Virgil in his woodworking shop, she suddenly had bouncy hair, a quick tongue that left him feeling witless. Where did girls learn these sharp comebacks? And how long had it taken him to realize she was flirting? Then he was fifteen and Hal was teaching him to drive, letting him take the old Dodge truck down to Virgil's on his learner's permit, a farm kid privileged with an early license.

Soon he was driving Billie in a powder blue 1958 Chevy Impala that Billie named Nadine. Billie was almost a year younger but managed to end up in his class, where he remained the biggest kid in his room. Someone needed to be the tallest, Hal told him. "It suits you, son. You're level-headed." *Gravitas,* Tyler's colleague Howard called it years later, a word he did not feel in the least worthy of.

Then it hit. He was sixteen when he told his father, never his mother. He was sweet on Billie Markham and didn't know what he should do. "Ask her out," Hal said. So he took her to that odd rite of passage—the junior prom. She was dressed in a pale pink dress that looked like a cloud. She smelled lovely, too, having applied her mother's Shalimar too liberally. By the end of the evening, he felt more deeply smitten. He'd repeatedly stepped on her toes while dancing, and she didn't hold it against him, making jokes, riding on his feet during one slow dance, which struck them both as hilarious. Only later would Billie put on the bulk common to women who'd borne children, weight that would vex her throughout her adulthood but which Tyler never thought of as unattractive. When he left for his stint in the navy, Billie and Bud Harrington were already considered *an item*. Boot camp did not allow for brooding, and the pain of that loss quickly dissipated.

Billie married Bud when she was twenty and Tyler was still overseas. Likable Bud. Funny, fast-talking, joke-telling Bud. Helen Markham had never been crazy for Bud—news his mother conveyed. But Tyler liked Bud. Who didn't, besides Helen or Delia? His own mother found fault with most men not under her direct supervision, which left virtually no one but her sons to approve of. Billie was finishing her college work, Delia wrote, "but Bud has dropped out and is employed in an auto shop full time, and also works for Virgil. Poor Billie." Tyler wrote her back: "Don't worry about Bud Harrington. He'll land on his feet. He always has." Delia never brought up the Harringtons again.

He'd hoped to find a job a little farther away, but Billie's high school was the first to make an offer. After a speedily arranged interview, the principal told Tyler, "The position is yours if you want it." It took his breath away. He wondered if he ought to slow down, shop and compare. But he was twenty-six, and the possibility of no other offers flashed briefly through his mind. He accepted the position, shaking the principal's hand. That was thirteen years ago, thirteen years before Baby May was delivered to his door. Tyler never taught anywhere else.

Over the years the industrial and fine arts department had grown. Washburn-Shawnee High School featured the vocational and technical arts and was affiliated with the main industrial training college in eastern Kansas. More than one person had called it a plum of a job, in a state-of-the-art shop: classes in basic wood working, finish carpentry, technical drawing or drafting, fundamentals of home repair, plus the occasional geometry and algebra class. Several hours a day he did what he loved. So popular were the technical arts that a new wing was eventually added.

He discovered a knack for explaining things simply, an advantage in a field where school counselors routinely dumped the unscholarly, falsely assuming if you were slow in history you'd be fast at shop. He could sort them out: this one carpentry, that one plumbing or electrical, a third to the auto shop while yet another quiet boy ought really to be in an art class with Howard Shay. Background talk never bothered him, as long it was purposeful. The atmosphere in a shop should be collegial, he thought, unlike an academic class. If you could talk, he reasoned, problems tended to dissolve, and the hyperactive were given physical tasks to complete. The key was making sure everybody stayed busy.

By the time his students were seniors they were headed for technical or vocational careers. He reminded his students—boys mostly—that developing a work ethic was a stated goal of his classes. The upperclassmen came into his capacious shop and got down to work, kept their lockers tidy and their work spaces free of dust and wood shavings and pencils, shared cleanup duties, and treated all tools with respect. Nothing was left out of place at the end of a class period. The boys claimed that a person could eat off the floor of Moose Manning's wood shop. "Moose mops it himself!" they bragged. Next door, in Jeff Kornacki's metal and auto shop, the squeal of compressors and high-powered metal tools made silence not only impossible but hazardous. Howard, in his cavernous art room, spoke about "the continuum of noise" in their new arts and industry wing. As far as Tyler could tell, the noise was never as oppressive as Howard claimed.

"We have the temple of High Art," Howard joked, "which is my room. Then we have the shop of the artisan, the honor-

able guildsman. That's you, Ty. Then you have the third level
of purgatory. That's Jeff and the damned au-to-mo-bile shop. "
Howard had already renamed the new arts and industry wing,
the Mother Ship.

"This is where creative things happen," said Howard.

If Tyler ever went out for a beer on a Friday, it was with
Jeff and Howard and sometimes Billie. None of them jokingly
called him Moose. They left that to the coaches, who thought
Moose was a compliment, and to Vice Principal Con Andrews,
a man Tyler found smarmy and unreliable. Early on, a squirrelly
sophomore, trying for cool, called him Moose in the middle of
a class. Tyler paused and gave the boy a penetrating look. Then
in a quiet voice he replied, "To you I'm Mr. Manning. Always."

Not another student called him Moose within earshot.

Yet the Moose part of his identity had its advantages, for
Tyler's size seemed to mitigate behavior problems. As for those
for whom no words helped, they ended up in study hall or in
Jeff Kornaki's auto shop. It helped that Jeff, an ex-marine, tat-
tooed and sunburned, looked as though he'd done hard time in
Leavenworth. "Send 'em on over," Jeff told him. "You can't do
much damage to an old chassis or a used engine."

In the fullness of time they formed a special club—the three
men of the Mother Ship. At first, Howard Shay seemed a little
impish and fey, a short dark-haired man with horn-rimmed
glasses and a preference for Reeboks. In time Tyler discovered
Howard's droll sense of humor came from a place of astounding sorrow, something to do with being mostly closeted or
possibly his divorce, even though his daughters were always at
his house. Howard heard and saw things no one else seemed to.

"Yeah well, that's what happens in the creative classes," he'd
say. "The kids let their hair down. And you can see it in their
art."

During lunch in the staff room Howard startled them with
his tales. There was the boy who surreptitiously ate clay and
poster paints because there was no food at home; the girl who
used acrylics to varnish her toenails because she never had

spending money. There was the incident with South Pacific posters painted by an enthusiastic group of juniors for their prom. The posters had been left in the Mother Ship courtyard to dry where they were destroyed by an unexpected hailstorm. The girls had wept inconsolably.

"Teenagers, you know," Howard said. "They take everything to heart."

For four months he commuted from the farm to Washburn-Shawnee High School—"Washaw High" to the kids and staff. In March he found the airplane bungalow for sale in the Kenwood neighborhood of Topeka. He liked the Craftsman style, the limestone foundation and wood structure, the newer composition roof. Fish-scale shingles accented the triangular space above the front porch and above the dining room windows. The only exterior updating had been the addition of a back deck.

He did not share his plans with his mother and had only one brief conversation with Hal about leaving the homestead. He stayed at the farm reluctantly, doing so only as a practical matter while he acquainted himself with the city where he now taught, a city he'd lived nearby all his life but now realized he didn't know.

"If you want a proper life," Hal had told him, "strike out on your own. I did."

Tyler did not take this remark as permission, which he didn't need, but as understanding. Without anyone in the family having seen it, Tyler bought the bungalow. One afternoon after classes, he brought Billie over to check it out. He asked her not to tell Bud since Bud, the tippling gabber and yarn teller, might inadvertently say something without ever remembering he'd promised not to tell. But Billie knew how to keep her own counsel. The day after he closed on the house he told his father in the barn. Hal nodded and asked, "Have you told your mother?"

"Not yet."

"Better let her think she's the first to know."

That evening he made the announcement at the dinner table, phrasing the news to include them both. Delia's fork stopped midway to her mouth. The gesture struck him as something theatrical—a pretend gesture. Fortunately, only the three of them sat around the kitchen table since Mickey had gone out with friends. As soon as Delia Manning lowered her fork, the grilling began.

"Didn't you think it might have been a good idea to ask your mother's advice over something as important as the first house?"

He asked her why she felt so strongly and then unspooled the reasons he had carefully rehearsed: The bungalow was closer to his job, and he would be the only one to live in it. A bit of a fixer-upper, so the price was right; a bargain, in fact, considering the good neighborhood. Hadn't she taught her sons to appreciate a bargain? (At this, his mother softened and allowed herself a smile.) He'd actually hoped to spare her all the nonsense that came with buying a house, he said. Besides, he wouldn't be that far away. He offered her one of his rare smiles and glanced at his father whose face was tilted downward, as if absorbed in the crumbs on his dinner plate.

"What do you think, Hal?" she said. "Did you know?"

"The fact it's a surprise doesn't make it a bad thing, does it?"

Delia kept her face expressionless as she discussed the merits of his decision with his father. He'd simply wanted to avoid giving her the chance to intrude, for he'd grown afraid of her. He thought she might be angry but hadn't counted on her feeling hurt. When had he so foolishly convinced himself that her concern for Mick eclipsed any concern she might have for him?

The bungalow had a fireplace with a hearth and mantel composed of Italian tile. On either side were beveled glass windows and built-in oak bookcases. Hardwood floors covered the ground floor. A galley kitchen ended in a breakfast nook looking out over the back garden. The detached garage at the very rear of the property could be turned into a shop. Two bedrooms downstairs and one large rectangular room up, reached by a steep flight of stairs: it was enough space for one man. Tyler planned to convert one of the upstairs closets into a bathroom for what would become the master bedroom.

During that first year, when the teaching day was over, Tyler drove wearily home to the bungalow. He parked his truck in the drive and walked up the few steps, across the deck to the back door. A surge of energy pulsed through him as soon as he entered the house, as if he'd just awakened from a nap. Over the course of that first year, he poured most of his disposable income into the bungalow, building cabinets and shelves, painting, stripping paper, rewiring, re-plumbing, sanding, and staining.

When the spare room downstairs was nearly complete, he invited Mickey to spend a weekend. To his surprise, his brother accepted. He decorated this guest room in blue-gray shades and sturdy masculine furniture, and thought of it briefly as "Mick's room." Over the years his mother's reports would have you believe that Mickey was flourishing. "He's very popular," she liked to say. "Always out with his friends. Not as shy as you were, Ty." The report from Hal gave a different story. The friends were a mixed lot as far as Hal was concerned.

"I don't like them much," his father told him when they were alone in the barn. "Bunch of ne'er-do-wells if you ask me. Michael barely scraped by in school. He's smart enough, he just doesn't try."

But now Mickey was nineteen and worked part-time for Virgil Markham and part-time somewhere else. According to his father, Mick spent all he earned. By the end of any given pay period he didn't have two nickels to rub together and would ask his mother for spending money. Moving away from home never occurred to him. Where was the incentive?

"Why would a young man do that?" Hal asked. "I could hardly wait to be on my own."

Mickey arrived driving the red El Camino his parents had given him. It was the only thing he bothered to keep in good shape, other than himself. When he climbed out of the truck,

Ty was hanging the last curtain in the guest bedroom. Mickey's glossy black shirt and tight blue jeans showed off a fit, trim figure. He also wore what looked like new black boots. The updated cowboy look, Tyler thought. Country swing. Ty climbed off the stool and went to the front door to let his brother in.

Mickey grinned, and the brothers went through an abbreviated version of the old, silly handshake they'd invented years ago. The boots elevated his brother noticeably, but Tyler still stood over him, taller and broader like their father. Tyler threw an arm around Mickey's shoulders and pulled him into the house.

"I've been looking forward to this," he said, melting under the influence of Mick's disarming smile. "Let me show you your room."

"Wow! My own room!" Mick teased.

"Hey, whenever you want to use it. It's here."

Mickey punched his brother lightly on the shoulder. "Thanks, man. So, whaddya do on the weekends?"

"We'll find plenty."

"Nightclubs. Girls?" Mick laughed.

Tyler felt a small deflation. He'd never been one to trawl for entertainment. He'd worked on his house or had an occasional beer with Howard and Jeff. He'd thought of showing his brother where he worked, but the inappropriateness of this hit him. Mick was a party guy, a country playboy, and Ty was going to entertain him at the Mother Ship?

"I'll phone some friends," Ty said hurriedly. "Howard knows the bar scene better than I do."

"Cool." Mick bobbed his head and grinned as if it were a pleasant revelation—his older brother actually had a fun side, his brother actually partied.

"Let me show you around."

There was an instant's misunderstanding when Mick thought he meant Topeka, not the house or workshop.

"Just a quick look." Tyler smiled, trying for a light touch. So much of himself was invested in the house he couldn't resist showing it off. "Virgil helped with the second floor. Come on up, this won't take long."

And so he gave Mickey a brief tour until Ty grew conscious his brother was bored. When he finally showed him the guest bedroom, he pointed out the framed aerial photo of the farm, hanging over the dresser.

"Remember this old thing?"

Mick stared at it and took a step forward. "Where'd you find it?"

"Dad found it in the attic."

"Where'd it used to hang?"

"In the living room. Over the couch."

Mick laughed. "I can't even remember what's hanging there now. Something with flowers probably. But I like this one." He pointed to the aerial photo. "This one's cool, bro."

Ty made them sandwiches for lunch. His brother saw the beer Ty had bought for his visit and asked for one. They sat awkwardly at the small table in the breakfast nook, saying little. Whenever Tyler asked about his life, Mickey laughed and joked. It was like watching someone dance away from you on tiptoe, like talking to a cloud. If he reached out for his brother, would his fingers pass right through like an object through vapor? He'd hoped Mickey might be more self-revealing away from the farm, more himself, whoever that might be.

"Thought I'd give you a tour of town, if you wanted one."

"I know the town. Come here all the time."

"Oh? Maybe there's a special place you'd like to go."

"Nah. I come with my friends. Visit *their* friends. Big parties, you know. Lots of people, falling out the doors. This is where my buddies score their dope."

He'd learned enough from his students, and Jeff, to know it circulated freely. *Cannibas, weed, dope.* The last place he wanted drugs was in his house or car. He was a school teacher, for crying out loud! He hoped Mick wasn't carrying any, hoped he wouldn't have to say anything and appear more square than he already was.

Tyler stared at his brother. Mick had no interest in "the sights," only in the possibilities of being in a place he associated with pleasure. What foolishness had made him think otherwise?

Howard and Jeff were seated at a table in back when the Manning brothers arrived. Howard waved them over. An updated country and western establishment, The Stable was the only bar Tyler ever frequented, and only with his work mates. A layer of smoke wavered under the low-hanging faux-Tiffany ceiling lamps. The bar itself was a narrow horseshoe in the middle, with booths along one side and back, movable tables across the floor. At nine each night, the dance floor was cleared.

Howard was nursing his signature gin and tonic. A half-consumed Guinness sat in front of Jeff. Tyler introduced his brother who transformed himself into Charming Mickey with the infectious smile. He shook hands, made all the right noises of welcome and pleasure, followed by the small appealing joke. ("Wish I'd worn my hat. So this is where you school teachers unwind. Pretty classy.") Tyler felt a moment's relief and pride: Mick knew how to meet and greet, so different from the Mick of Delia's kitchen.

A young waitress with kohl-lined eyes, spilling out of a black halter-top, sailed toward the table to take the newcomers' orders. Mick leaned back in his chair, sizing her up, flashing the disarming smile. The rest of the table was then given a small lesson in male flirtation. Suggestive words, languorous body posture, crooked smile and just enough of the strong white teeth. Sexual pheromones seemed to waft out from his brother, flustering the waitress, making her blush and shake her head of long brown hair. She swiftly returned with their drinks, slighting a table of four who'd come in just before the Mannings. The foursome glanced their way in annoyance. Some of us have it, Ty thought, and some don't.

"Okay, Howie," Ty said. "Tell us about some interesting, weird places no one has heard of."

Howard tilted his head back, smiled, and let his eyes shut

briefly. At that moment the band arrived through the rear door. A clatter arose as they set up on a small stage. Whatever Howard said, beyond a few preliminary Howardisms, was lost in the general noise of amplifier-testing, guitar riffs, excessive volume, and laughter. At precisely nine the waitresses and bartenders, with the help of patrons, moved the tables to the periphery of the floor. A familiar Mickey returned, easily distracted, eager for something beyond the limitations of their table. Howard addressed his remarks to Ty, whose ear was inches from his mouth. Jeff leaned over to hear. Meanwhile Mick had forgotten them. The noise level rose precipitously, and Tyler found the electronics unbearable. When the dance music began in earnest, Mick turned to the group and asked if they were going to dance. Laughter and hands flew out in protest. "No way!" Tyler said.

"Bull on the dance floor," said Jeff.

Then Howard, "You don't want to see me, man, it's a terrible sight!"

Mick grinned. "You guys don't mind if I go out?"

In unison the teachers urged him on. "Off you go, kid," Howard said. "We'll tap our toes from the sidelines."

Mickey sprang from his chair and made a beeline toward the buxom waitress, taking her wrist. He leaned across the bar first and said something to the older bartender, as if he knew instinctively this was the person who granted permission. The man appeared to be about fifty and behaved with the alertness of a manager. The bartender nodded, and Mickey and the young woman swung onto the dance floor.

"Do you dance, Jeff?" Ty asked.

"Not if I can help it, but Peg likes to, so…"

"Tyler?" Howard asked in a voice that seemed to smirk.

"Not since my junior prom, never really learned how."

"Cheap entertainment for the lad," said Howard, nodding toward Mickey. "How much younger?"

"Nine years. Almost ten."

"You two don't look much alike."

"He favors our mother."

Howard shook his head. "God, I can't even remember when I was that young."

His brother was a supple dancer, and Tyler watched him with a mix of envy and appreciation. Mickey looked relaxed on the dance floor, lithe. So why did Mick always shun anything physical on the farm? Watching him now, you would have thought Mick might take to farm work like a duck to water. Maybe digging postholes or ponds, ear-tagging calves did not bring out the dancer. Yet a dancer's instinct, Ty thought, would be useful.

From time to time, Mickey returned to the table to catch his breath. He shared a few jokes but didn't linger. Mick was having fun in his company, and that's what counted when in fact, Howard observed aloud, Mickey was moving to his own rhythms. The "old guys" at the table were only incidental. Each time he returned to the table, his eyes seemed a little redder, and as the evening wore on, Tyler watched more closely. Mick was going to the bar for drinks between numbers instead of ordering a beer from the table, and he was drunk.

"Getting past my bedtime," Jeff said with a yawn.

Howard made leaving noises as well. Mickey had insisted on driving the El Camino when they went out, and now he understood why. When Mickey made one of his appearances at the table, Tyler told him they were going. Mick should come home when he wanted. The back door key was under the mat. His brother oozed thanks and gave that little punch on the shoulder he'd given earlier in the day, except now it felt disingenuous.

"Howard will drive me home," Tyler said.

"Hey, guys, great to meet you." Mick shook hands all around with heightened words of thanks.

When a car in the street woke him at three, Ty got up to check. The El Camino was not in the drive or parked out front. When he finally got up at six, the guest room remained empty and unused. His shoulders drooped. He'd imagined a late breakfast with guy talk before his brother returned to the farm. He puttered in the kitchen, then wrote a note and placed it prominently on the kitchen table in case Mick returned. Then Ty went to the garage workshop.

So what if Mickey liked to dance? He liked to work with wood. What was the difference, except the medium? When he returned to the house for lunch, he'd hoped there might be a phone message from his brother on the machine but there wasn't, and the note was untouched. He pulled beef and cheese and condiments from the fridge, took a croissant from the bread bin and composed a sandwich. Everything that gave Tyler pleasure and sustenance was, to his brother, dry as old bones. They were so utterly different it was a wonder they came from the same parents. He supposed Mickey had gone home with one of the waitresses. He'd heard from the Harringtons that Mick had become a ladies' man. He never took his women to the house, though, and he never told Delia.

"As far as your mother's concerned," Billie told him, "the kid's an angel. Your dad knows better."

Tyler learned later that Mickey did not make it home until Monday morning, in time for work. When he told Howard what he'd hoped for from that weekend, Howie shook his head.

"He is who he is, Ty. Don't expect so much."

Why, if he knew better (and he did), had he thought he and Mick might achieve some brotherly accord? The possibility of that had been dashed when Mick was seven years old, so why had he chosen to forget? Perhaps it was the bungalow that had derailed him, the very place that made him feel whole at last. How could he be so foolish as to think Mick might be "restored to wholeness" when he didn't even feel divided?

With his students he didn't expect anything large except that they follow the shop rules, respect the tools, and pay attention to the lessons. He had no illusions about the power of his words to influence. If he grew fond of the occasional student, it was the student who'd strived for his approval. He didn't keep track of the students who were fond of him, and these were numerous enough if not demonstrative. Moose Manning did not require demonstrations of loyalty. But a man's only brother was a different matter, and he had been beset by hope.

When Tyler turned thirty-one, he drove to the farm for a birthday dinner his mother had planned in his honor. He drove expectantly up the long drive and parked his truck behind the house, relieved that Mick's El Camino was gone, the kitchen table set for three. The aroma of roast beef and onions scented the air. Just that Friday Howard told him he was lucky to have parents eager to see him and cook for him.

Delia was at the stove, stirring the contents of a small saucepan when he walked through the door. He hung his jeans jacket on the hook and went to kiss her cheek.

"What's Mick up to?" he asked. He couldn't help himself. He needed to be sure.

"He went to Arkansas with some friends. To the races."

"Where's Dad?"

"He'll be here directly."

He went to the sink to wash his hands, looking out the window at the bird feeders. The sky was turning a deeper blue in the approaching dusk. High, thin cirrus clouds ripened from pink to lavender as the sun set. He never paid as much attention to the sky in town, where it was only an uninteresting canopy hemmed in by trees. Besides, city lights spoiled the sky.

Tyler dried his hands and moved toward the back door, glancing out in search of his father. He offered to make coffee and his mother agreed. He shared small talk from school while Delia offered stale news of Mick and the Markhams and other neighbors along the road. He scarcely listened. Ten minutes passed and then fifteen. Tyler glanced out the window and inquired again about his father.

"I'm sure he'll be in soon," she said.

"I'll go check," he said and headed out the door.

He could see the barn light through the side window and the spaces around the door. He couldn't imagine his father getting stuck in a project so close to dinner time. Hal had an inner clock that would have brought him to the kitchen door precisely at 5:30.

Tyler reached the barn and went in through the small side door. He didn't see his father at first until he crossed the main space and saw him sprawled across the barn floor next to the new Ford tractor. The vehicle was still running. Hal had fallen on his side, one hand against his body, the other reaching toward the tractor. Tyler ran to him, rolled his father on his back, calling his name, before shutting off the vehicle. The older man seemed to be breathing, and then not. Tyler tore open his father's jacket and then his green plaid work shirt, popping buttons. There was a faint pulse. Tyler clambered to his feet, furious they still had no phone in the barn, and ran to the kitchen.

"Call 911," he yelled at his mother. "Now!"

Delia laughed, fanning the air above the stove where a dollop of lard had burned in the pan. "I don't think that's necessary, son. A little burned—"

"Please! It's Dad."

He dashed back to the barn where Hal remained motionless. A moment's hesitation, and then he began the CPR he'd learned in the navy and never used since. He recited the steps aloud, in between repeating his father's name. *Push, push, push, pause.* A three-stepped dance, a waltz of life and death. Despair overtook him, as though some sustaining floor inside him had dropped away. *Push, push, push, pause. Breathe in.*

He only became aware of the dark outside when he heard a large vehicle crunching across the barnyard. No siren wailed, or if it had, he'd failed to hear it. His mother's voice instructed someone to cross the back yard toward the barn where the lights still blazed. Two figures approached, and Tyler stood up. Two young men opened a gurney and lifted his father onto it. A hand placed a mask over Hal's nose and mouth. He followed the attendants to the ambulance, a walk that felt like a marathon, and then insisted he would be riding with his father. One of the young men told his mother the name of the hospital. He heard, but the name flew out of his mind the instant it was spoken. He would remember later the few moments of elaborate hooking up, even an injection. Of what, he didn't know and didn't ask. Something to stimulate the heart. Tyler could not be certain whether that heart was beating.

He was seated, head in his hands, elbows on knees, gazing at an unattractive gray and white tile floor when his mother arrived in the waiting room. Had he really expected her not to come? The sudden sequence of events addled him until his judgment felt impaired, like that appalling moment in the navy. If it weren't for Manny... Tyler shivered, reached over and embraced her. For a moment they clung to each other until she pulled way.

"Do you know anything?" she asked, her face bewildered.

"Not yet. Here." He pointed to a chair.

He was talking but was only minimally aware of what he said. It finally occurred to him that he was in shock, with no idea how long they waited when a doctor arrived and told them what Tyler sensed in his heart all along: a massive coronary. Immense damage. Hal had been hanging on by a thread on arrival—thanks to his son—but was too weak to carry on. The heart appeared to be enlarged. Did Hal Manning have a history of heart problems? His mother conceded the point. This was the first Tyler had heard of any heart problems, and a heavy swell crashed over him.

"And you never told me?" he said.

"If he'd wanted you to know, he'd have told you himself," she said, her own ire rising.

She was right. Ashamed, he turned from her.

"I want to see him," Tyler said and rose to his feet, ignoring his mother.

"They're cleaning him up. A nurse will come for you shortly."

Tyler stared at the man, towering over him, eyes narrowed in anger and grief. "Shortly isn't good enough. I'll go now." He'd been aware since high school of the unsettling effect his size could have on people, but he'd seldom made use of it. It felt like cheating. Hadn't Hal taught him a man should earn respect. But today was different. Tyler took a small step toward the surgeon, still glowering.

The doctor dropped his gaze. "Follow me then."

Tyler turned to his mother. "Will you be all right? Alone?"

"I don't know."

"I won't be long. You stay here and I'll be back for you directly."

She did not question him, only nodded. The person he admired most in the world, the one person who embodied all the lessons he'd come to live by, was gone, and he was totally unprepared for the loss. He followed the doctor into the room. Hal's worn plaid shirt was the first thing he saw, the colors faded and the cuffs frayed. Tyler's eyes filled with tears; no effort on his part could hold them back. He wanted that old green work shirt.

Mickey was unreachable. Delia refused to offer any contact information, and Tyler assumed, at first, she didn't know. When Ty suggested they call the police in Hot Springs, Delia put her foot down.

"We're not calling. Calling won't bring Hal back. Michael will return soon enough. That's all I can say."

Didn't she realize that *soon enough* for Mickey might be a week or two? He was more than willing to pay the morticians for each additional day, but his mother's refusal to find Mick was baffling and infuriating. And then it struck him she knew exactly where he was.

"You're not going to tell me, are you?" he said

She didn't look at him but raised a grim face and gazed out the window above the sink and said, "I have to fill the feeders now."

Women with casseroles arrived daily: neighbors, church people, Billie leading her deaf mother, Helen. Molded salads filled the fridge, tuna casseroles ready to heat. The women sat with Delia awhile, some holding her hand. Tyler stood discreetly in doorways or visited with men on the back porch. The men wanted to reminisce, and he let them. "Remember when Hal

wrestled that skittish steer? Remember when Hal scared the shit out of that sheriff's deputy? Hal was in the right, too..."
Remember when? Everyone knew to come around to the back except his colleagues who arrived, to his surprise, in Howard's late-model Camry, parking in front. He let Howard and Jeff in through the seldom-used front door and led them into the living room.

"Let us pay our respects to your mother first," Howard said. Tyler took them into the kitchen, recently vacated by a neighboring farm couple Ty hadn't seen in years.

It sounded callous to have to tell people that Mickey didn't know yet about his father, everyone in a quandary and unable to plan, awaiting Mick's return. Tyler's concern slipped out as his friends were making their departure.

"She wouldn't phone. He's in Arkansas. At the races, I thought. Someone could announce his name over a loudspeaker. She'll have none of it. Like she's afraid it might interfere with Mick's fun."

"I doubt that very much, Ty," Howard said. "He has to come back some time. Let it be soon."

"But it can't be very nice for Ty's mother," Jeff offered.

Howard shrugged. "If you need us...if you just need to get out of the house for a drink, call."

On the fifth day, a Wednesday, Tyler took his mother shopping. When they returned, crawling up the long drive to the back, the red El Camino was parked near the house.

"You go in," he said. "Tell Mickey. I'll bring in the groceries."

His mother gave him a bleak look and nodded.

Since the preceding Friday he'd felt as though he was suspended over a black pit. His mother was still in the living room with his brother when he brought the last of the groceries indoors. Slowly he put up the contents of the bags. When neither appeared in the kitchen, he phoned the mortuary and arranged to hold the service on Saturday. For nearly a week, he'd tried to relieve his mother of as many arrangements as possible, had even asked the mortuary people to handle the flowers. His mother had not succumbed to tears but appeared distant or distracted, confused even about how she should react; he wondered if she, too, might be in shock. Yet the moment they saw Mickey's car she changed, becoming Michael's hovering and solicitous mother, as though she'd relinquished her parenthood when Ty was present, reclaiming her mother's role only when Mick walked into the house. More than ever he wanted to return to the bungalow where he could grieve his father properly.

Mickey's response to the death mirrored his mother's: a stunned surprise, as if the bull had trampled the fence and escaped the pasture. Their confused silence left him feeling bereft. Then he was overcome by the frightening heat, the cauldron of anger—*the righteous feelings*—that he'd spent so much effort tamping down. The unwelcome memory reared up again: the Black kid in the parking lot of the bar when he was still a seaman.

Before Saturday's service he looked through his father's room and found an old trunk. From it, he removed several old photographs: his youthful father in his army uniform, Delia and Hal's wedding photo, a photo of the senior Mannings with Tyler, and one with all four Mannings posed on the front steps. Mickey looked about seven. Tyler arranged the photos on top of the television where visitors could easily see them—a small memorial gallery celebrating Hal's life. When his mother discovered them on display, she called him over.

"Why did you put these old things up?"

He couldn't fathom why she'd object. "People like to remember their friends. It's an homage to Dad."

"Nobody wants to see old photos."

"You're wrong, Mom. They do. They're good pictures." The dismay he'd been controlling all week rose to the surface. "People admired Dad. And everyone respected him. *Everyone!*"

Furious now, his voice came out in a hiss. "Someone in this house needs to honor Dad."

Delia's mouth dropped open. Tears suddenly shone in her eyes, and she spoke in an astonished whisper: "Whatever you may think, son, I loved your father. And I love him still. What would make you think otherwise?"

After the service, traffic to the farmhouse was constant. Billie came early with her colleague, Eppie Gordon, to relieve Delia of hostess duties. The two women spread out the salads and meat trays and sandwich fixings, plates of carrot sticks and celery, the pies and cakes and cookies. The buffet covered every inch of counter space and the entire kitchen table. Eppie stationed herself beside the beverages, dispensing lemonade and iced tea or refilling coffee cups and undertaking the washing up, so that mourners would not need to rummage through cabinets for a clean cup. A committedly sober Bud Harrington traveled the house picking up napkins and paper plates and putting them in the trash or placing the glasses and cups in the sink.

A knot of young men stood in the backyard with Mick and smoked, passing a bottle among them. A basketball appeared and two of Mick's friends began shooting baskets at the old net-less hoop attached to the barn. The dull *thwup* of the ball against the backboard sounded like a mallet against Tyler's head.

His Washaw colleagues attended the service, offered Tyler their condolences at the church, and then politely excused themselves from the remaining events that seemed so neighbor and family oriented. He wished he could join them. At the farmhouse Delia remained seated in the kitchen. Ty thought it would do her good to walk about and thank folks for coming to the house. When he mentioned this to Billie, she gave him a severe look.

"Let her sit, Ty. I've never seen her so exhausted. Besides, she is talking to people."

Chastened, he looked over and saw his mother speaking with a neighbor woman who'd pulled up a chair and sat beside Delia, holding her hand. If Billie, who was not fond of his mother, could sympathize, why couldn't he? Until now, Delia simply looked puzzled, even at the hospital when told her husband had died. Maybe it took the funeral, the finality of burial, to elicit the grief.

He watched her carefully for a while. His mother had never been one for strong emotions, only strong convictions, as though her Free State ancestors, of whom she was so proud, would cringe at any sentiment except justice. His father once loved this woman of strong principles before she'd been derailed by a colicky son. Did Hal love her to the end?

Oh, how she'd once held forth! He should have introduced his mother to Eppie Gordon long ago: two women cut from the same sturdy Kansas cloth. *Free Soilers*. Tyler had once loved his mother's stories.

Billie stopped beside him at one point: "This is the saddest I've seen your mother."

Tyler nodded but his mind was full of Hal. He didn't know how to manage whatever grief Delia might be feeling, and he still felt bruised that he'd been the one to make her cry. He turned his thoughts to the bungalow and the work of his heart. Nothing remained for him here.

"You've been very dutiful," Billie remarked, but he heard an edge in her voice.

"Is that a bad thing?"

Billie took his hand and squeezed it. "Soften your heart, Ty. She needs your love and support more than ever because she'll never get any from Mick." Billie turned away from him to speak with Eppie and then abruptly turned back. "There's something else I want to tell you about your mother and Mickey. But not today."

Billie moved off to help with the buffet. No, this wasn't the day to tell him, but she must do so soon, before Ty's feelings for Delia needlessly hardened. One evening when Billie and Helen were alone in the kitchen, with Bud and Virgil in the back room watching TV, the subject of the Mannings had come up. She couldn't recall the context now, only the message. Her mother stood at the sink, her hands submerged in soapy water.

"No harm in telling you, I suppose," Helen began. Her daughter turned and looked at her. "Because someone really ought to tell Tyler."

"Tell him what?" Billie asked.

"You wouldn't remember but Michael was a colicky baby. Which meant Delia got no sleep. Plus, Hal thought she had the postpartum depression. Anyway, Hal stumbled onto Delia one night. She was in the baby's room—Mickey was a bit over two months. Delia had a pillow over Mickey's face and was pressing down. Hal stopped her."

Helen turned on the water for rinsing, and Billie held her breath.

"Two things, and these are only my opinion," Helen continued. "First, Delia has felt such guilt about this incident that she'll let that boy do anything. And second, if that child's brain was deprived of oxygen… Well, it's clear to me that Michael Manning never developed normally."

Billie leaned in toward her mother. "Are you saying Ty doesn't know any of this?"

"That's what I'm saying."

5

HOME VISIT

JULY 1992

If a man abandons his child, can he return later and claim her? A moot point since Sherlynne Smith didn't even know where "Mike Mann" had gone. Yet Billie learned that Mick was liable for child support if paternity can be proved. Sherlynne might only have been fourteen when she got pregnant, and certainly unmarried, meaning Mickey had committed a crime. But Mickey had skedaddled. Ty slumped in his chair while something heavy dropped to the floor of his heart.

"You know what I think?" Billie said when he first expressed his fear. "I think there's no such thing as an illegitimate child, only illegitimate parents. And we're not going to think of her as an orphan or a foundling or any other such word. We know she's family, so... How's that crib working out?"

Now Billie was in his kitchen preparing iced tea and lemonade. Two baking sheets of snicker doodles filled the house with the aroma of nutmeg and sugar, the oven fan whirring noisily to distribute the heat. Bud looked especially dapper since Billie trimmed his hair, the usually riotous blond hair falling neatly around his face instead of spilling over his forehead and ears in a manner Tyler had been told women found irresistible. The baby lay in her playpen in a lovely yellow dress Billie had made, with eyelets and just the right amount of ruffle and flounce on the little panties. Her dark hair was behaving today, tamed with a yellow headband with a large white flower.

Was there ever a more beautiful child? He reached over and lifted her up. The silly voice popped out, the one he used to coo at Delia May, and he dropped the volume, fearful the Harringtons might hear him and tattle on him. *Did ya hear Ty baby talk May?*

Her small weight and softness, her fist moving toward her mouth, her large eyes on his face. An electrical current seemed to flow from her to him, pulsing through his blood. She was eleven weeks, according to the documents he'd finally received. The unimaginable fatigue of the first weeks of parenting had settled into ordinary tiredness. Whenever he looked at her—the cause of all his spoiled nights—the fatigue slid away into a bemused gratefulness. He had not felt so purposeful since his first assignments in the navy or his first year teaching.

Now the metallic heat of July hammered the air, drying out the soil and the foliage. The vegetables in his kitchen garden wilted daily unless he watered. The only significant rain they'd had this month was two weeks ago—a spectacular electrical storm. The thunder had been so close, it had caused the baby to waken and cry, the only time she'd been startled from sleep. He installed an air conditioning system for the baby as soon as the weather warmed. Billie had complained for years that the farmhouse was too hot, that Hal and Delia had made do with fans except for a window unit in one bedroom, and Tyler admitted to himself (but not Billie) how much better he slept.

A plume of dust signaled the car's arrival. Tyler charted its progress along the dry roadbed, uncomfortably reminded of the dirty cloud that followed the battered Ford carrying Baby May to his door. In his mind he saw Sherlynne Smith with her cutoffs and dirty hair, her stick-thin limbs and fierce expression painted over her desperation. *Mike said I should call you if I ever got into trouble. Well, I'm in trouble.*

An aging silver Toyota came to a stop in the parking area in front of the house. Geraniums and petunias and coleus, recently watered, sat erect in their containers. The grass around the house still retained some color and was neatly trimmed. Care had been taken to impress the driver of this Toyota. Billie made a note to ask Bud to repaint their front porch. Meanwhile, Tyler sat on the sofa, with an unimpeded view of the parking pad. A somewhat plump woman of medium height and uncertain age climbed out of the car, reached back in and removed a briefcase. She wore sunglasses. Her taffy-colored hair appeared unnaturally wavy and longer than it should have been, a headband keeping it off her face. She wore large hooped earrings and a filmy blue-green summer dress.

"She's here," Tyler called to the Harringtons fussing in the kitchen.

The social worker approached the house with an odd, humping gait that Tyler thought might be the fault of the overburdened briefcase, throwing her off balance. He lost sight of her once she reached the porch steps. By the time she rang the bell, he was already at the door, little May in his arms so that the baby would be the first thing she saw. The woman smiled and pushed her sunglasses atop her head where they disappeared into a thicket of curls.

"Well, hello there!" she said in a large, perky voice, addressing the baby. "This must be Delia May!" He wondered if jauntiness was a job requirement. She introduced herself as Heidi something and finally looked up at him. "I'd shake your hand but I see they're busy." She threw back her head and guffawed.

A laugher, he thought. He'd rather have a laugher than someone too self-contained with suspicious eyes that traveled over you, searching for flaws. The trouble with laughers was that they sometimes couldn't make up their minds and deferred to sterner voices, a lesson he'd learned from students and colleagues alike. Tyler invited her in and escorted her to the living room. To his relief, the woman scarcely stopped talking. He hoped she would size up the room, observe the gladiolas in a vase atop the television, the unblemished windows letting in the bright light, the cleanliness of the space, the newer carpet. Then his eyes became hers and swept around the room, wandering over the walls and furnishings as if he were a stranger here himself. The sofa was not new but well-preserved, sitting three easily. Above it was the long framed aerial photo of the farm that his father had admired. It struck him now that that the photo was too small for the wall space.

Above the television hung a large painting of two horses in a field that Howard had painted. He was especially fond of this picture, had even made the frame but now wondered if the woman would find it too rustic. What he most prized was the Van Gogh print hanging above the little bookcase: *Starry Night*, it was called. The swirl of color and sky still made him smile. He hoped she noticed it, the one worldly item in a room of pastoral sentiment.

The social worker dropped down onto one end of the sofa and removed papers from her briefcase, arranging them on the walnut coffee table. The conversation had not yet moved beyond chat when Billie swooped in with a tray of glasses and a platter of cookies. Bud followed in her wake, a thermos of iced tea in one hand, a pitcher of lemonade in the other, slices of lemon floating among the ice cubes.

"Ah, more family?" the woman exclaimed in a voice that begged confirmation.

"Old friends and neighbors," Billie said and introduced herself and Bud, her face stretched into a smile of such enormous proportions, Tyler was taken aback.

"Godparents," Bud offered.

The woman cocked her head, eyes widening and her smile still intact. "Lovely. And are there any other relatives?"

"None nearby," Tyler said, thinking of a scattering of second cousins in Colorado and Iowa. "No one knows where my brother is, I'm sorry to say. But that's in my report."

In Billie's view the woman's deep nods seemed affected. Hadn't Tyler repeated this information often enough, in written and oral form, and the very reason a social worker was here today? Billie poured iced tea and handed her the tall glass. The woman had hair like Bud's, and Billie wondered if it was natural or one of those Afros for white women: You go to your hairdresser and ask her to give you a perm with your limp, light white lady hair. She couldn't tell the woman's age. Well over forty, surely. Still there was something about her that put Billie on edge, something too jokey to be making such essential decisions. A rumble of discontent formed in the critical corner of Billy's brain. She sensed the words massing and her tongue eager to say them in her emphatic schoolteacher's voice.

The woman then picked up a sheet and slowly handed it to Tyler, looking at him meaningfully. "The mother signed her consent."

Tyler's legs weakened. He sat down heavily in the rocking chair facing the sofa. Bud appeared ready to sing out a "waa-hoo!" until Billie rose and threw him a look. Billie stepped toward the rocker and took May out of Tyler's hands and put the baby in her playpen. The child raised her feet and reached for her toes covered in her jingle booties.

"She's precious," the woman said, watching. "Love those jingle toe socks."

He leaned over and read the document but his eyes kept blurring. The woman clucked her tongue.

"The girl was only fifteen. But you know, sometimes mothers that young want to keep their babies. It's the first time in their lives someone needs them or makes them feel important."

He did not want to hear this. "Well, she brought the baby to me."

"So I understand. Hard to fathom but probably for the best. Have you ever been married, Mr. Manning?"

Surely she knew this. The question was included in the lengthy form he'd filled out long ago. Hadn't she read it?

"I was engaged once but had to break it off."

A wretched stillness settled over the room. Billie sat stiffly at her end of the sofa while Bud, who'd retreated earlier to the doorway, shifted his weight and slowly pushed his hands into his jeans' pockets. Then Billie reached for the platter of cookies and passed it around. "And just in the nick of time, if you ask me," she said.

But nobody asked, Tyler thought and stared earnestly at the

woman. The baby gurgled, reaching out for the jingles on her toes, and he felt the tension slide out of the room.

Billie kept her eyes on the woman who'd sipped a bit of iced tea, eyed the snicker doodles with longing but virtuously raised a hand with bright red nails and passed. Billie settled back onto the other end of the sofa, reached over slowly for a napkin and took a cookie with a cook's careful entitlement. Bud hulked in the doorway. Tyler was too nervous to eat and clasped his hands between his knees and kept leaning over the coffee table to read and sort the documents the woman pushed his way.

"We checked your references, Mr. Manning. School officials and colleagues, doctor, pediatrician. I think you wouldn't mind if I said—in front of your friends—that you came out with flying colors. No one had an ill word. No one doubted your ability."

Tyler flushed deeply and looked over the other papers flowing in his direction.

"Now, the awkward part of my visit," she said and threw back her head, laughing so broadly he could see her tonsils. "The required tour of the house and child's room."

Tyler and the woman left the room and took the stairs to the nursery. Quietly, Billie followed to the bottom of the stairs and listened. The Heidi woman was telling Tyler that the crib was old-fashioned and unsafe. "See how far apart the ribs are on the side? Baby could get her little head stuck between them while you're still asleep. You need to buy a new one."

Billie wanted to shout out, "That crib was just fine for my kids—that's two rambunctious boys and a girl. And not one stuck his head through the slots!" The woman just wanted an opportunity to show off, to tell Ty what to do, prove her expertise—poor helpless man. Tyler might be overly earnest, but he was the least helpless man she knew. The woman reminded Billie of a dog circling the premises—ingratiating as a hound—sniffing, sorting out the scents, searching for the right spot to squat down and plant her own scent, right on that crib!

Meanwhile Tyler chose not to tell the social worker about

the large barn workshop. He could imagine her first question: what will you do with Baby May when you're busy out there? Head cocked, eyes widened, the broad inquisitive smile still frozen on her round face. He hadn't worked that out. Instead he showed her the smaller repair workshop in the basement. She clearly knew nothing about carpentry or shop work, and for this ignorance he was grateful. He was even more grateful that Bud had managed to keep his mouth shut about the barn. Billie must have coached him. When the tour ended, Ty and the woman returned to the living room.

"And when you return to your job?" she inquired with the paralyzed smile.

"I'm taking a semester's leave. Call it paternity leave," he said and forced a laugh. "In January, I'm arranging for a babysitter and then the Montessori school in town."

Billie sat up straight and looked at him. He resisted looking back, keeping his eyes on the Heidi woman. He hadn't yet told the Harringtons about his so-called paternity leave. By January, May would be almost nine months and better able to handle a caregiver. Today the thought of a daylong separation left him strangled with anxiety.

Heidi nodded and made notes on her yellow pad. There would be some waiting, she indicated, and an adjudication. Technically, he would be a legal guardian. Not enough time had elapsed to terminate parental rights, and the mother must be given three months to change her mind. (Ridiculous! Billie thought. Like a return-by-this-date washing machine.) Theoretically, the woman rambled on, the father would have to sign as well. But if enough time passed and he could not be located and did not appear...well, that was a different matter.

"But that's way down the pike." The woman smiled.

Adoption was being dangled before him like a rabbit in front of a foxhound. And no one could tell him how long it would take. He was the only one willing to care for this child, and still the State of Kansas dithered about parental rights. Why should they cherish the rights of people who had cast off their responsibility like an old sweater? It wasn't as if he were a complete stranger. He was Delia May's uncle. Why, the child didn't even have a proper name before she arrived on his porch. *Baby Smith.* Those were the words on her birth certificate. No *Manning* anywhere. Or *Mann.* Tyler had thought agencies preferred to keep children with family members. Billie thought so too. They'd both encountered such arrangements among their students. Legal guardian: grandparents. Legal guardian: older sister. Adoptive parent: maternal aunt. So the woman was zeroing in on the Real Issue he had not wanted to face: how can a bachelor care for an infant girl?

"I met Sherlynne Smith's aunt and cousin," Tyler said. "I believe I wrote that down. There was no information forthcoming about Sherlynne's parents." He cleared his throat before continuing. "As far as I can tell, I'm the *only* family this child has who cares about her."

"We did a little rundown on your Sherlynne Smith. Her mother took off when she was four. Her father's in and out of prison. Still 'in' as we speak."

"Nice," Bud muttered from his post in the doorway.

"Sounds like Sherlynne Smith is continuing a pattern," Billie said in a quiet voice.

The Heidi woman made a humming noise in agreement. It struck Billie then that Ty was appalled at the injustice of it. How could anyone abandon a child and that included Sherlynne Smith, abandoned by her mother? He might have taken May in if the child had been found at the side of the road, just as a boy he'd raised orphaned kittens or birds. He should have been a woman, Billie thought and glanced at him: Moose Manning, the least feminine-looking man she knew. Why, even Bud had a "fey" aspect. Most men did if you knew where to look, but not Tyler. Even the velvety dark eyes radiated virility.

Daughter, I saw the most amazing thing. I was over visiting with Delia Manning, and Ty was in the kitchen baking a pie. A pie! You should have seen him crimp that crust.

"How long does the review process take?" he asked as the

social worker reassembled her papers and files, placing them back in the large briefcase.

"Hard to tell. I should think six weeks. Maybe a tad longer. It needs to make its way across several desks."

How could he wait six weeks? The anticipation was killing him. And the situation, with all its attending paperwork, was an *it*? That infuriating expression: across several desks. He would like to know exactly how many social workers and supervisors would be reading Heidi's report and passing judgment, never having met him or seen the child or visited his home or talked with the underage and ill-prepared mother or known the spineless Mick? At some point Billie had put May back in his arms, and he cradled the sleeping infant. He excused himself and said he wanted to put her down for her nap. Heidi stopped organizing and stapling papers and said she'd like to see his bedside manners. Another laugh. She meant it as a little joke, but it wasn't funny. She trailed after him, speaking in an absurd whisper that was more penetrating than if she'd spoken quietly in her natural voice.

He placed May in her crib on her back. Heidi sighed and whispered her approval and started to say something about SIDS. His indignation flared. He'd read up all he cared to about sudden infant death syndrome. He would never put an infant on its stomach. Had Heidi simply missed the fact he was schoolteacher? As far as he was concerned, he was May's legal guardian since the day Sherlynne Smith shoved May in his arms. He certainly didn't need the State of Kansas to tell him so.

Back in the living room, the woman put the last of the papers in her valise and latched it. Billie came in from the kitchen where she and Bud were cleaning up. Later he would never be able to reconstruct what the woman said at the end because the words sounded so inconsequential, like chat. Besides, he had one ear cocked for the baby. The woman suggested he keep her door open to let natural sounds surround her sleep.

"You don't want a fussy baby."

"She's not," he said.

Now she was in the doorway, then on the porch, still making small talk with Billie, taking with her the yellow pad and notes, signed copies of assorted documents, leaving copies of Sherlynne Smith's release and other items on the coffee table. The woman turned at last and shook his hand and wished him good luck. Then she was crunching across the gravel car pad in her odd lurching gait that reminded him of a camel. Tyler and Billie remained on the porch steps until she had turned around and driven back down the long drive. He couldn't put his finger on why he felt so disheartened.

"I thought that went very well," Billie said and went indoors, holding the screen door open.

"You did?" Incredulous, he followed her indoors.

"And you didn't?"

He shrugged. He didn't know how to express what weighed on his heart, that he dreaded the State would come and snatch her away because the State would not leave a little girl in the care of a single man even though he was family, even though Bud had made a totally convincing if untrue statement about the Manning family's long connection to the Bethany Methodist Church. The Harringtons had slipped in enough information about themselves to give an impression of dependability and easy access. "Just a phone call and fifty yards away." More like two hundred yards, but he was grateful for the compression. Even Bud seemed upbeat, but Bud was good at upbeat. They sat at the kitchen table where the platter of cookies remained. Tyler popped a cookie in his mouth. The Harringtons exchanged a glance.

"It seems like the more time elapses," he said, "and the more people have to have their say, the more likely things are to go wrong."

"Not necessarily," Bud put in. "The State of Kansas would be happy to find a guardian. Cheaper for them. A foster home costs money. You don't cost them a dime."

Billie nodded. He tried to let this line of thinking comfort him. Yet these decisions weren't about money. They were about suitability, and he did not know whether Heidi found him suitable. She was so completely neutral when she left, not giving a word of encouragement or discouragement. Only small talk.

6

WHEN LOVE GOES AWRY

I was engaged once but had to call it off.

He'd felt compelled to answer, to assure the woman he had normal impulses, whatever that meant. Tyler tucked the little girl into her crib for the night, with Nancy still in his thoughts. He supposed the baby had triggered those dismaying memories of what might have been.

Nancy had come into his life in the fall of 1987, one of the new math teachers. She was an attractive woman. When she entered a room, people first noticed the striking figure, made more impressive by three-inch heels, tailored clothes with wide belts that accentuated a narrow waist and flaring curves. Boys would play-act swooning whenever she walked past. They would deliberately stroll by her classroom and peer in, amuse each other with dramatized acts of weaving, staggering against the lockers, gesturing outward the exaggerated depth of her breasts, daring each other to whistle. So dramatically gorgeous was that Rita Hayworth figure, no one noticed, by design, the relatively plain face. Carefully applied makeup enhanced, or concealed, the small eyes and too prominent nose, emphasizing the high cheekbones and long neck. She wore her wavy, honey-colored hair sensually long, or in an elegant French twist, arriving each morning so nicely turned out that the unremarkable face didn't seem to matter. Much later he learned it mattered to Nancy.

She'd taken an interest in him late in the fall. In the back of the first floor staff lounge, near the sink and fridge, a large pot perked fresh coffee throughout the day, mugs lined up, some with names painted on. One morning in late September, she arrived at the coffee pot first. When he walked up, she filled his cup with a smile and asked, "Cream? Sugar?"

There were only seven single people on staff at the time, most of them "ineligible," including Howard.

Visiting near the coffee pot expanded to include the larger lounge, the hall, or their respective classrooms before or after school. Tyler felt himself grow light, then nimble in ways he'd never observed before. He wasn't a clumsy man but would never have called himself agile. His fingers were trained and obedient, but his body was a different matter—tall, broad at the shoulders as though slightly top heavy. Here he was, livelier of speech than he could recall. Chatting, making someone laugh, hearing himself laugh.

He was thirty-three, a schoolteacher since his mid-twenties. When the last school year ended, he'd felt stale and discouraged. "Typical," Howard opined. "You're just suffering the seven year itch. Same thing happens in marriages."

Maybe he should revive the farm, a thought he dismissed as soon as it popped up. Not enough acreage. His father had planted much of the farm in fescue and rented out the back pastures to ranchers short on grazing land. Then Billie urged him to be a full-time carpenter, but starting a business daunted him. He could rejoin a construction company, which he used to do during summer holidays but gave it up. Who wanted to work for another boss? Besides, developers only expected adequate, not quality, work. Get it done and do it fast. Attention to detail was all a craftsman had to call his own. At least during the summer he could work on the bungalow, plant a garden.

Howard suggested he put an ad in the paper for part-time work, and so he did. You can pick and choose, he said. Say *no* when you want to and still earn a little more. That summer he received one call to build some basement cabinets. Only afterward did he realize how much he'd undercharged the client—a fussy matron of comfortable means, her husband a shrink at Menninger's. The next summer he revised the ad, with Howard's help, and more calls came in. For every satisfying project, there was a tedious one. For every satisfied customer, there was a complainer. Billie encouraged him to raise his prices, which were still too low. But some women seemed prone to disappointment. So after four summers of carpentry, he removed his ad and stayed home, fending off calls from people who had heard, secondhand, about his inexpensive work. From then on, he only did jobs for friends.

"How much money do I need?" he asked an incredulous Billie, who was in chronic need, with two and then three young children.

What he really meant to say was: who needs the hassle? Carpentry was too precious to squander on unappreciative clients. But the summer after Nancy's first year, she hired him to convert an old mudroom into a utility space and refurbish the kitchen. She'd bought an old house with her older sister, a nurse. Two tall, self-possessed women who'd always assumed they'd have careers.

Nancy was teaching six weeks of remedial math in summer school. His plan: he would work on the sisters' kitchen while they were away at their jobs. The older sister, Joanna, was gone ten or twelve hours a day, four days a week. Nancy taught in the morning but stayed late to prepare her lessons for the new fall classes.

She gave him a key to the house. At eight the first day he let himself in the side door and through the mudroom to the kitchen he would be altering. Both women had already left, as expected. He reassessed the space, checking the walls and floorboards. As he stepped into the room, a black and white streak shot across the floor and through the doorway into the adjoining dining room. He followed the cat into a formal dining room that gave way to an adjoining living room. Perched on the back of the sofa sat the cat, and in the well of the sofa another one, an Abyssinian. His eyes traveled around the living room and then the dining room. Back in the kitchen he took a scrap of paper and drew a rough sketch of what might look to the untrained eye like a coat tree, except this one was taller, sturdier, with two perches, a slanting scratching post on the bottom, a circular entry between two platforms where he might hang a toy, and an enclosed box with a narrow entry where a cat could hide. It would take him a few evenings to construct the cat tower, another evening to cover appropriate parts with Berber for the scratching post. As he began work on the mudroom, he whistled.

He'd decided to work until one or the other sister returned, so they would know how long he was on the job. Besides, he suspected Nancy would arrive home first. Shortly before three, her car pulled slowly up the drive. Soon he heard her come in the front door. "Tyler? Hello!"

On the morning of the fourth day, he arrived with the cat tower in the bed of the truck, carting it into the dining room, which had struck him as the most promising room. Three mullioned windows bayed out over a narrow side garden where a dogwood grew. He placed the tower to the side of the right-hand window. One high perch jutted out from the tower, allowing the cats a good view of the out-of-doors.

At 2:40 her car pulled into the drive. Soon he heard footsteps cross the living room and into the dining room. "Oh, look at you!" she exclaimed. "And you! Tyler?"

"In here," he called. When she walked in, he was standing on a ladder in the mudroom, plastering the ceiling. She did not often smile with such abandon but usually let the ends of her lips lift, mouth shut. Her thanks poured forth. He felt his face heat up and his heart swell. "Come see," she said.

The Abyssinian was perched on the platform looking out into the yard. The little tuxedo cat peered out the small round door of the privacy box.

It took him two weeks to convert the mudroom, and another three on the kitchen, adding counter space along an unused wall and new cabinetry after leveling the floor that sloped. During the project a simple pattern emerged. When Nancy returned they fell into school talk, mostly news of colleagues and kids, renovations to the school building. Nothing significant, but Tyler found the bulletins thrilling, coming from her. He hadn't been to the building in several weeks.

"Howard says to stop by," she said, and he made a note to visit Howie. She never stood in his way, but off to one side, leaning against the fridge or in the doorway. It was easy talk, and he began to look forward to it. Each afternoon he cleaned up thoroughly, leaving around 3:30, so she could enjoy her house and prepare a meal.

He did not ask her out until the job was done. His father had once cautioned him against mixing business and pleasure or turning a client into a friend. *Never put your pecker in the payroll,* Hal said. When he completed the project, and the two women expressed satisfaction with the results, and paid him, then he would consider. He waited a week, and then phoned.

"I think Ty has a girlfriend," Billie told Bud over dinner.

She'd gone into Washaw with Eppie Gordon the first week of August, to prepare for the new school year. The women scoured the kitchen even though it hadn't been used for eight weeks, refreshed the bulletin boards, inventorying their shelves and pantries. Howard taught summer school that year and wandered up at noon to gossip, after the summer school kids had gone home.

"Miss Nancy has a crush on someone we all honor and adore," Howie joked.

"Who does?" Eppie blurted out.

"Our newish math teacher."

"Oh yes, that pretty woman," said Eppie, counting spools in the thread drawer.

Any woman smartly turned out automatically earned Eppie's respect, especially if that woman shared Eppie's generous proportions and covered them well, which Nancy did. Billie doubted the two women had ever had more than a passing conversation. But Billie had observed Tyler's interest, his sudden lingering in the first floor staff room, conveniently located between the Mother Ship and the math classes. She and Eppie favored the second floor lounge, but as soon as this new development caught Billie's attention, she began to make at least

one daily appearance downstairs, covering the obviousness of it
by joking with Howie and Jeff and finally chatting with Nancy.
The new woman was cordial but left Billie with the feeling she
either did not like or was not comfortable with other women.
Billie knew she should be happy for Ty but instead felt protective. After she told Bud, he'd chuckled and said, "Now don't
get envious."

"Envious?" she trumpeted. "Why on earth should I be envious of someone who might do Tyler some good?"

"Because you've had him to yourself all your life. Sisters can
be jealous creatures."

He should know. Bud had two, who supervised and pampered as though his own wife couldn't care for him, which had
irked her throughout their marriage. But at that moment she'd
been thankful that was how Bud thought of her—as Tyler's
surrogate sister.

Tyler and Nancy dated for a month, both of them shy and
a little formal. In retrospect, Tyler would acknowledge that it
was Nancy who made the first move. Since Nancy's sister did
not return until late, they climbed the stairs to the second floor
and collapsed across Nancy's bed. As the affair progressed they
came to Tyler's bungalow so that she might spend the night.
The first weeks of lovemaking were full of flying garments,
heat and passion. Under the carefully selected clothes was an
even greater beauty. Her curves and ampleness excited him—
here was a woman of glorious substance. He loved watching
every part of her. The controlled and formal woman of the
classroom and lounge was transformed into a woman more
feral than tender. He marveled at the transformation, feeling
his own sexuality respond. They could be ardent and lustful
together, he thought.

After a few months he became aware of a trembling,
self-conscious quality in her response to his overtures, as
though she thought his was a critical gaze and not a loving
one. Perhaps he was being too forceful or too fumbling. When
she told him months into the affair that she felt stared at, he

assured her his gaze was one of complete appreciation—admiration even.

She laughed and joked. "Not sure that's a moment to be admired."

"No? What then."

"Ravished!" she said, laughing, and grabbed his shoulders, pulling him toward her.

Once a week he drove to his mother's to check on her. Mickey was still using the farm as a home base but often gone. Where to, Tyler never asked. Delia still planted a kitchen garden but arthritis made stooping and bending painful. He wondered if he weren't so attentive, whether Mickey might be motivated to pick up the slack, do for his mother what a favorite son should do.

The summer he worked for Nancy, he was laid low for a week by a debilitating cold. He phoned his mother Thursday to say he would not be coming that weekend. On Saturday she phoned anyway. "Where are you, son? Does that mean you won't be stopping by at all? Mickey? No, he isn't here. He had to go to Wichita." Against his better judgment, he roused himself. He drove down to the farm, pumped full of decongestants and carrying a box of tissue. As soon as he walked through the kitchen door, with scarcely a how-do-you-do, Delia delivered a list of needs: would he water the garden, check the spinach, reach up and get her saltines from the top cabinet?

"Why not keep your crackers down here?" he said, indicating a shelf easily reached by his mother.

"But that's not where they belong."

He wondered if she ever asked Mick for a single thing or simply did without. He'd noticed the small step stool beside the basement door. After an hour of chores—not that she didn't thank him, for she did—Tyler pointed out he was still feeling poorly and needed to go home and rest. He hadn't thought it wise to come in the first place, afraid of passing his cold on to her.

"But this is your home. Why don't you spend the night? I'll make you some lemon tea. Then we can have dinner."

The old vise-grip seized him and squeezed. He took a few slow breaths and told her he really wasn't up to it. Not today. He was working another job and needed to get to the lumberyard in the morning. Would she like him to call Ellen Markham? Or maybe Billie could stop by.

His mother made a disdainful noise with her lips. "Ellen's mind has just about gone. Half the time she doesn't know where she is or who she is."

Tyler looked away, embarrassed for her. It wasn't true. Ellen was deaf, not demented. Delia's loneliness was her own doing. She'd become tactless with her old friends, and Virgil kept track of the offenses lobbed toward his family as scrupulously as Delia Manning kept track of hers. Still the old pity welled up. She looked as though she'd lost weight, which concerned him. She was such a small woman.

"You taking your painkillers?" he asked.

"What do you mean?"

"The Tylenol. For your arthritis."

She nodded. "As needed."

He nodded his approval. "When's Mickey coming back? Did he say?"

"He didn't say and I didn't ask. Don't want to intrude on a man's privacy."

He caught the laugh before it burst out.

He agreed to stay for dinner, helping her in the kitchen, hoping this would soothe her. He owed her that, surely. In silence, they ate the chicken he'd baked, the peas and carrots and salad. He had tried a little conversation, telling her about his current job for the sisters, even about the cat tower he constructed for them. He thought it would amuse her. In earlier days, it would have. Instead his mother put down her fork and knife and gazed at him with a stricken look that compressed her lips like crushed foil. "You mean to tell me, you can build a toy for a couple of cats but can't spend a few moments with your mother?"

"I've just spent more than a few moments with you."

Later he decided it was because he felt so ill that the flash of clarity had such an impact. He understood why Mick had driven to Wichita—fled, probably—and why he was about to leave. Still Delia did not usually burden Mick, preferring to smother him with favors. In that instant Tyler saw that he was supposed to mother Delia, the child becoming the parent, and yet he felt he could never do enough, was never good enough. What an odd delineation of roles his mother had invented. Without realizing it, he'd kept the knowledge in that hidden place where the mind seldom ventured. When she cut him a large slab of chocolate pie, he raised his hand. "I'm full."

He felt drained by the old sense of loss and rose from the table, took the dishes to the sink, rinsed them all, and carefully put them in her dishwater. Then he turned and announced he was leaving, patting her shoulder on his way out the door.

He did not tell his mother about Nancy. Billie knew, of course, because Billie somehow learned everything about him, but she'd never tell Delia. Ty planned to introduce Nancy when he felt it prudent, and not before.

By March of Nancy's second year at Washaw High, 1989, talk turned to marriage. For Ty, the affair had settled into something wonderfully comfortable and warm. He didn't know what she'd said or suggested that made him fearful that, given his size, he might be hurting her. Whatever it was, he deliberately tried to make his lovemaking gentler, softer. Only in hindsight did he realize this may not be what she desired, that his odd fear of hurting her had made him cautious.

After school one Friday, they drove into downtown Topeka to look at engagement rings. He had not wished to surprise but to give her exactly what she wanted and that would require her presence. At the jeweler's the only other people in the store, a mother and daughter, spoke in voices so hushed one would think they were in a cathedral. Tyler and Nancy circled the glass display cases in silence, moving slowly up one side and down the other, together and then separately, until Nancy stopped her perusal and came to stand beside him, taking his hand.

"Tyler, I have just now admitted something to myself. I'm not the engagement ring type. When friends showed theirs off, I thought they were bragging. As if the whole marriage thing was about the rings, not the person. I'm sorry. Have I offended you?" Her eyes were moist.

"Not at all." He was relieved, in fact, but confounded by the tears. "Are you okay?"

"Yes, but I'd like to get out of here."

He drove her home, reassuring her he was only eager to give her what she wanted. For the moment she seemed appeased, yet the ring outing had pulled a curtain over her that he could not quite gauge. When they reached her home and he waited to be invited in, she turned to him and said, "I feel a migraine coming on. I'm going to bed."

He urged her to do so, asked if there was anything he might do, but she said there wasn't. He kissed her cheek and started to get out and walk her to her door, but she hastily grasped his arm.

"Don't," she said. "It's not necessary. I'll be fine."

He waited until she was safely indoors before driving away. For the first time she did not turn and wave.

He'd long ago stopped following Mick's activities but thought it safer for his mother to have his brother maintain a presence on the farm. When Tyler went for a Sunday meal, he would check the barn and gates or walk the fence line since no one was making repairs or taking care. He reminded himself that Mick had never been handy; it wasn't his nature. The condition of the grass was a different matter. Once, when it appeared Mick had mowed, Tyler remarked, "Mick did a good job with the grass."

Delia looked up. "Bud Harrington did it. Michael has asthma, you know."

This is the first he'd heard of the asthma. But his brother was selling off his father's tools. Tyler had taken the few tools he wanted immediately after Hal's death, with his mother's blessing. The tools that remained were intended for farm repairs. When he last checked the basement workshop, Tyler found the table saw missing, as well as the power planer and sander, a power drill and the miter saw. He cautioned himself against saying anything. It wasn't as though he needed them. He had his own tools. Casually, he mentioned the absent tools over a Sunday meal.

Someone Mickey knew had asked after them. Since the tools were just gathering dust, Mickey sold them. Ty nodded, as though it was relief to learn they'd be put to use. Yet his stomach tensed at the casualness of the tools' disposal. His father had worked hard to acquire them, piece by piece, and Ty thought his mother understood the need to keep a reasonable number of tools on hand. Instead she'd absented herself from the discussion, getting up to find something in her pantry. He drove home after the meal, still unsettled, telling himself it wasn't his business any more. If he did not live there or use the tools regularly, it wasn't for him to comment on their disposal. Here was another lesson from Hal who would have stated the matter more succinctly.

He waited before telling his mother about Nancy, hoping for her blessing. She received the news cordially, but without excitement. She knew he had a girlfriend because she'd asked. Then he broached the subject of having his mother over for dinner. Nancy's sister would join them too. He didn't plan to invite Mickey this time, but Delia thought otherwise. Two guests were all Nancy could handle at the moment, and he reassured his mother that Mickey would be included soon. He laid out his arguments as convincingly as he could.

"And who do you suppose will drive me?" she asked.

He stared at her. What a silly question! His mother drove her Chrysler everywhere, including into Topeka.

"I'll come get you," he said finally, hoping to put an end to the matter.

But it wasn't the end. When he came to fetch Delia, she was

seated at the table, clearly unprepared to leave. It wasn't fair to Michael, she said, to leave him out of a family event. His exclusion left her so upset she didn't think she could come.

"Nancy and her sister are waiting for us. Dinner is to be at their house, not mine. It's her decision."

"I find it very odd."

But he did not and strived to make a joke of it. Mickey wasn't even home. His car was gone. "I think a future daughter-in-law might like to meet you without all the other family. If Dad were alive, of course he'd be invited too. Just imagine, confronting the whole family all at once! Look at it from her point of view. It's overwhelming."

"Yes, I see your point... And have you met her family?"

"She only has the one sister. Her parents are gone."

Delia nodded, got up slowly and took her sweater off the hook, dragging herself to the bedroom to fetch her pocketbook. He felt a swift stab of pity. She'd aged noticeably since Hal died. She kept a brave face, but the loss shone through. He'd been so engrossed in Nancy, he'd neglected Delia, avoided witnessing her sorrow. Thinking of his mother meant thinking of Mick, and so he preferred to think of neither.

Tyler said as little as possible about his brother. Nancy knew he had one, but he'd stripped his remarks of the complicated feelings Mickey evoked. Instead he kept to the facts: "He's nine years younger; he comes and goes... I don't know what he does for a living, actually, but he isn't farming... He resembles our mother... We're not close." Later he'd wonder why he'd shielded Mick, choosing instead not to speak of him at all. Still Nancy would periodically ask. She was so attached to her older sister she couldn't imagine anyone not cherishing a sibling. Tyler's one attempt to reestablish a brotherly connection had been derailed by alcohol and a voluptuous waitress. As far as Ty could see, nothing had improved since. How could he tell her that to bring his brother close would be as dangerous as placing a scorpion on his chest?

The day he took Nancy to see the farm Mickey was there, a

Mickey he scarcely recognized. A Mickey who shook his hand and then gave him a quick bear hug as if they were pals; a Mickey who pulled out Nancy's chair before Tyler had a chance, who sat up straight instead of lolling; a young man dressed in form-fitting jeans and a new green flannel shirt that flattered his hair and eyes; a Mickey who kept up a steady patter of commentary and jokes, laughing and teasing his mother and Nancy with what passed for affection. Tyler didn't know this brother because he'd only seen a brief version of it when the Manning brothers had gone drinking with Howie and Jeff. He finally recognized the competitive parry and jab, dressed up in public garb: a light banter wreathed in crocodile smiles.

Then Delia began the storytelling: amusing childhood tales of "my boys." Ty recognized that he was getting the worst of it, but an outsider like Nancy would be clueless, unable to see it for what it was, a circuitous taking of sides, putting forth one boy ahead of the other, making the older boy seem capable—"Tyler never does anything in half measures"—but hard. Tyler's face was burning. From that dinner at the farm he kept one other memory: Mickey's eyes devouring his fiancée.

"I finally met Ty's family," Nancy told Billie during a lunch hour break. They were seated in the first floor staff lounge, mugs of coffee in their hands. Tyler was not in the room.

"Thought you'd met Delia already," Billie ventured, instantly alert to the words *Ty's family*. What family? She felt suddenly indignant. Ty would, of course, introduce them because he had to and because he was dutiful, not because they behaved in any way she would recognize as family. Since Hal's death, her parents, Virgil and Helen, were more like family to Ty than anyone. She regretted not telling Nancy this.

In the hall the class bell rang loudly. Teachers moaned and rose from their chairs like weary soldiers, depositing their coffee cups in the sink or quickly swilling the last drops of cola from cans before depositing them in the trash.

"He'd scarcely mentioned his brother." Nancy gave Billie a

rare smile. "Don't know why Ty has been keeping him a secret."

"One day I'll tell you why," Billie managed to say, but Nancy had turned away, reaching for her handbag, walking toward the door.

A month after that family dinner, Tyler observed a change. He inquired finally since his fiancée seemed both edgy and pre-occupied. Was she feeling well? She seemed tired. She laughed it off, but the last time he asked, she snapped. Was he completely thickheaded? And why did he keep at it?

"Yes, I'm tired, Tyler. Of you asking. You're so predictable."

The remark was uncharacteristic and confirmed what he had dreaded, that women were unknowable and mercurial. One evening she might be wild in her lovemaking and the next so uninterested she opted to stay home alone. He'd noticed the tapering off of her sexual interest. Had he been too careful? He felt as though he were on an elevator, never sure whether he would be speeding up or down. He mentioned the moodiness to Billie, a passing remark he hoped sounded humorous.

"Maybe it's time to tell her the truth of your family," Billie said.

"What does that mean?" he asked. "*The truth of my family?*"

"I had your brother in mind."

He dismissed her with a shrug. "Least said soonest mended."

"You sound like your dad, Ty. What good did discretion do him? After years of silence and unhappiness, he drops dead of a heart attack."

"There's nothing to say. They're my family. Am I supposed to hide them? It's not like we're going to spend a lot of time with them."

Throughout one long weekend Nancy didn't call and even phoned in sick on Monday and Tuesday. He considered calling her sister at work but decided that might be construed, by both sisters, as intruding. Needy. Meanwhile his concern mounted. His imagination enlarged the situation to include a serious health problem: Her doctor had informed her that she had cancer, MS, a heart murmur. Yes, she was a strong, self-possessed woman, but why was she trying to handle it on her own? He left a message on her answering machine, urging her to call when she felt up to it. Still she didn't phone. When she was absent from school the next day as well, he drove to the house after school. He pulled his truck into the drive and let himself in through the side door with the key she'd given him months ago. He couldn't refrain from glancing around the mudroom, pleased to see that his renovations were holding up.

He walked silently through the kitchen and into the dining room. The tuxedo cat was perched on the tower, gazing into the dogwood outside. He went through the living room and into the front hall where a flight of stairs led to the second floor. Overhead someone laughed, and then a voice murmured indistinctly.

"Nancy?" he called up the stairs, remaining at the bottom.

The air didn't stir, and a feeling of dread opened up. Then Nancy called back.

"Ty? I'll be right down."

The laugh was not hers. Perhaps from the television she kept in her room. Then Nancy appeared at the top of the stairs in her bathrobe and slowly made her way down.

"Sorry if I woke you. I was worried," he said.

Was it the gesture of concern or the apology that made him weak in her eyes? Her brows and mouth immediately knotted in irritation.

"I told you I'd call."

"But you haven't." He stood, resolute, at the bottom of the stairs while the realization dawned that she was not alone.

"I'll make us some tea," she said and took the stairs slowly. Her feet were bare and her toenails were polished a deep red. She'd never polished her nails before.

She had almost reached him. He was about to step aside and let her pass, when a different figure appeared at the top of the stairs. He glanced up and saw Mickey, dressed only in trousers.

"What the fuck?" Tyler's voice was a husk of rage and he turned his glare on her.

No one spoke, or moved, and then Nancy said, "We need to talk."

"Get him out of here!" Ty said.

"No."

"What?"

Tyler lunged past her toward Mickey. She grabbed him with both arms, clinging to him with her full strength, screaming, "Stop it!"

His brother ducked back along the hall and disappeared. A door slammed shut. She clung to him, dragging him back with her whole weight until they both collapsed lengthwise along the stairs. Tears had sprung into her eyes. To get to Mick, he would have to somehow push her aside, and that he could not do. He pulled her to an awkward sitting position. Their faces were inches apart.

"What have you done?" he said, conscious that tears filled his own eyes. "Did he tell you that you were the most beautiful woman he'd ever met? You're not the first, Nance. And you won't be the last."

She couldn't answer him, couldn't look him in the eye. A sob shook her body, and she cried silently, without signaling the slightest need for comfort.

"You believe everything he says, don't you?"

"What do you know, Tyler?" Her voice shook.

"More than you think."

She lifted her head, and then her chin, in what looked like the defiance of a small child. The gesture was so pathetic he wanted to embrace her, but couldn't. So it was over, just like that. When had she planned to tell him? He saw their future snuffed out, as if it were only a candle flame you could easily extinguish between finger and thumb. She was still clinging to him, restraining him.

"I need to leave," he said. She relaxed her grip.

They were wedged together, and the lack of intimacy chilled

THE MANNING GIRL 107

him. He drew away and climbed to his feet, using the banister to pull himself up. He took the last few steps down and landed heavily on the hardwood floor, his back to her. His fingers flew to his eyes and wiped them free of tears. He turned so suddenly that she gasped, throwing out an arm. Without taking a step he leaned against the newel post and yelled up the stairs.

"Mickey? If I ever see you again, I'll kill you!"

Neither he nor Nancy appeared at school the next day. When he returned to teach on Friday, he steered clear of the staff room, staying close to the Mother Ship where Nancy would not likely appear. Soon after the final bell rang, Howard strolled into the shop.

"Missed you Thursday. Feeling okay?"

Tyler nodded and mumbled, "Things came up."

"You don't look diseased."

"Nothing like that."

"Some other affliction perhaps?"

Tyler shrugged, unable to look Howard in the eye.

"The Lady Fair seems under the weather too. She's been out too."

Tyler turned away abruptly. He grabbed the handsaw a student had left on his desk and hung it on the nearby pegboard.

"Well, if you want to shoot the breeze or just need an antidote for the cares of the world, mosey on down to the Art Cave." Howard patted his arm and left.

He couldn't have talked if he'd wanted to. Words stuck in his throat as if they were coated in fur, as if the event had unmanned him in some inscrutable way. He felt raw, his skin an open wound, his senses heightened except the brain, which seemed impaired.

Billie waited two weeks after the breakup, phoning Nancy at a time the older sister was sure to answer. When she asked for Nancy, Billie learned she was currently not in residence. Billie asked for a phone number but the sister resisted, giving Billie the school number instead. Billie left her own home phone and asked to have Nancy phone "Wilhelmina"—Billie's proper name. So Nancy was still with Mickey. *More fool you*, Billie thought after hanging up. Only three weeks remained in the school year, which was a blessing for Ty but made her own small project more urgent.

She found the documents in the courthouse and on library microfilm of old Topeka and Lawrence and Wichita newspapers, in public records, duplicating items until the large envelope she used to store her clippings was filled to her satisfaction. She even found the document from Hot Springs, his thirty days of jail time reduced to thirteen when the Arkansas authorities finally confirmed that his father had, indeed, died and that the mother was not just pulling a scam. So this was why Delia had refused to search for him. Billie was certain Tyler didn't know. How many of Mick's nefarious acts had Delia kept to herself?

Last, Billie typed up a chronology of Mick's sins and signed it, "Billie Harrington, who's known the Manning brothers their whole lives," slipping this on top as a guide. On Thursday she lingered after school, feeling guarded, her neck and shoulders tense. When she finally walked down to Nancy's classroom, she found the classroom door open, but Nancy was nowhere in sight. She had hoped to hand it to her in person. She didn't want to behave cowardly, an "anonymous tipster." She walked to the windows and waited, looking out over a patchy green playing field. When it became clear Nancy would not be back directly, she left the file on top of her desk, wrote across the top of the folder, "For Nancy Trotter...sorry I missed you, Billie." She secured the folder in the lower left hand pocket tab of the desk blotter. Billie's heart pounded as she left the room. Nerves set her stomach aflutter. She'd made two copies of every document—every arrest notice, every conviction and DUI, going back to Mickey's early adolescence. How could Mickey, or Nancy, deny these? Billie included a mug shot from a minor drug charge.

Still jittery, she walked to the staff parking lot, unlocked her small Toyota truck, and drove home to the farmhouse she and Bud now shared with her parents. How she wished Tyler still lived down the road. It wasn't the same with only Delia in the house. Billie felt a brief stab of pity for the older woman, now abandoned by the profligate son she cherished most. Evidently, Mick had returned once to the farmhouse, immediately after the incident, gathered his belongings and driven away, leaving his mother dumbfounded. Shacked up with Nancy somewhere, Billie thought.

The weeks that followed Ty's break with Nancy dragged by with languorous sameness. The most trivial events marked the summer holiday and included, to Billie's dismay, the discovery of her first gray hairs. Ty, too, she noticed. He'd be like his father, prematurely salted and peppered. She made note of Tyler's semi-weekly visits to his mother, sometimes spending a weekend night with her. He'd even spent one entire weekend repainting Delia's kitchen, something she gleaned only because Bud had stopped by to say hello. She'd become reluctant to intrude. Since the abrupt break with Nancy, darkness hung over Ty, a gloom she couldn't penetrate. He seemed impervious to humor, his gaze wandering off as soon as he acknowledged you, as if he couldn't look folks in the eye. Bud reported after his brief visit to the farmhouse that Ty had little to say, and whatever Delia said made remarkably little sense.

"Why don't we bring her over here for dinner?" she said.

"Don't bother. I invited her and she said something about not needing anyone's pity. Ty didn't say a word, just kept painting."

He shrugged and closed his eyes the way he did whenever something ought to be dismissed. She'd take Mom over. Deaf as she was, Helen was still capable of carrying on a conversation even if it was one-sided. Mother could appreciate the new kitchen decor and cheer Delia up if that was possible. They would stop by on an afternoon Tyler wasn't visiting.

Billie marveled that her mother was as sturdy as she was. Virgil had become frail and stayed in his room to watch the TV or sit at the kitchen table talking to the kids, occasionally carving toys for three-year-old Aaron. Virgil's legs had betrayed him, grown afflicted with neuropathy until he was scarcely aware he had toes, but as long as he was stationary her father seemed content. But Helen kept busy, fully capable of caring for Aaron while Billie taught school. So she approached her mother, urging her to put in her hearing aids while she explained that Delia needed company. Well, of course they must go over, Helen said, and Billie phoned the Manning house, waiting six rings before Delia answered. Delia only agreed to the visit when Billie said that her mother was eager to see Delia's new kitchen decor, and besides, Billie lied, Helen was a little lonely.

An hour later, Billie parked her truck behind the Manning house and helped her mother down. Helen didn't need much help, except with hearing, but ever since Virgil had become tremulous, she hovered over her mother as if sparing her mother unnecessary steps might prevent her from aging. Billie tapped on the back door, anticipating as long a wait as the answering of the phone. Delia opened the door right away.

"You don't need to knock, you know," Delia said. Billie didn't know if this was the old expression of hospitality speaking or the new voice of impatience they'd been hearing of late. Except it wasn't impatience, Helen told Billie later, but a vagabond desperation from a woman alone and at loose ends. Billie leaned over and gave Delia a peck on the check. Helen grabbed her neighbor's hand and held it. Billie stepped away from the older women, making pleased and surprised noises as she gazed upward, admiring the kitchen.

"That's a lovely green, Delia," she said. "And, by god, the cabinets are new too. Look at those ceramic drawer pulls, Mom."

"Well, you know Ty," Delia said, her voice suppressing any pride. "He never does anything in half measures."

They sat at the kitchen table which Delia had set with coffee cups and plates. On the table was a platter of store-bought cookies. There was a time when Delia Manning would never have been caught serving a guest anything from a store.

Helen also remarked on the decor, complimenting the painter and the house owner, threatening to overpower the conversation. Billie leaned slightly left and glanced at the side of her mother's head: the older woman had neglected to insert her hearing aids. Billie's heart sank. When Helen paused, Delia began, interrupted at increasingly frequent intervals by Helen asking Delia to repeat or speak up.

"Mom, you forgot your hearing aids again," Billie said in a loud voice. She turned to Delia and offered an apology. "They're uncomfortable, evidently."

"Then she should get better ones," Delia said in a sharp voice, her face dark, the impatience returning.

Billie sat up and forced a smile. "I'm sure you're right."

And then it began, the recitation of Michael's nonexistent virtues, Delia's puzzlement over his departure, the list of possible reasons for his extended absence, as if his behavior was never to blame. She no longer called him Mickey. When Helen Markham finally interrupted Delia's lengthy monologue, *What was that, dear?* Delia nearly threw herself across the table in anger. Billie would recoil at the memory for weeks to come.

"Good god, woman! All you can say is 'whatwhatwhat?' Where is your brain?"

Exhausted, Delia sank back in her chair, astounded by, if not ashamed of, her own words. Billie felt as though time had stopped. Her face burned yet her hands felt strangely cold. Helen, meanwhile, looked merely puzzled. Slowly, Billie rose. "Mother? It's time to go." She took her mother's arm and raised her firmly from her chair. At first Helen resisted, uncertain as to what was happening. It wasn't clear how much Helen had actually heard, but as far as Billie was concerned, all that mattered was getting her out of the Manning house. When they reached the back door, Billie turned. With the greatest effort, she kept her voice low.

"You should be ashamed. My mother is not demented, she's

deaf. And she is your oldest friend. Probably your only friend."

Delia lowered her gaze the moment Billie began to speak and rested her head in a fork of fingers, her elbow propped on the table. She was still looking down when Billie closed the kitchen door. In the truck neither woman spoke until Billie pulled out of the drive and onto the county road.

"She's not well," Helen said.

"You can say that again!" Billie shouted. "She's nuts."

"That's not what I meant. Didn't you see her face? Her hands? She is seriously unwell."

"Didn't you hear a word she said to you?"

Helen turned and gazed pointedly at her daughter. "I heard enough. There's a reason I don't wear my hearing aids to Delia's house. Delia's been saying regrettable things since Hal died."

Billie remained too upset to fully absorb her mother's observation. How could her mother be so detached, so understanding? Even if Helen hadn't heard all the words, someone had. Two people had—the speaker and Billie. While Bud and Billie assumed it was Mickey's departure that had unhinged Delia, Helen Markham was steadfast in her belief that her neighbor was physically ill.

"Call Tyler," she told Billie. But Billie did not call Tyler, convinced their neighbor's ailment was not only psychological but of her own choosing.

The new school year began, but still Billie did not see Tyler except for his occasional appearances in the staffroom, filling his coffee cup. It wasn't like her to resist contact, but something continued to hold her back. She asked Jeff, who shrugged and told her to give him some breathing room. She asked Howard who shrugged and closed his eyes like Bud did, as if to shut out the foolishness of the world. "You've known him longer than anyone here. Why don't you ask?"

She knew she should but couldn't bring herself to do so. Whenever she considered approaching him, something pushed her back like a strong wave heaving detritus to the shore.

"Maybe he's grieving," Howard said later.

"That's not what I see. I see anger. And that's not like Ty."

"Oh, but it is," Howie answered, and Billie gazed at him in dismay.

Was this how grief looked, angry and dark as an oil fire? She would have to breach the gloom one day, if for no other reason than to convey her mother's concern over Delia. Perhaps he was too lost in his own sorrow that he hadn't perceived his mother's condition. She'd guessed long ago that Tyler dealt with his mother by shutting her out, going through the motions, divesting.

Nancy Trotter did not return to Washburn-Shawnee High School in the fall. Billie learned she'd transferred to a different school and had reclaimed her original address with her sister. When she casually mentioned this to Tyler, he didn't respond. Then Billie suggested Nancy might like to hear from him. He gazed at her with that dark and stubborn look she remembered from when they were teens, and walked away.

In late September Billie went down to Howard's room during lunch. She found him stocking large sheets of colored paper into a vertical art cabinet. Her thoughts had gathered into such a knot that she forgot to announce herself and spoke abruptly to Howard's back.

"Did you know Nancy Trotter's back with her sister?"

Howard started and whirled around. "Good grief, Billie!"

"First off, do you suppose Nancy Trotter has Mick Manning out of her system? And second, do you think she can repair the damage?"

"Why are you asking me?"

"Because I know you've remained friends with her."

Howard gave her a cautious look. "I'm friends with many people, including my ex."

"Look, Howie. I think it was a huge mistake." She was speaking too hurriedly, as though the thought would vanish if she didn't lay it out for him now. "I know what Mick Manning's like. I'll bet you good money she's choking with regret."

"You really think they can move on? Just pick up where they left off?"

She didn't like the sarcasm in Howard's voice.

"And why are you getting involved?" he asked.

"Because Ty was happy with her. And until Mick interfered, she was happy too."

"I think you need to ask *her*."

She was afraid he would say this. Still, she'd come to an understanding over the summer, ever since she'd left the folder of "evidence" on Nancy's desk. She'd bet good money that Nancy had been—until Mick—a woman with limited experience who'd never been willingly seduced, a woman always in control who'd never taken a risk, always done "the right thing." For once in her life, she'd had a chance to be naughty, deliciously uninhibited. Who wouldn't grab it?

"Do you hear from her?" she asked finally.

Howard resumed shelving the sheets of art paper. "I'll give her a call. But it's not entirely up to her, you know?" Howard sighed. "This wasn't some little household burn. They scorched him good."

In early October Tyler found a small card in his mail box at the bungalow and recognized the handwriting. He left the letter on the dining room table for a day before opening it. The card was feminine, with two cats on the cover page. Nancy's message inside was brief and included an apology—if not exactly abject, an apology nevertheless: *I very much regret hurting you.* She had returned home, she wrote, which Ty already knew, thanks to Billie. And she included the old phone number. *If you ever want to get together, have some coffee, please phone.*

He read the card through a second time, then tore the note in half, disposing it and the envelope in the kitchen trash.

After Mickey vanished, Delia Manning lasted less than a year. She'd concealed her malady and then refused treatment. In her final month, when the cancer had finally incapacitated her, Tyler moved back to the farmhouse to look after her, reclaiming his old room upstairs. While he was at work, a hospice worker helped her during the day. He checked in on the bungalow every afternoon after school and spent an afternoon there each weekend. He missed his home when he wasn't there. It had become the one place he felt fully himself.

Near the end, Billie and Bud and Helen came and went, preparing meals, comforting and distracting Tyler as best they could. Delia showed no sign of recognizing any of them except Ty and the hospice nurse. On her last day she summoned Tyler while Billie and Bud were in the kitchen, cleaning dishes.

Tyler entered his mother's room and pulled the chair close to the bed. In the last days her pain had been so acute Delia had allowed the nurse to increase the morphine dose until she mostly slept. But the nurse had told him she'd requested no morphine that day. She was facing the wall when he sat down. He leaned over and took her wasted hand. She turned her head toward him and whispered his name. Her face was knotted in pain, and his throat felt clotted. He leaned over and kissed her forehead. He did not expect to suffer any heartbreak, but the sight of her in her final hours, and in such pain, made him feel undone. How he wanted to talk in earnest about the family, about her memories of his childhood, of Hal.

"You're a good son," she said slowly, pushing each word out as though it were a marble. "You're your father's boy, Ty. Always good...so proud of you. You need to forgive Michael. He's lost...all my fault."

The words came slowly, and she squeezed his hand. He held it firmly, squeezing back and whispered that he loved her. He needed to say it, for he now felt overcome by something larger than duty. She released her grip at last, her hands scrabbling along the sheets as though she was searching for a pin, and then she was gone.

When her will was read, he learned he'd inherited the farm property and house. This was his father's doing, he felt sure, Hal's final gift to his older son. Delia had left a nest egg for his brother—insurance money, her hoarded inheritance, savings—should Mickey ever return to claim it. Ty was startled at the amount. Every day of the last two years she'd pleaded penury. He'd used his own money for services he now realized she could easily have paid for herself.

A decision needed to be made. Sell the farm? Rent the bungalow? For the longest time he felt as though he were two people, caught in two distinct lives, town and country, uncertain and undecided.

It was spring of 1990. Visiting the farm, he walked the fence line with his retriever, a youthful Rusty, when a flock of Canada geese flew overhead, honking. He stopped to listen. They were headed for the pond just beyond the small stand of timber that stood in the southwest corner of the farm. The pond straddled a stretch of pasture on one side and a field of corn on the other where, after the summer harvest, the geese would feed on the gleanings. High cirrus clouds feathered a sky slowly losing its daytime color. A redwing blackbird flew up to a telephone wire and sang. The air smelled fresh and fecund, full of the odors of grain.

What moved him above all was the quiet. Since Nancy's departure, he'd come to need quiet, to crave it like some people crave nicotine or sugar. His neighborhood in town wasn't noisy, but he'd begun to find all human sounds jarring: car horns, neighborly voices, sirens, distressing laughter. He'd once hoped he and Nancy would live together in the bungalow. "The starter house," they'd joked. The loss of that dream—and the death of his mother, if only he'd admit it—made each room feel cramped, and he began to feel lonely there as though nothing remained of him that he could recognize. He didn't understand how a place where he'd once felt most at home now made him feel hollowed out.

He followed the fence line as far as the southwest pasture where other people's cattle now grazed. He turned and looked back toward the farmhouse and outbuildings. It would be a worthy project to convert part of the barn to a proper shop, and the orchard needed attention. With judicious pruning the fruit trees could be revived. In his mind's eye he could see the farmhouse as his father had maintained it, tidy and attractive, a solid structure that had been allowed to slump into decline. He could return the house to its previous glory, raise his own beef cattle and some poultry, get some goats and make cheese. The food co-op in Lawrence was always looking for goat cheese and organic produce. As his mind ticked off the possibilities, his spirits rose out of the cellar they had lived in for months.

He might teach in town, but he need not live there.

When Howie told her Ty had sold the bungalow, Billie felt suddenly weak.

"He loved that place," she told Bud. Ty would be their neighbor again. Like old times. It was as though someone essential had reentered their lives after a long absence overseas.

Billie watched the improvements to the old Manning place whenever she drove by: Ty on the roof, Ty replacing a window frame or the boards of the neglected front porch. A tractor tire appeared on its side near the mailbox by the road. In a matter of days seedlings germinated into a fringe of green, then stalks, finally blooming into a circle of marigolds and zinnias. Along the drive and around the house, Ty plowed the coarse Johnson grass and replaced it with hardy fescue and rye. When she drove around to his back door to deliver a pie, she heard chickens cheeping. She didn't know why she bothered with a pie. His pies were as good as hers, his crust flakier. She'd bring a casserole next time.

She missed her mother dreadfully. Helen now resided in assisted living ever since her once sturdy memory broke: Bud had found Helen wandering along the side of the road, destination unknown. Billie visited daily at first and now twice a week with one of her children, even if her mother didn't know who she was. She wanted to spy on the help, assure herself that no one was neglecting her mother, pinching her. She'd read about nursing home abuse. She looked for bruises, checked to be sure Mama was still wearing her rings. On her drive back home, she could pass by Tyler's place and see how he was coming along with the porch or the roof shingles or the new fancy all-climate windows. She amused herself by imagining Ty putting solar panels on the roof. He'd even made the school add some high-tech improvements when they rebuilt the new art and technology wing. How Howie and Jeff and Ty loved their classrooms.

When Tyler commenced his second year of isolation and mourning, as Billie thought of it, she wondered if he was ever going to emerge.

"How long d'ya suppose he's going to lick his wounds?" she asked Bud one evening. Tyler had just driven by with a load of lumber in his truck.

"Why do you want to interfere? He's a grown man. I imagine he knows what he wants."

"I don't think it's healthy."

Bud dropped the dish towel on the counter top. "And you know what's best for him, I suppose. Ty's never been out-going like you. And when folks don't want to socialize—like you—why do you suppose something's wrong?"

He was staring at her, and it made her uneasy. She kept her eyes focused on the dishes in the sink, then sighed.

"You're probably right," she said to avoid an argument.

PART TWO

7

A Day in the Life

From January fourth until the end of the school term when she turned one, Delia May spent her days at a babysitter. When Ty's summer vacation began, he wondered if May might miss the young woman's care. How did a child sort out the difference between family and sitter? She was still a baby when she first stayed at the sitter's and had taken her first steps there. In her second summer it thrilled him to be at home with the child. He modified a hiker's backpack and took her everywhere. "The Cadillac of backpacks," Bud joked.

If visitors stopped by while Ty was doing chores, they might see two heads bobbing across the barnyard. When he worked in the shop, he placed her at a safe distance in a playpen he'd bought secondhand. But she was unhappy when confined. The playpen made her fuss, even when surrounded by her dolls and blocks and musical toys. He decided to place the dog in with her, which made Rusty miserable but delighted the child for perhaps thirty minutes.

Next came the rope. Of course it didn't help that Billie had seen the rope and harness and flown into a snit. "Why do you have that child on a leash, Tyler? She's not a dog."

When had Billie taken this turn? He didn't remember the Harringtons being so strict with their kids. But the rope had been a disaster: that horrible moment when he'd found her playing under the circular saw. Immediately after, he made a blueprint for the "corral." Meanwhile Delia May grew apace. Before he could catch a breath her second birthday had come and gone.

In early fall he left her one Saturday morning in the playroom with Rusty while he vacuumed. She had her blocks out and her musical toys. The little toy piano plunked in the background, and her voice crooned to the dog. His mind had wandered off like a beagle on a scent and when it stopped tracking and he shut off the sweeper, the house was too quiet. He went to the playroom near the kitchen. The gate was open and both rooms empty. He flew out the back door and saw her in the yard, on her bottom, surrounded by a flock of curious chicks. The dog had plopped down in the shade of the old locust tree a few yards behind.

What Tyler could not know was that the child had been observing the dog for days. The animal walked up to the back door, pushed a flap with his nose and slowly disappeared through a wall. Sometime later—often only a moment or two later—the dog reappeared to the child's delight. The flap rose, a nose appeared, then a head, shoulders, and the whole of Rusty. The child was enchanted, and the urge to follow the dog grew. The next time Rusty approached the door May was ready. As soon as the animal pushed through the hole in the door and vanished, May crawled after. The flap gave way with the slightest pressure, and there she was, on the porch! Rusty was trotting across the barnyard toward the grassy verge beyond. The dog saw the child and waited. May turned and climbed backward down the steps that were too steep for her two-year-old legs. She ran to catch up with the dog until the appearance of the chicks distracted her, and she reversed course, back into the center of the patchy yard where the chickens liked to scratch. She reached for a small yellow chick, but the bird darted away. May gave chase until a too sudden turn brought her around so quickly she sat down with a thump. Immobilized and lower to the ground, she became an object of interest. The chicks ventured toward her to inspect a shoe, a leg, a hand. Thrilled, she reached out and plucked a slow moving chick off the ground.

Elevated above the flock, the chick beat its useless wings and cheeped. She brought the soft feathery body to her face and stroked her cheek with it and kissed it. It pecked her ear, and she dropped it. "Bad!" she said. When she looked up again, her father was standing on the back porch. She waved her hands.

"Daddy!"

He counseled himself not to panic, not to come flying at her as if she'd done something wrong. He told himself to relax, just bring her indoors. She stood up and waved again, calling, "Come see, Daddy." Then she sat back down. One of the chicks had come so near that she picked it up and held it out to him like a gift. He walked as slowly as he dared, took the chick out of her hands and put it on the ground where it ran off with its flock.

"How did May get out here?" he asked in a play voice and put his hands on his hips as if he were play-scolding.

She gave him a puzzled look, smiled, and raised her little arms in the universal gesture of "who knows?" Was she so smart she knew how to open the door? It wasn't the end of the earth, after all. She hadn't strayed. The dog was with her, and she'd spent maybe five minutes enjoying the chicks. No harm done. Still, inside his chest the bird of danger beat its heavy wings. He must remember to lock the door.

Within days it happened again, girl and dog escaping out the back. He'd gone upstairs to take a rare nap. The little girl was across the hall in her youth crib, also napping, except she was not. Quietly she'd slipped off the bed and down the stairs after the dog, her mind focused on the little door inside the big one. When he awoke and went to check, both May and the dog had vanished. Forewarned is forearmed, he thought.

Tyler raced downstairs, calling her name, but there was no answer. He grabbed the door and turned the knob to be sure it was locked. It was. He stepped back, mystified, and gazed the length the door, stopping only at the canvas flap at the base of the wooden door. *Surely not!* He unlocked the door and ran out. Neither she nor the dog was in the garden or barnyard, and he felt sick. He raced toward the barn, but the doors were closed. No child could open these doors or even the small side door to the shop. He made a fruitless search anyway. He moved beyond

the barn, calling her name, hoping she had not wandered down
the long drive to the road. He thought he heard a voice and
followed it, trotting along the bumpy trail to the orchard. He
stopped and bent over to catch his breath, stood back up and
called her name.

"Here I am!" a small voice called out.

He moved in among the trees toward the back, adjacent to
his neighbor's pasture. She was seated on a tussock of grass,
surrounded by windfall apples.

Not wishing to alarm her, he approached slowly. "How did
you get outside?" he asked.

"The door," she said clear as a bell.

Ah, but which, he thought.

He sat down with her on the grass and glanced toward the
fence thirty feet beyond. Three curious Holsteins stood in a
row, gazing over the fence. His neighbor the dairyman's cows.
The dog was sniffing a few yards off, wholly engaged in some
animal scent. May had built a small pile of apples, gathering
and returning, picking and choosing. She'd placed the ripe fruit
in neat rows, then small heaps. She'd only picked up the best
fruit, he noticed, leaving the rotters. She held up an apple as if
offering him a prize.

"Make a pie, Daddy."

"Shall we get a basket?"

"Yes!"

Still light-headed with relief, he took her hand and led her
back to the house. The dog noticed their departure and left
off his tracking to follow behind. When they reached the back
porch, Ty grabbed one of the soft plastic fruit baskets he left
piled along the porch wall.

"I take," May said.

"It's too big for you."

"No." She reached out her hands.

He handed it to her and gripped her collar, holding firm,
while she walked back toward the orchard. When she dropped
the basket a second time, he scooped it up.

"Daddy's turn, okay?"

She nodded, taking his hand.

Back among the fruit trees, the dog resumed his search, sniffing along the base of an old Jonathon tree. May pulled his hand toward the gathering spot. One at a time she lifted an apple and placed it in the basket.

"This way," she instructed.

As they set to their task, his mind played over the full range of her exploit. She'd somehow managed to reach the orchard by following the dog, presumably out its door. Again the bubble of mirth, and suppressed panic, popped up. Once there she'd invented a game of pick-the-pretty-apples until he found her. The adventure filled him with awe. She saw everything, imitated everything. He could take nothing for granted. He couldn't remember himself before school age, his earliest memories being ones of sitting in a circle before a kindergarten teacher, singing a song, teased for his size, and then cherished for his size when he was able to reach a shelf his little schoolmates could not.

It was miraculous any of them survived. When he was six, he'd gotten into the pasture with his father's bull. The animal had turned its heavy head and stared at him menacingly, and then turned back to graze as if Ty were not worth his attention. He didn't remember how he left the pasture or who found him. He did remember his mother had swatted his behind for "that stunt." But May was only three, not six.

They left the basket of fruit on the porch and went indoors.

"Can you show Daddy how you went outside?"

"There." She pointed in the general direction of the door.

He shrugged his shoulders. "So?" He needed to see her do it, to confirm his intuition.

"Rusty's door. See?" She walked over and then went down on her hands and knees and crowded through. "Hi, Daddy," came a delighted cry from the other side. The dog immediately shot through, and May squealed at his arrival.

He called out, "Come back in, okay?"

May pushed herself through at the same time as the dog,

causing a brief bottleneck. "Rusty, wait!" she instructed. The dog pulled back, waiting for the child to complete her awkward half-crouch, half-hands-and-knees entrance. Then the dog pushed in after. Tyler laughed out loud.

May's voice floated into his room and pulled him awake. His eyes flew open and he grabbed the bedside clock. *Six.* Something lay on his mind. His head cleared as he crawled up out of the cave of sleep, remembering there was something special about the day.

"Now here's Rusty and here's Daddy and here's Bub'nBee-bee…and here's May."

Her voice unmoored his heart and sent it sailing around his chest like a drunk and happy bird. Most mornings he awoke to the flute-like voice playing a game of her own invention, trilling the names of all she knew and could pronounce. She had developed at an alarming pace and his mind played over the continuum of her achievements. The memory of her early steps—making a beeline toward the dog—still filled him with awe. How did a child learn what to do and do it so fearlessly?

Her voice sang through the air. The dog was probably in her room by now, trotting up the stairs when she called his name, and she did call it. Every morning. The baby had puzzled Rusty at first until she was old enough to sit on the floor and coo at him, grabbing his abundant golden fur, patting him, lolling against him, falling asleep at his side. Tyler didn't imagine Rusty had had this much attention since he was a pup. He felt attached to the dog but in a more circumspect way: an occasional pat or rub of the ears, talking to him, taking Rusty on his rounds around the farm. But the baby had turned the animal into an object of desire, and the dog had grown to love it. Tyler quickly dressed and went to May's nursery.

"Now who could be in here?" he announced, stopping at the threshold and clasping his hands, the same words each morning, the same gestures, as if each morning were a surprise.

The little girl laughed. "May's in here," she chirped and put her little hands on her hips. "And Rusty." Except the R was still a W: *Wusty*.

"Do we want up or down?" he asked.

She climbed up, reaching out her arms. "May wants up *and* down."

He swung her out and onto the floor while they both called out "Wheeee!" as if the action was not complete without the sound effect. The dog's tail thumped back and forth across the floor. Thus the morning ritual began. She was perfectly capable of getting herself out of bed but usually waited for him to arrive, as though that swing from bed to floor was required to launch the day

"What clothes today, miss?" The night before he'd laid out two sets of little girl trousers and tops on the play chest in her room. She ran to the chest, which he had made, and grabbed the purple and pink set. He nodded his approval.

"PJs off," he announced and May shot her hands up in the air.

Down they eventually went to the kitchen where he hoisted her onto her booster chair. She had not stopped chattering, half of her narrative some private story, the other half quite plain. Out came the Cheerios, the milk, the grape juice and cheese buds. Always the same, except for the occasional grape or apple pieces or bit of scrambled egg. She was monitoring him with her lopsided smile, sneaking tidbits to the dog whenever he turned his back.

Once breakfast was accomplished, they walked out into the side yard where he let her toss grain to the chicks and ducks. Frank, the irascible drake, had once taken a peck at her bottom, and the little girl had whirled around and shaken her finger at him and said, "No, no!" in a loud voice. The drake cocked its hand, took a step back and a step to the side, did a little duck turn, and waddled away.

Hand in hand they made their way to the workshop in the barn. As they opened the workshop door, May released his hand. He'd made the wood corral eight feet in diameter where she could play in the middle of the shop. A large hook rug lay across the floor inside this elaborate playpen.

"Play time!" he called and opened the little gate to the corral. Inside were her toys: building blocks, a jack-in-the-box and a top, wooden farm animals and buildings he'd made himself, simple puzzles involving shapes, toddler musical instruments, and baby books that popped up.

"Shall we let Rusty in?" he asked.

"Yes! Rusty, too."

She dashed into the corral and the dog shuffled in after. He handed May the toothless old brush so she could "groom" the dog without causing him discomfort. "Comb your hair, Rusty." The radio remained silent these days so he could listen for May. She still had Ty's dark curly hair and dark blue eyes—his father's eyes and hair. She was a healthy, active child but small-boned and fragile-looking. Like her mother Sherlynne Smith. Like his own mother as well. Like Mickey. She certainly had Mick's pointed chin and dimples.

Tyler drilled small holes through the delicate balsa birds he'd painted the day before: a cardinal, blue jay, Canada goose, mourning dove, redwing blackbird, an owlet, and one Monarch butterfly for good measure. The only task remaining was to string and balance the birds along the four short dowels of the mobile he planned to hang in May's bedroom. This might be a good project for his students. The stringing up part might vex some of the boys, since more than a few seemed to suffer from some attention disorder. How many times had he warned school counselors that a child with no impulse control should not be in a shop with tools? They should be in a PE class, exhausting themselves, shooting baskets, climbing ropes, or swimming laps. But who listened to the "shop teacher"?

For support, he finally sought out the new boys' gym teacher, and Rudy Ortiz had given it. "Big O," they called him: short, solid, yet somehow imposing. Rudy was only the second Latino teacher on the staff. Tyler didn't know whether the counselors listened to Rudy because he was a member of a minority or because he was the high school's winning wrestling coach. The only wrestling coach, in fact, for Rudy started the squad as soon as he joined the faculty. He reminded Ty of Manny, even if the two men didn't look at all alike. Rudy had bulk, and Manny was thin and lithe as a cat, a welter weight.

May was murmuring and he turned to check. Dog and child lay across the cedar-filled animal bed he'd put in the corral. The dog lay on his side, dozing, and May leaned against the dog, opening and closing the pages of a pop-up book, narrating the story aloud, a story they'd read a thousand times. She wouldn't grasp what a mobile was until he hung it above her bed, and she could see it turning in a breeze. She would like the bird colors and shapes. She knew all her shapes and colors and could recite the name of birds she admired. Hopefully there would be a nap before the afternoon party Billie and Bud had planned. It was Independence Day and there would be fireworks.

8

THE FOURTH OF JULY

Billie pulled the sheet cake out of the oven, placing it on the wire rack to cool. If anyone had asked her three years ago whether Tyler Manning could be a father, she might have laughed. How do you consider someone's fathering skills when there isn't even a mother in the house?

She couldn't help but feel a little proprietary. From the first day the child was deposited in Ty's arms—a bundle of rags and a flight bag of Pampers—she'd been within shouting distance, giving parenting lessons over the phone, offering Ty what she knew in her blood and bones about caring for an infant. Did he feel it now, the great surge of energy when you touched your child, sponged and bathed her sweet round body, placed the tiny shoes on her feet, gripped her and put her limbs in the rompers or tights or jeans? He had to feel it. She'd long thought that without that surge of mystery energy no child would ever survive.

And that backpack! He was still using it. She'd stop over and see the two of them in the garden or back in the orchard or coming out of the barn workshop: two heads bobbing, Rusty trotting along behind. The retriever was getting a little long in the tooth. Ty ought to get himself a young shepherd and train it to be May's babysitter. Someone had told her Newfoundland dogs made good nannies, but how could you bring such a huge, thick-haired dog into all this Kansas heat? Billie had a Staffie as a child—a sweet, droll, devoted animal and the love of her grammar school life. When that dog died, breaking her heart, she'd wanted another but couldn't now remember why her parents hadn't gotten one. Bud was dead set against them. He claimed you never knew if a "Pit" would mix with other family dogs. Seemed to her it depended on the people and the training. Didn't he remember the dog in *The Little Rascals*? That was a Staffie or a "Pit" (take your pick): an affectionate companion that sat smiling for the camera, the original nanny dog.

Billie chased the thought from her mind as she beat the sugar into the cream cheese frosting. She was interfering again, trying to organize his life, just as she had done since she was a little girl.

Billie had scheduled the picnic for late afternoon. This year was no different from past Independence Days when summer finally lowered its appalling weight onto man and beast alike. Cattle suffered in the fields, sought refuge with the horses in the timber or stood, up to their flanks, in the farm ponds. Yard dogs lay panting in the shade or under moist porches. Farmers greeted each other at church or the Philips filling station—"Hot enough for ya?"—as though it didn't happen every year.

The temperature was still ninety when she threw a red checkered tablecloth over the picnic table. Bud was removing ribs from the smoker. Choked to death by smoke, Billie thought. She hoped by fireworks time the temperature might have dropped. There'd been a steady breeze all day, but the sun remained high, a ball of white heat, and the wind felt unpleasant against her skin. If need be, folks could come indoors to cool off. She'd set the central air down a couple of degrees to accommodate a group. She weighed the tablecloth down with salt and pepper shakers and walked over to her husband.

"I invited that new PE teacher from school. The woman," she told Bud.

"Okay by me. Do I know her?"

She shook her head. She doubted Bud had met her. They hadn't gone to any staff events recently, and Billie's interest in the young woman had only been piqued this past spring when Jeanne expressed some interest in Ty. Wasn't it about time the man started dating again? Or at least looking around? Jeanne was attractive and single, and she needed a group. Billie even ran the idea by Howie who gave it his approval: "Nice girl, that

Jeannie." Billie allowed herself a moment's in-breath of cer-
titude. Tyler needed to meet some women, and that was that!
Besides Jeanne was as different from Nancy Trotter as anyone
could be: small, compact, short dark hair, a brilliant smile, and
light-hearted. A pixie. Billie had never seen the statuesque Nancy laugh.

"Does Ty know you've invited her?" Bud asked.

"No," she said after a pause. "But I didn't think he'd mind."

She'd tell Ty later. Ty was usually the one who reached out to
new staff. Like Rudy. But he hadn't reached out much to Jeanne,
she didn't think, and Billie could guess why. *Fooled me once, shame
on you. Fooled me twice.* Perhaps he didn't trust his own judgment.

Bud finally looked at her. "He might mind if he thought you
were fixing him up."

"This is a party. Not a date. Just a chance for them to chat.
Besides, this group needs another woman."

Bud chuckled and turned his attention back to the ribs.

Billie was setting the table when Tyler and May drove up in
the truck. Ty helped the little girl out, her legs churning before
she'd hit the ground. She called out, "BeeBee!" as she raced
across the yard and threw her arms around Billie's legs. The
little girl was dressed in her ballerina outfit—bright pink tutu
and pink ballet slippers. It made Billie smile to see it. At least
Ty had gotten the child to forgo the white tights. May had worn
the same outfit to her third birthday party, two months ago in
this very garden. Most of the same folks would be here today.
The old crowd—Tyler's cohorts from the Mother Ship and Billie's colleague Eppie Gordon. Plus spouses. Rudy had declined.
He'd be in Garden City, yet again, with family. Why that man
hadn't found a teaching job in western Kansas, she didn't know.
She hated to think how many miles he'd put on his truck.

Nowadays when the guys from the Mother Ship went out for
their Friday beer, Rudy went with them. Ty had pieced together
a little of Rudy's life from casual comments he'd made. His
parents had come up to work the meat packing plants on guest
worker visas but eventually achieved green cards, and Rudy was

the first in his large family to go to university. Besides the usual holidays, Rudy went back to Garden City for every quinceañera, Mother's Day, or christening. Still single, he joked his parents had a few marriageable women in mind. He'd nudge Ty and laugh. "I'm gonna ask 'em to look for a girl for you, Ty."

Bud had gone indoors before the Mannings arrived and now came out the back carrying the bulky cooler. May squealed out, "Bub!" and rushed forward to wrap his legs in a hug.

"Who'd a thought?" Bud had quipped when May first called his name. "I've become a Bubba at the age of forty."

Billie wondered if these were their forever names as far as May was concerned. *BeeBee* had a sweet quality, and May would say the names together, *BeeBee'nBub. Bub'nBeeBee.*

"Where's Aaron?" May asked, fuddling the consonants.

The Harringtons youngest, almost nine, was the first person May turned into a friend. Billie's oldest, Wesley, was gone from the home. And her daughter Ginny was too much there, annoying her mother with her draggy Goth looks and her dark moods. Only Aaron remained a child—buoyant and funny and at home in the world. No wonder May adored him. Billie didn't know what had possessed them to spread their family out over so many years. Why hadn't they bunched them together sensibly and gotten the baby stuff over with in six or seven years? As it turned out, Wesley learned to drive the same year Aaron learned to use the pot.

Ty went up on the porch to help Bud while May stayed near Billie, asking if she could use the swing. The Harringtons had never taken down the old swing set and slide. Now May dashed over to it and stopped, delicately pulled up the skirt of her pink tutu and positioned her little bottom over the swing seat, grabbed hold of the chains and called out in an astonishingly large voice, "AA-won!"

Billie's son burst out the back door in his ragamuffin jeans, holey tennis shoes, and Green Hornet T-shirt. He was the smallest of her children, small the way Bud said he'd been as a boy before he shot up in high school.

"Hey, Maypole!" Aaron yelled back, and May shrieked with delight.

Everything he did or said made her laugh. When he realized this devotion, he became a little clown, a performer, a tease, and raconteur. In short, her slave. Was there ever an odder pair, Billie wondered, a third grader and a three-year old? Where did a boy that age find the patience?

Aaron reached the swing and the two children went through an elaborate greeting involving flat palms and twirling thumbs that Aaron taught her, some ridiculous made up thing that was never performed the same way twice. May sat back down and Aaron pushed her from the front so he could make faces at her.

"Be careful, you two," Billie called. "Don't let her fall backward, Aaron."

She noticed how Ty went absent whenever he brought May over, as if he was off-duty at the Harrington household, which meant the duty fell to her or Bud or Aaron. She couldn't blame him. How does one survive being a single parent, every hour of the day? Even if she did most of the childcare, Bud was there to take up the slack: keep up the premises (more or less), throw a load in the washer, fix a toilet or discipline a child. But Tyler did it all. He put the babe in her backpack and carried her along on his chores, narrating everything he did, talking and talking until she learned to talk back. No wonder the child had become a chatterbox, surprising them all with what she said and understood. Perhaps this is what happened to children surrounded mostly by adults.

Billie hadn't been fussy about the start time. "Just show up any time after five." Later was better, she thought, when the heat of the day was beginning to abate. She'd been organizing the salads, filling bowls and plates, squeezing the hated Cheez Whiz onto celery sticks, Bud's favorite. Something the Harrington clan couldn't live without. When she looked out the kitchen door she saw Peg and Jeff Kornacki standing with Bud and Ty by the grill, the men all dressed in jeans. She wondered how any of them could bear the heat. At least Peggy was smart enough to wear shorts. The children were still on the swing set, playing some game that involved the slide. Her hands full, Billie came down the porch steps, making her way to the picnic table. Peggy turned and waved and walked toward the house, calling out, "Can I help?"

Howard's Mustang convertible arrived at the same moment, with two passengers—the Gordons. As Howie parked, Billie unloaded the food on the table and followed Peg who'd veered off to greet the newcomers. Howie climbed out first, dressed in his faded paint-stained jeans and a short-sleeved shirt. Billie wondered if he even owned a pair of jeans that wasn't covered in acrylics. He'd just put on the joke beret for May's benefit: *Howard zee French Arteest.* How corny could one man get.

Howie had driven with his convertible top down and his hair was windblown. Eppie sat in back wearing vast oval sunglasses and a blue chiffon scarf tied securely under her chin. Eppie's diminutive husband Roy had only a fringe of hair and looked the least ruffled of the group. Roy climbed out, holding his wife's red handbag and opened the back door for Eppie. When she saw the two women approach, she stretched out her arms in welcome.

"Howie didn't tell us we'd have an open air ride," Eppie exclaimed with a laugh.

"Stop fussing," Howard said. "You loved every moment of it. Said it made you feel like a teenager."

"'Cept for my hair."

"Your hair looks fine. You never once took off that scarf."

Eppie got out, unfolded, and finally stood, towering over her spouse by a good head. She reached back and carefully removed a large food hamper. The pies, Billie thought and smiled.

"Rhubarb-strawberry, lemon meringue, and French silk," said Eppie. "Think that'll do?"

Eppie set the hamper down long enough to give each woman a hug. Billie felt the laugh pop out. Except for little May, the Harringtons and Mannings had never been huggers. Now she worked with a woman who hugged everyone indiscriminately.

"I'll just slip these in the fridge," said Eppie.

Billie could make out Howard's little flask of rum, tucked into his waistband under the shirt. Folks knew theirs was a dry house, even though Bud had been off the sauce for years. If a person wanted something a bit more invigorating, no one minded if you brought your own. Howard and Roy Gordon made their way across the newly mowed grass to join the men. Bud was poking at the meat with a long-handled fork, wearing his ridiculous King of Barbecue apron. Tyler at least looked as he always did—Levis, boots, blue chambray shirt with the sleeves rolled part way. Howard waved at the children just as May sailed skyward. The child called out, "Howie!" May told Aaron to stop the swing and climbed down, running toward him. When she reached Howard, she threw her arms around his legs. Howard scooped her up and into the air, resting her on his shoulder.

"What's a cookin,' good lookin'?" he sang out.

"'Grits and guts,'" she yelled and giggled.

Grits and guts? Billie wondered if she heard them right. He'd have to teach her something nicer, and soon. Billie walked back up the porch steps just as Eppie came out the kitchen door. Peg joined them.

"Is that Delia May out there with Aaron?" Eppie waved at Tyler. "I swear she's grown since her birthday party. She's got Ty's hair, doesn't she? They sure look like family."

"She's got his eyes too."

The rest was left unsaid. No one knew Michael Manning except the Harringtons. Eppie was going on about the chocolate in the French silk, and Billie listened while her eyes wandered over to the children who'd left the swing set and were driving around the yard inside the little pedal-driven car Jeff had built May for her third birthday. May's piping voice rose up from time to time, ordering Aaron about.

Eppie was still talking and Billie glanced at Peg. Years ago Eppie had commented, "Who'd have guessed that grease monkey would marry a girly girl." The Kornacki's had raised two children, but the younger child, a boy, had died of cancer about the time May arrived. They had taken a keen interest in May Manning, often babysitting for Ty.

Billie took hold of Peggy's thin arm and squeezed it gently. "How's your girl?"

"She's almost grown. Can you believe it?"

Howard pulled the flask out of his waistband and poured a measure of rum into Roy Gordon's Coke. A gust lifted the skirt of the tablecloth on the picnic table, making it snap. Dishes and silverware and condiments weighted down the cloth, preventing it from flying off across the yard like a checkered sail.

Eppie's smartly fitted dress fluttered around her legs. Billie didn't think she'd ever seen Eppie in trousers and knew she made most of her own clothes. "Julia Child's my model," she'd heard Eppie say more than once. Billie assumed it was Eppie's height that kept the girls—and now the occasional boy—in line. Her culinary classes were orderly and quiet. It was Billie who had to bark at the girls in her sewing and family planning classes. What was it about a needle and thread that loosened a girl's tongue? When the same girls cooked, they turned solemn as chemists.

Not for the first time, Billie wondered if Jeanne had gotten lost, but it did seem odd. When she invited Jeanne, she'd provided directions and phone number, telling her to call if she needed help finding them. Now she felt anxious that the young gym teacher had taken a wrong turn and ended up on an unpaved road near Clinton Lake. She hadn't thought to get Jeanne's number, nor had Jeanne actually said she'd be here. She'd thanked Billie and said she'd try to make it.

"I invited the new girls' gym teacher," Billie said. "Jeanne... Potts, is it?"

"Good for you," Eppie said. "We could use some younger blood."

The women laughed, and Billie handed Eppie two platters. "For the meat."

Eppie took them and marched purposefully off the porch

toward the grill, calling out, "All right, you men. Time to gather and eat."

Eppie shoved the platters toward Bud who gingerly transferred chicken breast and brats with a pair of monster tongs. Tyler took the second plate and piled it with ribs from the smoker, carrying it to the picnic table. Bud had placed a card table at one end of the long trestle table. Room for everyone, if May sat in Tyler's lap. Billie and Peg emerged from the house carrying large bowls of potato, three-bean and trembling Jell-O salads.

Slowly, the men sauntered toward the table, quipping as they came. "What, no place cards?" "My, look at that spread!" "Let's start with those pies." Billie called the children who disengaged from the little car and raced toward the table. Again Billie wondered what had happened to Jeanne.

When May reached the table, she made it known she would only sit near Aaron. Meanwhile, Billie carefully maneuvered Peggy and Eppie into the comfy tall-backed chairs at either end of the communal board. Eppie started filling the plates, taking orders, piling on the meat and salads and rolls and passing them down each side, amidst teasing calls of "don't stint!" and cautionary ones of "not too much!" When the group finally settled, Billie stood.

"And who would like to say the blessing?"

She sat down and turned immediately to Eppie who'd been waiting for the honor with a beatific smile.

The breeze had finally died down, and a few cotton ball clouds hung in the sky. Two red tail hawks circled and soared, so high up they appeared to be among the clouds. House finches sang in the tulip tree and under the eaves. Along the length of the table, the meat platters lay emptied, and bones collected in plates. Dinner rolls chased the last of the potato salad and meat drippings while clumps of unwanted raspberry Jell-O melted slowly. Billie tilted her head back, uncomfortably full.

Billie grabbed an empty platter. "Be right back," she said so

Bud could hear and headed for the house. Throughout the meal Billie glanced toward the road. In the kitchen she placed the empty platters on the side board. Her daughter was standing at the sink filling a glass. She didn't know why Ginny was avoiding the party. The girl knew everyone here, had known them her whole life.

"Honey, why don't you join us?" Billie said.

Ginny rolled her eyes and muttered, "No thanks."

A silence rolled out between them until the girl spoke again. "Oh, I almost forgot. You got a phone call."

"When?"

"I don't remember. About 4:30? Some woman called to say she couldn't make it to the picnic. She said something about a migraine."

"Jeanne," Billie muttered and stared out toward the road. Abruptly Billie turned back angrily on her daughter. "Since it's after seven o'clock, when did you plan on telling me?"

"Mom, I'm telling you now!"

"Didn't it occur to you we might worry about someone who didn't show up? I thought we taught you better!"

"Jesus, Mom! Cool your jets!"

"*Cool your jets?* What kind of talk is that?"

The girl dashed out of the kitchen and up the stairs, calling over her shoulder. "You are such a witch, you know that? You're nice to Aaron. Why aren't you nice to me?"

"What?" She stared at her daughter disappearing up the steps. Her arms fell limp by her sides, her face on fire. Bud tried to calm Billie down, but it never seemed to work. Her own behavior was as inscrutable and unpleasant as her daughter's. She hadn't a clue why she couldn't deliver her own corrections in a softer tone. Something fierce took hold of her and squeezed, making the words as hard as the tone of her voice. The boys had never been bothered, but this child was different and traveling through a sensitive phase. It wasn't as if Bud contradicted her in front of the girl. It was just this desperate feeling she had that he disapproved.

She needed to slice a piece of Eppie's French silk and take it up to her. What was it Bud always said? "Someone needs to make amends here." She took Eppie's pie from the fridge and cut a sliver. The girl would complain her mother was trying to make her fat. Slowly she climbed the stairs and knocked on Ginny's door.

Her face still felt warm and her head light while she talked with Ginny, offering up her apology while the girl remained silent until she muttered something Billie couldn't quite hear. The conversation was brief but had felt unendurably long.

"Come on down for the fireworks, why don't you?" she ended, patting Ginny's hand. "May would love to see you. She adores you. They all want to see you."

"Maybe," the girl answered. There was no inflection in her voice.

"We love you, you know. And you're missing Howie's silly jokes and Eppie's tiresome stories."

The girl offered up a tiny smile. Billie leaned over and kissed her daughter's forehead and left the room.

When she approached the picnic table, Howard and Eppie had already started up, engaged in familiar banter. The performance was a little late today, which usually appeared midway through a meal when conversation began to droop. Delia May and Aaron were back inside the little car, peddling and bumping over the clumps of Johnson grass. She'd expected the children to tire by now but perhaps the meal had simply refueled them. Their voices drifted over the air like bird song. Aaron appeared too large for the vehicle, his knees rising up. If he was cramped, he didn't show it, making a *vrrroom-vrrrooom* noise while May urged him to drive.

"Here we go!" their voices rang out. The small car began to move in little jerks toward the picnic table. May laughed and clapped her hands.

"You're riding shotgun, Maypole!" Aaron yelled.

"Time for a Free State story," Howard goaded Eppie. "Don't disappoint me."

"I'll tell you something else instead," the older woman said. "Do you know the Kansa Indian word for Topeka?"

"By all means tell us," said Howard. "Especially since I didn't know there was such a tribe."

"'A good place to dig potatoes.' And all those spuds are in our classrooms."

Billie could see Eppie's molars when she reared back and laughed.

"Now we want one of the real tales."

"Oh, Howie, you've heard 'em all."

"I can't believe that. We have to squeeze 'em out of you."

"Why are you so all fired up about one now?"

"It's the Fourth of July, Ep. What better day for a Kansas story."

"Okay. Here's my favorite. But my mother always said it was made up. So take it for what it's worth. It's a story about my great-grandmother, a Border War tale, mind you—about nightriders coming over into eastern Kansas, shooting livestock or pets or anything that moved, even men and boys. My people were homesteading between Lecompton and Lawrence when a group of those bushwhackers rode onto the premises, right through the kitchen garden, their horses kicking up the produce. Those men shot the family dog, most of the chickens in the pen—the ones they didn't steal. They even shot the little milk cow. Then they torched one of the outbuildings. Evidently the father was away, leaving only the mother and children. One of those children was my great-grandma Molly who peeked out between the curtains of their darkened house. The moon lit up those bushwhackers faces. She memorized every face but recognized only one. A Lecompton man. The others were strangers to her. Everyone assumed they'd come over from Missouri, except the one she knew."

"Is this tale suitable for children?" Howard asked.

"You asked for it, Howie, and the children aren't even listening."

The car and its young occupants were negotiating a turn around the swing set.

"As I was saying," Eppie went on. "The following Saturday, Molly was assigned to take the wagon to town to sell what few eggs were left and buy the basics. She was a young woman of fifteen or sixteen, wearing a homemade apron over her dress and a sunbonnet. In that apron she'd placed her father's hammer and two ten-penny nails. She took her younger brother along for good measure. The young people put their rifles or shotguns, whatever, at their feet, out of sight. Molly had discovered she had a knack for shooting. A crack shot, in fact—"

"Why of course," Howard interrupted. "All Free State heroines were crack shots."

"Hush up, Howie," said Jeff, and Eppie nodded her thanks.

"So…Molly and her brother joined the men folk at the shooting contest that often took place in a side alley near the courthouse. Men who didn't know her laughed at the poor-looking girl with the gun. Teased her and the younger brother, but they let them shoot. They stopped laughing when she didn't miss a single target and won the silver dollar that was the prize.

"Just as the group was breaking up, she turned her weapon on the young man she knew, the one whose face she recognized from that violent group of bushwhackers. The other men drew back. Her brother stood behind her, covering her, with his shotgun pointed at the crowd of marksmen. Then she marched that Lecompton man to the huge cottonwood tree beside Farrell's Dry Goods and Outfitters. She took the hammer from her apron pocket and one ten-penny nail. She grabbed his right hand, lickety-split, and nailed that hand to the tree trunk, her shotgun still cocked and leaning precariously against the tree. The man screamed bloody murder."

"I should hope so," Howard murmured.

"'That one's for the dog,' Molly said. Then just as quickly she grabbed the other hand and nailed it against the trunk on the other side. 'And that one's for the little cow.'

"The bushwhacker had fainted by that time and several

horrified onlookers rushed toward him, but she grabbed her shotgun and swung the muzzle around, and they slid back like water. Her brother pointed his weapon in the air and fired once, and the remaining group yipped and dashed away or dropped to the ground. She pointed her gun to the crucified man and then to the onlookers and yelled, 'You're nothin' but a bunch of slavery-loving cowards. All of ya!'"

Eppie leaned back dramatically.

"Gee," Howard mused. "I wonder how she made it home without someone peppering her backside with buckshot."

Preparing her retort, Eppie looked down the table toward Howard in time to see the little car headed to the edge of the steep berm. She jumped to her feet.

"Oh my god! Children!" she yelled. "Children! Stop!"

The adults whirled around and rose to their feet as one, just as the little car disappeared, nose first, into the drainage ditch. Cries rose up as Tyler and Jeff ran to the edge of the hill and scrambled down to reach the children first. The others, arriving at the top of the berm, looked down and saw the car pointed toward the culvert, the children unhurt and still seated comfortably, while little May clapped her hands and yelled, "Do it again, Aaron! Do it again!"

The two men reached in and pulled the children out, assuring them that everything was okay. The children knew this all along but doubted it for a moment as they were yanked abruptly out of the little car and saw the adults' worried faces. As for the vehicle, it was also unharmed. Grunting, Jeff slowly pushed it up the side of the hill while Bud rushed down to assist. The drainage ditch was dry, the toy car's descent slowed by un-mown grass and wide clumps of thistle and dandelions.

"Well!" Bud drawled. "A little roadside drama never hurt a party."

Shrill laughter broke out as the adults traipsed back to the picnic table. Still shaking inside, Billie scolded her son.

"Honey, that was a dangerous stunt."

"It wasn't a stunt, Mama."

May rushed to her and wrapped her arms around Billie's legs. "Don't be mad, BeeBee."

"Enough car riding for today." Billie took each child by the hand, walking them back to the picnic table.

Eppie resumed her vigil at the head of the table and waited for the partiers return. One by one the adults dropped into their seats, laughing. Tyler lifted May onto the bench. Then Eppie stretched out her arms as if to embrace the group as they dropped, relieved, into their seats around the picnic table

"Are we feeling peckish yet?" she asked, and meticulously sliced the pies. "Don't disappoint me, Jeff. I don't want to take anything home but empty pans."

The evening light faded slowly, turning the sky a deeper blue, while a red-gold sun appeared caught in the branches of a distant hedgerow. Aaron reached across the table and helped himself to a piece of his mother's cake while May climbed into her father's lap. Conversation had already mellowed when the Kornackies rose from the bench to prepare the fireworks— Roman candles, rockets, firecrackers and a small Catherine's wheel. Peg brought over sparklers for the kids. Tyler held onto May's, for the little girl was too tired to take hers. Bud stood up and whispered to his wife, "Why don't I get Ginny?"

For an instant the shame of her earlier temper returned. Did your children forgive you your harsh words, or did they remember for all time? Billie could not at the moment recall anything she held against her own mother except silly things, fodder for jokes and family stories. Her gaze drifted toward the Mannings. In the gloaming May was sleeping peaceably in her father's arms. She remembered when Ginny slept in hers.

Jeff called out that he would now test the first Roman candle. The table fell silent. She heard a *swoosh* and a whistle while the rocket arced skyward, and then the deep *boom*. A shower of colored sparks bloomed across the night sky.

"Ahhhh!" the group exclaimed and then laughed.

Billie glanced back and saw her husband and daughter descend the porch steps and make their way toward the picnic table. Bud's arm circled Ginny's narrow shoulders. *Do they forgive you your harsh words?* Billie waved and scooted over on the bench to make room, her emotions equal parts fear and relief.

Jeff lit a second candle. It rose, hissing, into the sky and exploded into red and silver and blue stars that crackled and winked before falling away. Awakened by the sound of the rocket, May Manning cried out, "Ohhh," and clapped her hands.

Aaron, twirling a sparkler, wrote sputtering letters in the air—A, A, R, O, N— and called out, "Mama, guess what word I'm spelling?"

9

MAY AND MAUDE

In only a blink of an eye May outgrew the pink tutu, the white tights and pink ballet slippers. At the end of her fourth year, she'd outgrown an entire wardrobe. By the time she entered kindergarten at age five, ballerina attire had lost its appeal. She'd discovered that dressing like a boy gave her more freedom and that little girl jeans, even peacock-colored ones, were a charm against the jostling of the world.

Tyler missed the ballerina clothes and the dresses with bows. Where was that little girl who awakened his heart each morning, as if the adult heart were an organ that aged and hardened overnight? She'd known what she wanted at three and knew, with equal confidence, at four and now five. Some mornings he thought he was talking to a child twice her age, for his daughter seemed endowed with entirely too many words and mannerisms that made her sound uncannily old. He didn't want her to grow up so fast or lose one minute of her childhood to the expectations of adults

He felt sure she was receiving all the correct instructions—the dos and don'ts, the table etiquette and courtesies that had somehow been imparted to him and to his parents and grandparents before him—that long trail of teaching that stretched backward in time until it disappeared from sight like a Kansas highway receding westward across the Plains. On the rare occasions she was contrary—"No, Daddy, I hate that dress… These carrots are mushy. You cooked them too long!"—her disobedience was so ordinary it made him laugh.

As for his good neighbors, Billie had remained *BeeBee* just as other children throughout their lives called a beloved grand-

mother *Nana* or *Mimi.* But when she was four, "Bub" disappeared and the correct name took its place.

"I miss ole *Bub,*" Bud Harrington confessed to his wife.
"Made me feel kinda special."

No one doubted May had passed out of babyhood. Tyler
wondered if this child was the person she would essentially remain: courteous but strong-willed, bright, tidy, and animal-lov-
ing, rushing home with injured sparrows and dying voles, eager
to help. He'd pull a chair to the sink each evening so she could
stand up and wash pots and pans. She seemed at home on the
farm, cherishing the farm animals and house cats, the birds at
the feeders and, above all, Rusty. He rejoiced that the farm delighted his daughter, but a small irrational part of him offered
up its free-floating dread that a farm, always a joyous place
for him, was somehow dangerous. What if an old water well
unsealed its jaws and swallowed her or a discarded blade cut
her foot or a length of barbed wire grabbed an ankle, tearing
her flesh? What if a neighbor's rogue steer trampled her or a
startled snake, sleeping in the woodpile, struck?

The fears did not abate as she grew. She dashed out the
backdoor and *explored.* He could see her in the small orchard,
picking windfalls, or swinging on the tree swing or haphazardly
weeding the kitchen garden or singing to Rusty on the porch.
To ensure her safety, he walked the fence lines, repaired gates,
and swept the property as carefully as he was able, keeping the
barns and workshop tidy. At the same time he didn't want to
infect her with his fears. His mother had been anxious with
Mickey. *Watch out! Be careful! Don't take chances!* It wasn't right for
a parent to distort the world, turn it into such a hazardous place
that joy was lost, discovery was lost, and all that remained was
dark and grim.

May was on the porch swing one evening, reading aloud to
Rusty from one of her numerous picture books, telling Rusty
the story she knew by heart. Tyler grabbed the kitchen phone
and dialed. As soon as Howard answered, he rushed into a lita-
ny of concerns, scarcely giving Howard a chance to say, "How

are ya?" Did all fathers of daughters feel this way? Tyler wanted to know. Would he feel this protective of a son? Why did he feel he had to face the world with a shotgun in one hand and a Louisville slugger in the other? The world would never be safe enough, clean enough, or right enough for this child. And if anything went wrong, how would he forgive himself?

"Relax, Ty," Howard crooned. "The world is not a *problem*. Life is not a *problem*. Maybe you feel this way because you're raising a child alone. And that is tough."

Tyler eased into a kitchen chair. Perhaps he just needed to hear Howard say the words. He needed to talk to a man about daughters, and Howie had two girls whom he loved and understood thoroughly.

As she grew May took on more responsibility because she wanted it, but the morning ritual had not changed. He still came to her room to help her start the day. At 5:30 she might be up and dressed, reading or dressing a doll, talking to herself or to Rusty who still obligingly climbed the stairs to join her. On this morning, however, the ritual was turned upside down. He heard steps by his bed. A hand gently nudged his shoulder.

"Daddy? Can you get up?"

He opened an eye. She was in her pajamas, standing by his bed.

"Please. Something's wrong with Rusty."

He was instantly awake and pulled himself out of the bed. May led him out of the room. Both of them in bare feet and pajamas, he followed her down the hall and stairs. Rusty lay at the bottom as though he'd tried to climb up.

Alone, Tyler thought with sorrow. Why had every dog he'd ever owned died alone? He'd come to think dogs preferred it that way, as though dying were an intensely private affair. It was humans that needed to comfort the dying pet, or cling to it as if the clinging could defer the loss. He stooped over the dog and searched for a pulse, knowing he wouldn't find one. The smell of fluids was strong.

"He pooped," she said.

"He's gone, May." He should have used the proper words: *Rusty is dead.* No child living on a farm should be afraid of death. In no time she understood what he was saying.

Tears welled in her eyes. "I didn't get to say goodbye."

"But he knew. They don't like to upset their people."

Her face collapsed. She fell into him and sobbed. He could bear the death but not this sorrow. She'd wept for animals before, but this loss was larger, not the trifling drama of an afternoon. Together they stroked the animal's fur while Tyler talked and talked. *Remember when Rusty… Remember when?* Gratefully the dog's eyes were closed, so the fiction of sleep could be maintained. Rusty was having his final, much-deserved rest. But his spirit was with all the other dogs that had come to earth to help people be better people. Was he actually saying all this?

May looked up, her face solemn. "Do I have a mother?"

He thought his heart might stop. His breathing stilled. "Of course. You know that."

"Where is she?"

"She was too young to take care of you. She made a great sacrifice and gave you up. To me. But that's a story for another day."

"Dad? Were you adopted too?"

His mouth hung open and he closed it. "No."

"It's like Rusty was adopted, isn't it? You aren't his dog father but you're *like* his father and he's like my brother, but not *really.*"

"Something like that." He could not possibly tackle this now. In her world Rusty was as valued as she was.

"I want you to do something for Rusty," he said. "I want you to go outdoors and find his favorite place. We'll bury him there."

Her sobs started again, and he pulled her close. They remained this way awhile, and he gently patted her back. Her hand reached out to touch the dog's head.

"Where's your wagon?" he asked.

"On the back porch."

"Get dressed first, and then you'll find that special place. Okay?"

She nodded and dragged herself up the stairs, turning to look back at the old dog as she went. By the time May came back down, he'd wrapped the animal in old towels and moved him to the porch.

"Where's Rusty?" she asked, alarmed.

He took her out back and she kneeled beside the red wagon, folding back the towels, and stroked him. Her first friend, if an animal could be said to be a friend. He'd always thought so. A small child was as inarticulate as a dog, and whatever communication took place between them happened on some intuitive plane that defied explanation. But it did take place. Love took place. Attachment.

"Honey, go find that special spot while I dress."

She looked up at him. "I want Aaron to come."

"Why?"

"It's like church, isn't it?"

What had she learned from their infrequent church visits? She'd never attended a funeral but knew what a grave was, having been to the cemetery every Memorial Day when he and the Harringtons decorated their parents' graves. And who knew what she talked about with Aaron. Billie told him she was precocious, but since he lived with May, the comment had little meaning. Who did he have to compare her with?

May ran toward the orchard, and he sighed with relief and climbed the stairs. He didn't want to dig a hole near the house, to be dug up by a coyote or feral dog. From his bedroom window he followed her as she traveled among the apples trees to a tussock of grass bordering the orchard and the north pasture. Hurriedly, he changed, pulling on his work boots at the back door. In long strides he went out to join her in the orchard. She was standing on the tussock, pointing down.

"This is a very good place," he affirmed.

He reached out his hand, and she took it. They walked to the barn where he kept his yard tools. He took the shovel, and they walked back to the spot at the edge of the orchard. Neither spoke while he broke ground.

"We'll make the hole extra deep and wide," he said finally. "That way Rusty will be comfortable."

"Can he feel it?"

"Not now."

If he kept this up, he'd make her feel worse, not better, more confused, not less. Wasn't death confounding enough?

"It will make us all feel better," he added, "to know Rusty's sleeping place has lots of room."

"Like a big bedroom."

"That's right."

Stop now. He widened the grave. She crouched down to watch and asked if they might put some of Rusty's toys with him. She listed the ball and bones that must accompany him to "the new place." She talked on, asking if she might put something of hers inside too. So he wouldn't forget her.

"His favorite book," she said. "The one I always read to him."

He drove the shovel into the dirt pile and turned away. To be laid low by a child's words—who'd have thought? When he'd buried his parents, he'd not considered the metaphysics of their remembrance of him. He retained strong images of his father, but his mother brought forth discordant memories. There was the mother he knew before Mickey's arrival, and then the altered mother, after. He preferred to think of his father. Those memories gave him strength.

Back at the house May gathered Rusty's gifts and piled them on the kitchen table. Then she reminded him, "Call BeeBee and Bud and Aaron."

He dialed the number and said, "It would be nice if you told them."

When Billie answered, he told her to hang on and handed May the receiver. He leaned against the sink while she told them about the dog and invited Aaron to come over to say goodbye. Finished, she handed the phone back to Ty, who asked, "You folks still have any river rock? We'll need to cover the grave."

May went out onto the back porch while he washed his hands. When he stuck his head out the kitchen door, he saw her sitting in a porch chair beside the red wagon, her hand on the dog.

"What are you doing?" he asked.

"Keeping Rusty company."

Bud's truck churned up the drive to the back door. Aaron hopped down, and May ran down the porch steps to greet him. The boy had shot up in height during the last year. May brought him up onto the porch to see Rusty resting in the wagon. She became more animated, less solemn. Now with her closest ally the pain of first loss seemed to lessen with the sharing. He kept one ear trained on the kids. Aaron seemed curious, pleased even, at the chance to touch a dead dog. Tyler came out on the porch and asked Aaron to take one end of the wagon. Together they lifted it down to the ground. Bud had driven off to the orchard to unload the river rock. Aaron offered to pull the wagon up the path.

"No," May announced. "I want to pull him myself."

"Might be hard over all this grass," Tyler said, pointing to the uneven track.

"Aaron can help then," she said.

The children took hold of the long handle and pulled the wagon along one of the tire tracks toward the orchard. The wagon trembled and bounced, jostling the body, but remained upright. He could see Bud in the distance, unloading. When they reached the hole, the children pulled the wagon to the lip of the grave and stopped. Bud had just finished and was climbing up into his truck.

"I'll bring Aaron home," Tyler said through the driver's window.

"Make yourself useful, son," Bud said and backed the truck away from the mourners before turning around.

The children stood uncertainly beside the pile of dirt. Tyler took the dog in his arms and, kneeling awkwardly, laid him gently on his side in the bottom of the hole. The children stepped to the edge and gazed down. One by one, May handed Tyler the mementos she wanted to accompany the dog. Once finished, he told her he would now cover the dog with earth and then rocks. Did she want to go to the house with Aaron now? Make them some lemonade?

"No," she answered, without hesitation. "I want to stay. Rusty needs all of us."

"That's my girl," he murmured.

Tyler pulled the shovel out of the dirt pile.

Slowly he placed the earth over the dog, letting the dirt slide gently off the tool. No one spoke. Tyler glanced at his daughter. She stood resolute, watching him fill the grave. He wondered at this point if the kids were more curious than sad. Perhaps the process of burial, the ritual of it, allowed her to comprehend her loss. He hoped so.

As Rusty disappeared under the accumulating dirt, a tremulous sigh rose from the little girl. The grave grew into a mound. Tyler turned to the children. "I want you two to tamp down the earth nice and firm. Use your feet. Like this. Then we'll put on the rock."

Thankfully, she hadn't asked why. Aaron would understand, but Ty wasn't up to telling his daughter about scavengers. Then he pointed to the rocks Bud had deposited near the fence, and Aaron lent a hand.

"Delia May, can you find some smaller rocks and lay down a circle around Rusty?"

For ten minutes they worked in silence, paving the grave site while May formed a tidy ring of small stones around the mounded dirt. When the surface was covered, Ty turned to the pile, staggering slightly under the weight of a particularly heavy stone he placed like a head marker.

Aaron thrust out his arms, signaling everyone to stop and wait. He threw out his chest and pointed his head heavenward and announced, "Here lies Rusty. A good and loyal dog."

"Amen!" May added loudly.

"Okay, Maypole." Aaron put a hand to May's back and pointed her toward the wagon. "Let's go."

"Stop!" she said. "I want to ride in the wagon like Rusty did."

"Well, get in then."

She climbed in, stretching out her legs, and announced with a giggle, "All right, horse. Get going!"

Tyler felt his shoulders droop in relief. Aaron was doing everything Ty had hoped he would. Now the kid turned and made a face at May, whinnied, and lurched forward, pulling the wagon back along the rough track toward the house. Tyler grabbed the shovel and followed, his heart lighter.

Scarcely a week had gone by when Billie phoned at suppertime. May was setting the table. "Okay, I have a question," she said. "Don't you think you ought to get May that nanny dog we talked about?"

Whatever "talking about" she was referring to had been done a year ago. And if he remembered correctly, Billie had been the only one to speak. He paused, glancing at May.

"Don't you think we ought to let the person involved get over this one first?"

"The person involved has got dog love to spare. She needs to give it to some poor pup that needs a home."

"Shall I put her on?"

"No! This is a parent's decision, Ty."

"What if the person involved doesn't want another one."

"That I simply do not believe! Do you?"

"What did you have in mind to improve our lives?" He couldn't keep the sarcasm out of his voice. He was hungry. Had she phoned *after* dinner, he might feel less provoked.

"The animal shelter. Aaron and I used to go there and volunteer. I took all my children one time or another."

"In Topeka?"

"Where else? I suppose we could go to the one in Lawrence. They probably have a better class of stray dog over there. The university, don't you know?"

When she'd come to the shelter with Aaron, the first thing that
greeted them was the noise. Billie supposed people got used to
it, but to her it was always jarring. She escorted Tyler and May
through the greeting area to the desk. The receptionist remembered her even though she and Aaron had stopped volunteering
two years ago, after the acquisition of the foul-tempered cocker
spaniel that Aaron loved. May reached the desk, put her hands
on the counter, pulled herself up onto tip toe and announced,
"I'm here to get a puppy."

The woman smiled down and made small talk presumably
suitable for a child, irritating Billie. She glanced at Tyler who
looked back stoically. There was a dearth of puppies, the
woman said, but plenty of young dogs of about a year or less,
desperate for homes.

"Breaks your heart," the receptionist went on, a substantial
woman with short graying hair. "People get their kids puppies
for Christmas. By Easter or summer they bring them back.
They're not cute anymore. They chew and tear things up because
they're teething." She shook her head with disgust. "Owners are
always the problem."

Throughout the rehearsed speech May remained at the
counter, scarcely able to see over it, her fingers resting on the
edge as she looked up at the woman.

"I'll see those puppies now," May said firmly.

The woman gazed down at the little girl, then got on a phone
and spoke to someone in back among the kennels.

"There is one mother dog back there with a small litter.
Someone brought her in—the family pet, mind you—because
she'd gotten herself pregnant. Gave her up, just like that." She
snapped her fingers. "Didn't occur to them to spay her. The
pups are only eight weeks. We don't generally like to part with
an animal until ten weeks. But I know you, Mrs. Harrington.
Have to warn you. They're part Pit."

She got up and led them toward a swinging door that opened
onto a corridor of kennels. Billie had grabbed hold of Tyler's

arm briefly when the woman identified the animals. He felt clueless.

"What's she talking about?" he asked. "Part pit?"

"Pit bulls."

"Right. Do we want one? I mean, everything I hear about pit bulls is negative."

"And wrong. Don't you remember Buster? Most wonderful dog in the world. Just the right size for May."

A kennel employee met them just beyond the swinging doors, a young man with blond dreadlocks, smiling, wearing a green apron with the shelter logo.

The receptionist spoke up. "Frankie, they'd like to see the puppies. And maybe some of those young dogs along the way? Suitable for the little girl."

"Gotcha," he said and winked at May.

He led them down the row of kennels. Billie winced at the noise. Tyler felt his heart swell. There was a reason he'd never taken a dog from the pound. He glanced at May who had taken his hand and looked purposefully after the kennel attendant. When Frankie reached the last kennel, he stopped and pointed. Billie came to the gate and grunted.

"Those aren't pits. The mother's too big. They're American bull dogs and something else."

"Boxer," said the kid, smiling.

May stooped down, gripping the mesh door, and peered in. "May I go in, please?"

They'd brought along a box, a ball, a squeaky toy, and a blanket, just in case. May sat strapped in the backseat, the box strapped in beside her, the brindle and white puppy in the box with the squeaky toy and blanket. Tyler's head filled with pictures of the tedious training that loomed ahead. The puppy was cute enough, unlike the mother dog, but May was enchanted. Since he was eleven he'd trained every animal that came into the house, but never this breed. He'd fashioned a small kennel in the kitchen composed of a carrier inside a corral—a smaller

version of May's barn corral. Thick layers of newspaper covered an old shower curtain stretched over the linoleum floor.
How he dreaded the messes, the whining at night. That first
night he set the alarm for one a.m. but never heard it.

When he came downstairs at five, May was wrapped in a
blanket and squeezed inside the small corral with the pup rolled
up next to her. The animal had made a discreet offering in one
corner of the corral. He roused his daughter and suggested she
take the dog out to the backyard.

After breakfast, after the puppy had eaten and was taken out
again to "the spot," it was allowed to run free in the kitchen,
fenced in by small gates. Ty grew solemn with instructions:
"You have to watch her at all times or confine her; you cannot
let her go outside without close supervision; you cannot let her
into the rest of the house until she is housebroken and crate
trained."

"When can Maudie come upstairs?"

"*Maudie?* Where'd that name come from?"

"It's Maude, actually." Her words were crisply enunciated, as
if she'd taken a course in elocution. He stared at her, holding
in the laugh.

Among her books was a funny storybook about a dog
named Maude—a cartoon animal with a huge round head and
body, tall pointed ears, and a wide grin. The only thing the living
Maude had in common with the illustrated dog was the grin.

"Nice name," he said finally and left the room. He closed the
door to the little half bath near the kitchen, leaned against the
wall, and burst out laughing. *It's Maude, ac-tu-a-lly.*

The long slog of dog training shaped the following weeks. He
was grateful it was summer, and May was free to help. In due
course the animal took to her large crate and did not fuss, indicated when she wanted to go out, until accidents became a
blessedly rare occurrence. Best of all, she loved Tyler and May
totally. For her part, May wanted to take the dog everywhere,
for the devotion was mutual.

Maude turned out to be affectionate and unalarmed by most of what she encountered on the farm. She obeyed instructions, tolerated one house cat and befriended the other, did not chase the chickens or sneak off to bother the cattle. She was cordial to the Harringtons and other visiting friends such as Howard, and developed a fondness for Aaron, which pleased May. In no time she was willing to go to her crate in the kitchen when asked, and by the fall, the dog had made her way to May's bedroom. *What harm?* Rusty had trudged up there whenever called. Why not Maude?

By the time school reconvened in late August, it seemed safe to leave the dog in her large crate while he drove off to teach, and May, under Aaron's supervision, caught the bus for the all-day Montessori school. On a day he left his truck in the shop, he drove to the high school with Billie. As Billie swung off the state road and onto the highway, he remembered the question May had posed.

"Remember the day Rusty died? May asked me about her mother."

Billie glanced over. "You haven't told her anything?"

"Yes, she knows she's adopted but not every hairy detail. I read her those books you gave me. She asked me the same day whether I was adopted."

"Time for a sit down talk." She looked at him. His hair had grown into a mass of dark curls drooping over his collar. "You need to tell her who you really are, or were, before some kid at school says something stupid."

"What do you mean, *were?*"

"Your transformation from uncle to father."

"She knows that. If I tell her more about her mother, won't I have to tell her more about her father too?"

"You're her father."

"Billie, you know what I mean."

That evening Billie made the chicken and dumplings Bud loved above all other dishes. As he savored the meal, she relayed her conversation with Tyler.

"Let's turn her adoption day into a special event. A big deal," he said. "Like maybe all of us in the kitchen with balloons and cake or candles. Have Ty pull out the baby pictures and make a display. Hell, I don't know. Maybe we tell her how she came, how Tyler put her in the drawer to sleep, that social worker with the big hair—the whole nine yards. Doesn't every kid want her life to be a special story?"

Billie gazed at him. He kept surprising her, and her eyes misted. Who else had the imagination to suggest it? Hadn't he once brought her two bright yellow ducklings for Easter? Hadn't he thought up the theme for their senior prom and talked the most unlikely students and staff into helping out: decorating, driving kids without cars, or baking cakes? Of course, he'd been drunk as a skunk by the end of prom night, and she'd thought it funny, even cute. Now, stone cold sober, he could still come up with the needed burst of juice, pushing the rest of them off their complacent butts. Billie reached across the table and kissed her husband on the mouth.

"Yuck!" Aaron said and, with a dramatic flourish, shielded his eyes. "Mush!"

10

THE MERCEDES

Bud noticed the cream-colored Mercedes while mowing the slope of his front yard. Who wouldn't notice a car of that quality, he told his wife later. The event was especially noteworthy since the Mercedes had driven by the Harringtons' going south, then returned shortly moving north. As Bud painstakingly maneuvered his riding mower along the steep berm, he saw in the distance that the car had stopped near Ty's place. What puzzled him most was the fact it parked on the shoulder, like someone lost or looking for an address, and not taking the drive up to the house. If the car were closer, Bud would have gone over and asked the driver if he, or she, needed help. Still, the Mercedes was worthy of mention at dinner, and then dismissed. His younger son and daughter were at the table, and Aaron expressed disappointment that he'd missed the Mercedes altogether. He'd never seen one up close.

It remained a topic of interest the following day when Aaron reported at dinnertime that he'd seen the car in question parked again down near Ty Manning's property. When asked how he'd come to see, he replied he'd been on his bike.

"You asked me to go over and watch May while Ty ran some errands. Remember?"

"I hope you're careful on the road," Bud said.

"Nobody's on that road, Dad."

Aaron's parents glanced at one another, telegraphing the same fear. *It only takes one lunatic in a car...*

"You wear your bike helmet?" Billie asked.

Aaron, aged twelve, rolled his eyes, which gave his mother all the answer she needed.

"Are we going to have another one of these *borrrring* conversations?" This from seventeen-year-old Ginny whose adolescent scorn lay as heavily on her tongue as the eyeliner on her lids.

"What conversation are you referring to?" Billie said tartly and gazed at her daughter, praying she might survive the girl's adolescence without strangling her.

Her beautiful Virginia, diseased by hormones, mouthy beyond tolerance in her need to be "cool." The girl was so touchy and weepy that Billie had begged Bud to tell the girl, every day, how much he loved her and that he liked her dress or her hair or whatever. Ginny didn't need to hear it from her mother, evidently.

"Moira's mom lets her do what she wants and Moira tells her everything. They're best buds and share secrets."

Billie did not wish to be her daughter's "best bud." She did not want to share secrets and wished her daughter did not have any.

"There was a guy in the Mercedes but he was wearing shades," Aaron broke in.

"Wearing what?" asked Bud.

"Sunglasses, Dad." Ginny again with disdain. "Why are you so suspicious?"

"Someone ought to tell Tyler," said Billie.

Later, after Ginny turned down the peach cobbler and her brother ate her share as well as his own, long after the table was cleared and the dishwasher loaded, only then did Bud phone Tyler and tell him about the Mercedes. As soon as Bud spoke, a dark cloud gathered, unsettling Tyler's mind. It was the two separate days that made him wary. He'd been waiting for years, he realized, but had never admitted it. A week passed, during which time the neighbors put aside thoughts of the strange car and its dual appearances. Maybe a property appraiser from the county. Then the cream Mercedes returned. Tyler did not notice, but the Harrington household did and alerted him at once.

"Don't you think it's time for the 'don't ride with strangers' conversation?" Bud said over the phone while Billie coached, just out of earshot on the other side of the kitchen.

"We've already had the conversation," he said, knowing Bud would accept this in good grace, unlike Billie who'd want to know the exact wording of his admonition. May had been five at the time of his talk, which had had no discernible impact.

While Tyler talked with Bud, May and Aaron played out back, if a twelve-year-old could be said to play with a child who'd just turned seven. Ty gazed at them through the open screened door. He'd bet good money Aaron would grow up to be a teacher. He was already practicing on May. This was what happened when you lived on a rural route. May had made preschool friends and kindergarten friends, but most of them were town kids whose parents were not inclined to drive them out a county road for a play date. She preferred Aaron anyway, and her dog Maude, BeeBee'nBud and Howard, the house cats and the occasional new calf. She'd become used to the company of adults. It was at Howard's suggestion that Tyler had put her in the all-day Montessori preschool, kindergarten, and first grade, but in the fall she would be attending a regular elementary school. Perhaps it was the relative safety of their lives that had made him put off a more substantial beware of strangers speech? It had simply never come up. Yet someone in a fancy car was staking out the farm, lurking, and he did not like having to look so closely at who that person might be.

Tyler opened the back door and asked the children to come inside. Slowly the two youngsters trooped in, laughing, and sat at the kitchen table. Tyler opened the freezer and pulled out packaged ice cream cones and handed one to each child.

"Wish you lived at my house," Aaron said and thanked Tyler while May giggled. "Say thank you, Maypole."

"Thank you, dear Father," she said, bursting into laughter again.

Tyler sat down opposite Aaron and folded his hands. Aaron immediately settled while May continued to tease Aaron, giggling over a piece of peanut that had dropped off the surface of her cone. "I know you've heard this before, Aaron. So has May, but you're going to hear it again." He paused and cleared his throat. May looked at him with a puzzled expression. "Honey, even if you don't realize it, there are people in the world who do not wish you well." Thus the cautionary advice was repeated, and to May's evident dismay.

"Maudie will protect me."

"But Maudie isn't always with you. Besides, she likes people."

"Daddy, I don't like it when you talk like this. Who are these creeps?"

"Weirdoes," Aaron added, not to be outdone. "There're lots of freaks and weirdoes in the world."

"You get the message, May?" said Tyler. "Do not accept a ride. Do not open the door."

"And if Howie asks if I want a ride?"

"That's totally different. I'm talking strangers. People you have never laid eyes on or been introduced to. Even if they say, 'I'm a friend of your father's.' They're probably lying. You understand?"

"I understand." She dropped her gaze to her cone and picked nervously at the nuts, placing each small shard in her mouth. Under the table, she kicked her legs back and forth.

His heart went out to her. Why did grown-ups have to spoil the day with their chronic anxieties? He hoped neither child had made the connection between the cream-colored Mercedes and this unpleasant conversation. But the thought he and his daughter might be stalked filled him with indignation, with an urge to purge the streets so that Delia May and Aaron would walk safely down any block in any town. Surely somewhere in the world there was a country that cherished and protected its young. He remembered himself early in his military service, naive and trusting. What an awakening the navy had been. *Cracker. Peckerwood. Nigger.* If it hadn't been for Manny...

He looked at the niece whom he now considered his daughter. The topic, and the memory, soured his stomach.

The following week Tyler brought home a load of lumber and found it more convenient to leave the truck in the barn where he could shelter the wood and unload it at his leisure. Later Tyler would think that the absence of a truck behind the house might have emboldened the stalker. He was considering the unfinished project on his worktable when the phone in the barn shop rang. Hurriedly he answered.

"Daddy, there's a man on the front porch. He's looking in the big window. What if he knocks?"

"Don't open the door. I'll be right there."

He left the shop on the run and arrived winded at the kitchen door. He couldn't remember if the front door was locked and when he reached the back, his stomach sank. The kitchen door was open. He pulled the screen shut and latched it. May was standing by the phone in the kitchen and mouthed the words, *On. The. Porch.* She pointed her finger toward the front room, and Tyler stopped momentarily to catch his breath and then strode into the front hall. He peered through one of the glass panels that ran the length of the door. The beveled glass was colored and distorted the figure that now stood to one side, looking out toward the road. Then the man retreated down the steps to the Mercedes parked in front. All Ty saw was the man's back, dressed in boots, jeans, and a black leather jacket, wearing a Stetson the same color as the Mercedes. Tyler stopped breathing momentarily.

He walked into the front room to look out the large window. By this time, the man had reached the car and opened the door. His right hand and arm rose up to protect the hat as he ducked into the vehicle. Tyler couldn't get a good look at either his face or profile. If it was who he thought it was, he'd put on weight over the last ten or so years. Still, Tyler recognized that figure and gait. The driver pulled the car carefully around the oval parking area and then drove slowly down the drive. A picture of the old red El Camino flitted through Tyler's mind.

He stared out toward the road, watching the vehicle turn

onto the road and left toward the Old Stull Road. When the vehicle was finally out of sight he retreated to the kitchen. May sat at the table, segmenting an orange, painstakingly separating the sections. Her dog Maudie sat expectantly at her feet. Tyler took hold of the top of the chair opposite and leaned toward her.

"Until I can figure out who's stalking us, I don't want you out of sight. I want you and Maude in the shop with me, or I want you to be at Bud and BeeBee's. Okay?"

"Aaron can stay with me."

"No. You're both kids. Against one determined grown man? No."

"Who are you talking about, Dad?"

The mystery of *who* was more distressing to her than his safety instructions.

"I don't know who. But I think we'll find out soon enough. For all I know it's some real estate agent." He faked a laugh. "Those guys are getting very aggressive these days."

"Who are they?"

"People who sell property. Probably asking if I want to sell our farm. Ha ha." The forced laugh embarrassed him. Still he'd heard all the stories he wanted to of farmers closer to Lawrence and Topeka, approached by developers urging them to sell their land. So they could put up another row of tacky McMansions.

"Are we going to sell the farm?" she asked.

"No way!"

"Are they dangerous?"

"Not the way you think. But I still don't want them approaching you or talking to you. They're unscrupulous."

He was making matters worse, offering a phony diversion so the child had something concrete to hang onto, something less scary.

"Okay, Dad. What's *unscrupulous?*" By the tone of her voice he guessed she was getting more exasperated with him than the man on the porch.

"Unscrupulous means you got no standards. No respect. You'll do about anything to get what you want."

May gazed at him perplexed, then shrugged and held up her hand. "Want some of my orange?"

He phoned the Harringtons that evening and told them, describing the man he knew to be his brother.

"Time for Tyler to have the other little talk," Bud told his wife after Tyler's call.

Billie cocked her head. "She knows she's adopted. It's the mother she's asking about."

"Did he ever tell her about Mick?"

"She knows Ty's her uncle and he has a brother out there. I think he's leaving her to put two and two together."

Bud pushed his chair back from the table and left the kitchen, returning a moment later. He sat down at the table near his wife and slipped two fingers into his shirt pocket, pulling out the small photo he'd taken out of Sherlynne Smith's wallet: the girl and Mickey, their heads pressed together, smiling at the camera of a photo kiosk. He handed his wife the photo.

"You took it?" Billie said. "I thought you said she'd grabbed it back?"

"She did. But there were three photos stacked together. Figured she'd be satisfied with two and wouldn't miss the third. I took the best. Sherlynne's eyes were closed in one. Mickey was a blur in the other."

"I wish you'd swiped that one. Then May could have a photo of her birth mom, and screw Mick!"

"She might want this as an adult."

"Why? Her mother gave her up, and we all know what Mickey's like."

"Yeah, but we don't know what the human heart is like. She still might want it."

"She might not! Would you? Mickey doesn't even know she exists."

"I think he does. I think he left li'l ole Sherlynne when she began to show with May."

"Does Ty know you have this photo?"

"Yep. Showed it to him the week he became May's legal guardian." Bud slid the grainy photo back in his shirt pocket and patted it. "What I hear is, girls sooner or later want to find their birth mothers."

"Not their fathers?"

"Haven't researched that."

11

SCHOOL DAYS

The specter of his brother hung over all Tyler loved. He insisted on driving May to her new elementary school, even though the school bus drove by the house and Aaron would be on it. He took Aaron whenever the boy wanted to come, but Aaron preferred the bus where he could swap comics with a small knot of friends. The boy had told Tyler he would look after May if she chose to ride the bus, and Tyler did not doubt for a moment that the kid would do just that. The fact that Mick—he was certain it was Mick—would be driving a luxury car merely confirmed that his brother was involved in something suspicious. Yet his imagination was not quite elastic enough, or willing, to consider how Mickey might be earning a living. Still he was afraid. Children were kidnapped every day, often by estranged parents, and then whisked out of the country or worse.

Meanwhile, the Harringtons held their counsel. Surely Ty's overprotectiveness would one day pass. Bud thought it came from having only one child, a father's hopes and fears wrapped up in a single package. Lose May and he lost everything.

For Tyler the new school year was utterly ordinary and by the end of the second week, the comforting rhythm of work was reestablished. When he was in his own classroom, he didn't ruminate over his daughter. Thoughts of May might return during lunch or his planning period, but he was seldom distracted while he taught. When he picked May up after school, joining an impressive line of SUVs filled with busy mothers collecting kids, he was eager to hear about her day. Every afternoon she clutched some artwork or a sheet of sums or simple spelling words. But the small person climbing into his truck, he soon discovered, was not filled with the thrill of learning. She was bored. She'd learned to read in her Montessori preschool. Her little classmates now were generally less skilled and less engaged.

At his first parent-teacher conference in early October, he learned that May liked to help the other children with their reading and sums. The attractive young teacher, who had painted both her lips and nails an alarming fire engine red, told him this with mock-enthusiasm. Tyler sensed she didn't care for a child with so much initiative, and he took a dislike to the woman. Such was his first experience with parental dismay at public schooling, where the luck of the draw could make a child's education a pleasure or a chamber of horrors. May had been so puzzled at the onset of school when her new teacher found fault with her.

"What did I do wrong, Daddy?" she asked early on, while they sat together over afternoon snacks. Tears stood in her eyes.

Nothing! He wanted to tell her: *You've done nothing wrong!* He would have another talk with her teacher. At the end of October he met with her again and explained May's previous schooling, which only made the young woman more defensive. He then wondered aloud if May might need a special place. He had in mind the advanced-placement classes available at his high school. But what would be the equivalent at the early primary level? He feared he'd offended her until he gleaned from some remark that she'd taken an interest.

In January May was placed with a small group in a special second-grade class, mostly children of Asian descent, Ty observed. Perhaps other graduates of Montessori. His hard feelings toward May's first teacher softened since she'd clearly been involved in the creation of this class. Half of May's school day was spent in the new group while the other half was spent with her other classmates doing music and gym and art. Now when he picked her up, she climbed into the truck excited and talkative, telling him about her classmates, about the solar system and the animal kingdom and the game where she'd learned to spell *fish* as *phish*. A stone lifted off his heart. Did the mothers lining up in front of the school feel this same weight? Or were their constitutions more resilient? He wondered if the weight was more evenly distributed—and thus reduced—when there were two parents instead of one. A moot point, he decided, now that May seemed happy.

In the fall, the mother of May's new friend phoned Tyler to invite May to an afternoon play date. The girl jumped up and down and clapped her hands. Tyler had been hearing about May Lynn for weeks. The weather remained warm but the little girls would probably be playing indoors, according to the child's mother. He would meet her when he picked May up at five, giving the children two hours to wear each other out.

The mother had not asked to speak to Mrs. Manning or to May's mother. Tyler concluded that May had conveyed to her schoolmate the absence of a mother. He appreciated the woman's discretion, underscoring his regret that, overall, discretion seemed to be a disappearing habit of mind. When he recalled the conversation later, he realized that she had addressed him as soon as he answered the phone: "Mr. Manning? I'm May Lynn's mother." Nor did the woman need to explain who May Lynn was. May Manning could not stop talking about her.

"Her name is Chinese," May said eventually, leaving him to reasonably assume the child was Chinese as well. It had not occurred to him that the parents were not. He'd observed that the special class had been filled with exotic-looking kids, the offspring of doctors at area hospitals, Billie opined. He had only one question: What did May tell her little schoolmates about her father's occupation? Teacher? Carpenter? Farmer? He stopped pondering the issue after he met the parents of May's other favorite friend, Danny Patel, son of a large Indian family who operated several motels.

"You think seven-year-olds go around comparing their parents' pedigrees?" Billie said.

"Well, that's why I'm asking."

"Relax, Ty. She's making friends."

He simply did not wish people to judge May because of

what he did, or did not do for a living. Surely Billie was right. What did it matter? When had he ever cared what strangers thought?

The Two Mays. That's how he thought of the children until his daughter spelled out *M-e-i L-i-n,* in her carefully articulated voice. "You spell and say things differently in Chinese."

"What are you wearing today?" he asked the morning of the keenly awaited play date. He was leaning into May's room while she rifled through her drawers, still dressed in PJs.

"Mei Lin and I are wearing our twin pinks."

"And what might that be?"

"You know, Daddy."

Did he? Since when had the Two Mays coordinated their wardrobes? She came to the doorway, which he was blocking, clothing in hand.

"Excuse me." She looked up and he stepped aside.

He called through the closed bathroom door. "What do you mean by twin pinks?"

"We have the same outfit. You'll see."

When she emerged, she was dressed in her dark pink girl jeans and a lighter pink knit top with the white and gold dog stitched across the front.

"Ah, so that's it."

She nodded and preceded him downstairs to the kitchen where he'd forgotten to set out the milk or anything else for that matter. She reminded him of his omissions, removing the milk carton from the fridge herself while he laughed and made *ooops* sounds, pulling bowls and spoons out of cabinets and drawers. She was behaving as if this were an ordinary day. Why, then, was expectation making a fool of him? She had been to several birthday parties as a preschooler, and after-school playdates as a first grader that seemed to involve small groups of little girls, but this was the first event with a "best" friend. Somehow she'd crossed a threshold when he wasn't looking, yet he was the one with butterflies, not his daughter.

"Mei Lin's mother will pick you up after school. Have you met her before?"

"Yes. She comes to our class to help out."

"Oh?"

"Some mothers do that, you know."

"No fathers?" He felt it again— the swift stab of inadequacy.

She paused, thinking on this prospect of volunteering fathers, and smiled at him. "Not yet."

Here was proof of the very thing that gave his fears legitimacy: Mothers helped out. Mothers were visible and ubiquitous; mothers were indispensable, or at least considered so. He was only a father who went to work and pinch-hit as a mother. Perhaps he should take a morning off and volunteer.

"I'll come for you at five."

"I know, Daddy. You told me already. Twice!"

"Machinery malfunction," Billie said to herself as she unthreaded the Singer and removed the bobbin. Eppie Gordon hung unhelpfully over her shoulder, humming. Why did the equipment always break down during the last period of class, requiring her to stay late? Billie assumed that, with its connection to the nearby vocational and technical college, Washaw High was the last high school in Topeka to offer the "domestic arts." She and Eppie were a dying breed: Home Econ teachers. Pterodactyls. She stifled a laugh.

"Suppose it's the wall outlet?" Eppie asked.

"Doubtful," Billie answered.

More likely some shard of cloth wedged up in the bobbin hole, jamming the works. Neither woman heard Tyler enter the sewing shop and make his way toward them.

"Can I help?"

The women turned abruptly. Eppie gave a startled yip that made Billie smile.

"Maybe you can help," Billie said, teasing. To her knowledge, the multi-talented Ty had never taken up sewing, a fact she couldn't resist bringing up. "If you've ever used one of these."

"Can't say that I have," he said finally. "I keep my Singer in the closet, mostly."

Eppie laughed out loud. "I have coffee cake baking in my classroom as we speak. Want some?"

He declined and thanked her.

"Why're you still here?" Billie asked and got up from the machine.

"I'm hanging around till five. May has a play date."

Eppie clasped her hands as if she could not have thought of a more thrilling event. Billie regarded him with a bemused expression.

"Oh my!" Eppie exclaimed. "Are you having fun with that sweet girl? Roy and I married so late that kids were out of the question. My one sorrow. I just love your Delia May."

An oven timer rang loudly from the adjoining classroom. "Gotta run."

Eppie squeezed Billie's shoulder and threw Tyler a kiss over her shoulder as she strode quickly toward her classroom.

"Play date, huh?" Billie said as the bemused look bloomed into a smile. She turned back to the machine she'd been working on and fussed with the bobbin.

"Do you suppose I should volunteer at her school?" he asked. "May said something about other kids' mothers always being there to volunteer. But no dads."

"Why not? Could be fun."

Tyler began shuffling around the room, fingering a finished apron on a work table, then another garment. He passed another sewing machine and looked down at it, pulling out the drawer, opening the bobbin tray, before wandering on to pause at Billie's bulletin board and read the contents.

"Tyler, I have never seen you at such loose ends."

"No, no. Just killing time."

"You never just kill time. You are the most purposeful person I know, other than Eppie. Fess up, Ty! You're nervous."

"What would I be nervous about?"

"I don't know. You'll have to tell me."

He was being cryptic again, holding it in, unwilling to sort out the facts of his feelings.

Finally, he spoke. "I have to meet the mother. My guess is the family is *rich* and *important.*" He emphasized the two prominent words.

"The mother will love you, I promise."

"I hope not." He feigned shock.

"Oh, you're impossible!"

"Just joking."

"Go downstairs and bother Howie. I have to fix this machine and it's making me cross."

Tyler wandered out of the Home Econ suite, down the stairs to the Mother Ship. Was it that obvious? He was about to meet Mei Lin's mother, and pass muster. They'd had pleasant enough telephone conversations, but never met. But now, at seven years of age, his daughter had a best girlfriend, and other parents were in a position to judge May on the basis of her one parent. The thought completely unsettled him.

In Howard's Art Cave overhead lights blazed. He heard laughter, but no Howard. Then he spotted him near the back of the vast room, working with two students. All three were bent over what appeared to be a large sculpted head with prominent ears but no face. He approached, announcing himself.

"What do you think of the puppet?" Howard asked.

"Show me how it works."

"I'm not sure it does yet." Howard told the boy, whom Ty recognized as a senior, to elevate it. The head was lighter than it appeared. When the student turned it around, he saw the face.

"There'll be three puppets. Jill's making one now." Howard indicated a tall, reedy creature in torn jeans.

"There's going to be a St. Patrick's Day parade, and we're carrying these," the girl said.

"Recognize the culprit?" said Howard.

Ty cocked his head. The puppet bore a vague resemblance to President Clinton. They'd managed to achieve the spud of a nose, the dome of hair, the squinting eyes and smile. "I'm creating the Hillary puppet," the girl said.

A man of no politics, Tyler didn't know why you'd want the Clintons anyway but didn't say so. "And the third puppet?" he asked.

"A generic Irishman, I guess," the boy said.

"That'll be the easiest," Howard said. "Lots of green and ruddy cheeks."

"Where's the march?"

"A parade," the girl corrected. "Downtown."

"The way they work is," Howard explained, "you hold the giant heads up on large sticks and bounce them around. As if these faces were floating above the crowd."

"Are you going?" he asked Howard.

"Probably not. Don't want to give our illustrious vice principal more ammunition. I'm already on his bad boy list."

"Yeah," the boy drawled. "Con is such a right-winger."

"*Con?*" Tyler gave the kid a pointed look before he could stop himself.

The kid dropped his gaze and turned away, toward the puppet.

"Con Andrews," Howard said hurriedly, as if Ty's response had been a question. Howard tapped him on the arm and mouthed, *Cool it.*

How could Howard feel comfortable talking so personally with students? He supposed art students were different from the kids who signed up for carpentry.

"These are really neat," Ty said hurriedly. "Hope the news channels get photos."

"You're sworn to secrecy," Howard said. "You don't know these were built here."

"How are you going to hide them?"

"My inside office." Howard turned and spoke to the students. "Darken all the features."

He took Tyler's arm and steered him toward his desk on the far side of the room. Howard perched on it while Tyler balanced himself on Howard's stool. The seat struck him as precariously high and teetery.

"Do you actually sit on this thing?"

"For exactly five minutes, while I take attendance. I don't sit much. Do you?"

"No." He fell silent, working a large callus on his right hand.

"Let me guess. You're brooding."

Tyler broke out laughing, glanced up briefly, and then avoided Howard's eyes. "Yes."

"Don't."

"Easy for you to say."

"Try telling people you're a divorced father. And I certainly don't tell them I'm gay."

But a divorced father still made sense. What made no sense was the non-father father, the father whose daughter was vaguely aware you were her biological uncle. The concept of *niece* had long ago been covered over in heavy layers of filial sediment. In front of May, everyone referred to Tyler as "your dad." Nowadays the words *niece* or *uncle* appeared only in documents composed in a dry language that seldom dealt with subtle truths.

"Look, Ty. If the other mother asks, tell her the truth. With as little additional detail as possible. It's nobody's business anyway. People are just naturally curious."

"So I've noticed. My dad used to say, 'Discretion is the better part of valor.' What happened to it?"

"Nothing's happened. It never thrived except as a personal principle among a tiny group of men. Marcus Aurelius had it, but his wife and son and most of his relatives and descendants did not. Your father's one of the few. You're one of the few. And I'm sorry to tell you, I'm not. I'm one of the great unwashed. I'm curious as hell about other people's dirt. And I'm likely to ask."

"But you've never been nosy with me."

"That's because we're friends. Sooner or later you'll tell me."

"Now I'm totally confused. What are you doing with Marcus Aurelius? Doesn't sound like your type of reading."

"I've been reading his *Meditations* for years. It's my bedtime ritual."

Tyler smiled.

"I read a little every night to improve my character. Then in the morning I forget it all and go back to my wicked ways." Howard looked at his watch. "I need to chase those two out of here and lock up. And you need to pick up May."

Tyler parked the truck in front of an attractive brick home set back from the street. He followed a flagstone walk across a well-groomed lawn and up to the large two-story residence. Tall stocks of yellow canna stood at both corners of the house. Beneath the canna grew giant elephant ears and, in front of these, colorful pygmy zinnias. He'd never planted canna and now thought he might. Before he rang the bell he turned and took in the safe, well-heeled neighborhood. A distinctly western woman answered the door, and once he'd identified himself, introduced herself as Mei Lin's mother, Sara Robertson. He followed her down a hall to a large, airy kitchen. Behind the kitchen he glimpsed a family room where the little girls were playing.

She invited him to sit for a moment, "to get acquainted," she said. She'd just brewed a pot of tea and offered him a cup. A plate of cookies sat on the table, arranged on an expensive-looking glass plate. He estimated Sara Robertson to be his age. A smattering of silver filament ran through her hair. She was an appealing-looking woman, if not pretty. *Well-turned out,* his mother would have said.

"Your May is my little Mei's first best friend," she said as he sipped his tea.

He could hear the children's voices behind them—a laugh, a trill, a playful protest, and then silence.

"Our Mei came to us when she was about five months. Or rather we went to get her in Sichuan. Since Mei Lin is an only child, we want her to have as many friends as possible."

He had never dwelled on his May's solitary status. Perhaps

he should. She'd had Aaron's company since babyhood, plus
BeeBee'n Bud, and the dogs. But that wasn't the same as a best
friend. He cleared his throat. The woman had given him a cue,
and he'd best take it.

"My May's situation is similar," he said. "She's also an only
child…" He hesitated a moment. He didn't like sounding so
tentative. "Not to put too fine a point on it, her parents abandoned her, and each other. Her birth mother was virtually a
child. May came to live with me when she was less than a month
old, so I'm the only parent she's ever known. Her 'father'"—he
made air quotes—"is my brother, but no one knows where he
is. As far as I'm concerned, May's my daughter. I'm her legal
guardian, and in due course, the state will make the adoption
final. For now, they're dragging their heels."

When he finished, he felt he'd been slugged with adrenaline.
He'd never explained the situation to an unofficial stranger, nor
told the story so succinctly.

The mother nodded knowingly. "Try dealing with the Chinese. I've never jumped through so many hoops. I finally decided it was all about the money."

They stared at each until the woman smiled, and Tyler
dropped his gaze. Was this why the little girls felt such an affin-
ity? A shared loss? A sense of difference? How would an infant
know this? A biology teacher at the high school talked once in
the lounge about cellular memory. Even if our heads can't recall
some trauma or significant event, even if our heads can reason
it out, our body cells remember and influence our actions. An
extraordinary concept, he thought. He hadn't scoffed at the
theory as some of the staff had. He'd mulled it over. Why not?
It might explain his visceral response to his brother.

Tyler brought up the subject of volunteering in the children's
classroom.

"You'd be a hit," Sara Robertson said. "They don't see
enough men in their school lives. I'll speak to the woman who
organizes the volunteers."

Tyler promptly invited Mei Lin to the farm for the next play date. He would happily pick the children up and also return Mei Lin, so the mother would not need to drive at rush hour. Suddenly, the invitation expanded as he rattled on. Perhaps she and her husband would also like to come. The children could play and he could show them the farm.

"I'd love to have Mei Lin visit your farm," she said. "But my husband's an obstetrician. He's seldom home, I'm sorry to say." She smiled and took a sip of her tea. If her husband's absence from home bothered her, he couldn't tell. Perhaps she was used to it. He admired her restraint in any event.

Tyler leaned across the kitchen table. "I assumed you might want to see the farm for yourself. You know, parental worries."

The size of her laugh came as a relief. She'd struck him at first as overly controlled. If her husband was seldom available, her situation was much like his: she was laboring alone in the trenches of parenthood.

"Why don't *I* pick Mei Lin up from your farm?" she said. "Then I can see for myself."

The two parents went to the family room.

"May? Your father's here."

The little girls looked up. May waved.

"Hi, Daddy. Come see our game."

He stepped down into the family room and crossed the large carpeted space. When he reached them, he bent down to see. Mei Lin stared at him.

"Mei, honey. This is Mr. Manning."

The little girl stood up and curtsied. "I'm pleased to meet you."

He'd never seen a child curtsey. It struck him as charming and completely otherworldly. After some hesitation and foot dragging, the little girls followed the grown-ups out of the family room, through the kitchen and down the hall to the entry. Amid the goodbye chatter, May Manning managed to pull on her jacket. Then the most extraordinary thing happened: the two girls hugged each other. He was speechless, charmed. Mei Lin's mother glanced at him and quickly looked away. He was still so overcome by the embrace that he hadn't paid as much attention as he ought to May's departure etiquette. Only when it was over did he realize May had said all she was supposed to say, thanking the hostess and her little friend. His daughter then took her leave with a happy, "See you tomorrow, Mei-Mei."

Mei-Mei. For an instant he thought he might dissolve. How did a person cherish such innocence? The two Mays wouldn't be seven forever. There were trolls out there waiting to wipe their muddy shoes on anyone too innocent to know better. The task that tangled his sleep and any un-corralled thought was how to prevent such a sacrilege from happening. A picture of May's hapless young mother came into his head. At what age had Sherlynne Smith been wrenched out of childhood? Two? Four? He couldn't imagine her childhood being anything but wretched. As for Mickey? Well, he'd dwelled enough on that subject.

Tyler would look back on his day in May's classroom and struggle to find the correct word to describe it. Surreal? Howard offered. But *surreal* was a Howard word, not his.

May's teacher was the first hurdle, a pretty but fussy woman in her thirties, a twelve-year veteran of the classroom. She wore a flowing green and tightly belted shirtwaist dress, hoop earrings, and loops of colorful beads that bounced against a flat chest. She was tiny. Pert, Billy would say. He noted the wedding bands with the ostentatious engagement diamond, even though her behavior would not suggest she felt any need to honor her commitment on a superficial level. He found her a coquette. No woman in recent memory—certainly not since Nancy—had flirted with him so strenuously. His face flushed and his hands began to sweat. He ignored the batting eyelashes, astounded that women still did this. She also had a little habit of tilting her head down so her eyes appeared larger when she gazed up at him. She let her fingers touch his when she gave him construction paper or chalk to hand out. He kept himself as calm as possible, allowing himself the occasional smile, the neutral or amusing comment. But she was becoming a hindrance to his help.

At one point, he found himself perched on a ridiculously low stool, reading aloud from a story book while the children circled his feet. He heard himself drone boringly on until his daughter piped up, "Use your Rusty voice, Dad." This was the silly scratchy falsetto he used to imitate animal characters when he read to her. It had not occurred to him to use this voice in public. It was early enough in the story that he could adjust his reading, introducing the cartoon "Rusty voice." As he did, the children squealed and laughed, encouraging him on. The kids would call out the answers to the questions posed in the story. They knew the story by heart. By the time he finished, the children were unusually wound up. Sensing this, Mrs. Twining suggested a floor game of Duck-Duck-Goose.

He'd played this as a child and marveled that such things stayed the same. When it was his turn to be the goose—which was entirely too often, all the children wanting him to hop up and chase them—he clambered to his feet and ran around the circle in a crouch, feeling as large and cumbersome as a bear. Afterward, little Danny Patel decided Ty was a jungle gym and tried to climb him. Mrs. Twining admonished the boy in a soft voice, which had no impact at all. Then May pulled the boy's arm and said, "Stop that, Danny! That's my dad and you're being a dork!"

The boy stopped.

On a Friday, early in the new millennial year, Ty's teaching day got off to a rocky start. Three sophomore boys arrived fifteen minutes after the hour. They'd been outside, hiding behind the Mother Ship with their smokes. Once in class they didn't settle down. Mischief-makers, he thought, placed in his class by that consummate opportunist, the VP, Con Andrews, perhaps as a favor to someone who didn't want them in their history or social studies class. Instead of separating the group, as any savvy teacher would do, Con slapped all three in Tyler's Fundamentals

of Woodworking. Tyler glared at the three boys clumped together in back. He stepped down between the worktables and
pointed to the troublemakers, one by one.

"You. Up here." The first kid rolled forward, smirking all the
way, ending up in a table by himself next to Ty's desk.

"You." He pointed to the second boy, the ringleader. "Right
over here. With Mark." A tall, fearsome-looking kid, Mark had
once been a troublemaker himself. Now a model of responsibility, he worshipped Moose Manning.

"And you." He pointed to the final kid, placing him at a
middle table with his most reliable worker.

"You three act up again," Tyler said, "your bench mates have
my permission to eat you alive. And, you'll stay after class, miss
your lunch period, and clean up the entire shop."

The class hooted. If they still acted up, he'd send them to
Jeff who would eat them alive. Boys who ended up in Jeff's
mechanics classes—not the genuine mechanics, just the screw-
ups—did not always come from families who cared if Jeff
knocked a ball cap off a miscreant's head or grabbed a collar
menacingly or punched a shoulder to get his attention. Tyler
would never get physical, but Jeff seemed to know when to
draw the line. Neither Ty nor Howard said a word against him.

The project of the day cranked forward, but the three tru-
ants had interrupted the work mood, throwing the class rhythm
out of whack. Tyler struggled to regain the momentum, to no
avail. Restlessness permeated the air.

A quarter-hour before lunch, a tall boy in paint-spattered
jeans ran into Ty's room and yelled, "Mr. Manning, can you
come quick? Mr. Shay just keeled over."

Tyler pointed to the imposing boy named Mark. "You're in
charge till I get back."

As Tyler ran from the room following the art student, Mark
rose from his table and strode ominously to Tyler's desk. Tyler
faintly heard him announce, "All right, guys. Listen up."

"What happened?" Tyler jogged along beside the kid, down
to the Art Cave.

"I was standing right by him. Mr. Shay was talking to Violet about her sculpture. Then he said something like, 'Oh my god.' Then 'Jeez no'—right out of the blue. He rubbed his forehead with one hand, then both hands. Then he just…crumpled." The boy emitted a strangled sob.

Tyler grabbed the kid's sleeve. "You're gonna be okay."

The boy stifled the sob and nodded. They reached the art room and crossed quickly to the rear where a knot of kids hovered near the floor.

"Where's Mr. Shay's phone?"

A weeping girl, crouched over Howard, raised her hand. "In his office." She pointed to the glass-fronted space at the back of the large classroom.

"Call 911. Ask for an ambulance. And you." He indicated the boy who'd come to fetch him. "Run down to the office. Tell them."

The boy took off. Tyler told the kids to stand back so Howard could have some air. He then knelt beside Howard. He quickly placed fingers against Howard's neck and discerned a clear pulse. He leaned over, felt the breath. He was unconscious but alive. It did not look like a heart attack, no CPR was required. A stroke? There was no clothing to loosen since Howard only wore loose clothes and had never been seen in a tie.

"Mr. Shay is alive and breathing."

They'd acted quickly and that would likely save him, he added. Several more of the girls were crying. How had he and Howie and Billie taught such delicate creatures, day in and day out? It was as though adolescence was a medical condition, those afflicted always close to anger or tears, confusion, depression or jubilation. Yet on a good day, their energy could revitalize and even reassure you that another crop of fledgling adults was on its way. And here hovered a small group, witnesses to the worst thing a kid could endure, the laying low of a significant adult.

He told the kids to stand in the large hall atrium outside Howard's studio, explaining that the medics would need space and not onlookers. He'd stay with Howard and even go with him to the hospital. At that moment, Principal O'Brien burst through the door, VP Andrews trailing behind. While O'Brien looked appropriately concerned, Tyler thought Andrews simply looked addled. The kids hung back, still huddled in the doorway. Ty waved at them and slowly, one by one, they pulled out into the hall.

"Can we come to the hospital too?" asked the girl named Violet and the tall boy who had remained near Tyler.

Later, he reassured them. Definitely later. Howard may need surgery. He told the two students to write their name and phones numbers down. He would call each of them personally, and they could notify their classmates. The girl smiled through her tears. The boy nodded solemnly and grabbed a sheet of paper off Howard's desk.

Tyler was still kneeling beside Howard when he heard the siren. He spoke briefly to his two superiors, telling them what little he knew, deferring to the two students who described, once again, the event. He announced he was going to the hospital with Howard, and he would need someone to cover his classes. He also needed to tell Billie to pick up his daughter after school.

The principal turned to his vice principal. "Con? Would you mind? It's an emergency."

A clattering at the door announced the medics who stormed into the Art room like Navy SEALs. Unable to help themselves, the kids bulged back through the door, blocking it. Tyler called out to them to clear the way, and again they reluctantly pulled out into the hall atrium. A gurney unfolded. Oxygen, tubes, and needles appeared. The two young men worked quickly, asking questions. Tyler told them what he could, assuming it was a cerebral hemorrhage. A wave of desperation struck him, leaving him short of breath. He wanted to scream, "Just get him to the hospital!" but could say nothing. A picture of his collapsed father flashed into his head. The medics told him which hospital and wheeled Howard toward the door. No, Tyler could not ride with them, but he could certainly follow.

"I'm leaving," he told his superiors and jammed the paper

with the two phone numbers into his jeans pocket. He jogged behind the gurney, waving his arms, cautioning the students further back, calling out as he ran, "Mr. Shay's alive and breathing. We have high hopes." They wanted to watch, and yet were horrified. They didn't want to miss one second of Howie's inglorious exit. God, let him live. Tyler ran out of the Mother Ship and up to the Home Econ classrooms. He blew into Billie's cooking class without knocking. She whirled around, ready to scold, and then saw his face.

"A word?" he said, raising an index finger.

He turned back to the entrance of her class and explained as soon as she joined him in the hall. He was on the way to the hospital now. Maybe he could be of use. Would she pick up May after school? "I didn't want to say anything in front of your girls. Half of Howard's class saw him collapse. The girls are very upset."

"They can come in here if they want," she offered.

"Then more students would know and get upset. O'Brien is with them now."

Tyler took the nearest exit. He looked around for his car and felt strangely disoriented until he remembered his truck was parked on the other end of the school. Later he would learn that, after a brief "visibility run," the vice principal left Tyler's shop in the hands of the stalwart Mark, excusing the young man from his afternoon classes in order to continue as Tyler's surrogate. No incidents were reported.

Meanwhile, Tyler sped to Stormont-Vail, his heart in his throat. He invoked God's mercies, and then chided himself for such feckless foxhole prayers. Howard would live or he would not. Tyler's feeble pleas would not help. Then again, prayer never hurt, and he prayed once more. He parked in the visitor lot nearest the emergency entrance, locked the truck for once, and ran across the pavement toward the ER. His thoughts kept breaking up, like a window shattering. *Howard, we still need you. May needs you. I need you!*

The receptionist in ER sidelined Tyler to a tacky, airless

waiting room with two glass walls. He felt he was in a zoo cage. Stranded. Beached. Prominently posted on one solid wall was a sign: *No cell phones. Please go outside to call.* He willingly left the room and walked through the crowded ER lobby and out of the building.

"Diane?" Tyler identified himself to Howard's ex-wife. Howie had long ago given Tyler her number. "We're still friends, you know," Howie said often. A good thing, Ty thought, if you share kids. Diane would come to the hospital and handle the legal and insurance matter that Ty could not. The hospital had managed to glean quite a bit from Howard's untidy wallet. Yes, he was alive. Hopefully, he'd be conscious soon. But they needed a relative. An "ex" would do. They told Tyler next to nothing.

When he wandered back in, he approached the window at the ER, inquiring when he might visit Mr. Shay. The reception-ist was a stickler for the rules: a doctor would have to authorize it before Howard could have any visitors except immediate family. "But I brought him in. I'm his best friend. He's single, divorced."

She gave him a weary look and shook her head. "Sorry. Please wait over there."

Diane Shay found Ty slumped in a corner of the ER waiting room, flipping through a health magazine. His Oxford cloth shirt looked as though he'd removed it, wadded it into a small ball for an hour, and then put it back on. She slipped into an adjoining chair. "Tyler?"

He didn't know Diane well. She and Howard had divorced early in Ty's teaching career. She'd remarried but that had also ended in divorce after only a couple of years. "A control freak," Howard had described husband number two. "He couldn't stand our girls." Howard's sympathy was entirely with his ex, and their relationship as friends burgeoned after her disastrous second marriage. She never changed her name, Howard said. She was still a Shay. Said it would be easier for the girls.

"Howie's out of surgery," she said. "It took him a while to

regain his wits. But he's already sassed one nurse, so I'd say he's alive and well."

Tyler felt the tension subside as though his entire body were sighing. The heavy wings that had beaten inside him for hours grew still. Would there be any long-term damage?

"They won't know until he can get up. If there is, it will affect his right side only. His right eye looks a bit droopy."

"Visitors?"

She nodded. "Tomorrow."

He phoned Billie. May was fine, she said. All was fine. "How's Howard?"

Then he phoned Howard's students.

A month passed before Howard returned to Washaw High, driven by his former wife and aided by a motorized wheelchair.

"If you need the chair, Howie," Tyler implored, "you're not ready. You've got more sick-leave saved up than I do."

"The chair's just for effect," Howard said. "Besides I was bored. Missed the action." He flourished a cane he now kept beside the desk.

On the first day of Howard's return, Tyler wandered down to the Art Cave during his planning period to check on him. Before he entered, he glanced through the narrow window in the door in time to see one of Howard's students shoot by in the wheelchair, do what amounted to a wheelie, and drive back in the other direction. The room usually roiled with students strung out around the room, talking, fetching materials, while others hunched over worktables. Today, a larger than usual knot of kids hovered around the desk. When the group parted, Tyler caught a glimpse of Howard seated atop the desk, gesturing with the cane. So, it was business as usual. He opened the door and crossed the cavernous space.

"Thought you might feel tired. Want me to bring you some lunch?"

"No, no. Thought I'd limp on down to the lounge and enjoy some adult company."

He was being brave for his students, but he looked drawn. The affected eye sagged. Kids drifted away to let the teachers talk, and Howie leaned forward, his head tilted conspiratorially.

"I made Con Andrews a proposal. Rename the industrial arts wing—our Mother Ship— the Art and Industry Campus. Whaddya think?"

Not bad. Ty nodded.

"I'm not industrial arts," Howard complained. "Neither are you, technically."

"At least you're never called 'the shop teacher.' Like it's a remedial class."

Howie patted his arm. "Pay no attention to the philistines. They're beyond help. Speaking of which, Con liked the idea. Thought it had a classy ring. Art and Industry Campus. I think it's the word *campus* he likes. Makes him believe he's in a college."

Howard slid off the desk, propping himself up on the cane.

The class bell rang. Voices whipped into frothy peaks of laughter as students swirled toward the door in a river of denim.

"It's like a bath drain," Howard said. "Ring the bell, pull the plug, *swoosh*, they're gone."

A dry winter gave way to a wet and dreary spring. Howard's right leg grew stronger, which he attributed to early and vigorous therapy, as did the arm and hand although these seemed less affected. Whenever Ty asked, Howard answered with a smile and a cavalier wave of the cane.

"Fine, fine! Leg's improved by leaps and bounds. I'm returning the wheelchair Friday. The kids'll miss it more than I will."

The truth was the leg would never fully recover. The doctors claimed he could manage without a cane, but it offered stability. Howard appeared reconciled to this fact. Considering Howard had started his rehabilitation in a wheelchair, Tyler allowed himself to share his colleague's optimism. And contrary to Ty's predictions, Howard diligently exercised.

"If I don't, my girls get after me. Nothing worse, Ty, than a daughter on a mission."

Howard would carry on, joke about his new limitation, use the cane as a prop, and jokingly threaten his students with it.

"I'll give new meaning to the word *caning*."

In early May, Howard's seniors came to Tyler to ask for permission to use his tools. They presented Tyler with a length of wood, which he milled and readied, buffing it so the kids could work it with ease. Before and after school and during lunch hours, they slipped quietly into Tyler's shop, carving Howie a stout and elaborate souvenir. Ty watched the cane evolve. It reminded him of a hand-sized totem pole. Some of the students painted or carved faces resembling their own. Others worked animal faces or special icons into the wood. A bird's head, with a sturdy pointed beak and a ruff of carved feathers formed the handle. A crow, someone told him. Howie reminded them of a crow. And in tiny, precise letters along the shaft of the cane, a young woman carved Howard's signature remarks: *Start over* and *Persevere*. On the last day of school, they presented it to Howard during class.

"I choked up," he reported to Tyler. "Imagine what would've happened if I'd broken down. A colossal weepfest, right here in the Mother Ship."

What must it feel like to be so liked by your students that they presented you with an irreplaceable gift, made by their own hands? Howie's gift cane was a marvel of invention, crowded with images. When viewed from the left, the carvings were beautifully balanced but from the right, slightly grotesque. What Ty admired most was the crow's head handle, with two pitch-black glass beads for eyes. When he told Howard how much he admired—no, envied—the cane, Howard looked at him, astonished, and blurted out.

"But you were always the one getting homemade gifts, Ty. Remember the ebony napkins rings? That little lamp and the wren house? What about those dog bookends? Maybe not elegant but still. I used to envy you."

What a perfectly useless emotion envy was, like a dank mist. Like mold. The bookends had come from a student from the early days of teaching: rosewood carved to resemble the heads of two long-eared hounds. The boy—a quiet, sandy-haired waif—had left them on his desk one Christmas, clumsily wrapped in holiday paper. He still had the rosewood hounds in the living room atop his mother's antique chest, holding up a dictionary, an atlas, *The Workman's Guide to Carpentry,* and Zornow's *Kansas: History of the Jayhawk State.*

The year after Howard's stroke when May was nine, she asked about "those dog bookends." Could she have them in her room? He looked at them closely for the first time in years. The dog shapes were a bit clumsy, the ears uneven, but the boy had taken pains with the polishing. When May proudly carried the hound bookends upstairs, he thought about the boy who'd now be an adult. He noticed the hounds' absence from the old chest more than he had noticed their presence. Whenever he needed to go into May's room, he admired them anew, holding up her favorite books.

PART THREE

12

THE TWO MAYS

When Delia May and Mei Lin were still seven, a trio of school boys caught Mei-Mei Robertson alone on the soccer field and menaced her, calling her a *gook* and a few other words. Delia May, who was a short distance away, saw what was happening and flew across the playing field in high dudgeon, threatening the boys in return. Or so she reported to Tyler later.

"I called them boogers. Told them I'd box their ears if they ever bothered Mei-Mei again!"

Box their ears? Did anyone actually say that nowadays?

"BeeBee says it to Aaron. 'A-ron! If you don't straighten up, I'll box your ears!'"

When he asked if she knew what the boys had said to Mei-Mei, she gazed at him thoughtfully and then replied, "No, but it wasn't very nice, was it?"

Because May could not stop talking about the insult to her friend, he phoned Sara Robertson, concerned whether this had happened before and no adult had intervened. Sara Robertson took a broad view of the incident. No, the bullying hadn't happened before that she knew of. More often elderly church ladies or cashiers at checkout counters cooed at Mei-Mei and remarked, without batting an eye, "And where did you find this beautiful child?"

"Right in front of Mei Lin," she said. "As if we'd lifted up a cabbage leaf and there she was."

Sara Robertson sounded stoic, and Tyler laughed with her but felt disheartened. He wondered if one incident was enough to harm a child, and he asked his daughter to tell him if it ever happened again.

At the end of their third-grade year when she was eight, May came home with a different story: One of the girls in her class had called her "a little orphan girl." She didn't mention the incident right away. It only came to light a day later as he was considering what to prepare for supper.

"How do you become an orphan?" she asked.

He felt a cold hand on his heart. "You lose your parents."

A pause. "Am I an orphan?"

"Heck no! It usually means both parents are dead. And you've got me, and I'm certainly not dead."

A small titter of relief.

"In fact, you also have BeeBee and Bud…and of course your original parents." He said this last part quickly. He couldn't remember when he'd started using *original*. At the time it had seemed a less vexing word than birth parents. "So you have more parents than anyone."

She threw back her head and laughed.

"Why do you ask?" he said quickly.

She finally told him. This child was as circumspect as her grandfather, concealing her wound in her eight-year-old heart. Ever since Mei Lin had been bullied, he'd wondered if his daughter might also become a target. Only May's ferocity kept the bullies at bay, but those who took pleasure in belittling were less easily discouraged. How could a kid reply to malice cloaked in pity?

"Shall we make PB&Js for dinner? Maudie likes PB&Js."

She gave him another small laugh, offered as a consolation prize. He didn't know if she was old enough to reason out why someone would take pleasure in calling her "an orphan girl." In any event, it didn't end there. Not long after, an unwitting boy called her "little orphan Annie." She bore down on him and offered to bloody his nose. Tyler pictured her, fists balled, ready to pounce like a duck on a June bug. And then he pictured himself, wild with rage.

"I asked him how he supposed it made a real orphan feel," she said. "I told him I had five parents. My original parents,

then you—my real dad—and then my godparents. The stupid
kid was so mixed up he just walked away."

When she finished, she thrust her hands on her hips and
threw back her head. Tyler was speechless. This was the first
time she'd referred to Sherlynne and Mick.

"Good job," he said finally. "I'm proud of you for *not*
bloodying his nose. And I want to tell you a story."

He sat her down in her kitchen chair and gave her an abbreviated version of the day he lost his temper so totally that
he'd seriously damaged another person's most important feature—his face. While he spoke, she did not take her eyes off
him. He wasn't sure she believed him. She'd seldom seen him
angry, certainly not with her. Annoyed, perhaps. Impatient. But
never wrathful.

The next day he phoned her teacher and inquired of the
incident. No, she hadn't witnessed the scene. It must have taken
place on the playground. "That's where our children learn to
interact, don't you think, Mr. Manning?" The condescending
tone stunned him. When he remarked that this was the second
or third incident, her voice grew noticeably defensive, her tone
arch. "We can't be everywhere at once."

If she'd expressed even the smallest concern, offered to be
alert to the situation, he might have respected her. So this was
how devilish behavior flourished: the grown-ups weren't paying
attention. The grown-ups were disengaged.

"Seems to me," the teacher remarked, "May handled the
situation well enough."

He agreed. He also sensed this woman didn't altogether
approve of May. And on this unsatisfactory note he concluded
the conversation. Perhaps the woman was more alarmed by
May's self-defense than the original provocations. Perhaps she
wanted May to come crying to her for solace, something his
daughter would never do. Why should she? Her principal model was Billie Harrington, and Billie would never cry or expect
someone to intervene in something she could handle herself.
Cross Billie and you might just get your ears boxed!

The thought cheered him considerably.

Was it any wonder, then, the Two Mays developed a social conscience?

His daughter was nine when the World Trade buildings went down. He wouldn't have thought that 9/11 would affect school children so young, although it had clearly affected their parents. Some middle school boys crossed their playing field, entered the elementary school playground and threatened Danny Patel, who happened to be alone on a swing. Outraged, the Two Mays recruited their teachers and a corps of schoolmates to protect Danny and a handful of other Indian and Pakistani children.

Tyler spent more time on the phone that September than he could remember—calls to and from Sara Robertson, the school principal, the children's teacher, an idealistic young man who inspired the little girls to strive. The Two Mays would not let their friend Danny go anywhere without them, needlessly escorting him from class to class as if they thought his tormentors planned to follow him into the building. The "Two Musketeers," their teacher called the girls. But the incident brought to mind the bullying of Mei Lin when the girls were seven.

It struck him that May Manning's reaction to Danny's bullies was exactly the same. She was as fierce as Maude if someone had been foolish enough to menace May in front of her bulldog. As fierce as Billie.

Still, he found it odd that the little girls had become such crusaders. This was Topeka, after all, not San Francisco. Then Sara Robertson reminded him the girls' school was full of the offspring of university faculty, physicians, and Menninger psychiatrists. Smarty-pants, in other words. Living with people who actually read. "Environment is everything," Sara said.

A pattern soon emerged.

At the age of ten it was animal welfare and the environment, with recycle bins in their school. The campaign moved on to carpooling and bicycle riding, and she announced to her father she would henceforth ride the bus. "You and BeeBee really ought to carpool," she said in her new voice of Lifestyle Improvement.

By sixth grade, the Two Mays reopened the door to social justice first activated in third grade. They performed an anti-bullying play for their classmates, an awkward little drama of their own creation. "Someone has to stand up for the geeks and gays, Daddy!" When they rehearsed it at the farmhouse, he admired the sentiment and the girls' courage but thought the play sounded embarrassingly preachy.

"Maybe it should be a wee bit shorter," he suggested. "Tighter."

Before he had a chance to catch his breath another election year rolled around and, of course, the Two Mays had an opinion. His own answers to May's daily barrage of questions were mostly apolitical, which did not stop his daughter's constant opinionating: "Dad, don't you think the war is an absolute disaster...? Don't you think it's all about the oil...? You *are* going to vote, aren't you?"

In his own mind he knew what was fair and what wasn't, and most of what he believed was not advanced by any politician he knew of. He came from a long line of Kansas Republicans, moderates by nature, who dated their political affiliation to the age of Lincoln. Someday he would tell his daughter about her abolitionist lineage, her Free State grandmother. He'd have to ask Eppie Gordon to tell May some of her own stories. Yet whenever he invoked the word *Republican*, she acted shocked, flounced dramatically, and used her new favorite words: "I'm *appalled.*"

Twelve years old and she's *appalled*? When she first said it, he'd had to excuse himself to the back porch and stifle a laugh.

"We're going to make shields and protect the family. You're a veteran so you ought to come."

He listened while the small dagger of dread entered his heart. This year alone, 2004, the two Mays had baked cookies for an animal shelter fundraiser, sold raffle tickets for a seventh-grade project, and performed another awful anti-bullying play. He was proud of her in his undemonstrative way, but she was only twelve. He'd hoped she might do little girl things a while longer and not tackle the problems of the world so soon.

The latest endeavor troubled him. He phoned Howard, whose name had cropped up as one of the organizers. Ty wanted to know the nature of the event. And why had May linked the event to his veteran status?

"*Mea culpa.* I was just going to call you, Ty."

Howard confessed he didn't know how the Two Mays had gotten wind of it, perhaps through Sara Robertson. He knew some college kids who would be there. And veterans. Lots of veterans.

"Can you just spell it out?" said Tyler. "Delia May can't stop talking about the 'shields' but no details."

"The Westboro Baptist Church people are going to picket a military funeral."

His heart sank.

"And before you even ask—because I know you will," Howard said. "The dangers are minimal. The Westboro people are religious thugs, not physical thugs. They follow the rules, stand behind the proper lines, and they bring *their* children."

"I've seen the photos. So they're offensive. What's the big deal?"

"Have you seen their signs, Tyler? *God Hates Gays.* Or how 'bout, *Pray For More Dead Soldiers.* They're heaping abuse on the whole US military because it accepts gays."

"I know, Howie! You can't watch the Topeka evening news and not see Fred Phelps."

"They don't just use signs, Ty. They have these disgustingly loud bullhorns. The church people are going to harass a grieving family at their son's funeral."

"I'm not sure I want to subject my child to this. She won't understand it."

"Are you kidding me? All kids understand unfairness. And

who in Topeka doesn't know about the Westboro Wingnuts? That includes your kid. Let her see some compassion in action. She's a very compassionate kid."

"I know."

"Besides, Tyler. You're a vet. This should disgust you."

"It does."

"Can we count on your support then?"

Where had this annoying political strain in Howie come from? Tyler didn't recognize it. "I'll be there. I wouldn't let May go alone. I'll even bring the Harringtons."

"Terrific! The more the merrier."

"It's a funeral, Howie."

"Christ, Ty! A figure of speech!"

The event was scheduled for five days hence. They'd already wasted one day just talking, May complained. He asked if Mei Lin and her mother were still onboard.

"Of course!" Spoken with a petulant toss of head and hair. There seemed to be a great deal of hair tossing these days. ("Tween behavior," Billie said, not bothering to explain the word.) "We'll all be there."

"Who's *all*?" he asked, patience waning.

"Miss Eppie."

"Eppie Gordon?"

"Yes, Dad." She rolled her eyes. Her voice had dropped down to that world-weary tone she now employed whenever she had to explain the obvious to an idiot. *Yes, Daaad!*

"Miss Eppie has the parachute fabric for the shields. They'll look like wings."

And now she was off to BeeBee's where the construction was under way. Could she ride her bike down?

On the day of the funeral, Bud insisted on driving. The cloth shields were wrapped in canvas and secured in the bed of his truck. Ty sat in front with Bud while Billie and the kids squeezed into the back seat. Other women in other houses had been busily constructing white cloth shields so the family of the dead soldier would not have to see the placards that announced, *Fag Troops, You're Going to Hell!*

"Think we'll see old Phelps himself?" Bud asked.

"He doesn't show up much anymore," Aaron said. "Sends his daughters out with the rest of the church. Which is pretty much his extended family."

"How do you know all this?" Ty asked. It seemed an odd bit of knowledge for a teenager.

"I Googled him."

A puzzled silence filled the truck. Aaron gazed at each adult in turn. "You people have *got* to get on the internet."

Tyler glanced at Billie. She'd turned her face toward her window, her mouth a rictus of suppressed mirth.

Bud's truck bumped over a culvert and entered the cemetery grounds. The site was made conspicuous by a group gathered in the northwest corner, some of them holding tall white objects—more "shields." The truck shuddered as it traveled the unpaved road. Bud didn't see any parked cars even though the group standing under a large locust tree was considerable and growing. At last Howard emerged and limped toward them.

Bud said, "There's your man."

He pulled on the brake and the others piled out. Billie and Tyler walked around to the back to gather the shields while Howard came over to greet them. Bud leaned out the window and asked about parking. Howard pointed: you couldn't see the cars from where they stood. The landscape swelled up in a rise and then fell away to an older, rolling expanse of ground that included the resting place of several historic figures. Topeka founders. Movers and shakers, Tyler thought. Right now, Tyler struggled with the meaning of this demonstration, hastily shaped and brought to life by the restorative belief that free speech might take unconventional forms, including the two separate groups that would soon face off.

A brisk breeze riffled hair and shirts, tossing a few hats. In these early days of October, the weather had remained mellow, and so it was today. The sun was growing warm as noon approached. May was casing the crowd, searching for her best friend. Soon after Bud drove off to park, Mei Lin and her mother arrived along the same rough track. May jumped up and down, waving her arms. Mei Lin's mother had scarcely stopped the car when Mei-Mei leaped from it and into Delia May's arms. Howard approached, leaned into the driver's window, and Sara Robertson drove away, following Bud.

"So where's the opposition?" Tyler asked as Howard glanced at his watch.

"We're early. By design."

Howard dove back into the larger group and was soon locked in serious conference with a tall, thick-chested, kerchief-headed man with a skinny gray ponytail, sunglasses, and leather vest over a blue shirt. He looked like a biker, but two military medals hung from the well-worn vest. People continued to arrive, and Howard seemed to know a fair number of them. Perhaps he didn't know as much about Howie's life away from Washaw High as he thought. According to Howard, Ed, the biker-vet, had rallied a fair number of his veteran biker pals, and Howard finally introduced the two men.

"Tyler's a closet vet," Howard said, and Ed laughed.

"A peacetime vet," Tyler quickly added.

Two older men joined them, one wearing a cap with the insignia, VFP. "Veterans for Peace," Howie told Tyler when he asked. The talk turned to platitudes of military service and as the men bantered, a jeep bounced up the uneven track.

"There they are!" Ed said, breaking out of his monotone. Howard pointed toward the parking area and they drove on, walking back a few moments later, both dressed in their army fatigues.

"Two of our young Iraq War vets, God love 'em… Hey, brothers!" Ed greeted them.

On the hat of one was the logo IVAW. "A brand new organization," Howie muttered in Ty's ear as Ed embraced the two veterans. The little girls were watching, fascinated, and Tyler glanced at them. When had they grown so tall and skinny? They'd become two string beans, without a curve or a bump between them. One of the two Iraq veterans looked too young to shave, his cheeks a remarkable pink. When the kid noticed the two girls staring at him, he winked at them and smiled, and the girls broke into giggles, falling into each other, whispering. The young men were swallowed up inside the crowd, calling out to friends further back. The Two Mays watched with expressions of awe. Billie nudged Ty and pointed slightly to the girls with her head. "A crush already."

"Some of our people will be riding their bikes with the hearse, fore and aft," Ed said. "An honor guard thing."

Ed gazed over people's heads and shoulders when he talked, as if to look you in the eye was an act too intimate to bear. Calls on Ed's cell became more frequent. He flipped open the mobile, stepped away from the group, said a few words, paused, muttered an "okay," and the call was over. A news bulletin would follow: the cortege had not yet left the funeral hall; the "Westboro crazies" had not yet been sighted. Meanwhile the Two Mays tried out their wings—open, close, open, close. Watch this, Mei-Mei!

"Girls, stop! You'll break them," Billie said sternly. "Save them for when we need you."

The girls stopped, enchanted by those magical words: *We need you.* Billie suppressed a grin and whispered to Tyler, "They're wound up tight."

Suddenly, Ed lifted his arms and announced that the funeral party had left the mortuary. Then the man posted near the entrance to the cemetery trotted up the winding path.

"The Phelps people are on the move," he called as he approached. "The one daughter is leading them."

A palpable tension ran through the group. People gripped their cloth shields, and nervous laughter broke out here and there. Bud was saying something to Billie, and Tyler could not imagine, ten years ago, either his friends or himself hanging out with a crowd of protesters. Tyler turned and scanned the crowd again, spotted Howard, and walked over.

"Shouldn't we line the drive and then regroup around the site?"

"Let's see what the Phelps people do," Howard answered.

He'd learned a bit more while standing around. The young soldier had been killed in Afghanistan. He had a wife but no children. Both parents were living as well as an older sister and brother. All would be attending the service, plus several nieces and nephews.

The group was noticeably larger than when they'd arrived. No longer tightly bunched, the "defenders," as Ed now called them, were moving outward into a loose oval of protection in front of the grave site. Tyler left May with Billie and Bud and wandered up to look at the prepared grave. The funeral people had set up a canopied seating area for the family with additional chairs behind. The grave area was festooned in military colors, the electronic mechanism elevated to its highest point, like a bier, above earth level, waiting to support the casket. At the appropriate time, he remembered, it would descend.

Memories of his father's burial besieged him, and he was un-expectedly awash with feelings he thought were long settled. He tried to visualize the Phelps people yelling out their contempt while his stricken mother watched Hal's casket descend, but it was too much to take in. The *why* of their behavior eluded him. "How do you get that spiteful?" he murmured to himself and walked back to his daughter and friends.

The scout by the road phoned Ed once more. Phelps's daughter was here but no Fred; there were ten people in all, including a couple of teens and one kid. Ed shared the news. A different voice—a woman's—answered back from the midst of the group.

"We've got a *hundred*. They don't stand a chance!"

The group broke into applause, cheers, whistles, broken laughter. More likely seventy, Tyler estimated. The Two Mays jumped up and down in their excitement, and Tyler laid a hand on his daughter's shoulder. She looked up at him, undaunted, her face shining with expectation and certainty. At the moment she was smiling, her eyes ablaze, and all his protective instincts reared up.

"Ready for this?" he asked.

"Yes!" She pumped a fist.

She wasn't a little girl anymore. Nowadays, any question he asked was carefully calibrated, for hormones were already spreading their delirium throughout her body. Her gestures, her choice of clothes, all declared her a teen, even if she wasn't, quite. She was growing up too fast, and the days passed with electronic speed.

Then they heard it—a voice projected through a bullhorn, the word *God* distinct but the following words blown away in a gust of wind.

A chill ran down Billie's spine. She glanced at her teenage son and wondered if this was his first encounter with raw, grown-up ugliness. You never knew with teens. Aaron might have ferreted out every photo and scrap of news of the Westboro church he could find. What upset her was the presence of children in the Phelps camp. What would they grow up to be? Her parents had never been beams of social enlightenment, but Billie never once heard her mother speak ugliness in the house.

The amplified voice was distinct this time: "God hates gays!" Ed raised his voice and announced that the Phelps people were entering the cemetery. Billie didn't want to read the signs. The voice in the megaphone was bad enough.

Suddenly a strong woman's voice started singing: "'Shall we gather at the river where bright angel feet have trod?'"

Billie felt herself inhale deeply. The voice continued. "'With its crystal tide forever, flowing by the throne of God.'"

Other voices joined: "'Yes, we'll gather at the river, the beautiful, the beautiful river.'"

Bud squeezed her hand, chuckling. "Now there's a good Methodist hymn."

"How would either of us know?" Her mother had loved the

hymns and the gospel, and there was a time when Billie loved to hear the Advent story. Her children had gone to Sunday school when they were little—their grandparents had taken them. But she and Bud had fallen away. The voices around them swelled.

"I know the hymns," Bud said. "My folks made me go to church until I was fourteen. A freshman in high school."

"I don't remember you then."

"Good. I was scrawny like A-ron and ugly. I played hooky from Sunday school, but I remember the hymns."

Bud sang along with the other voices. Amazing, Billie thought—he actually knew all the verses. More and more people joined in the chorus, following the woman with the rich mezzo voice.

"'Soon we'll reach the shining river, soon our pilgrimage will cease; soon our happy hearts will quiver with the melody of peace.'"

Tears stung her eyes, startling her. Yes, her heart was quivering, too. This is how church music ought to be—full of celebration and peace. Bud squeezed her hand and joined in the final chorus. "'Yes, we'll gather at the river...'"

Billie glanced down the line of defenders to Tyler. His hand was resting on Delia May's shoulder. The Two Mays had their arms around each other, their shields on the ground in front of them, swaying to the music, side to side. They were still little girls at this moment, unselfconscious in their devotion to each other. Any second now they would change, refuse to touch anyone or allow a single touch, certain that every eye was critically focused on them, devastated by the most infinitesimal blemish. But for now? How sweet they were! Billie glanced the other way. The girls weren't the only ones swaying to the hymn. She suddenly envied Eppie Gordon her sturdy faith. She wished Eppie had come, but Eppie had changed her mind.

"I'll be with you in spirit, honey," Eppie said while they sewed the parachute cloth into wings. "But I just can't abide confrontation. The more I think about it, the more I can't."

Between the shouts from the Phelps group and the singing,

no one heard the faraway rumble like a voice suffering from catarrh. The sound approached along the state road before turning onto the lesser county road to the cemetery, a procession led by a single state trooper on a motorcycle, followed by four volunteer motorcyclists riding two abreast. Ed's people. The somber hearse and two black limos followed, carrying family members, and then four more motorcyclists riding two abreast. Stretched out behind was a string of private cars conveying people who'd chosen to accompany the family to the gravesite. Two final motorcyclists brought up the rear.

Tyler noticed the rising dust, even heard the Harleys, the pitch and timbre of the Hogs cutting in over the shouts of the Westboro Baptist Church group. The earth seemed to vibrate. For the first time Tyler saw Ed smile. In a low voice he announced, "Here they come."

The Phelps group had advanced a few yards inside the cemetery gate, then a few yards more. Suddenly, the lot of them turned their heads and bodies toward the road. Seconds later the full metallic roar of the Harleys reached the counter-protesters, and the funeral escort turned and drove slowly, noisily, between the stone posts of the cemetery, drowning out the chants of "God hates the US army!"

Unable to contain himself, Aaron called out, "They're here!"

Slowly the motorcycles approached the grave site, moving at such a deliberate creep that Billie wondered how the men kept themselves upright. A collective sigh rose up from the group when the hearse turned off the road into the cemetery. The first limo followed, and then the second. Billie's knees trembled, her legs quaking under her.

"You okay?" Bud asked and put an arm around her waist and held her tightly.

"Until this moment," she said in his ear, "none of this was real. More like a carnival. That poor mother."

"Be strong, girl." Bud tightened his grip until she thought she was being squeezed by a boa constrictor, and a laugh popped out.

"If you don't let go, I'll faint from lack of air."

Bud chuckled his throaty *hehhehheh*. She felt briefly restored and not at all ready to collapse in an embarrassing heap in front of the children. Then again, maybe it wouldn't be a bad idea for the children to see a grown-up so moved by the death of a child she couldn't bear it. *Oh God*, she hoped Aaron never had to go to war. She hoped he never signed up for the National Guard or Reserves or any such nonsense. Once again her pulse raced and the heat rose and her legs weakened beneath her. A wet ball of sorrow pushed up, choking her.

Bud was smiling at her. He looked different for some reason, and she realized he'd put on his sunglasses. The sun beat down as the few remaining clouds drifted eastward. She felt the heat now on her arms and face. She ought to have worn a hat. Howard and Ed were waving their arms, exhorting the group to pull in and form a tight semi-circle between the Phelps people and the mourners.

"Shields at the ready!" Ed announced.

Bud snorted, whispering to his wife, "That guy needs to get a life."

The line of defenders stretched around grave markers, mumbling about "respecting the graves" and stumbling over the uneven ground in their effort to "tighten up." Those with shields positioned themselves in front. May looked up at her father with an eager expression, *Look at us!* Mei Lin's mother stood beside her daughter with a group of women. Tyler suddenly recognized Howie's ex-wife among that group.

Tyler leaned back and glanced at the Harringtons. Billie and Bud had pulled Aaron between them protectively. The boy was still all joints and skinny limbs, taller than his mother, and gaining on his father. After all these years Delia May still thought the kid walked on water. Tyler held his shield in one hand, then reached out and steadied his daughter's until she got a grip on it. Ed called out, "Link arms!" And they all squeezed close to one another.

Billie felt the pause, as if everyone had inhaled and held their breath. She counseled herself to remain calm, set an example for her son, and not worry her husband any more than she already had. Stand as resolute as the other shield holders and help the poor family get through this.

Then Ed shouted, "Shields open!"

There was a fluttery *shwooossh-ump,* as though thirty flimsy beach umbrellas had opened at once. The group cheered while a voice behind let out a triumphant yell, and then the group hushed itself—"the service...*shush,* the burial." From the front the Westboro people would see only tall panels of white cloth, one sail after another. Billie wanted to laugh out loud but dared not, hoping the line of cloth dampened the protesters' noise. She exchanged a thrilled glance with Aaron and then with Bud, while the Two Mays stood solemn as flag poles. From somewhere behind, the mezzo-soprano was still singing the hymn. Billie listened, aware that everyone around her was also listening, to the one pure voice rising up over the hate-fueled chants.

13

THE PRODIGAL

2005

"Can I drive in with you?" May asked. "The bus isn't fun without Aaron."

He would happily drive her to middle school as soon as he could work it out with Billie. May couldn't digest the fact that Aaron had graduated, worked for a year, and now attended KU, the only Harrington offspring with a scholarly bent. The day Aaron left home, with Billie's SUV loaded to the roof top, May had gone to her room and closed the door. When she didn't come out, Tyler went up to check. She was reading, with Maudie, stretched out on the bed beside her. He asked if he might come in and gingerly sat on the edge of the bed.

"You still have Mei Lin and Danny, you know. Besides, Aaron's only a few miles down the road."

"I wish I was old enough to drive," she said, folding her arms indignantly to stave off the sorrow.

Thank god she wasn't. He reached out and stroked the dog. "I suspect Aaron will be here often."

Her eyes teared and she pulled her legs to her chest and wrapped them with her arms. "Think he'll forget me, Daddy?"

Tyler smiled. "Not hardly."

But a new era had begun, marked by mood swings and frequent tears. Billie and Bud recognized the signs immediately. "The sensitive phase," Billie called it.

"But she's only thirteen," Tyler said, as if that could stave off the change.

"All those growth hormones in food," Billie said.

Even Howard weighed in. "A dreadful time! My ex threatened to send our youngest away to school. 'She can come home when she outgrows it.'"

Advice flooded in, most of it of little use. Tyler sifted through the received wisdom, saving what bits seemed relevant to May. There were days when she was constantly on the phone. Other days she used her allotted computer time sending emails. She did not suffer from lack of friends. Even the brainy Danny Patel remained steadfast. But Aaron was unique. Sui generis. Tyler often wondered who Aaron's friends were since he'd seen the occasional boy running through the Harringtons' yard or seated at the kitchen table. May was not always on his coattails but until now, Aaron was at least nearby. When May was younger, it occurred to him that Aaron was the sibling she didn't otherwise have. Now he was no longer available, and the loss hit her in ways Tyler had not foreseen.

The day Aaron drove off to Lawrence and May had left the company of adults to tend to her sorrow alone, he knew, unequivocally, that his attachment was so deep he might as well have provided the seed.

Now an eighth grader, the delicate 'bird bones' of her birth father and mother became apparent, if he remembered the girl correctly. May's hair remained curly like his, and dark, their eyes the same shade of dark blue; on this basis people thought them direct kin. He supposed Sherlynne Smith must have had blue eyes, but he couldn't remember. The one photo still in Bud's possession was black and white.

In early October, Aaron drove home on a Friday night—not for the first time—with plans to spend the weekend. Saturday morning May insisted on going to the Harrington's after breakfast, taking the dog with her. Tyler drove them down. When he returned, he went immediately to the basement to work out, fortifying himself for the day ahead.

He was flat on his back when he heard the vehicle approach the house. He glanced toward the small windows. The heavy tires of an SUV rolled past. An engine idled noisily and then stopped. He sat up, toweling off his face and neck, and then rubbed the towel over his damp hair. May would not return so soon. She'd be in BeeBee's kitchen, eating a second breakfast with the Harringtons, if eating were the right word. The child had turned fussy and picked at her food, honing her likes and dislikes. But Billie made cinnamon rolls, pecan and sour cream coffee cakes, and his daughter had developed a sweet tooth. Better a sweet roll than nothing at all.

With a grunt, Tyler lifted himself off the incline bench and climbed the stairs to the kitchen. His sweatpants drooped with moisture, and a V of sweat darkened the front of his T-shirt. He expected a knock on the back door or a familiar voice to call out before stepping indoors. Strangers went to the front door, not the back. He filled a glass from the tap and drank it down. Odd, the driver hadn't yet come to the door. Tyler gazed out through the back window, lifting the white lace curtain to get a better view. A black Jeep Cherokee sat in the yard, halfway between barn and house. The driver would know he was home by the truck parked near the barn. A man sat in the driver's seat, gazing straight ahead through the windshield. Then he tilted his head down as though he were looking at something in his lap. He wore sunglasses and a ball cap, but Tyler didn't recognize him. The man continued to sit motionless while Tyler gazed through the window until something passing for curiosity turned to impatience. The driver hadn't once glanced toward the house.

Tyler rubbed the towel over his face and hair once more and threw it over the back of a chair. He grabbed his windbreaker off the hook and opened the door. He stood on the porch gazing out at the jeep. The air smelled clean. House finches sang and flitted back and forth, from trees to feeders. In the side yard poultry cheeped and clucked while the scent of fermenting windfalls drifted down from the orchard, carried on a soft, steady breeze. He descended the step and crunched through the gravel toward the jeep. When he reached it, he tapped on the driver's window. Without turning, the driver touched a button and the window slid slowly down.

"Can I help you?" Ty asked. He wished he'd had time to take a shower.

The driver turned his head and smiled. "Maybe."

Mickey.

The two men stared at each other. A black chasm opened inside Tyler. How long had it been? Sixteen years? No wonder he hadn't recognized him. What hair he could see around the ball cap was clipped short. Mick had never worn his hair short. "The chicks like the long curls," he'd told Tyler more than once. His brother would be at least forty now.

"What are you doing here, Mick?"

"This used to be my home."

"Not anymore."

The smile faded from Mickey's face. "I thought after all this time we could talk."

A flock of sparrows lifted up from the row of junipers along the house. He inhaled deeply until the quivering inside abated.

"You might as well come in." Tyler pointed toward the house and turned back toward the porch.

Behind him, the jeep door opened and shut. He waited by the back door for his brother to catch up, opened it and let Mick in first. Mickey was expensively dressed: black designer jeans with a pink designer shirt. Around his neck hung a bolo tie—a western touch—the leather strings threaded through a large turquoise rock embedded in silver. The black leather jacket hadn't yet been broken in although the Tony Lamas lizard boots looked well worn. Against the posh clothing only the ball cap appeared ordinary, an Astros insignia above the bill.

"You live in Texas now?" Tyler pointed to the cap.

"Yeah. For quite a while. People I work for are moving up here. Branching out."

"Up where?"

"Omaha. I'll actually supervise a three-state area—Nebraska, Kansas, Iowa."

"What do you do?"

"Hard to explain. A complex business. I do personnel. Placing the right people in the right jobs."

Tyler took a mug off the cup tree and poured his first coffee of the day from a drip pot on the counter. Without asking, he placed another mug of coffee in front of his brother. Bowls of powdered cream and sugar sat on the kitchen table. He reached into the breadbox and removed three remaining cream cheese pastries he'd hidden from May.

"Looks nice in here," Mickey said indicating the room "You repainted."

"Several times."

"Exterior looks good too."

"I do it every four years. The weather's brutal on house paint. Dad used to complain. Remember?"

Mickey nodded. "You put in those cabinets, didn't you?"

"Made them too.

"You had the talent, that's for sure."

Tyler felt the hair on the back of his neck stiffen, prickling his skin, like the ruff along a fearful dog's spine. Mickey never noticed other people's things, or their environment, unless he coveted them.

"You didn't come back here to visit or make conversation. I don't mean to be rude, but that's not your way."

"It's been a long time, big brother. People change."

"Do they?"

"You did threaten to kill me."

"Under the circumstances, you might've done the same."

Mick hadn't changed. It took him less than a minute to place the blame on someone else. Without responding, only keeping his eyes on Tyler, Mickey lifted the cup to his lips and drank. He put it down and glanced around the room.

"You might be right about that. Been a long time. A lot happens in—what is it? Fifteen years?"

"Sixteen."

Mickey chuckled, newly confident. "You always were one for keeping track."

Tyler felt his blood rise, the anger hovering below the surface.

"Like I said, Mick. You wouldn't have come here unless you wanted something. So let's have it."

"I thought it might be nice to just visit before getting down to business. Catch up, so to speak. As a matter of fact, I was driving 70 when I thought to get off and see the old homestead."

"Highway 70 won't take you to Omaha."

"I was driving east from Colorado. Seventy will get me to I-29."

"Why not take 80? That's direct from Colorado."

"I was in Pueblo. Nowhere near 80. Aren't I allowed to visit my old home?"

"You visited once before, didn't you? About five, six years ago. You were driving a cream-colored Mercedes, if memory serves. Wearing a cream-colored Stetson to match. The Mercedes had California plates."

The smile spread across Mick's face, turning into a massive grin. Bud would have called it "a shit-eating grin." It was a calculated guess, and the fact it proved fruitful made Tyler feel momentarily light-headed.

"No one was to home," Mick said.

"Yes, we were. You left before I could open the door."

"Who's this 'we'?"

"Just a figure of speech."

Mickey's gaze traveled the surfaces of the kitchen, through the door to the dining room where he could easily see their mother's antique buffet, the middle drawer of which had once served as a crib, then meandered toward the basement door. As he measured the route of the gaze, Tyler's discomfort grew.

"You want a real breakfast?" Ty asked. "Eggs and bacon? Biscuits and gravy?"

The eyes stopped traveling, and Mickey looked back at his brother. His expression softened. He wasn't expecting a kindness.

"Nah, but thanks. I remember you were a good cook."

"Try to be."

Mention of May almost slipped out. If he was lucky, Mickey would be long gone before she returned. Tyler refilled both coffees and finally sat opposite his brother

"In case you're interested," Tyler began, blowing over the surface of the mug. "I still teach at Washburn-Shawnee High School. Jeff and Howard are still there—you met them—and Billie. She and Bud are doing well. Their son Aaron went to college this year. He's the youngest, if you remember, and the smartest. Their daughter Ginny married and divorced, with at least one kid. She's in Topeka. Wesley's up in Des Moines with a growing family. Anyone else you might know that I've forgotten?"

Mickey shook his head. Even if he never gave these people a second thought, he ought to know, Tyler thought. Force him to at least acknowledge the existence of neighbors who'd been a part of their lives.

"Sounds like everyone's all grown up and doing well," Mick said at last.

"Pretty much." Tyler nodded. What could he talk about if not May? Sherlynne Smith had told him that she'd never had a chance to tell Mike Mann she was pregnant. But Mickey had an uncanny sense of what was good for him and what wasn't. And he wasn't the sort to keep in touch. How many other little Micks had been planted in the Kansas soil and left to grow up unattended? Take and never give, although he did give a fifteen-year-old girl a child she couldn't care for.

Heart racing, Tyler leaned over his cup. "You don't remember a girl named Sherlynne Smith, do you?"

Mickey looked at Tyler, then upward, thinking, and shook his head. "Who is she?"

"Old student of mine," Tyler lied. "Some years back. She thought she knew you."

Mickey leaned back. "I knew a Cher once. Cher like the singer." He shook his head again.

Tyler watched his brother closely when he said the name. His face was blank, maybe puzzled at first but with no meaningful reaction: no tremor of nostrils or narrowing of the eyes, no hardening around the mouth. No comprehension. Mick had forgotten Sherlynne completely, even the name, unless Sherlynne had, briefly, called herself Cher. And now, still trembling inside, Tyler could not believe he'd asked. They drank in silence until the silence grew uncomfortable. "So tell me about this job," he said. "How long you been at it?"

"Several years now. My bosses are prosperous and they're branching out into other locales. I take care of some of the hiring. Like a branch manager."

"You like this job? It's been good for you?"

"It's been real good to me," Mick said with a grin.

The old brotherly concern had crept back without his permission. Sit with Mickey at the kitchen table—as if Ty had become their mother—and the old family feeling seeped in. Buried inside Mick's hurtful acts was the little boy he remembered before he'd changed, long before the betrayal with Nancy.

He felt incredibly hungry but wanted Mick gone, out of the house in his fancy duds and into his shiny new jeep. He wanted this brother, who'd turned forty behind his back, to drive out of his life once and for all.

"So what last thing can I do for you, Mick?"

His brother tilted back in his chair and laughed softly. No wonder women had once fallen for him: the dimples that appeared when he smiled, the eyes that grew charmingly small when he laughed, except Mick's teeth were no longer perfect, but yellowed. When Mick lifted the ball cap up to run a hand over his hair, Tyler saw how much hair his brother had lost, the hairline receded beyond his crown, the remaining hair thin and brittle.

"Something small. I have to carry around some valuable documents. I want a place to store them until I get set up in Omaha. Do you still have that old safe of Dad's in the basement?"

"I'm not sure it's big enough. But I've got my own safe in the barn."

"The barn?"

"My shop's out there now, completely weatherized. Got a pole barn for the hay."

Mickey eyed him with interest. "You're pretty handy."

"It's my job. I teach kids how to be handy."

"I remember Dad's shop in the basement."

Tyler's breath grew oddly shallow. Did Mick also remember the chisel and screwdriver he'd filched from that basement shop? "I moved it all out to the barn."

Mickey nodded approvingly. "I'd like to see it. Bet it's neat as a pin."

"I try. Come on."

Mickey was on his feet before Tyler had pushed out his chair. He would use the leisurely walk from house to barn to mull over Mick's eagerness. "So, your business partners—"

"—my employers. Wouldn't call myself a partner."

"I see. So they're legit?"

"Totally."

"Entrusting you with documents."

"Yes, which I need for my job. But I don't feel comfortable leaving the case in the car if I have to get out. And I don't want to carry it everywhere."

"But your bosses didn't feel uncomfortable having you carry the documents around in your car." He gazed at his brother whose eyes were narrowing. Never a good sign. "Wouldn't a safe deposit box better suit your needs?"

Mickey shrugged. "I'll get one eventually."

"So you'll go to Omaha and set up your—whatever."

"Office."

"And then you'll come back for the documents?"

"Right."

"You can see for yourself, this safe's also small."

Mickey turned away from him, continuing his appraisal of the shop.

"No problem, bro. In fact, the documents don't need to be in a safe. Just not in the car. They just need to be in a decent, dry place where I can get to them after I'm settled. And not necessarily on banking hours. See what I'm saying?"

He had to say it, let Mick know he was not in full accord with something off the boards. "I just want to know one thing, Mick. Are you putting me in danger?"

Mickey threw back his head and laughed. A brittle sound came out. "Nah. it's just that jeeps are thief magnets."

Then drive a different car, Tyler thought. "When would you be back for them?"

"Like I said, a week. Two at most. I keep the papers in a locked document box. Like a bulky briefcase. Someone would have to blow it apart to get in."

None of it made a lick of sense. "Sorry to say it, Mick, but this doesn't smell right."

Mick gazed at him and then glanced away. "I think you're being overly suspicious, and I don't know why." Mick sighed and returned Tyler's gaze. Tyler's eyes bore into him.

"I don't have a reason in the world to trust you," Tyler said.

Mick nodded. "I understand. But you're not giving me any credit for changing or for growing up. I now have a good job and I'm asking for a small favor since I don't yet have a home or an office. I'm only asking you to help out for a short period of time. Hell, I don't know anyone in Omaha. I honestly don't have anyone else to ask. Only some old pot-smoking buddies in Topeka—and I don't trust them. Two weeks, Tyler, till I can get settled. The case is a little heavy and it's useless to me until I get set up. This is a small favor I'm asking. And it'll be the last you'll see of me, I promise. Since that's the way you seem to want it."

"Follow me." Tyler led his brother across the shop and un-locked the interior door that led to the garage portion of the barn. On one side near the shop door stood a tall, sturdy metal cabinet where Tyler stored automotive supplies: cans of motor oil, brake fluid, chamois and sponges and turtle wax. He pulled

a set of keys out of his pocket and unlocked the cabinet. He
pointed to the top shelf.

"Will your box fit up there?"

"Perfect."

"I'll give you a key. You can come get it any time." He removed the key from the ring and handed it over.

"Thanks, bro. I'll get the case and be on my way."

Tyler remained in the garage while Mickey went out through
the shop to his jeep. A dank shadow of remorse hung over him
as he waited. He should have said no, but Mickey's appeal also
had the ring of truth. He suddenly saw himself as hard and
unforgiving in a way his father might have disapproved, even
though Mick's job sounded shapeless. When Mickey returned,
he was carrying what looked like a thick metal briefcase with
two combination locks. Mickey hoisted, then carefully slid the
case onto the top shelf, closed the cabinet door, inserted the
ordinary Yale lock, and snapped it shut.

"You don't have to come to the house when you return. You
can leave a note. Or you can phone. I got the same number as
we always had."

"Don't want to see me again?" The grin was not friendly.

"You're missing the point. I work in Topeka and I might not
be here." Tyler pointed to the smaller garage door at the end
of the dim barn. "You don't have to worry about the garage.
The little door's never locked. The shop is." He pointed to the
interior door. "I usually keep the truck outside."

The two men left the barn through that smaller door beside
the large double barn doors. Mickey headed toward his jeep
and Tyler followed. When he reached his vehicle, his brother
climbed in. Tyler took hold of the door, and for an instant he
caught his breath. He was allowing his brother to return to the
place his daughter lived. Their daughter. The words knotted inside him. He gripped the door of the jeep until his head cleared.

"I wish you the best, Mickey. I really do. But I don't want you
back here, except to pick up your item."

"I'd kind of hoped you'd gotten over your hard feelings."

There it was again, the blame. "I had good reason."

"I know. I just hoped we might put it behind us."

"Some things can't be fixed."

Mick leaned back in the driver's seat and stared through the windshield. "I was young and stupid and did a stupid thing."

Tyler stared at his brother. Mick's gaze was still focused away from him toward the barn yard beyond. This was as close to an apology as Mick had ever made. It came at him like a blunt object concealed inside a bouquet. His brother's expression was the most sober he'd seen all morning. Then Mick removed a pair of sunglasses stored over the sun visor and put them on, leaning his elbow against the open window. The dark glasses bowed away from his face. It was like looking at an enormous insect.

"Take care of yourself," Tyler said. He reached for his brother's arm resting in the window, then pulled his hand away.

"Thanks. I usually do."

Tyler stepped back and Mickey pulled the vehicle around, driving slowly down the long drive to the road.

He ignored the document case at first, never coming near the cabinet as if it were radioactive. But the longer it remained in the garage, the more disconcerted he felt. He kept the interior door to the shop locked, the exterior shop door as well. After a week he ventured in to check, opening the cabinet with the spare key. Mickey's metal briefcase remained on the top shelf. After ten days, he called the number that Mick had given him, but the number proved out of service.

A week later, Aaron invited his parents and the Mannings to come to Lawrence for Homecoming. Aaron had procured football tickets, and they could eat out after the game. Delia May could view his dorm cell, as he called it. When Billie phoned with the invite, Tyler readily agreed. May had already heard about the plans in an email.

At the back of Tyler's mind was the unfounded hope his brother might return for the case while they were gone.

The morning of Homecoming was clear and crisp with a few high clouds streaking an otherwise unblemished sky. The porch thermometer measured thirty-eight degrees, but it would likely warm up to the fifties. Before Bud and Billie picked them up, Tyler locked both doors leading to the shop, checked the windows of shop and house, basement too, and threw the deadbolt on the front door.

"How come you're locking everything up?" May asked.

"I usually do," he lied. "You just don't notice."

Like most people who'd grown up along the Old Stull Road, he had not been cautious or prone to lock up. Keeping a fence line secure was as close to locking up as he came. But it was a different age. Traffic had increased due to the lake. A year ago, someone had wandered up to the Harringtons late one night and walked right in through the front door. Bud, a light sleeper and armed with his shotgun, met the intruder in the front hall. When he pointed it at the man—a drunk who'd run his car off the road—the driver had slumped to his knees and soiled his pants. After the incident, Bud phoned Tyler and suggested he should start locking up. So Tyler dutifully threw the deadbolt on the front door and ignored the back. Anyone could pop that flimsy button lock in the back door or kick through the screen. When Bud beeped his horn and May rushed out the back door, Tyler reminded himself, yet again, it was time to install a deadbolt.

Since they would be sitting out-of-doors, the Mannings had bundled into layers, with gloves and caps and scarves that could be peeled away as the sun rose. They clambered into the back seat of Billie's Honda SUV, with Bud behind the wheel. Tyler didn't know why they didn't spend more time in Lawrence. He thought it an attractive town and certainly as close to them as Topeka, but their friends lived in Topeka. Lawrence had grown substantially in all directions, the same disconcerting sprawl that afflicted Topeka. As they traveled down the long Manning drive, Billie turned around and gave the Mannings an appraising look.

"Look at you two. You gonna break a sweat any second now."

They drove east, the sun in their eyes, the day falling open before them. Maples planted around farmhouses in the distance were turning scarlet and peach while locust and hickories, growing in the hedgerows, had turned a confident gold. It would be a good fall for color. As they entered Lawrence, the colors grew more saturated, especially the yellows, as if the leaves were made of butter. Until now he hadn't put it into words: October was the "golden month." The mood inside the car was buoyant. Tyler listened with half an ear to May teasing Bud about his KU ball cap and pinch-on earmuffs. There would be no need for earmuffs if the day warmed as he assumed it would.

"We'll pick up A-ron first," Billie announced.

She'd packed a hamper—a tailgate party, she said. Where they'd park for this picnic lunch remained unclear, for traffic into town had grown exponentially. They moved toward Aaron's residence hall at a snail's pace, the congestion worsening the closer they drove to campus, and they were left to ponder the absurdity of parking anywhere near the stadium.

"Let's get the boy first," Bud said. "We can worry about parking second."

As they inched along a residential street that skirted the university, May scouted signs in yards. "There's one for ten dollars!" Homeowners offered a spot in their yards for varying sums. Maybe we should reserve a spot, May offered.

"Boy first, parking second," Bud intoned. Eventually, the tall brick residence hall loomed before them, and Bud turned onto an entry drive.

"How can he stand to live there?" May exclaimed.

"Maybe he thinks it's exciting," said Billie.

Aaron had promised to be out front at eleven sharp, wearing his crimson and blue Jayhawk neck scarf. The group would then park, eat lunch, and walk to the stadium. May piped up in her new derisive voice.

"Will we be tailgating on someone's front lawn? Sharing our

fried chicken with another car parked three inches from our bumper?"

The disdainful, world-weary tone was a recent acquisition, and Tyler wondered how thirteen-year-olds became such scoffers. Certainly Ginny Harrington had been one, but he did not want his daughter to emulate Ginny. The cars in front blocked their view, and then May called out, "There he is!"

He looked like half the other young men swarming across the campus: pencil-thin legs encased in jeans, lank blond hair in need of a haircut, no hat. He'd draped the scarf around his neck like a sweat towel, his hands shoved deep into the pockets of a well-worn leather bomber jacket.

"Where'd he get that jacket?" May asked. "It's not Aaron at all."

What wasn't clear until they reached the curb was whether the tall, rosy-cheeked girl with a ponytail was with Aaron or simply standing nearby. A hush settled over the car. She stood too close to Aaron not to be a friend.

"Cozy, huh," Billie said in a near whisper. "He said something about bringing a friend."

"Did he mention a girlfriend?" Bud asked.

"Don't believe so."

May looked at her father and shook her head, mouthing the word *no*. If the girl with Aaron was no great beauty, she was attractive in a healthy-looking way. In Delia Manning's book, a great beauty was a liability while a pleasant-looking girl was not, especially if she dressed humbly and didn't put on airs, which is why she'd never approved of Billie. Delia Manning would have liked this girl. His own daughter, however, was struck dumb.

Billie opened the door and climbed out. Bud stopped the car and followed her, to the annoyance of the driver behind him. Aaron greeted his mother and father and introduced his friend. Tyler picked up the word "Linda." Then a shuffle began: May would have to perch on her father's knee to accommodate the young people, who proceeded to crawl up into the backseat.

May muttered her distaste at being moved around like a toy. Aaron pretended not to hear.

"Hey, Maypole!" Aaron grabbed her hat and gouged her side with a tickle.

"Don't!" she said, giving him a haughty look.

Aaron laughed, flung his arm around her neck, and gave her a squeeze, ignoring the dour face, and introduced her to Linda. If disappointment had an odor, Tyler thought, it would be of rancid cheese. The young woman greeted May and smiled, but May did not smile back and mumbled a chilly *hello*. He would have to speak to her later, a few words about civility. It wasn't the friend's fault, after all.

His daughter was not processing the afternoon in any useful way, and the hours filled with discomfort, even confusion. For the first time May Manning was consumed by jealousy, and not just the petty envies of a schoolgirl. Only when they walked through the gate and up into the stadium, only then did May seem to forget herself, caught up by the roar of the crowd and the band. Aaron had taken a girl on each arm, and May exclaimed over the size of the arena, the crowd. "Wow! It's huge!" Excitement filled the enormous stadium and his daughter as well. Aaron divided his time between his classmate and May, and whenever he turned away from May, Tyler could see in her face the fear slink back like a deformed animal.

Aaron and his presumed girlfriend declined to join his parents and the Mannings for a quick bite after the football game. One of his "buds" was having a post-game party. They'd promised to pick up a few snacks. The Harringtons took this in stride—Aaron would probably be home the next weekend, perhaps with Linda this time. The group said their goodbyes and climbed into the SUV.

"I thought that game was pretty exciting," said Billie.

"College ball usually is." Bud glanced into the rearview. "Didn't you love that band, Maypole?"

May hitched a shoulder. "It was all right."

"I liked the gymnasts," Billie said. "But what is it with cheerleaders? Booty shorts and big hair."

"Long hair, honey. Mostly in ponytails."

"What's the difference? There's so much of it."

Hair had become an obsession with Billie. In the last year Delia May had insisted on letting her curly hair grow, to Billie's displeasure. It was certainly not the floor mop Billie called it. It was attractive, Tyler thought, graceful in its length. For the first time, she didn't look like some little kid with a wild halo of curls. Then Billie turned and lobbed her question over the seat to May.

"What did you think of Linda?" She might as well have said, Whaddya think of my shoes? Tyler held his breath.

"She was okay," May said finally. "She likes horses, but she kept telling me about them as if I was six years old, in that Minnie Mouse voice."

"A-ron looks thin," Billie said, changing course. "Dorm food, I guess."

Bud vigorously shook his head. "Not true. He looks taller."

"What d'ya mean? You saw him two weeks ago. He's grown an inch in two weeks?"

"I suppose he's lost ten pounds in two weeks. I'm just saying he *looks* taller. I thought his weight was fine."

Off and running. The Bud and Billie Show. Tyler closed his eyes and leaned back into the car seat.

"What d'ya think, May girl?" said Bud. "Is our A-ron thinner or taller?"

"I don't know. I hardly talked to him. It was like I wasn't there."

Tyler opened his eyes. "That's not true. He spoke to you non-stop."

"He was speaking to his girlfriend too."

Billie laughed. "You just wanted him to yourself."

Tyler flushed hot. Couldn't she see May was surprised to the point of hurt? May gave Billie a dark look and flung herself back in the seat.

It was nearly 6:30 when Bud pulled the SUV behind the Manning house. May bounced out of the car and strode toward the backdoor.

"Could we be a little jealous?" Billie asked with smile.

"Live and learn," Tyler said irritably and climbed down, wishing his friends good night.

Once Ty closed the door, Billie turned to her husband and asked, "I just stuck my foot in it, didn't I?"

"That you did, babe."

"What is it I'm not getting here?" she asked and leaned her head against the window while he pulled out of the Manning drive.

Bud shrugged. "Discretion, Billie. You're not getting that."

Billie had her doubts that Linda was Aaron's girlfriend. Hadn't Tyler told her May missed Aaron in a big way, which didn't really surprise her? Even Aaron expressed concern about what his absence would do, and she hadn't been listening. Yes, she'd put her foot in it. *Speak in haste,* Daddy used to say, *and repent in leisure.*

May was standing in front of an open refrigerator door when Ty walked in. She looked at him and dramatically flung the door closed.

"He didn't tell me, Dad. Didn't phone or email. Why would he keep it a secret?'

"Maybe he was keeping it from his parents."

"I don't blab every little thing to BeeBee and Bud."

"Well, maybe she's just a friend. You know, nothing romantic."

"Are you blind? They were holding hands! He invited me to see his dorm room in his email, but you'll notice how that got overlooked. He was showing off! The nerd!"

She reached down to pick up one of the house cats and rubbed her face in its fur. Maudie lifted a paw in supplication. May leaned over and cooed at her, scratching the dog behind her ear.

"This doesn't mean you and Aaron aren't still good friends. I can tell Aaron thinks so. And you mustn't take it out on Linda. It's not her fault. I thought she was a horse-lover like you."

"Yeah, she had a pony once, 'when I was *your* age.'" May gave an unattractive imitation of Linda's reedy voice. Then the corners of her mouth drooped, her lower lip trembled. When her eyes suddenly glistened, she turned her face away.

"I'm going to my room."

She turned abruptly and left the kitchen with the cat in her arms, the dog padding faithfully behind.

Tyler picked up the phone and dialed the Harringtons. When Billie answered, he asked for Bud.

"Look," he said when Bud came on the line. "There's something I would have told you if May hadn't been in the car. Mickey paid me a visit not long ago. Left a briefcase in my care. He's moving to Omaha for a job, or so he says. Would you mind coming over?"

Soon Bud's truck crunched through the gravel of the drive and stopped near Tyler's back door. Tyler stepped out onto the back porch and indicated the barn. The two men walked across the yard in silence. Tyler went to the small barn door, entered and turned on an overhead light, which only made the barn garage seem more cavernous. Bud entered just behind.

"I don't want Billie to know this yet," Tyler said. "And Delia May most definitely not ever."

They trudged the length of the barn garage to the back.

"Does it sound right to you?" Bud said. "After umpteen years, your shifty brother shows up and wants to leave a valuable in your possession? I'm assuming it's valuable."

Tyler explained, even repeating Mickey's words, his reason for wanting to leave the case with Tyler, and then Mickey's plea for reconciliation.

"It's not that odd, is it? Wanting to make up with a brother?" Tyler felt conscious of how defensive his words sounded. "Even if *I* don't want to?"

Bud closed his eyes, sighed and shrugged. "I don't know. He's not my brother. But I don't trust him."

Tyler unlocked the metal cabinet and pointed to the top shelf. The briefcase remained where Mickey had put it. Bud pulled it down, whistling at the weight and then remarking on the two combination locks.

"My guess? He's got a lot of cash in here."

"Why me? He knows how I feel about him."

"Yeah, but he also *knows* you. Knows you're probably the most trustworthy person he knows."

"I threatened to kill him once."

"That was over fifteen years ago. So stop worrying, Ty. He'll come back and he'll take the case and he'll be gone. Look, I can't keep this from Billie."

Tyler nodded. "It's May I'm worried about."

"I'm betting good money he doesn't know your daughter exists."

14

THE DOCUMENT CASE

It was Tyler's custom to place a bowl of hedge apples and pine cones in the center of the oak dining table. The room went generally unused until May started middle school. She wanted to do her homework at the dining table so that she had easy access to her father, who might be in the kitchen or in the computer room or relaxing in the living room with the television turned low. She would call out with a question or simply read aloud something from a text: "Dad, listen to this!"

His colleagues might marvel at his ability to attach a cabinet to a wall, even more so to build it, but he did not. Being within sight and sound of your own kid—that was the marvel. As May stumbled over the rocky ground of her thirteenth year, through moods that changed at lightning speeds—sweet one moment, sour the next—the dining room table remained an anchor. To encourage her, he allowed her to leave her schoolbooks and papers scattered about, never rebuking her for the clutter. A thinking mess, he told himself. Creativity could be messy.

Telling Bud about Mickey's visit had brought him some relief, but not entirely. He assumed Bud had told Billie, which did not worry him. Neither would ever bring Mick up in front of May.

Aaron returned home the weekend after the Homecoming trip. May postured in a bored voice that she wasn't at all interested in whether *A-ron* was visiting or not. Tyler was ironing a rack of permanent-press work shirts that May had forgotten to pull out of the dryer. He listened as if she were rehearsing lines from a play.

"If he stops by, fine. If he doesn't stop by, that's fine too. What-e-ver."

Whatever? He could not think of a more meaningless expression. She wanted to punish Aaron, rake him over the coals before allowing him to stand in her pure and radiant presence. The wounded friend. The trouble was Aaron hadn't a clue he'd hurt May. He was just being exuberant Aaron. A good deal like Bud, Tyler thought, except Aaron seemed also to have acquired Billie's conscientious genes. Tyler had been Billie's companion from the time they were toddlers. Now his daughter was repeating the behavior as though there was a genetic marker predisposing the Manning offspring to one of two behaviors: complete loyalty or none at all.

Uncle. Tyler grimaced and rested the iron on its plate. He'd thought of himself as May's father for so long, the word *uncle* had vanished from usage. To May he had always been *Dad.* He exhaled in a single burst of air and picked up the iron. The five o'clock news droned in the background, and he glanced up from time to time, giving it his loose attention. Like a teething pup on a shoe, his mind could not stop gnawing on that insinuating word or the complex relationships inside his house.

The phone rang and May answered. He muted the TV. Aaron, evidently. Her answer sounded as though an invitation had been extended. May feigned disinterest, luring him like a trout. "No, I can't come now. Daddy's putting dinner on the table and I'm helping him… No, I can't ride my bike later, fool. It'll be dark… Yeah, I guess I'll see you next time. Have a nice visit."

Followed by a shameful yawn. Helping? His daughter was idling in the kitchen while he ironed the shirts she had left to wrinkle.

Perhaps it would dawn on her to perform her one task before dinner, currently in the oven. In what school did women learn to be so coy? He suppressed the urge to laugh.

"Delia May?" he called out. "Set the table, please. Dinner at 5:30."

With a great spatter of gravel and squealing brakes, Aaron arrived in Bud's truck. Tyler was putting away the ironing board when Aaron knocked on the back door. May let him knock twice before opening, greeting him in her new jaundiced voice: "Oh, hi. It's you."

How long was she going to continue this act of indifference? Tyler turned off the TV and walked into the kitchen. "Did you invite Aaron to join us?" he asked.

"Oh. Well, I thought he'd rather be with BeeBee and Bud." The bored drawl returned.

"Aaron?" Tyler pulled another set of utensils from the silverware drawer, another plate from the cabinet

"Sure," the boy answered. "That way I can bother the Maypole."

May shut her eyes. A melodramatic sigh rolled out. "I've been meaning to talk to you about that."

He wondered if she'd continue in that nasal tone if she knew how unattractive it sounded.

"I don't think *Maypole* or *Tadpole* is an appropriate name anymore. Especially in public. I'm not five, you know."

"So what would you prefer?" Aaron asked.

"How about my *name* name?"

Tyler put on oven mitts and removed the casserole. May had allowed the water to evaporate from the boiled carrots and potatoes he'd asked her to watch. Where had his eager helper gone? Tyler thought her prickliness had more to do with not having Aaron nearby. The girl was floundering.

"Bread?" he asked his daughter.

She got up with a flounce and fetched it from the bread box. She flopped the entire plastic-wrapped loaf on the table and dropped into her chair with a toss of hair. Tyler bit his lip.

"You know we never do that. Get the tray, please. And the butter."

May sighed loudly and rose with conspicuous languor, retrieving the bread tray and butter.

"You look like you should be eating more bread and milk," he said to the boy. "Your folks think you're too thin."

"He's always been scrawny," said May and eyed Aaron spitefully.

Aaron threw back his head and laughed, elevating himself in Tyler's esteem. To avoid a scene Tyler placed the bread on the tray himself and put the desiccated potatoes and carrots in a bowl, adding a spatula full of casserole directly onto each plate before passing them around. If Delia May sighed one more time... She was leaning on one elbow, spooning food into her mouth as though she'd tossed out the table manners he'd so carefully taught her.

"Sit up, please."

"I'm really not hungry tonight. May I be excused?"

"No. We have company."

"Aaron's isn't company."

"Yes, he is, as long as he's in our kitchen. Besides, I'm glad to see him even if you are not."

She sat up straight. "I didn't say I wasn't glad to see him. I just said I wasn't hungry."

Aaron gave her a plaintive look. "Mom wanted to ask you all to come back with me for pie and homemade ice cream."

The Harringtons had probably eaten at five, which meant this was Aaron's second meal of the evening. Tyler felt a rumble of mirth travel up the pipeline. He cleared his throat.

"If May wants to join you after dinner, she has my permission. I'll give your folks a call."

"You're not coming, Ty?"

A plea for help. How was Aaron to navigate around this surly stranger without help? The mirth continued its passage upward. He smiled at the boy. "I'm behind on a project. Otherwise I'd come."

The mention of dessert held May's attention. If he stayed out of it, perhaps the two kids could find their way through to some understanding. Right now, Aaron hadn't a clue why May was sighing and insulting and generally behaving as if she didn't care a lick for her friend of a lifetime. What he would like to tell the boy was this: the adored companion of her childhood had let her down by moving to Lawrence and acquiring a girlfriend. This, and only this, was the cause of her discourteous behavior.

She was, in fact, besotted. Hal Manning had once offered Ty a word of solace under similar circumstances: "Son, women know how to give vent to their feelings, which scares the hell out of men. Best not to take too much to heart."

The conversation threatened to die from lack of sustenance. Tyler asked Aaron about his university classes, glancing from time to time at his daughter. She poked her fork through the chicken casserole, shunning the veggies and salad, and brought a bite or two to her mouth, giving Aaron surreptitious glances. But he would not break the rules governing mealtime protocol for the sake of her adolescent snit. She would treat Aaron as a guest and nourish her body, or she could stay home. He looked at her as more food made its way to her mouth.

Aaron leaned across the table. "Thought you weren't hungry, Miss Delia May."

"I was until you came. You made me lose my appetite."

Aaron threw back his shaggy blond head and roared with laughter. "Still quick on the draw, huh, Tadpole. Oops!"

"I don't know about that, A-Ron. Oops, so sorry. I don't know but one of your hoity-toity friends."

"You know one? Who's that?"

Tyler inwardly cringed, wishing to warn the boy away from the subject. Delia May gave Aaron the stink eye.

"Weren't we just there to visit? And weren't you accompanied by a *friend*?"

"Oh, you mean Linda. She's my roomie's girlfriend. You didn't know that?"

"You hold hands with your roommate's girlfriend? Pretty good friends, I'd say!"

"So? I've held your hand too. Does that mean we're waltzing our way up the aisle?"

May squealed with laughter and let her fork fall to her plate with a clatter. The pressure building up inside Tyler leaked slowly out—a thread of steam from a canner.

Through the rest of the meal, the boy offered up a steady banter of predictable anecdotes: tales of eccentric professors, idiot TAs, snotty out-of-state students. May did her part, making suitable noises and murmurs of support. Tyler had heard the stories before. They were the laments, disguised as humor, of every farm kid who'd gone away to university and been made to feel a rube. By the time the meal was finished, the dark mood had lifted and Aaron rose to help clean up.

"I'll get it," he told the youngsters. "Stay where you are, Aaron, and keep talking. We've missed your stories."

When May got up to load the dishwasher, conscience struck, he hoped, Aaron followed, handing her the rinsed dishes to be put in the washer. Tyler dealt with the leftovers and told the children to go while there was still daylight. He needed to get to his workroom.

"Your mom will understand." He turned on the porch light and held the back door open for the chattering teenagers. When he closed it behind them, he leaned his head against the frame and muttered, "Yes!" The case of the disappointed—and sullen—daughter could be put to rest for another evening. He turned on the little radio, perched on the windowsill, and listened to the country music station while he scoured the scorched saucepan and washed the casserole dish. How light he felt now that May had recovered from her dark mood. Yet each new hurdle knocked him off balance.

When May first arrived, Billie had mused over his sudden fatherhood. "Now you'll know what it feels like to be humbled." He didn't understand why she felt compelled to say this. He was painfully aware of his shortcomings. He was shy, often stubborn, sometimes clueless, and a perfectionist in his work. But arrogance was not among the faults that came to mind. He did not lack self-confidence, only the ability to promote himself in the manner currently in favor. If you were good at what you did, and at ease with that, what need was there to flaunt yourself as if you were advertising an Italian suit? Yet Billie was right in one respect. May challenged every confident fiber in his being. Some days he pondered whether parenthood had strengthened him or made him weak.

He walked across the farmyard to the barn shop and flipped on the lights. He left the shop door open and got down to work on the new cabinets. He didn't mind the coolness. The day had been mild and the chicks were murmuring in their coop. His two rebel hens had flown up to roost in the branches of the dogwood. He had to trust they were high enough to escape the predations of coyotes or foxes. He'd installed motion lights on the house facing the yard to warn off predators, but loose dogs were not so easily deterred. The shop grew chilly. Tyler went to close the door when he heard an approaching vehicle. It was too early for Aaron to be bringing May home. She would stretch the bounds of her curfew until nine o'clock when Bud would shoo her home: "Bedtime, little girl." But his daughter often stayed up reading until all hours. How had it come to pass that he'd nurtured a night owl?

Tyler peered into the gloaming. A jeep crawled around the side of the house, its lights out, creeping slowly to the far edge of the parking pad near the barn and behind Tyler's truck. The vehicle had not activated the motion lights, and Tyler made a note to add more lights at the corners of house and barn.

Tyler checked the metal cabinet a few days ago, and the case was still there. The driver parked the jeep but no one emerged. Tyler's breathing slowed until he was holding his breath. The door finally opened and Mickey stepped out, bareheaded. For the second time, Mick's balding head came as a surprise. The kid wasn't so handsome without the hair, nor was he even a kid. Mick fussed with something on his belt, under what looked like the same leather jacket he'd worn three weeks before. He stood beside the jeep and looked in the direction of the house, where the kitchen and porch lights shone. Tyler grew uneasy until his brother walked around the jeep, opened the passenger door and removed something from the glove box. A flashlight, he guessed by the shape. Tyler found it odd that Mickey hadn't noticed the shop lights. Then again, maybe he had. Tyler waited.

Slowly, Mickey walked toward the garage end of the barn and opened the smaller door. Tyler moved quietly across the shop to the door that led to the garage. He stood near it and listened. Footsteps crossed the length of the garage, faint at first and then louder, boots scuffing against concrete. A key ring tinkled. The unoiled hinges of the cabinet door opened with a muted squawk. In his mind's eye he saw his brother reaching for the document case, and then he heard it—the scratch of a heavy object pulled along a surface. Mickey grunted. He had taken Mick at his word that it contained documents—papers, contracts, files. Bud had not, making some joke about bullion and cash. Now he felt a stab of fear, convinced now that the case was filled with contraband.

The silence stretched out. He imagined Mick kneeling on the floor, examining the contents of his case. Tyler wavered and then swiftly unlocked the shop door and flung it open. The open shop door flooded the garage with light. The open case and flashlight were resting on the floor, with Mickey crouched over them. Mickey flipped the case shut before Tyler could see.

"Jesus Christ!" Mickey jumped up and reached for his waist.

"Come on into the shop."

"You scared the shit outta me!"

"You didn't see the shop light?"

"You made it clear you didn't want to be bothered."

"Since I'm here, you might as well have some light."

"It's okay now. I need to leave."

Mick snapped the case shut and picked it up, moving with tentative steps into the bright shop. Tyler locked the door behind him. The fluorescent lights of the shop were unforgiving, and Mick looked colorless, his face worn and creased. What remained of his once sandy hair looked dry as twigs, and the recessed hairline made him look older. Lines were etched around his eyes and mouth. Mick had not seemed so aged when Ty saw him before, but today everything about him looked spent and eroded by the wind of a dry country. He remembered the boy with no callouses on his hands, with lush wavy hair, the boy who burned easily in the sun.

"Got a coffee pot in here," Tyler said. "Would you like some?

"No…thanks."

"Mick, that phone number you gave me—"

"—I'll give you a new one once I'm settled."

"You're not settled yet?"

"I have a place but I'm not moved in. You know?"

Tyler gazed at Mick, disbelieving each word, then walked to his work bench and took a recipe box off the shelf above, removed a business card, and handed it to his brother.

"I had these made up back when I was doing a lot of residential carpentry. There's an email address on it too."

Mickey looked the card over and briefly flashed the familiar smile. "And a cellphone. You're getting modern, man. Thanks." His brother slipped the card into his back pocket. "I probably won't be bothering you."

"Maybe not, but it might be useful to know how to reach each other."

Mickey nodded and let his eyes travel toward the open door and into the dark beyond. There was nothing left to say, and Tyler felt as if an invisible hand was closing a book.

A heavy engine made its way up the drive, moving rapidly, spitting gravel. Mickey flinched and reached for the inside door, pulling on it before realizing it was locked. Tyler went to the outside door to look. Bud's truck was turning past the corner of the house and into the yard, stopping with a jerk near the back door. Aaron piled out and ran around to the passenger door to help May. His daughter climbed down slowly. Tyler gingerly closed the door. His brother's face was knotted with fear, and he'd flattened himself against a shadowed wall.

"Who is it?" Mick whispered.

"Just the neighbor kid. Aaron Harrington."

He wanted the children to go straight to the house and stay there. His heart pounded. The kids were laughing, and Mickey cocked his head. Even with his back to the door, Tyler could discern their voices growing louder as they approached the shop. They'd seen the lights. Aaron had probably thought he needed to tell him May was safely home.

"Daddy?" May called out.

He glanced at his brother whose face had taken on a quiz-zical expression, mouth slightly ajar. The kids stopped halfway, and May's voice sang out again.

"There's my girl," she said. "There's my Maudie!"

The dog had evidently come out through the dog door to greet them. Now maybe they'd go to the house. Instead, they arrived at the shop.

"Dad?"

Mickey's face twisted into something resembling a smile. The kids pulled open the door and shoved into the shop.

"Whose jeep?" Aaron asked. He didn't see Mick standing in the dark.

"Kids, I want you to meet my brother, Michael. Mick, you knew Billie's boy Aaron as a toddler. And this is my daughter May."

The young people stared at Mickey, a ghost from an old photograph. The dog scratched at the door and whined. May reached back and let her in. Maude ran to greet Tyler, saw Mick and froze. Her spine arched and the hackles rose. A low growl emanated from the back of her throat.

"It's okay, girl," Tyler said.

"Come, Maude!" May commanded but the dog did not budge, placing herself between May and the stranger, and barked once. "Guess she doesn't like you."

"That's 'cause she doesn't know me," Mick said gamely. "She's a pit, isn't she?"

"No, actually, she's an American bulldog." May spoke in an aloof tone Tyler had not heard before. "People confuse the two breeds."

"Didn't know you had a kid, Ty. You hiding a wife as well?"

"I'm his only family," May said.

"Well, you look like a Manning," said Mickey. He hadn't moved out into the light. "You resemble both your grandparents."

"I think I take after my dad." She moved over and took Ty-ler's hand.

The tight band squeezing his chest loosened slightly. "No wife, Mick. Just May."

If Mick was expecting an explanation, he'd have a long wait. Aaron seemed stunned into silence. Tyler turned to the boy. "Thanks, A-ron. How're your folks?"

"Mom sent back some pie. I left it in the truck."

"Why don't you kids go up to house? I'll join you in a moment."

Mickey remained frozen in the shadows. May stared at him, her face stony. So intent was her gaze that Mickey eventually moved his eyes away from hers to Tyler.

"Go on." Tyler gestured and walked them toward the door. The young people left the shop, and the dog followed. Tyler watched. They walked across the yard, stopping by the truck to let Aaron remove a container and then continuing up the steps and into the kitchen. He turned to his brother.

"You're gonna have to explain this one," Mick said. A tentative smile had replaced the puzzled expression.

"It's a short and boring story. I'd like to lock up now."

Mickey seemed to return to himself, picked up the case and flashlight and stepped out of the shop. Tyler shut off the lights and locked the door. With the kids gone, the curiosity that had come over Mick's face drained away. Tyler wanted him off the premises. "I got the feeling you were in a hurry," Tyler said.

"I am. Maybe when we're a couple of old men," Mickey said, "we can sit down and have a beer. And you can tell me about your mysterious private life."

"If I told, it wouldn't be private."

Tyler pulled himself up to his considerable height and stared at his brother. Mickey laughed nervously and shifted his weight. The hunted look he had worn, when Tyler first flung open the shop door, had returned. Mickey walked in a nervous stride toward his vehicle. The band around Tyler's chest tightened once more, and his breathing grew shallow. He followed his brother to the jeep and stood like a wall between Mick and the house, his arms folded.

Mickey climbed into the jeep, hoisting the document case into the backseat. For an instant his jacket swung open, revealing the gun and holster. So he'd been right after all. Whatever Mickey was doing was under the radar, which shouldn't surprise him, but the gun did. He couldn't remember Mick ever showing an interest in firearms. He certainly had no interest in hunting. Mick turned the key and the jeep rumbled to life. Then Mick looked at him and raised his hand in a faint-hearted goodbye. Tyler raised his hand as well, but the look on his brother's face troubled him: sorrow was not an emotion he associated with Mick. Tyler stepped back as his brother turned the vehicle around and drove slowly away. He walked to the corner of the house so he could see the jeep turn onto the road. When Tyler finally climbed the porch steps, he felt weighted with stones.

The kids sat without talking at the kitchen table. The dog lay beside May's chair while May stroked the large tabby perched in her lap. Tyler pulled out a kitchen chair and sat down. May lifted her face.

"Isn't your brother coming?" Aaron asked.

"No."

"So that's the man," May said in the same hard voice he'd heard in the shop.

"Yes, that's Mickey if that's who you mean."

"Heard lots about *him*," Aaron said in a soft voice.

"That's not what I meant," May said. "That's the man who got my mother pregnant."

Tyler stared at her.

"I saw Bud's picture," she said.

"Can you explain, please?"

"Aaron showed me. The photo of your brother and the girl who is my mom."

"And what was Aaron doing with something that didn't belong to him." He gave Aaron an angry look.

"I found it in Dad's drawer," Aaron said, dropping his gaze. "He asked me to go fetch something and I found the photo."

"And showed it to May, not considering how it might make her feel."

"Daddy, you're behaving as if I don't know anything."

"Perhaps you need to tell me exactly what you do or don't know, and I can fill in the blanks."

"I know it *all*. You're the one who told me! I know *that man* is my birth father and *you're* my birth uncle, and no one seems to know squat about my mother."

He felt as though he'd been slapped. No one spoke, and the silence lengthened out into a painful barrenness that made him want to scream.

"He looks different," Aaron said at last.

"The photo is older than May," said Tyler.

"He could be prosecuted for sex with a minor," May said with disgust.

"True. But you're forgetting something."

"What am I forgetting?" Her eyes were wet.

"Your beginnings might seem undesirable, but there are many people, including the ones at this table, who would be very unhappy if you weren't here."

The children stared straight down at the table. Slowly, May rose and left the room, the dog following behind. Tyler reached over and gave Aaron's thin shoulder a squeeze.

"'Bedtime, buddy boy.'" Bud's expression.

"I did a bad thing, huh, Ty?"

"Not really. You just took me by surprise."

"She's known forever," the boy said, sounding so young.

"I know. But until Mickey became flesh, he wasn't real to her."

Aaron nodded.

He couldn't tell whether the boy understood fully. You never knew these days. He'd never been savvy the way the kids nowadays seemed to be. Even after his stint in the navy, where he had learned his own capacity for rage, he still did not fully understand his brother. He'd been derailed by hope, by wishful thinking. By that time there was so much physical distance between them it hardly seemed to matter, until he met Nancy.

Aaron stood up and Tyler rose with him.

"The pie is in the fridge," Aaron said.

"May and I will eat it for breakfast." He patted the boy on the back and walked him out the door.

Aaron got in the truck, retracing the route Mickey had just taken. Tyler locked both the flimsy screen and door. He checked the kitchen and turned off the lights, climbed the stairs to the second floor and tapped on Delia May's door.

"Can I come in?"

He awoke to the sound of grinding metal. He'd been dreaming about the school shop, something involving a giant piece of equipment he didn't quite recognize or know how to use. He lay on his back without moving, his eyes open, trying to sort out the source of the noise. The metallic sound devolved into the cough of an engine. He rolled off the bed and went to the window and parted the curtains an inch. There was no light to speak of, no moon to offer a glimpse, and he waited for his eyes to adjust. Across the barnyard, near the garage, two shapes rose out of the dark, eventually resolving into large vehicles.

He dropped the curtain and pulled on jeans, shirt, slippers, and removed a handful of shotgun slugs from the drawer in the bedside table. He dove into the closet and grabbed the Remington stored in back, then left the bedroom and crept toward the stairs. No one stirred in May's room. Not even the dog had alerted them. He clung to the railing, the gun in his left hand. The yellow glow from a nightlight in the downstairs half bath spilled across the hallway. In the gloom its light seemed as piercing as a strobe, guiding him through the dining room and into the kitchen.

Gingerly, he parted the curtain on the kitchen window. The vehicles were parked near the barn garage. One appeared white and loomed through the darkness like a misshapen elephant. He guessed them to be jeeps, like Mick's, and for a moment he wondered if Mickey had returned, with company. For what, he couldn't guess. Light from a flashlight winked across the window inside the shop. Tyler felt a flash of panic. The vehicles were too expensive for this to be a couple of kids on a lark. The light pulsed around the shop and across the windows again and briefly silhouetted a figure. Tyler waited, pressed between wall and window.

He had no notion of time gone by when two men emerged through the smaller garage door. *The door is never locked, Mick. You can get your case any time.* He glanced across the yard. The outside door of his shop remained shut, so they must have broken in through the interior door. Outside the building the two men appeared to be conferring, but he couldn't hear voices. Then one man walked toward the house. Tyler pushed four slugs into the magazine. Soon enough the approaching man triggered the motion lights that flooded the yard. The man froze. The lights brought the approaching man into focus. The one behind called out something in words Tyler couldn't understand. Spanish, he thought.

He heard the click of nails on linoleum. Before he could stop her, Maude ran through the dog door and out on the porch, barking her head off. The man closer to the house reached under a jacket. Tyler swung the backdoor open and fired a warning shot into the air. The man lingering by the jeeps yelled, "*Vamos!*" He then jumped behind the closest vehicle. In a flash the dog leaped onto the approaching man. Man and dog fell to the ground and rolled in the dirt, the man yelling and pulling while the dog snarled savagely, firmly attached to his wrist. The gun hung useless from his hand as the dog gripped more firmly and pulled the bloodied hand back and forth, back and forth, until the gun fell to the ground. The man screamed and rolled to his side, straining to reach the gun. The man in the distance reached into the jeep, and Tyler fired a second shot. The vehicle lurched and the door swung ajar and the distant man fell back, yelling in surprise.

"Daddy?"

He hadn't heard her come down.

She stood in the doorway, a perfect target.

"Get to the basement now! No talk!" He swept her toward the basement.

He stepped off the porch, shotgun pointed.

"Maudie! Off!"

The dog did not turn. She'd tear his arm off, and Tyler strode toward the unarmed man on the ground, his shotgun pointed at the other man crouched by the jeep. The gun remained in the dirt and Tyler kicked it sideways. It skittered, spinning, across the yard and under a shrub outside the perimeter of light. He grabbed the dog's tail and forcibly yanked her off, the man screaming in pain. He now pointed the shotgun at the man on the ground.

"Up!" he yelled.

The man tentatively raised an arm. The gun hand remained limp, blood streaming from it.

"*Vayamos!*" his partner yelled.

Tyler turned and fired a third shot into the dark vehicle. The jeep rose into the air as if taking flight and then sank down onto a flattened front left tire. The standing man ran the few yards and leaped into the white jeep. With a roar, the engine came to life. With Tyler's attention distracted, the man on the ground rolled over and scrambled to his feet, stumbling frantically toward the vehicle. The dog strained to be released, and Tyler gripped her collar. When the passenger door swung open, the white jeep was already in motion. The fleeing man grabbed the door frame, hung there precariously until he managed to pull himself in. The realization he had only one shot left dampened the urge to fire. He wanted them gone, not stranded. Two crazed men, armed and dangerous—no, he would not fire at all. The jeep swerved perilously close to the corner of the house. The driver overcorrected, and the vehicle careened to the left, off the gravel track and onto the grass lining the drive. Tyler ran back to the porch, the dog on his heels.

"Inside!" he yelled at the dog, shoved her indoors with his foot and slammed the door, just as a shot rang out. He heard a muffled thud as a bullet hit wood. The jeep left behind at the far edge of the yard looked suddenly ludicrous, a giant camel kneeling drunkenly to one side. The occupied jeep, engine rumbling, tore down his drive, weaving from side to side, and headed erratically for the county road amidst a shower of dirt and gravel.

He thought the slug had hit a porch post or a fascia board under the eave. He'd barely gotten a look at the man on the ground. The bill of the ball cap shadowed his face in spite of the yard lights. Mexicans, he thought, and young. He'd never be able to pick him out of a lineup, and he hoped the dog had shredded his arm. He needed more lights in the yard, more of everything—lights, locks, sirens. A great fury washed over him. If the man had reached the house, Tyler thought he could have torn him limb from limb. All he wanted was to raise his child peaceably in their country home without a couple of gangbangers, or whoever they were, breaking into his barn and firing shots at his house. And Mickey! He should have killed his brother while he had the chance. Nancy could have watched.

For a moment he thought his head would explode. *May!* Tyler ran down the basement steps, the dog at his heels. His daughter had dragged an apple crate over to one of the high windows and was looking out. How much had she seen? He was suddenly horrified.

"Is Maudie okay?" she asked. Her face was white.

"Yes. And so is your father."

She burst into tears and launched herself at him. He folded her into his arms.

"Who were those creeps?" she asked when she finally stopped sobbing. The dog sat quietly, waiting for recognition.

"I don't know, but I'm sure we'll find out."

She held up her cellphone. "I phoned 911 and Bud. He said he'd call the Feds. Those were his words. *The Feds.*"

She saw the dog at last and fell to her knees beside her. "Maudie! You're our heroine!"

He suddenly began to shake. What might have happened

swamped his mind in lurid color—dead dog, dead man—and he felt suddenly faint. He did not want her to see him this way and turned toward the basement steps. He heard her behind him, climbing the stairs to the kitchen. Before they reached the top, the phone rang. Tyler answered, and Bud began speaking at a rapid clip. They'd heard the shots.

"You all okay?"

"There's a shot-up jeep in my yard, a bullet hole in my porch, my daughter's scared, and I'm mad as hell... Yes, we're okay."

Within minutes the Harrington clan stood in his kitchen, Bud proudly toting a hunting rifle with a complicated scope and wearing his faded camouflage jacket. Tyler stared at the get-up. Was Bud hoping the thugs were still here? He couldn't tell whether Aaron was shocked or thrilled.

"What's the world coming to?" Billie said with disgust. "Nothing, but nothing has scared me more."

She didn't look scared. She looked as she always did—in control. She crossed the kitchen and put her arms around May, who clung to her. "I want the two of you at our house tonight."

"Only if I can bring my pets," said May.

"Drug people," said Bud, spitting out the words. "You don't know what they're likely to do. Come back and burn your house down."

"Nice talk, Bud!" Darts flew out of Billie's eyes. She motioned toward May with her head.

"I doubt very much they'll be back," Tyler said. "They know the law will be here."

The law arrived belatedly but in large numbers: state troopers, KBI, and a man purporting to be a federal drug enforcement officer. Even someone from Homeland Security phoned the house, informing them that Immigration was also taking an interest. How many times did he have to tell the story? How many stony-faced men had to cross-examine his daughter with their blunt questions and blunt faces, frightening her? When two FBI agents arrived, at some ungodly hour, the KBI men bristled. In the fullness of time Bud could be heard in the kitchen, muttering to the Kansas agents, "What a bunch of pricks!"

The abandoned jeep proved useful as did the slug lodged in his roof. It was a rental car from Dallas but the renters' names, although Spanish, were probably bogus. Nor were there any prints. Was the man on the ground wearing gloves? Tyler couldn't recall until May piped up. "Yes."

"The cartels are moving in," one of the FBI men announced solemnly while the KBI officers glanced at each other as if to say, *And this is news?* When the federal agents left, the state officials were free to joke at their expense and console Bud with their own opinions: "Fucking credit-takers. Notice how their heads swing? They're looking for the TV cameras."

Tyler finally got to his shop in the wee hours of the morning, still shaken, accompanied by state troopers with their crime scene people, while a relentless Bud dogged their heels. Nothing was missing. A few drawers stood open, a few tools tossed aside and shelves rearranged. Inside the garage the metal cabinet where Mickey had stored his document case had been left ajar. Nothing the intruders disturbed had been locked—except the shop doors—and no significant damage was detectable, except the psychological wound. The intruders had an object in mind, and so did Tyler. His anger rekindled. He'd never been able to accept that Mick had no moral compass. Mickey didn't care that he'd put his own brother in danger, and still he'd been unable to accept this.

"You're lucky they didn't check out the house," a young trooper said.

"My, my," Bud drawled. "Isn't that a comfort?"

An eyebrow rose.

"They were coming," Tyler said. "One of them was approaching the house when the dog and I intervened."

Remembering the intervention made his stomach heave. He hadn't fired a weapon in two years, when he'd taken Aaron squirrel hunting with their 22s.

"Got any ideas what they were looking for?" one agent asked.

"Yes." And so he told them: his brother's document case. Not knowing what was inside made him feel foolish.

The following afternoon, Tyler and May, who'd had little sleep, were invited to an office in Topeka where they pored through a thick book of mug shots. How many times had he explained? It was dark and no moon. His motion lights were barely adequate. He reminded them there was no ambient light in the countryside. The brief look he got of the intruder Maudie attacked was obscured by his ball cap. The man was wearing jeans, a jeans jacket, and the ball cap. Sure, he would try, but to no avail. And they could forget about the second man. He was only a voice and a shape, outside the circle of lights. They should look for a Mexican with a torn-up hand.

In silence he turned one page of mug shots and another and then another as he grew increasingly impatient. It was futile. Pointless. Then to his astonishment, May reached over and pointed to a face.

"Him."

Tyler and the officials leaned over the photo. He looked like a teenager, definitely a Latino.

The FBI officer nodded and sighed. "Yup…Sinaloa Cartel. They've established a presence in Chicago, we believe. They're sending the young ones up. Probably recruited in Nuevo Laredo or Southern California. Probably even a legal resident of the US of A."

"But they spoke Spanish," Tyler said.

"So does half the Southwest."

The mug shots were compliments of federal marshals in Texas. The agent said no more until they were about to leave when he added, discouragingly, "We'll probably never find him. Probably home by now."

After another bad night on Billie's couch, he woke with a jolt. The other gun.

"I'm going back to the house," he announced to a household scarcely awake.

His daughter's face was so crumpled with worry he couldn't bear to look at her. Hadn't the troopers suggested they stay away from the house? Billie asked. Yes, but he needed to have another look around since he wasn't sure the crime scene people had found the pistol. He was positive he'd told them the man on the ground was armed. The crime scene folks had fussed over the shot-up jeep, which had been towed away, and pored through the garage and shop, dusting for prints. But nothing was done in the yard. "Too dark, tomorrow," they said. Well, it was tomorrow, and nothing was said about a gun.

He parked his truck beside the porch and went to the barn for the rake, stepping over the yellow crime scene tape. He poked around the rose bushes and shrubs, lifting up small branches with the rake head, finally pulling the FN-57 out from under a thick juniper. The chunky ordinariness of it gave him a chill. He'd never been this close to a semi-automatic handgun. Hopefully, he wouldn't encounter one again. He raked it into a paper bag, wrapped the end tightly, put it on the porch, and dialed the authorities.

Enough of officialdom. Today he was moving back into his house. From now on he would keep the shotgun under the bed.

15

An End and a Beginning

May remained at the Harringtons, in Ginny's old room. Since Aaron had returned to Lawrence, Billie and Bud were more than happy to have a child in the house. Tyler alone would guard the homestead where even the house cats seemed skittish. At the Harringtons, Maudie never left May's side since May was too upset to attend school. Billie put up with the dog without comment. May expressed her dismay over the separation, loudly and often: "Why is Dad sleeping over there when I have to stay here?" He knew she was upset, but what choice did he have when it was a matter of ensuring his daughter's safety?

"What about your safety?" Billie asked him when the child was out of the room. "She's a kid with one parent. You fill in the blank."

Nothing more would happen, he felt sure. What kind of fool would return to the scene of his crime, especially one where the intruder had been harmed through his own carelessness? Still, he couldn't convince Bud of this, and Bud influenced Billie. He should at least spend the night at the Harringtons, they advised. For May's sake.

A week passed before the issue was resolved. The two KBI agents of their acquaintance arrived at the Manning residence at six in the evening. Billie and Bud happened to be in his kitchen, cleaning up after a meal designed to allow May guarded access to her own home. The child had taken both house cats and the dog up to her room. The adults had just sat down for a final cup of coffee when they heard the car pull up in the front. Bud glanced over at Tyler apprehensively, and then his wife, while Tyler got up and went to the hall. Through the narrow panel of glass he saw the agents climb the porch steps. He opened the door before they knocked.

"We think we've located your brother…"

For a long minute Tyler stared at them. "You know it's him?"

"We found your business card in his pocket."

He became aware he was holding his breath. He turned to get the Harringtons, but they were behind him, standing in the dining room doorway.

"I'll come too," said Bud. Billie would stay with May until they returned or phoned. The little girl needed time in her own home.

Tyler glanced back at the agents for reassurance. The designated talker nodded. "You'll be safe now. We'll go into detail downtown."

As dusk faded into twilight, he followed the agents in his truck, down the drive, onto the gravel county road, and west on 442. The county had improved the Old Stull Road over the years, but the short trip to Topeka had never seemed so long. Bud stopped talking as soon as he started the truck, which made Tyler uneasy. The steady patter of Bud's voice was the most reliable feature of his company. Tyler felt abandoned to his own imaginings that soon became sharp objects bumping against the thin lining of his skull.

They were escorted into an office and sat. One agent eased himself into a large chair behind a tidy desk while the other remained standing. The seated man pulled a folder from a file drawer and placed it on the desk. Was anyone going to speak or was it all a mime show? Tyler's temper rose in direct proportion to his fear. Photos were pulled out as well as typed reports, documents with small photos clipped to them, all of which he was forced to view upside down while the agent sorted through, deciding what to show him and what not to. The agent finally cleared his throat, leaned forward slightly, and looked up: Michael Manning, a.k.a. Mickey Mensa, a.k.a. Michael Monroe, a.k.a. Mike Mann had been found in his Jeep Cherokee. Unfortunately, the jeep had been submerged in Clinton Lake, and

Manning had been shot several times. The agent slid photos of the jeep across the desk. Tyler recognized the license plate. Then the agent slowly slid across the desk a photo of the ve-hicle with the door open and an arm protruding. Tyler blinked. He couldn't wrap his mind around it. Nothing appeared real. He might as well be looking at photos of dead gangsters from the 1930s.

"Some guy camping in the primitive area heard voices and saw two men push the jeep off a boat dock. The jeep drifted and sank. The camper was a bit alarmed, as you can imagine, and didn't phone till morning. He said you could see the roof beneath the surface of the water."

Bud leaned forward. "Where are your FBI buddies? Thought this was a federal investigation."

"They're working on it," said the agent with the high-pitched voice. "They like us or the troopers to contact the family."

"So they can keep their hands clean," Bud muttered.

The agent shifted his weight and the chair squawked. He turned his attention back to the photos on his desk and then to Tyler. "We're assuming it's your brother."

The trembling began inside. Leaning toward the desk, Tyler clasped his hands and held them between his knees, out of view.

"We need to ask you to identify him."

They sounded tentative, dragging it out, turning the inter-view into a soap opera. Tyler stood abruptly, startling the man behind the desk.

"Okay. Where is he?"

The drive to the coroner did not exist in any timeframe he knew of but in some parallel world, as though they were walking down corridors without time where the minutes on his watch had stopped. Bud didn't leave his side and began a narrative intended to distract until they reached the cold room that neither man wished to enter. Tyler could not remember a word of what Bud said, only the reassuring purr of his voice like a reliable motor. Finally, the agent opened a door, and they walked in, the agent following behind. An attendant in a white lab coat escorted them across this space to a huge cabinet with long, heavy drawers and yanked one out. Tyler's eyes blurred. A moment passed before a shape came into focus. Mickey was not shrouded. He was not cleaned up or improved. He was soiled and stained, a piece of meat on a rolling tray. Nor did he look bloated like people he had seen who were drowned. Puzzled, Tyler said this to the agent.

The agent replied, "Most likely he was dead before he entered the water. Killed elsewhere."

He was wearing the leather jacket, jeans, and a dark shirt, all discolored by the lake. There was a hole in Mickey's forehead, above one eye. There were other holes in his torso, but Tyler could not bear to look closely at them. His knees buckled, and Bud grabbed him before he hit the floor.

"Whoa, man!"

The agent yelled at the attendant to get a chair. He heard voices overhead, crows in the trees. When he regained his senses, he was sitting with his head between his knees. He didn't know how much time had passed before he spoke aloud. "That's him." The agent turned to Bud who nodded. Blood swirled through Tyler's head, blocking his hearing. He shook his head slightly to clear it, as if dislodging water from his ears, and looked at the agent. "Did you find a document case in the jeep?"

"No, but we have a good idea what was in it. Manning made off with thousands of dollars and a few drug samples. You don't do that to those boys and get away with it."

"That case was in my garage for three weeks. He came for it some hours before my intruders."

"Well, they found it all right."

"He said he was sent here to set up a new branch of some business."

"Probably, but he never checked in. He was also supposed to help plug them into the US meth trade. They assumed he'd jumped ship. With their funds."

Tyler steadied himself and stepped toward the shelf containing his brother. It wasn't Mickey, only the husk. Mickey was elsewhere, gone on to whatever reward he'd earned. Tyler felt an urge to touch the dark hole above Mick's eye, as though he might rub it away like a charcoal smudge, clean the forehead, brush Mick's hair back into place. He shut his eyes and the dizziness returned while he gripped the edge of the morgue shelf. Bud put a hand on his back for support.

"Some people are just born bad, Ty. Mick falls in that category."

Ty could never bring himself to believe that. Were people born bad or made so, somehow? That was the only explanation that made sense.

What was the word one of the FBI guys used? *Sociopath?* But the agent was talking about the whole culture of drugs and the people in it. *Thugs and sociopaths.* Tyler had suspected a connection long before Mickey dropped off his document case, back when he'd appeared like a ghost driving the pale Mercedes. The suspicion was confirmed the night Mick retrieved the case: the way he jumped when Ty opened the shop door, the look on his face when the kids drove into the yard, then again when he saw his brother's gun.

"I'm finished here," Tyler said, turning to the agent. "When can we have the body?"

At least he could put Mick to rest in the plot beside their parents. Mick wouldn't be disrupting his life again, or anyone else's. The agent said something about a mandatory autopsy and then they could release him. *Release him?* Tyler gave the man a blank stare. Mick wasn't a kid who'd just spent a night in a city jail on a DUI. He was dead, murdered. Tyler turned toward the door, his back to the agent.

"Anything else you need from me?"

"Just a signature."

Bud insisted on driving home, and Tyler felt too depleted to object. Throughout the drive he tuned Bud in and out like white noise, both a distraction and an accompaniment to his thoughts. He sorted through the words he might use to tell May and Billie until the words collapsed into a meaningless pile. Suddenly they were turning off 442 onto their own county road, and Tyler pulled himself up. The ride felt as though it had lasted five minutes, and now he would have to face the women. Bud cleared his throat. You had to give the women some credit, Bud said, because they surely knew what had happened. Tyler turned and looked at him.

"It's May I'm worried about. That guy in the morgue was her father."

Bud glanced over but didn't speak; he pulled the truck behind the Manning house and parked near the porch. Tyler reached for the door handle.

"Wait a sec," Bud said and flung out his arm to stop him. "Mick was *not* her father except in the most basic way. Did he even know?"

"That he'd fathered a child? I doubt it."

"So let's just leave it at that. Your brother is dead. Period."

"Yeah, but she knows."

Bud cocked his head and his eyes narrowed. "You told her, just like that?"

"Not just like that. We all gave her clues, and she put them together. Besides, your son showed her the picture of him and Sherlynne Smith. The one you took off her."

Bud's mouth fell open and puckered into a stiff O. "Jeez! How'd he get his hands on it?"

"You tell me." Tyler opened the door and stepped down, striding around the front of the vehicle to the porch.

Billie was in the living room knitting with the TV on, the late news playing softly in the background. Bud followed Tyler into the room.

"Well, did it make the local news?" Bud asked.

Billie gave him a puzzled look.

"Stop right there," Tyler said. "It's a federal investigation. It may not make the local news."

"Keep May away from the TV," Bud said.

When the men sat down, Billie put her knitting aside and lifted the remote. The TV blinked off. Tyler clasped his hands, leaned toward her, and told her all he could. Should they stay? Billie asked. *Oh yes!* Every onerous task of his life as a parent had been made less so by the Harringtons. But perhaps they shouldn't wake May.

"She's awake," Billie said.

The three adults looked helplessly at one another. Billie had just offered to get the girl and bring her down when they heard her footsteps on the stairs.

Tyler gave Bud a helpless look. "What do I say?"

"Only what you need to."

The girl walked into the room, the dog at her heels. Tyler stood and smiled at May. She sat in the rocking chair, and the dog plopped down at her feet.

"We need a little nourishment," Billie announced and retreated to the kitchen.

Tyler's shoulders drooped with relief. He knew better than to start without her. Then Bud moved in—water seeking its own level—striving mightily to entertain the girl with descriptions of the KBI agent with the high-pitched voice, the other one with the slight lisp, the broad desk and squeaky chairs of the office, lavishing his humor and scorn on any worthy detail. May listened guardedly as she moved the old rocker up and back, up and back. The urge to protect was muddying Tyler's head, interrupting any logical sequence of thought. The corners of her mouth lifted, for Bud had not stopped performing.

Billie returned with a tray laden with cookies, coffee, and hot chocolate with marshmallows afloat. She placed the tray on the coffee table and distributed the beverages. No one spoke or drank. The hot mugs remained firmly clasped as if they were only hand warmers. Tyler finally returned his to the tray and leaned back on the sofa. *Now or never,* he told himself. May was staring at him. The words he'd so haphazardly rehearsed on the ride home were now marshaled on his tongue and when he opened his mouth, they walked out.

It was after midnight when the Harringtons left. When he finally stretched out in bed, his daughter in her own room, he wondered if he would ever get to sleep. He had not yet switched off the bedside light when May tapped on his door and asked to come in. He got up and put on his robe. She lingered in the doorway a moment until he waved her in, along with the dog. He pointed to the bed and she sat on the edge of it while he sank wearily into the little bedside chair.

"I've wanted to know something for a long time," she began.

He waited. The dog hopped up on his bed beside her, and Tyler bit his tongue. She hesitated, unable to ask, and kneaded the corner of the bedspread.

"It's okay to ask, May. You're entitled to know."

"Did your brother know who he was?"

Was there ever a more loaded question? It took his breath away. If she meant, did he know who he was, in a philosophical sense, he would have to say *no*.

But that wasn't the question she intended. He waited for her to frame it.

She continued to knead the quilt. "Did your brother know he was my father?"

"He never said so. And Mickey was the sort of person who let you know what he knew."

"So he never knew about me."

"Probably not. We never kept in touch. For years no one knew where he was or how to reach him. Then he pops up when he needs my help. That was typical."

She wasn't listening, or more likely, only listening to the parts that involved her.

"Do you think I look like him?"

"You have his chin and dimples."

"You have dimples too."

She pointed at his left cheek where his one dimple might emerge if he ever smiled.

"Would he have wanted to know me if he knew who I was?"

He stalled, unable to find the words that might, decently, convey Mick's selfishness. She never knew him, and so his character would be only an abstraction. He didn't know how to explain to a protected thirteen-year-old the wretched behavior of adults. Nor did he know how a child could feel abandoned by a person who never figured in her life.

"But he didn't know about you, honey. There's no way I can answer that."

He didn't want to tell her that Mick would not have wanted to know her if it entailed any effort or debt.

"BeeBee and Bud don't like him," she said.

"Neither do I. Mickey did some terrible things. He did only what he wanted, and if anyone got in his way, too bad. He put our household in grave danger. Remember that, May."

She peeked at him through her bangs and then looked away, stroking the dog that remained comfortably stretched out on his bed—the first dog ever allowed on his bed. Now that Mick was dead, he wondered if she would immortalize him in some teenage way, turning him into a "misunderstood" icon like Jesse James or laud him the way some folks lauded William Quantrill—now there was a sociopath—as a Civil War hero. Clearly she was toying with the fantasy that if Mick had known about her, he would have taken an interest and loved her as a daughter. The dismaying thought of losing her to a dead criminal filled him with panic. The familiar chasm opened up once again.

"If I remember, you didn't have a high opinion of him when you met him in the shop," he said finally. A calculated risk.

"He was alive then."

"So?"

"I feel sad for him now, in a way."

He gazed at her. What a horror this pity was! It was the compassion of a little girl for a stray dog, except in this case the dog was a jackal. He felt helpless to navigate around that.

"I feel sorry for him too," he said, "because he didn't know you as I do."

She glanced at him again.

"He missed out because that is what he *chose*. He *chose* to miss you when he got your mother pregnant and then left her. He *chose* never to find you, if he even knew. And I *chose* to make you the most important part of my life. We all make choices, Delia May. But I made the better choice and have never regretted it. As far as I'm concerned, I'm your father, not Michael. And in case you haven't noticed, I love you."

He'd said too much, and now she was crying. He moved swiftly to the side of the bed and held her, murmuring words of consolation and encouragement until she fell asleep, the dog at her feet. He pulled the covers over her, turned out the light, walked out of the room and down the stairs, curling up with a blanket on the living room sofa.

16

Memorial

In the house down the road, neither Harrington was able to sleep. They lay side by side, staring toward the ceiling.

"What did he look like?" Billie asked.

"Dead."

"That's not what I meant."

"An older version of the Mick we all knew. A balding guy with a hole in his head."

"How awful," she murmured.

"Why? He stole from a drug cartel and thought he could get away with it. That's dumb, if you ask me."

Billie sighed. "That little girl may just turn him into a hero."

Bud reared up onto one elbow and stared at his wife through a gloom lightened only by the digital clock. "How so?"

"Adolescent imaginings. Once someone's dead you can always polish them up. Poor misunderstood Michael."

"Whoa! No one in our family or hers thinks Mick was anything but a shit. Not even Aaron. What he did to Ty was totally unforgiveable."

"But we've all spent the last thirteen years keeping the whole truth away from her. Protecting her. Now we're going to pay for it."

Bud threw himself on his back and, with a great show of disgust, folded his arms across his chest. "That's crazy talk, woman. She's smarter than that."

"We can only hope."

She reached down and pulled the tossed covers over them both.

Tyler slept fitfully on the uneven couch until it was time to rise

and go to work. At six-thirty he phoned the high school office
and informed them, again, he would not be coming in—a death
in the family. By the time he'd phoned May's school with a similar message, morning light had gilded the picture window, and
he opened the drapes to a cloudless day. He had no plans to
wake May and went to the kitchen to make coffee. When she finally emerged, it was after nine, and he heard her padding down
the stairs. She stood in her pajamas in the kitchen doorway with
disheveled hair and puffy eyes.

"Did I miss the alarm?" she asked in a forlorn voice.

"No. We're on compassionate leave. We'll go back to school
after my brother's buried. And if anyone asks, you can tell them
your uncle died. Period. Okay?"

She nodded and sagged into a kitchen chair. The calico
hopped into her lap, and she sat back and focused her attention
on the animal. In time she lifted her head and said in a voice
now fully awake, "What's that saying BeeBee always uses, Dad?
You've got enough on your plate."

He smiled and cracked eggs into the skillet for breakfast.
"Sounds like BeeBee. Yeah, we've got enough on our plates."

The state released Mickey's body on Friday. Tyler had made the
necessary arrangements, and the funeral home would have the
sexton dig a hole in the family plot in the Watson cemetery, a
village halfway to Topeka, where his mother's people were laid
to rest. The space would only need to be large enough for the
urn containing Mick's ashes. They would place the urn early the
next week. Something in Tyler recoiled against the thought of
Mickey's bullet-riddled remains residing in the earth. At least
ashes were clean, as though burning could make his brother
pure. There would be no service. He didn't know how to me-
morialize a man who had neglected his own family time and
again. He wasn't sure he could endure some distant neighbor,
who knew nothing of Mick's adult life, telling him what a sweet
little boy Michael Manning had been. His own feelings were
unsettled except for the trace of hostility, which he would not

realize until years to come was the body's way of forestalling grief. The two Mannings would gather at the grave site and if the Harringtons chose to be there, too, he'd welcome their company.

He was washing dishes after dinner on that Friday when May approached him. "You're all alone now, aren't you, Dad?"

He turned and looked at her, his hands dripping soapy water. He didn't feel more alone than at any other time in his life. Nor was it proper to say he was all alone. He told her he didn't feel lonely since that is what he assumed she meant.

"I mean, you don't have any other family left," she clarified.

"What're you talking about? I have you."

A smile flickered. "I meant no parents or brothers and sisters. You know."

"Losing your parents is sad, but it's natural. It happens to everyone. And Mickey and I weren't close. Besides I have you and my friends and my work. I don't feel lonely. Never have." He chose not to remember the months after he'd lost Nancy. Anger had allowed him to survive the full brunt of his loss. As far as he was concerned, anger had preserved his life, even if it had made him lousy company. As for selling the bungalow, so many years had passed that he could no longer conjure up that sorrow.

When May was perhaps six, something the child was doing made him think of Nancy after years of not thinking of her. The little girl had come home and put Maudie in a kitchen chair and an uncooperative cat in another in order to play school. She was so engrossed in her play teaching, her voice trilling out the lessons she'd just learned, that Tyler felt his spirit lighten and lift and float above the kitchen as if he were watching his daughter from above. He knew then he'd finally let Nancy go. You couldn't feel this much lightness and still harbor bitter thoughts. The resentment was gone, and life was good even if Nancy wasn't in it. Then something May, the little school teacher, said to Maude made him burst out laughing. May had turned to him and said, "What's so funny, Daddy?"

He gazed at his daughter. She was a young lady now, the

buds of her new breasts visible under her T-shirt, her face more sculpted and less childlike.

"But," he said gently, "I could use a hug."

His daughter stepped forward and wrapped her arms around his waist.

Aaron volunteered to pick up the urn. What a task for a boy, Tyler told Billie.

"He's not a boy," she reminded him. "He's a university student of nineteen."

Aaron would bring it along with his parents to the cemetery on Monday. Tyler was happy to have another day away from the classroom and the staff room. Even though it made no sense, he felt the need to get Mick in the ground before his workmates asked questions or offered their condolences. There had been a news report, something lurid on a late-evening broadcast, but the name had been withheld "until notification of next of kin." For once he was grateful for an official lie. The Feds were eager to keep it under wraps until "further investigation." When he asked if that meant they were going to seek Mickey's killers, he was met with a wall of silence and realized nothing more would be done. They were working on "a larger canvas." The once obscure picture became clear: Mickey was only a sidebar in a wider drug investigation. They didn't care about justice for one small crook. Mickey may not have been a decent man, may even have been a dealer, but he was not a killer, Ty thought. Yet two killers, men far more cold-blooded than Mick, had ended his life. There would be no closure for the family of Michael Manning, and Tyler felt an unexpected flicker of indignation on his brother's behalf. "Even a thief deserves better," he told the Harringtons.

Aaron decided the two families should ride together. After he made the trip to pick up Mickey's ashes, he returned home for Billie and Bud and on to the Manning homestead.

"Why waste gas?" he told his parents. "One car is more ecological than two."

Bud turned toward his wife sitting in the backseat and gave her a look but refrained from comment. Billie suppressed a smile while a balloon of pride inflated inside her.

It was mid-November and cold. October had been a blessing of mild and sunny autumn weather, but the temperature had dropped on Halloween, the first hard freeze of the season. The day would warm up, Tyler thought, but at noon when Aaron pulled into the yard, the porch thermometer read thirty-nine. Everyone was bundled into jackets and knit hats and gloves. The Mannings joined Billie in the back seat of her SUV, Aaron behind the wheel, Bud beside him. Aaron had placed the urn on the passenger floor near Bud with instructions to his father to take care of it. The Harrington parents anchored the conversation in the platitudes of weather, and Tyler tuned them out. May appeared lost in thought until she pointed and said, "Look."

An Osage orange stood out amidst a tangle of hedgerow trees like a barren Christmas fir laden with large round ornaments. The pale green fruit clung to the leafless branches, so many of them that the Mannings stared at the tree in wonder. He and everyone he knew had always called the fruit of the Osage orange "hedge apples." There were farmers in the area who could still point to hedgerows made up entirely of Osage orange, boastful that they'd never had to build a fence between fields because of this impenetrable barrier. Not a single head of livestock got through it. The thorns that grew along the bark were daunting, a lesson he'd learned in boyhood, to his sorrow. And the old wives tale that a hedge apple under your bed kept away spiders wasn't a tale at all. When he told Delia May, she insisted he put several under her bed.

His father had told him how Osage Indians would travel a hundred miles to find the tree the French called *bois d'arc*. The wood was so dense it made the best bows. FDR had the "hedge apple" planted throughout the prairie as a windbreak tree. Some WPA project, his father explained. Millions of trees in 30,000 shelter belts over nearly 20,000 square miles. Tyler thought he might come back later and ask the farmer if he could take a few of the fruit off the tree or the ground. Green hedge apples in a colored bowl were a pretty thing.

Aaron turned onto the unpaved track leading to the old cemetery. When Delia married Hal Manning and moved across the county line, you'd have thought she had done something bold and undesirable, like moving "back East." But her family had reserved space for her in the small cemetery near the tiny town that bore their name, and she in turn had made sure there was room for her husband and boys. In a youthful fit of pique, Tyler once told her he didn't intend to be stuck in the ground of the cemetery. He wanted his ashes scattered across the Pacific. He hadn't anticipated her shocked response. He was on leave from the navy and had observed the claustrophobic atmosphere in his mother's kitchen. A pampered Mickey hunched over the funny papers while he ate his breakfast, as if his mother had completely neglected Mick's table manners, while his father took refuge in the barn.

First Hal, then Delia, now Mickey. For the first time, when he thought of his family, no anger tainted his feelings, only sorrow.

Aaron parked the car a discreet distance from the path that would take them to the plot. Further down, a man in a truck drank coffee from a thermos. The sexton. Tyler stepped out of the car and raised his hand in greeting. The man waved back and nodded. Bud climbed out and removed the box of ashes at his feet. Aaron led the way and May ran up to join him, taking his hand. Side by side, the Harrington parents followed Tyler toward the family plot. Billie thought the kids looked like a young couple, and she wondered if she ought to be concerned. Probably not, since May was still a little girl trying to be a big one.

An odd little hole had been dug in the ground, and at the sight of it Tyler gasped. Alarmed, May turned back toward him.

"Daddy?"

"I'm fine, honey."

The group positioned themselves on one side of the grave,

opposite the small pile of dirt. Bud stepped forward and laid the container of ashes at Tyler's feet. The group stood silently waiting. Finally, Tyler bent down, picked up the box, and stepped toward the grave. He stooped onto one knee and lowered the box into the hole, then slowly rose. The children stepped forward unexpectedly and dropped artificial flower petals into the hole before scattering them around the general area of the grave. He wondered if this was May's idea, or perhaps Mei-Mei's.

The children stepped forward again. "Let's join hands," Aaron said.

The adults shuffled awkwardly together in a line, a child on each end. The young people moved them into a small circle around the tiny open grave.

"Who's going to pray?" Aaron asked. "Mom?"

It would be me, wouldn't it? Billie thought and cleared her throat. Thousands of mealtime graces flitted through her head. But this was not to be a prayer of gratitude but of sorrow and rest. What was it preachers said about ashes to ashes and dust to dust? If she used the words, they would sound ridiculous. Maybe her words should take the form of a narrative, and not something as biblical as prayer. And so she remembered the first story of Mick she could think of, his difficult entry into this world and his struggles through it, and what a pretty child he'd been at the age of three. When she was finished she said simply, "We hope and pray that Michael has now found some peace and that You will look over and protect him." *Amen.*

They dropped their hands and without a word walked slowly back to the vehicle, the children taking the lead. Tyler veered off and made his way to the man in the old Ford truck. He removed an envelope from his pocket. At least the ground had not yet frozen. The sexton opened the truck door and climbed down. He shook Tyler's outstretched hands. As he did so Tyler slipped the envelope into a pocket of his insulated coveralls, murmuring, "Thank you. We're done here."

The group in the car was unnaturally quiet until they reached the Douglas Country line when Billie opened her mouth and the reminiscences began. "Ty, do you remember when Mickey was born?"

He did. It was a difficult birth. "Mickey had colic."

"What's that?" May asked, and Billie explained.

"Mother told me something else I'll never forget," Billie went on. "She told me to keep it to myself but I don't have to anymore. If you remember that colicky period, you know your mother hardly got a lick of sleep. Up all night with the baby. Catching a few winks when you or Hal would help out. I know you helped because Mother said so. Your mother hadn't slept for a month, besides suffering from postpartum depression."

"What's that?" May asked, and again Billy explained.

"Mother thought Delia Manning never did get over the depression. Anyway," she continued, speaking hurriedly, "so the story goes, Hal found your mother one early morning, bent over the crib. He'd gone into look because Mickey had finally stopped crying. Instead, he found Delia pressing a pillow over the baby's head. Hal grabbed it away. Mick looked a little blue. The babe blinked at him and sucked in a great breath of air. Hal knew Delia was half-crazed from lack of sleep. All he had to do was look at her eyes, her face. A horrible moment for both parents. Plus the guilt over nearly suffocating her newborn."

Startled, Tyler leaned toward the front seat. "She did what?"

Billie went on. "My folks were of the opinion Delia pampered Mickey out of remorse, trying to make it up to him. No one knew but your parents and mine. And mine only knew because Hal told Dad. It scared the bejesus out of Hal, walking into the nursery and finding his wife trying to smother Mickey. Hal wanted to take Delia to the doctor, at least get her some sleeping pills, but she'd have none of it. You know your mom, Ty... Didn't your dad ever tell you?"

Stunned, Tyler realized his mouth was ajar and closed it. He couldn't answer, and the silence grew uncomfortable until he spoke. "No. This is the first time I've heard of it." His voice sounded unnatural.

"I'd have thought Hal might have told you so you might understand why Mick seemed so privileged. Mother also wondered if Mickey's brain had been deprived of oxygen during that incident, you know? What your mother never grasped is that she'd pretty much ruined three lives, if not her own."

"She didn't ruin my life," Tyler said "She just made it uncomfortable. Same for Dad. Especially uncomfortable for Dad. But I'd have to agree she ruined Mick. Maybe her own."

"Phooey! Nobody's ruined once they're an adult," Bud said.

Billie shook her head. "Delia kept her oar in long after Mickey was twenty-one."

"Well, that's his own damn fault," said Bud. "And Mick began thieving as a little kid."

"They say kids thieve when they want their mother's love," Aaron said, offering up his new learning. "They're stealing her love."

"For god's sake, boy!" Bud burst out. "Where do you get all this?"

"Just a theory, Dad. Settle down."

"Listen to him! The professor."

Aaron jabbed his father lightly in the side.

"I know that theory," Tyler said in Aaron's defense. "But the mother is usually cold and unloving, which doesn't describe Mom. Mick was stealing from Dad and me. Not Mom."

"Does that mean Mickey wanted *your* love?" Bud asked with scorn. "*Hal's* love?"

"He already had mine," said Tyler.

"Just proves my point," said Bud. "Born bad."

"We're home," May announced. She'd grown skittish the longer the adults talked.

Aaron parked in the Harrington's drive.

"We're having a midday dinner," Billie said. "And lots of dessert."

She gave May a wink.

May was unusually quiet when they finally returned home. In a moment he'd inquire if she wanted to watch a movie or read a book together, but May asked to use the phone. Tyler left the house to check on the poultry and then wandered across the yard to the shop. He wanted to go inside, to know it was there, a space so thoroughly restorative it gave him strength simply to stand in the room or touch the workbench and admire his tools. Muddled thoughts clarified themselves in the shop, as if carpentry were a form of meditation. Certain concerns involving May had been forming of late. Except for the hens and the few head of beef cattle in the back pasture, he had no other stock. He wondered if she would like to care for a couple of rabbits or a pony or burro. She spoke a great deal of animals and lavished the housecats and Maudie with attention and nursing. She and Mei Lin volunteered at one of the shelters near Topeka twice a month, although May enjoyed this considerably more than her friend. She was ready for more responsibility, longed for it, in fact. Besides, Hal used to say, "A change is as good as a rest." They needed some changes, an infusion of activity.

In the morning he began a careful examination of the *Capital-Journal* classifieds. Within a week he saw the ad—"Six-year-old sorrel mare with blaze"—for sale at a farm south of Lawrence. The only hitch, the mare came with a companion, a nanny goat. "Lifetime friends," said the ad, "sold as a package deal." Tyler wondered if this was a ruse on the part of the owner to rid himself of a troublesome animal. The goat, most likely. The chuckle started somewhere deep and made its way up until a laugh popped out just as he took a sip of coffee.

May stuck her head out of the computer room. "What's so funny?"

He carefully folded the paper, took the green felt tip pen he was reading with and circled the ad. "Take a look at this."

Tyler phoned the farmer, an elderly man, judging from the wavering voice, and the clack and whistle of loose dentures.

He asked the man to explain this odd arrangement—horse and goat.

"I can't separate them. The wife won't stand for it. They've been together since they was young."

They were the wife's pets, and when May and Tyler arrived at the small farm, the woman could not bring herself to come out of the house.

"I retired, you see," the old man said. "Can't afford the extra livestock. Economics, pure and simple. The grandkids like 'em, but my daughters can't take 'em. The wife understands, but she grieves."

He nodded toward the house. Tyler saw a face at the kitchen window where the curtains had parted. The farmer had a misshapen leg and limped in a slow, rolling gait toward the barn. The Mannings trudged slowly behind. There in one stall stood the sorrel mare with the goat lying in the straw nearby.

"Come on, Dolly. You too, Nanny."

He roused the goat up, placed a halter over the mare's head and led her out of the stall with the goat trotting at her side. May was enchanted.

"She's a sweet animal. Rides well. Your girl will like her."

The tasks ahead seemed suddenly daunting. He'd have to reclaim part of the barn, turn it back into a stable, or build a partition and a new door. The animals would need access to the range with the cattle, and he would need to plant more bluestem besides. He and May would have to walk the fence line immediately, repair the weak spots and replace rotting fence posts. He told May all this on the drive home, speaking more than he had spoken in days, itemizing all the tasks ahead. When he glanced over, her eyes had grown large and shiny and bore into him with rapt attention. A horse needs other horses to be content and sleep, he told her, and maybe that's why the goat was her bosom companion.

"We may even have to get a second horse."

17

A POSTLUDE

1

Thus began May Manning's love affair with horses. By fifteen, she was attending their vet whenever he came to the farm, learning how to give injections and tend to sore hooves and wounds. By the time she graduated from high school she'd been working in the vet's clinic every Saturday for a year.

Tyler had hoped Delia May might enlarge her circle of friends beyond the faithful Mei Lin and Danny and was relieved when she finally did so in tenth grade. She attended parties and sporting events with a group of girls and boys that Billie assured him were "the right type." Whatever that meant. From time to time she brought one or another or all of them home for popcorn and movies and pizza. But when he introduced the idea of a junior year abroad—"I've been talking to the lady from AFS. Would you like to consider a trip?"—she recoiled as though he'd asked her to consider moving out of the house. Since his brother's death he'd worried she was becoming a sheltered and solitary child. He remembered, with fondness, the travels during his brief navy career. So, they began the New Years' and June Trips: twice to California; once to Orlando; and one trip to Washington, DC, each accompanied by Mei Lin. In return, Delia May spent two weeks each July with the Robertsons, flying to Traverse City to join Mei-Mei at her parents' summer cottage on Glen Lake, returning from Michigan brown as a nut from days spent on the beach and in the water.

"I don't know why they call it a cottage," she said. "You could live there year-round."

When she announced, rather coyly, that she'd invited a boy to the senior prom, he inquired, "Don't boys usually do the asking?"

"Oh, Dad! That is so twentieth century."

When he told Billie, she smirked and said, "And I know who the lucky fella is."

Aaron? Why would a graduate student want to take a high school girl to her prom?

"Because he's her oldest friend," Billie replied. "That's what the kids do nowadays. They travel in packs and go out with their best friends. All that roses and romance stuff we lived through, Ty? That's so out of style!"

When his daughter was accepted into KU, Tyler wanted her to experience group living. He wanted her to have the chance to live away from home. May was aghast. Leave home? Leave Dolly and Nanny, the cats and sweet old Maude? "Not on your life, Daddy!" At the end of her freshman year Maude died, and May's mourning was intense. She assuaged her grief by building Maudie a shrine, covering one wall of her bedroom with photos. After this loss, May surprised him by taking up the notion of a junior semester abroad. It struck him with great force: As long as Maudie was living, she had not wanted to stay away from her dog for more than a couple of weeks. To do so would have been an act of betrayal. With Maude's death, she was free of that commitment, and the depth of her loyalty humbled him. And so she spent six months on a sheep ranch in New Zealand, coming home with a new accent and a new confidence and, soon after, a covey of new friends—classmates in Lawrence.

The Harrington children were also suitably launched, but it was Aaron who took their breath away. Who would have thought their youngest boy would take an interest in teeth? A-Ron? Dentistry? And not just dental school but oral surgery, with the most daunting schedule and career opening up. His steadfast devotion to the Maypole was another cause for won-

der. Wouldn't a young man want to "graze"? Bud opined. Act
up and sew a few wild oats? Billie thought Bud was projecting
onto his son regret over his own straight path, for Bud had
never strayed far from home, if you overlooked a few inconsequential flirtations.

For here came the most astonishing thing of all. In spite of
the six years between them, Aaron and May Manning planned
to marry.

"And you're surprised?" Bud teased his wife. "I saw this
coming when May was three."

Pooh! Billie thought. He had no idea! The man hadn't
changed a jot since high school.

Billie had also been monitoring the Manning house expansion.
Tyler began constructing an addition to the old homestead after
the kids had asked if they might live there so May could remain
close to her father and her animals as she completed her degree. She would be commuting to K-State for veterinary school.
They would throw a decent-sized wing off the computer room,
turning that space into his sitting room while the extension
would be his bedroom, bath, kitchenette, and storage. They'd
suggested the wing should be theirs, but Tyler objected. ("And
where do you propose to keep your kids when they come?")
He'd offered to make the addition onto the shop, not the house,
so the kids could have some privacy. Aghast, the children had
reacted as if he'd offered to move to Denver, so the suggestion
was dropped.

Aaron had admired Tyler for so long it would be no hardship
to live with him. Living at the old homestead made all the sense
in the world, the kids told anyone who'd listen. Meanwhile Billie
thought she might fall to her knees and give thanks but settled
for a good cry in the bathroom. The kids! Right here! She knew
Aaron was keeping an eye on his father. Since his minor heart
attack, Bud had aged noticeably, and his blond hair had turned
silver. Aaron could be found of a Sunday on the tractor, mowing his father's considerable expanse of weeds.

2

2013

But the singular event in these early days of May Manning's adulthood is her wedding, during this summer of her twenty-first year. The three parents have reached their late fifties. Neither Tyler nor Billie entertains plans for retirement, and yet it looms ahead like an obstruction in the road. The commute to Washaw High has grown tedious, even though Tyler and Billie share the chore. They joke but seldom complain. Besides, they still have the summers off.

The approaching summer offers this joyous prospect: the wedding will take place in the Harrington's garden. A county judge of their acquaintance will serve as justice of the peace. Their colleague Jeff Kornacki and his wife, Peg, have offered to construct an arched trellis, covered in flowers, under which the principals might stand. The widowed and retired Eppie Gordon, who seldom travels, will be traveling this one time: Howard will drive her to the nuptials. Eppie insists upon baking, proudly announcing, "May Manning will be the only bride in Kansas to have a red velvet wedding cake."

As for Howard, he has recently retired and claims to regret it even though he has all the time in the world to make art. ("Miss the kids. Can you imagine?") Aware that retirement has not been an unmitigated blessing, Tyler has plans for him. He needs Howie's help designing a website for May and one for himself, and more advice on decorating the addition. Since retiring, there's been a noticeable uptick in Howard's drinking, his younger daughter confides, and too much trawling in assorted bars.

Rudy Ortiz—Big O—gladly accepts the invitation to May's wedding. Since marrying, he has fathered three daughters and, finally, a long-awaited son. But Rudy is now under the supervision of his family-centered wife. Mercedes has laid claim to all his holidays, which are usually shared with her large Topeka family, to the sorrow of Rudy's Garden City family. However, the marriage of May Manning is a different matter, and he's looking forward to the wedding. Tyler Manning was the first staff person to reach out, and Rudy has announced he will be going, with or without Mercedes. So she concedes but only if they can bring the children.

Two days prior to the wedding, a truck pulls into the Harrington drive. A deliveryman emerges, staggering under the weight and breadth of an enormous, tissue-wrapped flower arrangement. The man helps Billie place the vase of flowers on the coffee table in her sitting room, which it dwarfs. She then calls May Manning. Before May drives over, accompanied by her maid of honor, Billie carefully opens the card and reads— *Congratulations! Love, Danny.* Billie believes the arrangement must have cost over three hundred dollars. She cannot even identify some of the exotic blooms, spears of which shoot up at ninety-degree angles from the base. When the Two Mays see the flower arrangement, they embrace each other, squealing like teenagers, and laugh.

"That is *so* Danny," says Mei Lin Robertson.

When Billie asks who this Danny is, May scolds Billie for forgetting her other "best friend." Ah, that Danny, but Billie does not remember clapping eyes on him in ten years. Danny Patel will not be at the wedding, May says, which saddens both young women. Danny is currently on family business in Mumbai, as well as checking out bride prospects, pre-selected by his parents. Both girls snicker.

The day of the wedding dawns clear and bright, with an auspicious forecast. No weather is predicted, except the inevitable winds that are as common to Kansas as chicken hawks.

Billie's daughter arrives early to help her mother arrange the borrowed chairs and lay out the reception table. Mei Lin Robertson, the maid of honor, is currently at the Manning's, assisting May with her hair. Aaron is upstairs in "the boys' room," arguing with Wesley who will be his brother's best man. Aaron does not want to wear the tux and tells his older brother that he would prefer the suit. The thought of a cummerbund leaves him in stitches.

"The Maypole will burst out laughing," Aaron says, although he no longer uses the nickname in her presence.

Bryce, Aaron's college roommate and best friend, is upstairs as well, while his wife helps Billie with the Harrington grandchildren. May and Aaron have made it clear that the wedding should be a small family affair with their own and their parents' best friends. Aaron tells his parents that Bryce has organized a celebratory gathering while they honeymoon in the city. Aaron's colleagues from the med center and May's college chums will meet up at a dumpling bar on Thirty-Ninth Street. Some place tasty and un-fussy, May says, "Where they fill the wine glasses to the top and not that cheesy four-ounce pour." Her remark startles Tyler. He has not seen his daughter drink at all, and so he asks.

"Wine at parties, Dad. Don't freak out. And I hate beer."

Tyler has told his daughter more than once about the time he lost his own temper so spectacularly that he destroyed another man's face. Only two other times, he tells his daughter, has he ever felt the incapacitating anger rise up—once with his brother, Mickey, and once when a drug-dealing thug approached their house with a gun.

Billie will serve as mother of the groom and surrogate mother of the bride, which amuses and perplexes her. BeeBee the fairy godmother, she thinks. How, exactly, is a godmother supposed to act? Whatever the kids want to call her, she'll answer. She does wonder what has happened to May's natural mother, wondering in what way May resembles her. At the moment, she pities the wayward girl who gave up her daughter. For Mickey Manning she feels nothing at all—may he rest in peace—and certainly no pity.

Howard is the first to arrive and pulls his red Mazda sports car to the front of the drive. He limps, cane-less, around the car to open the door for Eppie Gordon. There is nothing wrong with Eppie's agility, when you consider her age, but her vision is problematic. Carefully, Howard removes one cake layer from the backseat and carries it like a newborn to the kitchen door. When Billie realizes they've arrived, she lets out a welcoming whoop, rushing out-of-doors to enfold her old workmates in her arms, in an exceptional burst of exuberance. Once Eppie has been safely deposited indoors, Howard returns with Billie for the remaining cake layers.

"She fussed the whole damn way about my car," Howard says with a snort.

The instant Howie and Billie return to the kitchen, Eppie says in a dramatic voice, "Howard didn't tell me he was driving a roller skate these days. I could hardly get my legs in."

Stationed at the wide kitchen table, Eppie will assemble and decorate the wedding cake. Billie would have preferred a store-bought cake—less trouble all around—but Eppie insisted, and Billie did not have the heart to say no. As the women dicker over the icing, Howard slips a silver flask out of his trouser pocket and avails himself of a shot in a glass of wedding punch.

"Just so long as you can drive me home," Eppie says, glancing up at him, causing Howard to wonder, aloud, how she knows if her vision is supposedly so impaired.

"Nothing wrong with my ears," she says.

Gifts will be placed in the living room and opened after the reception. Billie has told Eppie repeatedly that the cake is gift enough. Yet as soon as they arrive, Eppie has Howard remove an enormous wrapped box from his tiny trunk. ("All the kitchen and guest towels she'll need for years.") Billie knows that Eppie will have personalized each guest towel regardless of the strain such delicate needlework puts on her eyes. Also elaborately wrapped are two oils painted by Howard: one of Maude the dog (now dead), and another of Dolly and her goat, from photos Tyler lent him.

"At least they'll have something to hang on a wall when they set up house."

Billie and Bud and their other children have combined their resources to provide the newlyweds with bedding and blankets for the millennium.

"I peeked into Ty's bed closet," Billie has informed her husband beforehand. "Don't suppose he's purchased a sheet in ten years."

Tyler is paying for the honeymoon weekend in Kansas City—"The Paris of the Plains," Howie jokes—a weekend being all the time the kids have to spare. The newlyweds will stay in the downtown Hyatt, wined and dined by their friends—"If you can call Chinese noodles fine dining," Billie sniffs to the adults—and visit the Steam Boat Arabia Museum. Billie suggests they may wish to visit the Crown Center Shops, but May, who detests shopping, turns up her nose. Undoubtedly, they will visit the zoo, even though Aaron does not like zoos, does not like to see caged animals stared at and heckled by idiotic adolescent boys, or daft adults for that matter. But he will concede because May will want to go. All animals concern his soon-to-be veterinarian bride. She will probably track down some unsuspecting zookeeper and pepper him with questions regarding the diet and well-being of the zebras or elands or pachyderms.

Suddenly, the noise of Jeff's muscle truck distracts the occupants of the kitchen. Bud, who has just come downstairs after checking on his sons, and Howard leave the house to assist. In the bed of the truck lies the trellis. It takes all three men to hoist it out and totter it over to the designated spot. "What did you use, for crissakes!" Bud puffs. "Cast iron?" Jeff's wife, Peg, follows with a large box of roses cut from her garden, plus an assortment of artificial blooms. Jeff hammers in the stakes to keep the trellis upright while Peg threads the flowers artfully through mesh that covers the structure. Peg thinks the Washaw senior class might repurpose the trellis for their prom. They have also brought a wrapped gift, a fancy coffeemaker with assorted bells and whistles. Billie is overcome at the generosity unfolding before her. She'd thought the cake and trellis were gifts enough. She must take refuge once more in the bathroom to weep and blow her nose.

Rudy Ortiz's family is the last to arrive. His three young daughters step out of the car with great care, wearing matching dresses of pink and yellow organza. The Harringtons come forward to greet them, for it has been several years since they have met his wife socially—even though everyone sees each other at the sporting events. The girls are eight, six, and four.

Meanwhile, Rudy proudly carries his ten-month-old son while Mercedes places on the coffee table a beautifully wrapped box from Macy's: a crystal fruit bowl. Mercedes believes that marriages must begin with beauty as well as towels. She will take satisfaction later from May Manning's pleased response to the bowl when it is finally unwrapped after the service. The bride will thank her profusely and guard the bowl against injury. At this point Mercedes will feel a fondness for the girl and a twinge of admiration for her father.

"He did a good job with his daughter," she will tell her husband on the drive home, to Rudy's considerable relief.

Billie and her daughter, Ginny, shuttle between kitchen and outdoor table with such frequency that Peg offers to help. The judge has yet to appear, and a nervous energy descends on the kitchen. His arrival will signal the moment Billie will phone the Mannings who are still at home. Not long after, Howard gazes out the kitchen window and sees a short woman in a legal looking robe examining the trellised wedding arch.

"I think your judge is here."

No one has heard a car, and Billie has a sinking feeling the judge has left his vehicle on the side of the road and walked the long drive up. Billie joins Howard at the window. The judge, she knows, is definitely a man, and she rushes from the house to inquire and invite the woman in. She is a substitute and provides a simple explanation and a query: "Didn't the office call?"

Billie phones the Manning house. Wesley's wife and younger son, as well as Ginny's two children, are in the family room doing crafts. Wes's oldest, the nine-year-old granddaughter, is trying to help but mostly getting in the way, calling out every few seconds, "Where does this one go, Gram?" annoying Billie in the process. She now urges those remaining in the kitchen to go out to the garden and find a chair.

Eppie, with her keen ears, is the first to alert the guests of the bride's arrival. "I'd know the sound of that muffler any-where," she says, referring to Tyler's truck.

"How would you know, Ep?" Howard quizzes her playfully. "It's a brand-new truck."

Mei Lin Robertson climbs down first to help Delia May, although the bride is not so elaborately clothed or shod that she needs much assistance. With a groaning heart, Billie sees that May has brought her two border collies and Aaron's mutt. The dogs bound out of the truck bed and approach the Har-rington property as if they owned it. May loathes high heels and has settled for the lowest pump she can find. In one early fit of pique, she tells Billie she'll wear her work boots if she feels like it but later apologizes in tears. Nor is the bride clad in white, but in a calf-length dress of the most delicious pale blue satin. It is a simple A-line dress without embellishments except for the folded boat-neck collar and a cloth belt with bow behind. Although she never says so, Billie thinks the dress is designed for a bridesmaid; it is the only bridal garment May liked. During the shopping trip, Delia May passes racks of long gowns with lacy sleeves and beaded bodices, dramatic strapless gowns, daring high-low white garments and endless trains. She has grown more downcast with each new rack, until she reaches the colored garments and found the simple blue dress. "I hate all the froufrou, BeeBee. And I hate white!"

Mei Lin, who accompanied them on the dreaded gown search, said to her best friend, "Then you should have *exactly* what you want."

Billie will not soon forget the remark or Mei Lin's calm delivery and Delia May's relieved response, hugging her friend for the simple permission Mei Lin has given. She marvels at these girls, one planning to be a vet, the other a pediatrician.

How does a child learn to be so certain, so early? She nips the self-reproach in the bud—gratitude, Billie!—reminding herself Ginny has proven to be a capable and generous mother.

May is also wearing a simple necklace and matching teardrop earrings with tiny diamonds and pearls that once belonged to her grandmother. Tyler has been saving them for her. As her wedding dress will testify, her tastes have simplified. Tyler remembers wistfully the pink tutu and ballet slippers she wore to an Independence Day party in this very garden. He remembers the purple corduroy little-girl slacks and bright T-shirts with puppy faces. But May has not been that little girl for some time and only last week helped deliver a calf.

Mei Lin and Billie hustle the bride into the family room where Wesley's and Bryce's wives and the smaller children are still braiding lanyards. The children *ooh* at the bride and want to touch her garment. The adult women give a stern *no*, but May doesn't mind and steps toward the children. Billie shuts her eyes and grimly imagines a toddler's greasy handprint on the side of May's lovely dress. May, she knows, couldn't care less, or more precisely, cares more for indulging the children than for protecting the satin. Billie hears the men on the stairs and guards the door, instructing the men to wait on the porch.

"Aaron mustn't see the bride," she whispers.

There will be no music, no processional march, a decision Aaron and May made some time ago. Instead, Mei Lin will play a song on her flute during the ceremony. The tiny woman judge is waiting under the trellis, and all the friends and family are seated or on their way. Tyler remains in the kitchen, waiting to be told what to do as Wes's wife shoos the little children through the kitchen and out into the garden to their chairs.

Billie embraces May quickly and leaves. How lovely May looks with the wreath of fresh flowers wound through her hair. Wesley is waiting to escort his mother to her seat in the front row. There are only three short rows of chairs, for the group is small. But she has already begun to feel the hummingbird wings in her heart. As Wesley offers his arm, she takes it, processing awkwardly across the newly mown grass. As she passes, she cannot help but note that Eppie's handkerchief is already in full use. Billie sits beside her husband, with Ginny and the babes on his far side, and looks up. The judge is smiling at her. It is such a reassuring sight that she feels the tears line up along her lids like soldiers awaiting marching orders. Wesley walks back down the little aisle, and she feels a small hand on her shoulder.

"You okay, Gram?" says the oldest granddaughter in her auctioneer's voice. "Are you crying yet?" Billie would like to spank her bottom.

Wesley returns with Mei Lin who takes her place to one side of the judge. Billie has turned to look at Bud who has gripped her hand. When she looks up, Wes and Aaron are suddenly standing side by side, and she gazes at her sons. How has it happened that they've become men? *Responsible adults.* She wonders if Bud feels as puzzled by this miracle as she does. It seems like only last year that Wes was married, when in fact over ten years have gone by.

Tyler wishes he had the power to stop time, so that their brief walk from kitchen to altar might last until the memory grows firm, and then indelible. Before they leave the kitchen he asks, "Are you happy?" She laughs lightly and says *yes.* What she has realized, in fact, as she takes her father's arm, is that everyone in the world who matters, everyone she loves, is standing beside her or sitting in Billie's ragtag garden. But she cannot find the words.

"I hope I don't look silly," she says instead, reaching behind her back to check the bow.

"That's not possible," he answers, which elicits another laugh.

She asks in a teasing voice, "Are you ready, Dad?"

Again, the moist ball lodges in his throat until he finally squeezes out the words, "Ready as I'll ever be."

Aaron suddenly smiles, and the judge says, "Please rise for the bride."

May is clinging to her father's arm as they slowly walk

toward the trellis. May is not only smiling but blushing. The bouquet in her hands, constructed by her best friend, matches the flowers around her head. When Billie glances at Tyler she is stunned by the quantity of gray in his hair. The graying has been so incremental and started so long ago—Hal Manning's hair exactly—that she has not noticed just how white he's become. The eyebrows remain dark and perhaps that is why she's overlooked his head. Billie wonders how silvery she might be if she ever stopped coloring her hair. The judge asks, "Who gives this bride away?" and Tyler answers: "I, her father, and her beloved godparents, the Harringtons, have raised her with love. But the bride gives herself away."

Did the kids write that? At first Billie is so transfixed by what she sees that she cannot initially take in the ceremonial words the judge recites. Sounds seem to dissolve as soon as they reach the air. Then Mei-Mei plays her flute, a lovely tune that Billie does not recognize, followed by a poem the bride and groom have requested, and her attention returns.

The vows are exchanged. The rings are placed. The newlyweds exchange a discreet kiss. How has it escaped her notice that a marriage ceremony is so brief? As soon as the judge pronounces them man and wife, the little children, coached by Mei Lin, throw quantities of paper flower petals in the air, the little boys hurling them in wads like balls while the girls toss them gently or drop them at their feet. The bride and groom, followed by Wes and Mei Lin, retreat down the aisle amid enthusiastic applause. The instant the applause fades away, the nine-year-old granddaughter asks in her deafening voice, "Can we have our cake now?"

They stream out toward the side garden where the reception table stands, covered in a white lace cloth. A large punch bowl anchors one end while plates of sweets and nuts covered in plastic wrap are placed here and there. On this mostly sunny afternoon, the wind has behaved, sparing them the bother of weighing down the napkins. The only culprits are the newlyweds' three dogs that have been patrolling the table for the last hour. One of May's border collies has taken up its post beneath the table, awaiting further instruction. Upon elaborate directions from Eppie Gordon, Wesley hoists the large wedding cake—with Billie and Mei Lin hovering nearby—and carries it carefully down the porch steps and around to the table. Eppie has iced and decorated it with spun sugar wedding bells, a tiny bride and groom atop, and pink icing flowers round the tiered edges. Eppie has not lost her culinary touch, Billie thinks, even if she's losing her vision. The guests bulge toward the table as Eppie stations herself by the cake, with Mei Lin at the other end, serving punch.

The newlyweds insist that their guests—children first—be served the cake. They will eat last. They want to visit with everyone right away. The children hover near Eppie who deftly slices one piece after another. Howard, who's been watching Eppie, can be heard whispering into Tyler's ear, "I don't think there's a damn thing wrong with her eyes."

May has been hugged more times than she can remember. She takes a moment to explain to Mercedes Ortiz and Ginny Harrington, once her babysitter, how she intends, in the fullness of time, to have her own veterinary practice. She even hopes one day soon to have a flock of sheep so she might work her collies. Tyler, who's conversing with Rudy nearby, is so startled he stands stock still. *A flock of sheep?* This is the first he's heard of sheep.

Not far off, Aaron is in a huddle with Jeff and Howard and his father, Bud. The older men are engaged in a session of *remember when.* Aaron must allow himself to hear their tales of his boyhood, his unintentionally funny remarks and childhood gaffs, his scrawniness—which he can now endure since he has become as tall and good-looking as his father and taller by an inch than his older brother Wes.

At this moment a tiny dark cloud pauses in its passage overhead, long enough to release its full payload, arriving just as the adults receive their cake. Thirty seconds of warning sprinkles precede a downpour. A shriek goes up, peals of laughter, and whoops of dismay. The well-wishers grip their plates and dash through the rain to the back door. The hostess and her assistants rescue the dishes of candy and savories and follow quickly. The cake, alas, is too large to hoist and run. Only Mei Lin has the presence of mind to throw a tea towel over the cake's skeletal remains.

In the kitchen everyone is so amused and talkative, wiping droplets from shoulders and hair, they have momentarily lost track of the bride and groom. Wesley's wife moves through the room distributing dishtowels to the guests. Most of the children remain on the porch, squealing and playing and pestering the two dogs that have crawled underneath for refuge. One small boy, a grandson, eager for attention, runs off the porch with a rebel yell, flaps his arms through the deluge, and returns, screaming as he goes.

When Billie looks around for the newlyweds, they are nowhere to be seen.

"Where are the kids?" she asks in an alarmed voice.

Howard Shay, who has wandered into the family room for another nip from the flask, glances through a side window and spots the newlyweds, still out-of-doors. May and Aaron have remained at the reception table, their bridal clothing growing damp and damper and then thoroughly drenched. The bride's hair springs into untamed curls while the white gardenia in the groom's lapel hangs its head.

"Why, there they are," Howard drawls.

The group taking shelter indoors rushes from the kitchen into the adjoining room and joins Howard at the window. The newlyweds are laughing as May performs a little jig while the border collie beneath the table follows May's performance with disapproving eyes. The shower has tapered off but the newlyweds hardly notice. According to custom, Aaron and May are feeding each other melting lumps of cake until their lips and chins are speckled with Eppie's red velvet confection. Then the bride and broom join hands, still laughing, and run toward the kitchen door to join their guests.

ACKNOWLEDGMENTS

My thanks to George Eliot who published her lovely fable, *Silas Marner*, in 1860. It all springs from her storytelling genius. The quote from Wordsworth appeared first as the epigraph for her book, and I acknowledge that I have purloined it for mine.

Good friends, accomplished writers all, read portions or all of the manuscript at various times in its evolution and offered their insights, making it a better story: John Mort, Tom Fox Averill, Margot Patterson, Linda Rodriguez, and Trish Reeves.

My special thanks for the great women at Regal House Publishing who chose the novel for their Petrichor Prize, in 2021: Jaynie Royal and Pam Van Dyk and the marvelous staff at Regal House who believe publishing can be a collegial and inclusive enterprise. It was my great good fortune to have found you, and to be found.

My deep gratitude to you all.